A HOUSE FOR ALICE

ALSO BY DIANA EVANS

26a
The Wonder
Ordinary People

A House for Alice

DIANA EVANS

Pantheon Books, New York

All rights reserved. Published in the United States by Pantheon Books, a division of Penguin Random House LLC, New York, and distributed in Canada by Penguin Random House Canada Limited, Toronto. Originally published in hardcover in Great Britain by Chatto & Windus, an imprint of Vintage Publishing, a division of Penguin Random House Ltd., London, in 2023.

Pantheon Books and colophon are registered trademarks of Penguin Random House LLC.

Library of Congress Cataloging-in-Publication Data
Name: Evans, Diana, [date] author.
Title: A house for Alice : a novel / Diana Evans.
Description: First American Edition. New York : Pantheon Books, 2023
Identifiers: LCCN 2023011376 (print) | LCCN 2023011377 (ebook) |
ISBN 9780593701089 (hardcover) | ISBN 9780593701096 (ebook)
Subjects: LCGFT: Novels. Fiction.
Classification: LCC PR6105.V345 H68 2023 (print) |
LCC PR6105.V345 (ebook) | DDC 823/.92—dc23/eng/20230310
LC record available at https://lccn.loc.gov/2023011376
LC ebook record available at https://lccn.loc.gov/2023011377

www.pantheonbooks.com

Jacket images: (top to bottom, left to right) Morsa Images/Getty Images;
Fabian Plock/Alamy; Omoniyi Ayedun Olubunmi/Alamy;
HuyThoai/Getty Images: MoMo Productions/Getty Images;
Guy Corbishley/Alamy; Santagig/Getty;
(background) Tahlia Russell/Getty Images
Jacket design and illustration by Tal Goretsky

Printed in the United States of America
First United States Edition
2 4 6 8 9 7 5 3 1

For my mother

and all of us who have found ourselves
in a strange land

Where is my rest place, Jesus? Where is my harbour?
Where is the pillow I will not have to pay for,
and the window I can look from that frames my life?

Derek Walcott, *The Schooner Flight*

ONE

1

Cornelius Winston Pitt, in the evening of his life, eyebrows white and wild, eyesight dysfunctional, moved with a dancy small-foot shuffle along his hallway, holding a pork pie. In the other hand was a cigarette shedding ash onto his route, over the slip mat, into the kitchen, where pausing he became freshly alarmed at the absence of his wife, an absence he felt most strongly in this room, its floor still sounding of her slippers, its toaster still evocative of her sadly buttered crusts. Where was she? Then he remembered. Kilburn. Was glad that he remembered, a whole crisp name. No chops anymore in this kitchen, no rice, rice being extremely complex, no Sunday chicken. Here in this land of the late and alone the menu was condensed. A pork pie was enough for a man, only it needed

Beetroot. Yes. That was why he was here. He opened the fridge immediately so that beetroot would not disappear again inside its name, "immediately" being relative to his particular nonagenarian physicality: a moment of slight forward falling, the grabbing of the low-down handle, the haul posing threats to his spine. Inside was a hollow ice cave, mist. There was milk in the mist, and a tomato (also good with pork pie), two meals in foil from a daughter to the north, butter, and the purple thing. He took it out, the cigarette now balanced on his lower lip getting smoke in his eye, the one that worked, so he closed it, couldn't see anything, opened it again, and was struck by another requirement round and flat in his mind and useful for carrying food. The fridge he left ajar in this new venture, reaching up to the cupboard for a

Plate. Words were occasional boats, sometimish, coming at him brightly sailed then passing by. What Cornelius was learning was that they are not always necessary. Abstraction is peaceful, like twilight, wide swimming in a quiet colour, and you can exist in a place without names, where nothing is labelled, nothing flaunts itself, but instead the words wait, so quietly, for a time like this when you become in need of a—yes . . .

Beetroot is wet. It slopped around the pork pie on the dancy shuffle back to the chair, a primordial green throne of once-abject patriarchy positioned in the living room directly in front of the TV where Cornelius spent most of his waking hours on this the ground floor of the house of many clocks. Around the chair were the apparatus of his daily proceedings. The table in front, individual-sized, for one eater, one smoker, one controller of remote control. Underneath the table the leather pouffe, for raising of feet when desired. To the left the dustbin, now half full, mainly with discarded post-its containing the names of fleetingly essential objects (WD-40, battery, sharpener, Adel—his daughter), and a shelf, also to his left, for beer coasters, glasses repair tools and the telephone, his conduit to the outside. Beyond all of this there were the clocks, everywhere, in every room, grandfathers, carriages, cuckoos, pendulums, collected over the course of his long working life in horology. The house ticked, and tocked, constantly.

At four o'clock today—it was Tuesday, sweltering, swollen at the windows the sick gold of a twenty-first-century June—he must call the tax office to find out about the implications of the recent changes to inheritance tax charges that might affect his will. The reminder was provided on one of the table's current post-its, phone number included. It was incumbent upon him, he felt, as he neared the milestone of a century (which of course would come with a congratulatory card from the Queen) to make sure his financial affairs were in order, what with the grandchildren, and his wife who was still his wife as far as money was concerned, and then the daughters and their way-ward ways through the arts, Buddhism, break-ups and vegan behaviour. Money is messy and at the end of a century it should be neat, a nice scout's knot, not flailing around like a raging octopus. He wanted to go neatly, like his father, himself a horol-ogist, who had died at exactly a hundred proudly in receipt of the royal note, leaving his family with only their grief to face, not an ensuing feud brought on by fiscal carelessness.

Before that, though, was this very adequate pork-beet lunch which did travel onto his shirt due to the additional forgetting of the floppy thing for residue that is called a serviette. Then there were ash streaks from the post-prandial smoke that didn't find the ashtray in time because he was watching a repeat of Natasha Kaplinsky on *Who Do You Think You Are?* He loved Natasha Kaplinsky. She was his favourite newsreader, always so well dressed and neat, always well powdered and matt. He'd missed her when she'd left ITN, had watched her on *Strictly*, *Have I Got News for You*, wherever she popped up, it was a shame she'd chosen to prioritise her family now but he understood that she probably had lots of ironing and washing to do while her husband was at work. Right in the middle of the show, annoy-ingly, sending more ash onto his trousers as it made him jump, the phone rang. Why did it ring at the most inconvenient moments, when he was busy? Why couldn't the world just leave him alone to enjoy the freedom of his retirement earned over more than fifty years of solid work, dutiful family-providing-for, tax-paying and pension contributions?

"Hello?" he shouted.

"Hi, Dad, it's Adel."

"Who?"

"Adel," she said more slowly, though still sounding rushed. A boat sailed in displaying her haecceity: eldest, visits too much, bit of a nag, eats meat (he thinks).

"Ah right," he said.

"Don't forget the carers are coming at five. And remember the dinners in the fridge in the foil. Just put one straight in the oven, no need to take off the foil, and don't forget to turn off the oven afterwards. Did you have one last night?"

"I've had a pork pie," he said.

"When, last night?"

"No just now!"

"Did you have one of the foil dinners last night? Oh it doesn't matter, I've got to go, I'm still at work. Carers at five, ok? They'll help you with the dinner. Just show them it, in the fridge, in the foil. I'll come round tomorrow."

He would like to say it would be all right if she damn well didn't come round tomorrow, seeing as the carers, those pointless people, were coming today and that would be too much visiting, he preferred it when they were more widely staggered, but he didn't want to be rude, she was doing what she thought she was supposed to do. Actually Cornelius had envisaged his old age in a home, sitting in a large lounge with light falling in and the other aged around him knitting, watching, waiting, drooling and playing draughts, but when it came to it the thought had seemed unattractive. What about his clocks? Where would he put them? The house was moulded around him. It was the shape of him. Moving somewhere else would be like trying to pour himself into another shape and at his time of life he lacked the liquidity to be poured. He would have to die here and that was fine with him. He just wished people didn't feel it was their responsibility to manage him and bother.

That was the reason, he remembered, for scheduling the tax call for four o'clock, to catch the afternoon lull before the busy lead-up to closing time and because the carers were coming at five (also stated on a post-it). He enjoyed the last few minutes of Natasha, and with infallible timing the grandfather clock in the hallway chimed four, a loud, reverberating gong, singing the hours, which after years of hearing he often easily slept through unless there was some appointment to keep that his subconscious was alert to. Likewise in the kitchen went the cuckoo. He tipped his ash, drained his stone-cold tea and picked up the phone with a quiver-prone beet-stained hand. The call was answered by a machine parading as a human, offering a list of options. Cornelius pressed two. No he did not want to take part in the questionnaire about his experience of calling HMRC.

"Ok. If you're contacting us following a death and you want to know what you need to do, press one. If you're calling about probate, confirmation, the online estate report, or inheritance tax, press two. For taxable trusts, press three. For non-taxable trusts, press four."

Cornelius pressed two.

"Now. If you've already sent a probate or confirmation application and want to check the progress, press one. For help with the probate or confirmation process, the online estate report, or Forms IHT205, PA1 or C5, press two. If you're calling to find out if we have issued Form IHT421, Probate Summary, or Certificate for Confirmation, press three. If you need help with Form IHT400, press four. If you've sent in an Inheritance Tax form and are calling for an update, press five. Or for anything else, press six."

Cornelius pressed five while muttering expletives.

"Just so you know, once we have received your form or

request, it can take up to twenty-five working days for you to receive our response. Now, if you've been waiting longer than twenty-five working days, please hold to speak to an advisor." Information followed on the routine recording of calls and the handling of personal data. Then some classical music, during which Cornelius lit another cigarette, having stubbed out the last one on the plate instead of the ashtray. The voice apologised for not yet answering his call and told him he was in a queue. In the midst of more music, and more high-octane swearing on his part, he began to suspect that option five was an empty office. It was the place for people with queries lacking in urgency and specificity, who therefore did not deserve to be answered. He slammed down the handset, resolving to try again tomorrow at 10:45. The post-it was amended accordingly.

They were strangers, these women who arrived at five, with their sandals and computer phones and cardigans around their waists and facial shine. Doreen and Emma, what did it matter there would be no boats. He wasn't even sure he hadn't met them before, they were interchangeable, he never settled on any of them with one eye. What right did they have to come in here and ask questions about his menu and domestic movements and tut at his ashtrays and empty his dustbins? Did they know him, who he was and where he had been? Did they know that he had served in the military ambulance during World War II and lost his brother whose name he just could not for the life of him remember which pained him, and that his father had fought in the first war and come back to Dewsbury crippled and partially blind in one eye but had never let that impede his horology? Did they know that Alice his wife whose name he could however always seem to remember which also pained him was still insisting on her new life in Kilburn when it was her duty according to their vows to accompany him on his journey to the final eclipse, and that he would much rather have *her* arranging his menu than these externals, these flat-eyed, borough-borrowed stand-ins from a town hall? Every fortnight or so he still telephoned Alice to tell her to come home, to end her sulky sojourn in Kilburn and return to Kingsbury, to reign with him in their empty castle, for wasn't now, in the cave of old age, the calling of marriage? To warm and shield each other from storms, inflation and loneliness? But she always refused, saying she couldn't live with him anymore, "we visit each other sometimes," "we keep in touch," as if that was enough, as if that was fair.

"It's very smoky in here, Mr. Pitt, shall I open the windows?" Doreen or Emma said. "It's always best to use the ashtray, for safety's sake. Have you tried cutting down a bit? Remember we talked last week about limiting yourself to, say, ten a day to begin with, then five, then three and so on?"

"Will you leave those boxes there, I need those." Cornelius was appalled at the enforced tidying of the area, the bulldozing of his stacks of Lambert empties, used for extraneous butts to help with ashtray overflow, and the violent wiping of the table disturbing his post-its. A helicopter stormed in from the hallway affronting papers, lifting dust—the hoover, whose existence he had forgotten about and only became reacquainted with via Adel or Melissa or the other one whose name currently escaped him. "Will you mind my slippers!" he yelled, grabbing for them beneath the table which was no easy thing for his vertebrae. There was a crushed baby tomato by the table leg that was mostly hoovered up, and some butts, and some toothpicks which he was finding were so much more convenient than the overzealous conventional dental hygiene methods. He was not aware of his kaleidoscopic halitosis. He was not aware of his stainage or emissions or the moulding debris down the side of his chair. He was aware of feeling rather sleepy at his core, of how he had come to respect the efficacy particularly in hot weather of the afternoon nap, today not yet taken.

"Now, what about dinner," Donna said, her face shinier than before, her accent Irish, her sandals disconcertingly open-toed. "Will I prepare something for you?" He told her about the foil food but that he wasn't hungry yet as he'd had lunch late, a pork pie with

"Still you'll need a proper dinner, won't you. Will I warm it up for a bit and leave it out for you to have when you like, put a cover over it?" From the kitchen she called, "Don't forget to close the fridge, Mr. Pitt, all your food will go off."

"Ah right," he said. He was out of his chair, approaching the slip mat, registering through the kitchen window the empty garden where little girls had swung, their voices still resounding at the edges of the air and sometimes as a high frill in the clocks when they chimed. Emma tried to take his mug but he went and washed it himself at the sink, his castle invaded, this his effort to assert ownership, MY sink, MY kitchen, MY CUP. Soon the smell of meat began wafting from the oven—chops, it turned out, with sprouts and potatoes, a meal he understood Adel had thought about, his favoured foods, and flanked by these carers he felt moved at her knowing and her authentic familial care. That was what it came to at the end of a century, those lasting ones, the ones whom you engender and the ones from whom you come, the web of blood. How he yearned to see his brother again. He could see his face, his inner eye was sharpened by the dwindling of the outer. He could see the last time he saw him. "A bright day, like today," he said to Emma.

"Yes?" she said.

"What was his name? What was it?"

"Can I help you, Mr. Pitt?"

"He walked down the road and stopped when he got to the postbox, to tie his—his shoe . . ."

"His shoelace?"

"Yes. That's it. Never saw him again."

The next time Adel was here he was going to ask her to write it down on a large post-it, his brother's name, because his inability to remember was like a deep dislocation from the roots of the earth. It was ok if you couldn't remember the name for beetroot or plate but it was different when you couldn't remember the name of your blood! He didn't belong here anymore! His tribe was extinct yet he lived in its wake, a ghost, faded into yesterday, his ticking house his only standing structure. Was that why he didn't like to leave it? If he went outside he would disappear, perish, be singed and swallowed by the uninhabitable heat and never get Her Majesty's card? Really it didn't matter, he could fall asleep happily in front of Natasha and never wake up again, but it was as if the clocks were inside him chiming, like a battery, automatically on the hour each hour encouraging him on to the end of his heart. There was nothing he could do about it but drift, and wait, and smoke, and sleep, until the last sleep.

He offered the women Eccles cakes, a delicacy he always offered visitors, but they declined, "not a fan of raisins," she said, "I'm off wheat," said the other, this he put down to veganism. He had one himself after they'd gone, before dinner, which she'd left covered on the table in front of his chair, knife and fork ready, oven officially turned off. On his final voyage back to the kitchen to put sugar in his tea (Adel would never have forgotten), he neglected to close the fridge again after opening it by mistake to look for sugar, and the dinner was left cold, a cigarette still burning on the edge of the ashtray, as he gradually entered an abyss of post-Eccles, post-post-prandial-smoke sopor, full of dreams and boats and clear crisp names that would evaporate as soon as he awoke . . . Sidney . . .

To the west of the city, in a bulging brutalist tower of twenty-four floors overlooking the electric London vistas, was another

11

man's fridge, a Hotpoint, and some hours onward during that long June night of passing clouds and a five-mile-an-hour breeze, this particular fridge on the fourth floor of this tower would turn freakishly aflame. All around the burning fridge there were lives preparing for Ramadan, there were lazing dogs and tender sleeps and families rich in entireties of love, there were wars remembered and seas remembered, and sections of homework completed and other sections pending, and rows of dolls in children's bedrooms and rows of Moroccan cushions on high-up over-sized corner sofas, and rivers of futures flowing through the shared water pipes, and trails of fairy lights along mantels and bookshelves and wrapped around picture frames enclosing English landscapes, and artists dreaming new pictures, and mothers lying on their sides with their headscarves on and their eyelids moist and warm and gently flickering. The fire brigade would come and put the fire out. Then they left, unaware of the rest of the fire licking diagonally up the side of the tower, along its newly adorned cloak of combustible cladding acquired to make it look nicer amidst the wealthier dwellers and wandering tourists of the Royal Borough of Kensington & Chelsea.

There were only two lifts in the tower, serving around three hundred and fifty people. There was one staircase (Britain being the only country in the EU whose building regulations allowed such a situation), no sprinklers, and no communal fire alarm. Such hazards were considered sufficiently unhazardous by the Kensington & Chelsea Tenant Management Organisation, which had been harangued and beseeched by residents of the tower to address these shortcomings in case there ever was an actual deadly fire a bit like this one and all those people had to safely get out. Safety was not a highest-priority requirement for a tenement block vastly occupied by immigrants, the working class and the no longer useful. Let them find their way down. Let them make ladders out of sheets and throw their babies out of windows. Let them stay in their flats and wait to be rescued by confused belated fire fighters and teasing helicopters. Let them organise little legions of finite survival on the upper storeys and unite in a peak of fruitless praying, and let them eventually slump inside their carbon-monoxide coughing, and hope that the terrible sleep would come before the terrible flames, particularly for the children. How to describe fire: without mercy, too fast, a horror of heat, a murderous orange sprint of thirsty arm-waving gods. How to describe this fire: a massacre by negligence, a criminal activity, a corporate atrocity, an obliteration of families.

Cornelius and Sidney were on the hillside overlooking the Welsh bay. They were visiting their grandmother who lived at the top of the hill. She was almost six feet tall and had been a schoolteacher. She called them inside as dark was coming and they walked upwards in the twilight towards the peak which was hotter. Inside it was hotter still and familiar in its furniture and its clocks, but the ticks were louder than the tocks, and there was another sound even louder than the ticks, a screeching, a wailing. At first Cornelius thought this was the sound of the tiny screams from the seventies that lived under the carpets and haunted him sometimes when he remembered his daughters as children and his patchy thunderous fathering of their little souls, but it was louder than that too, and he opened his eyes to see if his one eye could work out what his two ears could not. First of all he didn't know *what* he was seeing, or *where* he was seeing it. Was it the bombs in the fields? Was it the house on the hill? But he recognised things, the pouffe, the pouffe was on fire! The— the thing with the plate on it, the food on the plate, the fire was on the food, on the plate, on the thing over the pouffe. And *under* the pouffe, the *floor* was on fire, but *how* was the floor on fire? Now the sound announced itself clearly as the fire alarm, yes, and yes, fire, there was a fire, the *house* was on fire.

More immediately affecting his person was the problem with the chair itself, his chair, the old decrepit throne in which he was sitting, and which he understood with the utmost clarity was in flames. *That* was why he was so hot. This chair is burning. Over the course of the blaze it would burn right down into the ground, so deep that when it was over you could look down into the soil and envisage a geographical tunnel to an opposite place like Australia or the South Pacific. But before it got that far Cornelius leapt up, his spine unregistering, uncomplaining, for there were more important things at stake like breath, and the beat of the heart, and the batting of his cardigan. This in his panic he managed to remove and cast away, but with another shock he also understood that the phone was withheld in the fiery vicinity of the throne, there was no getting to it, no calling the fire brigade with three numbers that he couldn't remember, no calling Adel whose number was on a post-it disintegrating with all the other flammables such as the straw dustbin and the Lambert empties and the tax office post-it and the newspaper which had been underneath the ashtray and was in fact the first thing to catch fire, when Cornelius's last cigarette had rolled off the edge of the ashtray at a soporific leg shudder from under the table. Who knew that would be his last one? Who knew tonight would be the night, like any ordinary night, the pavements quiet, the clocks ticking, the river shifting, Big Ben marking time, and the moon a hazy half, softly coral and distant above.

Rania knew. She had told her sister that death was coming and she prayed in the peak at the top of Grenfell. Jessica didn't know; at twelve you likely don't know. Khadija didn't know; she had pictures to make and was fresh from the waters of Venice that had set her future sailing, and her mother Mary Mendy didn't know, that it was tonight, this very June, and that her daughter would go with her. For sixty hours the tower burned, full of waving phone torches at the smoky windows, full of bodies capitulating on the dark stairway, the cladding crashing down into the trees along the walkway, the water hoses pivoted at the inferno like far-flung upward urinations. People watched. They watched the failure of seventy fire engines and two hundred and fifty fire fighters to save seventy-two lives. They watched from the neighbouring flats and houses and could not believe that this was their local earth, this blazing height, this next-door scene. There were rushes back inside by the brave trying at rescues, some of which succeeded, some of which did not, or almost did, until death came outside on the grass instead, from shock, from smoke, from the final chime of inside clocks. Those who remained inside were ashes by sunset, difficult to identify in the midst of each other.

The last flame inside Cornelius was smothered from without. He coughed and danced in fright as the curtains caught. His old hands rocked. The old veins pumped. He asked his mother what had happened but she wasn't there anymore there was only silence—and then, within the flare, like a parting of the waves, caught in the doorway leading out towards the hall, the image of a little girl in a pale green nightdress, with upward burning hair. She appeared, disappeared, appeared again. She was standing completely still, gazing at him. That was when he knew. He knew exactly what had happened. He had known for a long time what it was. It was the fires of hell.

2

Kilburn. Wednesday. Alice Pitt was in her kitchen surrounded by her daughters and those of their children old enough to digest the night's dark matter; Warren had just arrived, his sister Lauren was already seated at the table with her thin gold chains and strips of tattoo eyebrow. There was not much eba at this table today. There was barely enough for a few mouthfuls each and the accompanying stew lacked zest and seasoning, but this was overlooked. What fine stew came out of grief? What good judgement of salt, of Oxo cube simmer? A related issue was that Alice had lately started using potato in her recipe instead of yam, a development requiring less effort with the pestle and mortar but which did not bear the same creaminess, the same compatibility with gari.

Aside from that there were crisps, a bag of alfalfa, some carrots, some chocolate muffins and white bread rolls culled frantically from Asda by Adel on the way here, in case there was no eba, no food at all, just Alice, bewildered in widowhood. Was she a widow? Did widows arise from marriages ended in everything but paper? She was a paper widow, fluttering in the British air, newly stranded, the cord to Kingsbury finally broken and catapulting her out towards the ocean. There would be no more pressured evening phone calls from that way north. There would be no more taut Christmases with the family gathered together. Cornelius was Kingsbury. Kingsbury itself therefore no longer existed. Except for the house. It did, the black burnt hole of itself, and that was something to face.

"We're going to have to *go* there," said Carol, "and see." She pictured the rooms, with a shudder of fascination; hanging smoke, bad silence.

"I'll come with you," Melissa said, sitting adjacent to her.

"You mean go *inside*," Adel burst into tears again, followed by Alice, more quietly, she had a private, silent way of crying, using her damp tissue, and Warren also resumed at the gravity of both his mother and grandmother overcome, he had never seen them cry in unison before. Lauren opened out another packet of crisps on the blue tablecloth in the communal fashion so that everyone could partake. "I was meant to go round there today after work," Adel said. "I *spoke* to him. The carers were coming. How could this've happened? They're supposed to check everything, didn't they check?"

"We can't blame the carers."

"Well who *can* we blame, Carol? When was the last time *you* visited him, huh? I've been doing it practically on my own. You don't help. You didn't help."

"That's not true, I was there last week . . . or, recently . . . Anyway it's easier for you, we're across the river, you're closer. It takes—"

"Just because I'm *closer* it doesn't mean I should do all the work. It doesn't mean I should be responsible, as per usual, for everything. Bushey doesn't really feel very close you know when I've been working all day and I'm tired and just want to get home. It's not about location. It's about making time. I have a full-time job and still manage to get over there almost every week. You teach pilates occasionally."

"Not occasionally, Adel, I run a business."

"Either way, your hours are flexible."

"That's not the point, though. The point is he shouldn't even've been living there anymore," Carol said. "That house was too big for him. He should've moved years ago, and I seem to remember you not being very helpful when I tried to make that happen."

"Did you? Really?" Adel scoffed.

Carol was about to reply but Alice interrupted. She was standing, leaning with her ringed hands on the edge of the table. She couldn't bear them arguing. How could they look at each other and argue when their father was just taken in the night like that? Adel the oldest behaving as youngest, and Carol the middle always chatting back, even at a time like this. "Is an *accident*," she pleaded with them. "Nobody's fault. Care for your sister. You cannot blame your sister—is me, only me . . ."

"Mum, don't cry."

They put their arms around her, the little hunched woman, who seemed overnight to have shrunk, become weaker, some solidity of being had vanished. Here was the revelation that had greeted them this burning morning, the deliverance of her life into their hands, like a late and second birth, a switch in direction. Now she was their charge, as they had been her reason to remain on this island. They had lived enough to make a raft and carry her. They all felt this and momentarily it calmed and united them.

"Mum's upset," Lauren said.

"I'm upset," Adel said.

"We're all upset."

It would emerge, from the inquest, that Cornelius was discovered intact, not ashes, it was smoke, not direct flames that took him. This had been a briefer, lesser fire than the bigger fire still raging in Ladbroke Grove. The tears for this fire were also tears for that fire, for one was stoked by the other, the black smoke meeting in London sky drifts, in the eastward direction of the bleak gold breeze. "What happened last night?" Carol said with her hands on her face, a slant-eyed architecture of jawline and cheekbone descended from her tall great grandmother of the Welsh bay. She was taller than her sisters, though they had all inherited their father's stout muscle and robust arms, and from their mother a look of innocence across the brow—in Adel it was sterner, older, in Melissa, distracted, in Carol, wilder, and there was a regal aspect to the way she carried herself, upright and earnest. She seemed to be speaking partly to herself, as if trying to comprehend. "There must've been some evil, some vicious force in the air last night. What's happening? It feels like the world is ending."

"The world *is* ending," Warren enthused, being prone to conspiracy theories, religions on the edge, stories of the dark centres of power. "It's happening, man. *Slowly*. Right here in front of us though. They're saying hundreds of people could be dead inside there by now. The media are downplaying it in case there's riots."

"If there's riots I'm rioting," said Lauren.

"Not that it makes any difference."

"It does make a difference."

"Maybe it does. I don't know," Melissa sighed and shook her head, closing her eyes.

"Hey, have you eaten anything yet?" Carol asked her. "You should have something even if you don't feel like it."

"You want akara?" Alice went quickly to her freezer, her city of ice, the chicken in reserve, the random renditions of rice (puddings, jollof). She had continued to inhabit her kitchen as if hungry mouths were waiting open. Every meal was badly attended, just her, aside from visits from family members, including Cornelius himself who had come on Wednesdays during the years of the after-marriage. He would kiss her dryly on the cheek in the hallway in the tradition of husbands, go on up into her single-occupancy living room and find things to criticise: flats are not as safe as houses, you know, these boilers they use are communal, aren't they, you can't control them yourself or turn them off when you want to. He had brought her for her seventieth birthday a porcelain Ansonia wall clock with a gilded rim, bright purple and flowered, which was positioned above the kitchen table and this morning had mysteriously paused, at 5:20 a.m. No one cared what time it was, it could be noon, three, five. Flames in their speed had taken time, all the ticks and tocks, and put them somewhere, perhaps given them to him, being an expert. Beneath the voices in the room, then, was a profound silence, no radio was playing, no music. Alice was finding it difficult to sit down. She had to keep moving, and what better reason than to feed a member of her clan, no matter how small a portion. "This only one I found in freezer," she said rising, holding a single, frosty akara in a corner-shop plastic bag. "I take it out for you." Now she must turn on the grill. Now she must get a small flameproof dish.

"Sit *down*, Mum, *we* can do that," came Adel's officious tone. Her life-stress was carried in her lungs, in her sinus, in the puff of her loosened skin, she was at that moment hotflushing, a rush of sickening heat all through which started deep within her upper back and shoulders, went down her arms and legs and up her neck, a furnace. "You need to *rest*," she ordered in this clammy surge; at least as far as Carol was concerned it was an order, and it brought on more backchat.

"Just let her be, will you?" she said. "Everyone has their own way of coping. If she needs to keep busy then let her keep busy." She was about to add that Adel was just like their father sometimes in the way she spoke to Alice, instructing and infantilising her, but she managed to hold her tongue. Adel was angrily ripping off her red and black zebra-print cardigan before the surge became unbearable, her cheeks awash with the heat, she snapped back, "Will you stop *arguing* with everything I *say*?"

Alice let them go on. She washed things, dried things. She switched on Radio 4. There was a programme on about Iraq in the wake of the US invasion. Awareness of such things leaked into her consciousness in passing segments, making a puddle of disconnected knowledge through which she noticed the world. "Want some alfalfa with that?" Lauren said to Melissa as Alice placed the akara in front of her on a saucer, with salt, it always needed salt. Melissa declined and stared at the food for a while. She still didn't feel like eating, but did so to please her mother, hardly tasting it, only registering the texture, a moist, air-bubbled doughiness. Since last night she had had no appetite. The phone had rung just after eleven and Carol's voice had come slithering down the line, not crying exactly, but slippery, unleashed. "Dad's gone," she'd said with brave resoluteness. The earth shifted, tipped sideways. Melissa had sat down on a step in her hallway as a numbed sensation came into her legs. Almost immediately on hearing the news, she had thought yet tried not to think of Michael. He swam up, out of a deep sea where he was submerged, never wholly drowned, the tendrils of him, the long hands that would hold and comfort (only he would know, only he would be the right one in this moment). She had cried in an expected, mechanical way, then stopped. In the morning she and Carol drove across the river to join with the relatives of the north, stopping on the way to buy cigarettes, of which they'd smoked one each, Melissa on an empty stomach. The numbness inside remained.

It was Carol whom Adel had bought the alfalfa for, and the carrots, in consideration of her avoidance of dairy, wheat, gluten (was there a difference?), meat, additives, spinach (what was *wrong* with spinach?), red peppers, yellow peppers, oranges, sugar, and salt if it was not either Celtic or Himalayan. But no one, not even Carol, wanted alfalfa today. Warren just looked at it, whiskery and unappetising in its bag. Alice was now sitting down, on a stool by the window, away from the main thoroughfare of the table. She had started peeling the carrots and would not stop until they were all peeled. Solitary and oily-eyed in her apron, she tried to listen to what Adel was saying about the house, something about insurance and papers and mess to sort out.

"The will's probably been destroyed. We're going to have to deal with the estate, the banks, household accounts, everything. Those insurance companies you know they'll do anything not to pay a claim."

"Innit. Tiefs," Warren said.

"We've got copies though, so at least that's something."

"I don't have a copy."

"You do. We all do, Melissa. He gave them to us, don't you remember? You've probably lost it. Maybe you misplaced it when you moved. I know where mine is."

Carol mumbled, "Yeah, I bet you do."

"What was that?"

"How can you be talking about a will, already?" she said. "How can you even be *thinking* about money and what you might get? There's people out there looking for their families, their kids . . ."

"I'm *talking* about *Dad*—"

"I know you are but has it escaped your attention there's an inferno going on down the road and how fucked up that is? Sorry for the language, Mum, but I'm just finding this so off-key. Where's your sense of humanity?"

Here Adel tightened at the mouth, her face stony, seeming to contain all the rigidity of her efforts to pretend and appease, about to lapse. "Watch the way you're talking to me, Carol.

Someone's got to be organised. This is not a normal way to die. It's not straightforward."

"No, it's not straightforward. What a shame. How inconsiderate of him not to die more conveniently."

Warren and Lauren were looking from one sister to the other with objections on the tips of their tongues. They were aware that their aunt Carol was the argumentative one, always the rocker of the boat, the rebel against authority. In their eyes their mother could do no wrong, they could never turn on her, but they did see that Carol might have a point. Maybe it was too soon to talk about paperwork.

"Know what I think, guys?" Lauren said by way of tempering. "I think at least Grandad died in his castle. He was at home, where he liked to be, where he was comfortable. So many of the old people at my work just want to be at home, and instead they're trapped in an institution with strangers. He went on his own terms. That's a positive thing, in a way."

"It's true," said her brother.

"Lauren, you have such a good heart."

"Yeah all right, Mum, don't get gushy."

"It *is* his castle, though . . . or—was. I liked going to see him there. I liked looking after him, even when he was being irritating and wouldn't listen or let me help. Whatever he was, however difficult, it was our duty to care for him." Adel gave Carol a short slap of a stare, going on to say, "*Now* it's our duty to manage his exit from this world, and we have to do it, all of us, together. I'm not going to be alone in it this time, that's all I'm saying. We have to deal with things properly and do it together. If you don't tie up the loose strings of your life when you go it makes for a bad time in the next world, in the after."

"The after," Carol said.

"The after, you know. After here."

"How do you know there's an after?" Warren asked.

"Déjà vu. That's all the proof I need."

Carol and Melissa glanced at each other but said nothing. Alice was thinking about her own next world and her own castle, which was not in Kingsbury or in Kilburn. It was far away from here, out in the fields near the edge of Benin City, a little house, long in the dreaming, which her relatives had been building for her for when it was time to go home to Nigeria. One day it would be time to go home, and perhaps now that time was closer than it was yesterday. She had never flourished in this UK. She had never been fully reborn or reconfigured as the immigrant must be in order to thrive, and leaving Cornelius had manifested less as a freeing actualisation of her whole self than as a greater yearning for the place where she began, so as to start again and reassemble, to remember herself before him, before the fog, before the children and the mountain of her life and everything it obscured.

She had left him slowly, with many suitcases. The same suitcases she had used for infrequent trips home over the decades. After one such trip, touching down at Heathrow Airport with the shine of the true country still in her head, in her cheeks, she had decided. Rather, *it* was decided. Her capacity for unhappiness was finite. If joy was so accessible from a short spell amidst her people, why wilt and decline in that old ticking house emptied of its children, with a man she had never understood and who had never understood her, often not even her voice, its thick Edo inflection? Carol had helped her, transporting the suitcases, arranging a room next to hers on Bantem Street in a shared house of women awaiting subsidised accommodation, where Alice became cherished for her akara and lemon sponge cakes and her plastic flowers. She was a mother to strangers and flailing girls, one or two of whom would come to visit sometimes once Alice had moved into her flat, all the suitcases finally unpacked, the parlour walls painted pink, the photographs and

the horde of ornaments on her shelves, disparate and imperma-
nent, like so many people waiting for a boat.

Pink as it was, and plastic flowers abounding, it was not the
castle. When she walked out into the streets with her orange
polka-dot trolley and her keys tied to the inside of her bag with
a safety pin as she was always advising her children to do to
guard against muggers and forgetfulness, she never felt that this
Kilburn was the place to meet her lord. She had found a church,
where she prayed on Sundays, Tuesdays and Thursdays. She was
a member of the four-lady choir, and she could buy all the foods
of Africa she wanted from bottled nuts to ground egusi to yams
and okra at the grocers and market stalls, but it was not the same
as walking the red-flecked paths of Benin, with the voices in the
air being her own kind of voice, the loneliness and exclusion of
foreignness erased. There, she did not have to remind herself
who she was because she was absorbed into the surrounding
multiple, and she could see and feel who she was. There, in her
castle, when she went and did her shopping, she would say hello
to neighbours and passers-by and they would not try to over-
charge her for plantain at the market and the young boys would
help her carry her bags and there would be no random British
curse words flying past her ears. Then in the evening, because
now she is an old, old woman, she would sit with her crochet
and spend the quiet, trickling time with death. She would not
be afraid. She would go towards it with her back straight and
her head bent, ready to be enfolded in its great dark cloak,
knowing that she was in the right place to receive it. Alice
believed in the cyclical life. We must end at the beginning.

As far as she knew, the house was not yet finished. She had no
idea how close it was to being finished. It had faded away, the dream
of it. Her brother who had been handling things had died. No particular instructions had been left for someone to take up the reins
and complete it. Suddenly the matter of the building of the castle

and where this long-lapsed project now stood was urgent. She broke into the conversation, tilted forward on her stool.

"That my house in Africa," she said, directing her question vaguely at Adel. "Is it nearly finish?"

The sunlight in the kitchen had shifted so that half of the table was in shade. As a result the shadow that passed over Adel's face was not visible, but there was a hesitation, a testing in her voice.

"The house? I don't know . . ."

This response annoyed Alice. Her eyes flashed. "What do you mean? You don't know? They must do it!"

"I don't *know* what's happening with it, Mum, you haven't mentioned it in ages. Why are you asking me? Why am *I* always the one people are always asking about everything?"

"Weren't you the one dealing with it?" said Carol.

"*Dad* was dealing with it."

"You had power of attorney."

"What's that?" Lauren said.

For some years Cornelius had sent money to Alice's brother to make this dream of hers come true. He loved his wife, even as he did not know her. He wanted to make her happy, to obscure his shortcomings with a lasting gift. He had even pictured himself in this house on the other shore, the crickets singing outside, the great settlement of the evening over the wide and beautiful terrain. He had loved Nigeria also, during the few years he'd lived there, and long afterwards he had missed it and imagined going back there to live one day. It had given him another possibility, a place to be someone else.

The foundations had been laid. Alice remembered, from one of her visits, three rows of bricks and mortar and the beginnings of partitions between rooms, no windows yet, but a solid ground, the green of the field surrounding and the teaching hospital in the distance. She had sat down there in the dust at the opening of a would-be doorway and envisioned it finished, filled with all of her mats and her crockery and her ornaments no longer waiting for a boat. Surely it must now have windows and a roof. Surely they had had enough money to do the walls all the way up.

"I wish you talk to them at home," she said, this time to all three daughters. "Ask them. Your daddy give them money for building, since many years. Talk to them. Call their number."

She scraped the carrot peelings into the bin next to her, mobilised by the castle vision, her faith in it, then she stood, placing the carrots in a pile on the table, their stubs cut off at each end. It was like an offering from the land, a declaration of roots, extracted and displaced, no fine stew or soup to enter.

Aware of the extent of Alice's upset—she was the closest child, the one who had come after the stillborn boy and there was a special love between them—Carol said lightly, "Don't worry, Mum, we'll look into it. I'll ask Clay to help, a little homework project. Do we have any of their numbers?"

"Use Facebook, it's quicker. Don't you know the long-lost aunties, uncles, fathers, brothers and sisters are all accessible on Facebook? Phones will soon be obsolete."

"Not my phone," said Lauren, clutching it out of her bag in its glittered cover and checking it.

"I was talking about landlines," Melissa clarified.

"Anyway I gotta go, people, I'm working today." Warren was getting up from his stool. He stretched out and yawned, flexing sinew, putting on his shades. He was twenty-seven years old but had a younger face, if tense around the jaw, a symptom of a lingering confusion about his future, a recent girlfriend lost. His mother took in the sight of him, approving of him and inwardly justifying everything necessary she had done to rescue him, while Melissa asked, "When you coming to see me? We never see you. Where are you working now?"

"At What!!!"

"What?"

"What!!! It's a shop, in Lewisham."

Laughter spread across the room, "Are you being serious?" Carol said.

"I'm *serious*. We sell pens, watches, wrapping paper, plates, combs, deckchairs. It's one of those warehouse shops. Just temporary. I need the money."

"Well, maybe I'll drop in and see *you* instead some time," Melissa replied, "seeing as you're such a stranger. I have to go now as well. Got to pick up Blake."

"Wait," said Alice, drying her hands on a towel. "I going to give you some of that oil from Africa. Michael can mash your back." By mash she meant massage. She made to leave the room.

"Mum, I'm not *with* Michael anymore, will you please try and remember? It's been eight years! I don't know why you can't just accept it or at least just *remember*."

It was true. Alice had a blockage when it came to Michael, which flared up in moments of distress or extremity. He was the finest boy who had passed through this wing of women, the good prince, the one a mother dreams of, although he wasn't a Nigerian but it didn't matter really at the end of the day. Carol she did not like men anymore but women so she was out of the picture. And Adel since divorce did not have time to waste on wastemen, as she often put it, having brought up her children alone, their father an infrequent visitor. Michael was respectful. He had always addressed her as Mrs. Pitt and offered his arm if she was getting out of a car or going up stairs. Good manners. Good family. She just couldn't understand why Melissa threw him away after so many thirteen years when he was far from a wasteman. What did she want? And their two babies, what about them?

"I don't know," she said shaking her head. "It's not good for you young people to be mum and dad. The children need their daddy."

"And they *have* him. He has them most weekends." This information had been delivered many times before, always to no impact. It did not appease her. How can you be a father just at weekends? It was not the same thing as a real husband who was there every day and who came home after work and put down his briefcase and grumbled over dinner then watched television and drank whisky and terrified the children, as had been her experience, which she had endured for the sake of the children. That was marriage. When you have someone who is decent and proper, you must be grateful.

"I miss him, though," Warren was shouldering his rucksack. "It's sad when people break up and a whole person just disappears out the family. It's not fair on everyone else."

"You should call him. I'm sure he'd love to hear from you," Melissa said.

"Maybe I will."

There was a messy gathering to leave. Adel and Lauren stayed behind for a while with Alice, who gave parting gifts of out-of-date popcorn, out-of-date Quality Streets left over from Easter and anything else suitable she could find in her cupboards. She said to the computer users, "Remember when you been computer for so long you leave it few minute at a time," to the electricity users, "Make sure you turn light off in the night," to the drivers, "Don't try to take shortcut just go major road," to the rearers of young children, "Remember not to shout at them. Give them a kiss," and to the tired, ailing or cramped, "Make sure you use hot water bottle and mash with that oil from Africa," a pot of which she did give to Melissa anyway. This remained her central purpose, to guide and mash the young. It was the only thing this country had given her, and now she was sewn into its cloth, by the fact of their birth, and when that flag waved in the air at Buckingham Palace and the Houses of Parliament, she was inside that flag.

Warren hugged her by the cooker, vigorously, even a little roughly, slumped over her, accepting the chance to be quite broken in that moment. He always hugged her like that, no one but him. Later when she was alone she sat by the lamp in the parlour and mourned Cornelius. All that he was. The life of a man. He was not perfect and not quite good. There was only one aspect in which she did not feel any guilt. He had spoken to death in his own land, where he knew the shape of the air and the language of the folds of the cloak. He was home, and maybe that would have been enough to deliver him in the flames.

3

There are no more gypsies in Gipsy Hill. Their dome-shaped tents are gone, their winter camps during the reign of Victoria, their travels among the farms picking fruit and September hops. Open fields gave way to railway lines and the swelling of the city, the dwindling of the Great North Wood, becoming Norwood, Upper Norwood, of which Gipsy Hill was now a part. In its hilly distances were the Eiffel shapes of the two towers, rising from Crystal Palace and from Beulah. Probably descendants of those old Roma still dwelled here, amid the quiet rows of low houses, the flats overlooking the bumpy greens. Melissa had stayed here, partly because she liked the name of the place, the way it evoked movement, and partly because the children had settled into schools, averting movement. She had a three-bed flat on the first and loft floors of a house owned by a former chef who lived alone on the ground floor. He baked a lot and never increased the rent.

It took an hour and a half to drive back across London during the rush hour, in time to pick up Blake by six. On the way she and Carol talked about the prospect of the house in Nigeria; it seemed an abstract resurrection from this distance of years and miles, a pipe dream, where to begin? They fell silent assessing the new reality of the world without Cornelius, which looked the same from the outside, the constancy of everything, but inside something was amiss, a section clipped off, an extraction of a root. Old white men in the streets looked just like him. They witnessed in a softer light passing dancy shuffles, bent white-haired crowns and swaying walking sticks. To the west at their backs as they crossed over Vauxhall Bridge the last of the flames of the bigger fire burned onwards. Carol got out near her place in Camberwell with tears in her eyes ("text me tomorrow"), and Melissa watched her walk away, her fierce and earnest sister, her wrap dress and the silver lights of her locks merging into the drifting summer din of Walworth Road.

How to explain it to the children, such tragedy—a violence so close, a vanishing—without a lie? Since it had been observed lately that Blake cheated at games and tried to deny midnight sweet sneaks when he got caught and was even prepared to steal from Costcutter to get football cards, Melissa had vowed to always demonstrate truth, so as to avoid the apparently real possibility of her son turning out to be a liar, a cheat and a thief. Far from it did he appear, rising from the Lego station amidst his yellow-shirted school mates, reluctantly advancing towards her against the pull of his playing, thin-faced, light-footed, big hands. "You're too early," he complained. He wanted to be the last, the very last, perhaps to stay in the empty school building and see what happened in here at night; were there ghosts? were there workers? was there food? was it the same as in *Toy Story*?

"It's quarter to," she said. "They close in fifteen minutes."

"I like it when Daddy picks me up."

And there it stood, the fracture of his life, much larger than him, repeatedly underlined. Michael picked him up most Fridays and took him, along with Ria, for a weekend stay in the green suburban summits beyond the bowl of Catford, returning them on Sunday evening for dinner. It was an arrangement established without lawyers or courts, outside the jurisdiction of a fallen marriage, that contract they had never dared enter and as it turned out wisely so, they had walked on without paper, eager for a smooth transition. The house they'd lived in on Paradise Row was a distant memory of slayed mice, dust and crooked walls, sold and split both ways. Given the weekend cameo, these Daddy-preferences were common, and met with mute endurance or sarcasm.

"Well, it's nice to see you too," she muttered, gathering his water bottle and his mislaid cap and feeling an affinity with both for being a receptacle of concentrated matter. On the way out there was a problem with her fingerprint, necessary for entering and exiting the building due to a high-level security system designed to keep out child murderers, paedophiles and any passing South London molesters. The print had to be re-scanned but wouldn't read. Philomena, after-school club manager, remarked accusingly, "You have a faint finger."

Under the circumstances Melissa found this disturbing. "Oh . . . do I?"

"Let's try it again. Hold it firm, right there. Press hard."

It still wouldn't read. A surge of get-my-money's-worth six-o'clockers with fully functioning fingers arrived to take the last children home and the re-scan got side-tracked, so they left, remaining faint, heading out to the car park where the murky green Vauxhall with the bodywork dents along the sides was waiting, a car that Blake was secretly ashamed of, Daddy's car was better. The dents had happened during momentary blanks, slights of the Highway Code, once on the way back from a night out with her friend Hazel when they'd shaved against a boulder in the rain. Beyond the car park the playing fields stretched out towards the woods behind the school, where the town quietened, giving air to its birds, among swathes of centurial trees.

Sliding up the hill past the petrol station, Blake said, "We've all got three holes in our faces, Mummy, and two more holes on the sides of our faces, you know, our ears. Where do they go?"

"Where do what go?" she asked.

"The holes. It's just because today at lunch a fly flew in my ear and I think it's still in my head."

"Don't worry, it's not in your head. It flew back out."

"How do *you* know?"

"That happened to me once with a wasp. I was convinced it had reached my brain, but it didn't."

"How do you *know* it didn't?"

"Because it's just not physically possible. Things that fly like air."

"That's not a proper reason."

Such dilemmas and questions of existential biology, cosmology, ecology, ontology, etymology and the animal kingdom came regularly from the back seat, requiring subsequent Google checks and reminders to Blake to consult the hard-cover encyclopaedia, mostly ignored out of laziness. Why consult a book when the parent oracle is at hand with smarterphone and accompanying food, finance and secretarial services? Melissa was constantly faced with the limits of her own knowledge, compelled to filling her head with disparate useful trivia, on hand to present to this eight-year-old boy when met with his everyday befuddlement. What *is* this place? he still felt. What does it *mean*? What does *everything* mean?

At fifteen, Ria could be assumed to have advanced from such wonder. She was tall and stretching treelike to a higher stature, slender of limbs and fingers, lush rose-lipped and natural-lashed. Yesterday the teenage boy who worked at the till in Costcutter had given her the eye, her blooming prettiness, her tight black coils and frightened shining stare, so unlike the girls with the fake lashes and edge-controlled baby hairs. She was a creature facing her gender, everything that it posed, its performance, its humiliation and restriction, and she *was* frightened, at the same time indifferent. She was still beset with marvel such as why her gums were different colours and whether darkness was alive, separately and in itself. "You know balloons are basically just hovering time bombs," she might say at a random moment, or, "You know celery is just crunchy water, right?" or "Last night I had a dream I ate the internet." She favoured the boys department of H&M, hated skirts, lipstick, bras, high heels and pink. When Melissa and Blake got home she was playing Despacito on her keyboard, sending notes like a bright shower spilling down the stairs leading up to the flat. She also hated Justin Bieber but was not discriminate in her song choices.

"S'up, sis," Blake said.

"Hey."

"What did he make today?"

Melissa was referring to Calvin who lived below. There was a smell of ginger and heated sugar.

"Spice bun. I had some with cheese."

"I'm having some."

"Wait 'til after dinner. Go and put your stuff away and get changed."

Whenever Calvin baked he shared it. Walnut and pineapple cakes, breads of the world, at Christmas fruit logs laced with rum. Melissa was coldly aware that it was because of Calvin that she had acquired her excess stone, now tipping towards a stone and a half, the evening chewing of his shared creations and left-over wedding cakes, offered continually to the storey above and never declined, not by these children. In fact they imitated him, baked also, fried pancakes, quesadillas. If it were up to Melissa she would eat keto and fend off her menopause, but it was hard in this situation, her life orchestrated by other people's batons, their cymbals and triangles. They played in his garden too, which was reached via a metal staircase off the tiny kitchen balcony, and he watched over them sometimes when she was out. Calvin had bought the house thirty years ago for the modern equivalent of a song and paid off the remainder of the mortgage after selling his parents' house in St. Kitts, so he no longer needed to work. Food was his work and he carried on with it.

"You heard about the fire?" he said.

Melissa was out on the balcony, having glimpsed him in the garden bent over his herbs, navy-blue polo shirt tucked in by a brown leather belt. Further down along the row of lawns was a Union Jack waving in the breeze, attached to someone's conservatory. After the referendum last year it had become ragged with the temper of the weather, like a shredding manifesto, to be quickly replaced with a fresh new flag, foolishly fluttering with intent.

"It's horrific."

"I know that block, it's too tall, was always too big and tall. They don't care about them people in there. It's breaking my heart. People burning up, burning up! What are they going to do about it now? It's too late, man. They never took the time to mind the accident and look the accident done happen."

"Does Ria know about it? I didn't want to say anything this morning."

"Must be, it's all over the news. It'll be just like Katrina. You watch."

"Do I know about what?"

Ria had come up behind her. "What happened, Calvin?" she said, leaning out.

"Nah, I let your mother say, you'll know about it soon enough. I don't want to tell you everything on my mind about this damn country as you still got to grow up and live in it."

"It's ok, I'm going to live in LA."

"LA? Since when?" Melissa said. "But Trump."

"I'll deal with him."

This made Calvin laugh but then cry a bit, "Ha, what are you going to do about Trump?"

"I have a plan. His days are numbered." Ria had a strange wide smile on her face, housing her eccentricity. Calvin gathered his herbs in his hands and said, "Well, I hope you get through with that one—there's another catastrophe!," and he returned to his kitchen to make more food, something savoury this time.

"So tell me then," Ria said coming back inside.

"Wait. Help me with this. Have you done your homework?"

"If you don't tell me now I'll get some mud one day and put it in your sock."

"You're crazy."

"I'll tickle your feet in the middle of the night. And I won't go to school tomorrow."

"I thought you might know by now anyway. The fire . . . didn't you hear about it?"

"No."

"I thought your teachers might have told you."

"We didn't have assembly today."

They made pasta as they talked, in the orange light of the kitchen. The room was separated from the living area by a half-height wall so it was more a segment, once part of a back bedroom. Two small rooms at the front, looking out on the tight-packed terraces and the railway lines heading for London Bridge, had been fashioned from Calvin's old master suite, now the children's place of dreaming. In this house, unlike the upstairs-downstairs of Paradise Row, their dreaming did not have a floor of its own and breakfast was not descended into, instead walked across to, past the bathroom, which, for Melissa, however, was still downstairs. She slept in the loft at the top of the house. It was like ascending to Alaska in the winter months but she had become accustomed to it and was stoically frugal with her supplementary electric heater. In the summer it was by contrast acrid and stifling. Wasps flew in through the skylights and smashed against the ceiling fan, spiders nestled in the sloping corners, when they ventured out she faced them with an upside-down cup and a postcard, the way Michael used to do. Arachnophobia was for lovers, a luxury.

From the dining table by the window they could see Calvin watering his grass and picking up landed fruit, his movements riled and brooding, while the evening sun moved backwards towards the slump of sunset. A deep pink frowned in the expanse, laced in smoke-grey drifts enflamed. Fire was everywhere. Death was all around. The food tasted chalky and bitter in Melissa's mouth, rejected by an inside tremor, the lingering numbness, borne from the comprehension that her father was no more of this ground, but skyward, extinguished. There was so much she felt and did not feel, a relief, a sense of retribution, in the next instant nothing. Sitting between the children on the sofa after dinner, she told them the news, about the earlier fire, which was smaller, much smaller, last night in their grandfather's house. He was not burnt, she told them, for a gentler picture, it was the shock, he was too old for such a shock.

Blake immediately began to weep. Ria gasped, as if she had been tapped on the shoulder, as if she walked among ghosts and had half expected it. That man who gave them Eccles cakes, ginger nuts and crisps and let them measure their own Ribena, they would never see him again. Ria would never again be able to study the mercury volcano of his hands or jump off his garage roof, and Blake would never swing on those old broken swings with the uneven ropes. It was over, that part of their lives, and that was what was hard to take. Not so much that they would yearn for him—he was polite, aloof, mostly, exotic in his northernness—but that he *no longer existed,* which was the impossible thing about death. Nobody did not exist, but everyone ceased to exist, taking bits of the people around them, leaving holes.

"Who *started* the fire," Blake said, appalled. "Was it started by a, a pyromaniac?" This was his latest new word.

"Was he by himself?" Ria said, as guilt crawled thickly around Melissa's shoulders, circling her voice in her attempts to answer their questions.

"Where will he go?" Blake said, thinking again of the fly in his head.

"We'll have a funeral, and he'll be buried. Or maybe he'll be cremated."

"What's that?"

"Burnt and scattered on the sea," said Ria.

"But how can you be burnt twice?"

"He wasn't burnt."

"I bet some of him was burnt. I bet his trousers got burnt."

"Ok now listen," Melissa said, taking their hands and clenching them in hers; Blake folded into her, she was still his warmest cave. "We should try and think of him alive, the good things about him. Remember him that way instead. What are the good things?"

They thought about it together.

"He did good barbeques."

"Yes. He did."

"Good sausages."

"Yes."

"He was kind," Ria said.

Melissa pictured her father in the garden, sitting before his grill with his back to the house. They would visit him there with beer-refills and chat for a while, but he was very much alone with his meat, caged in its browning, in the ever-churning primal tasks of men. She was trying to concentrate on the good things but the bitter taste in her mouth made it difficult. She

39

could feel a far-back darkness gathering, coming closer, bringing old pictures she could not quite make out. On the TV across the room, David Attenborough was narrating the lives of lions. There were bison chasing. When they caught the lion they started to eat, while that steady, familiar male voice went on in the background, observant and detached.

"Imagine if that was you, being eaten alive to death," Blake said to his mother. "If I was watching that happen, I would sacrifice myself."

The lion capitulated and closed its eyes.

Ria said quietly, "That's a horrible way to die."

Later, when everything was still, Melissa went upstairs to her room. She turned on the fan and the bedside lamp and pulled in the skylights, leaving them ajar. There was a message from David on her phone that she hadn't replied to yet. Are we still on for Friday? Want to see you. She should cancel, she thought, but didn't quite want to. They might have a nice time. He might say something right and rescuing or they might walk, one of those shadowy Dulwich walks with the lit trees. Still on, she wrote back; he replied straight away, Great! 7 at Patchwork?, which made her want to change her mind.

David had never been in this room. No man had, apart from Calvin who once had fixed the fan. Here was her fort of solipsism and higher dreaming. The singular space she had yearned for in the red Paradise master where Michael had lain next to her night after night. Here she lay alone in a carefully chosen queen-size pushed against the wall, not stranded ship-like in the middle, leaving space for morning yoga and occasional leaps of simulation ballet. In the corner of the room to the right of the skylights was her desk from which she delivered her subedits to Gower Media on Wednesdays and Thursdays. On Fridays she took the train to Clapham Junction and walked from there to

Battersea to sit in a very white room off a college IT area help-ing undergraduates with their essays. The rest of the week she was back at Gower, in the office this time, a subdivision based in Blackfriars, which was underneath a cosmetic dentist. They shared the letterbox. Sometimes Melissa went up there to give them their post. All the dental people seemed contented, the receptionist, the passing orthodontist in his jeans and open-collared shirt. They led clear, fixed, uncomplicated lives, given to the care of mouths. They operated in a clean blue purity full of light and glinting metal with benevolent sharp points. Lin-gering, she would get to wondering if she should pursue a different kind of work from her current portfolio arrange-ment, something practical and instantaneously impactful or redemptive, in order to feel her human usefulness on a more consistent basis.

As it was, the words were the teeth. She cleaned them. She scraped the plaque, filled the holes, flossed, advised interdental brush measurements to the contributors who misjudged their linkages between paragraphs. She liked to say something over the phone like "I don't think your semicolon has been fully jus-tified here," or "the whole weight of this piece is becoming lopsided because of abandoned logic," or "I'm afraid we have to return yet again to the problem of your comma splice." She massaged, not massacred, the words, keeping tone intact, sharp-ening intention, and she had great admiration for the plural apostrophe. After six years of teaching full time at the journal-ism school, a fashion expat, retired to the has-beens of low-level sartorial columnists, she had surrendered to her hack and sought a position, something that would mean she didn't have to use overhead projectors anymore in front of the staring Genera-tion Z. "They're customers, not students," Luander, another lecturer, would say. "They want to buy their 2:1. It's not their fault. The monetisation of education is a disaster for everyone, for *society,* that fucking Nick Clegg. Traitor." One-to-one they were softer, the students, less masking of their fright. She would say similar things about the comma splice and spend no more than five pounds on lunch at the campus café, sometimes with Luander, who was in remission from cancer now, was a little quieter and wore scarves, had started writing poetry, which they talked about and shared recommendations.

Melissa still wrote them, her dripping stanzas (she was thinking of taking classes), a funnel for her woes (it was only when she was sad that she wrote them), and an antidote to journalism with its eye on the big cataclysmic world. She had deliberately chosen current affairs over lifestyle, commentary over glossy magazine, but the work left her with a similar lack and compartmentalisation. She lived, she felt, on two levels; one was louder than the other. One existed in a place of deep thought and retreat, the other was full of jump and beat, throwing itself outwards, wanting flight, action, a crowded room. But in her yellow wingback armchair, carefully positioned in the opposite corner from the desk, she retreated with the poets, a line of them on the bookshelf including Anne Sexton ("Some women marry houses"), Derek Walcott with his blue birds, and Neruda. She would dip into their verse and find a trail for her thoughts. Poetry was like religion, a current that drew the searching towards it. There was a kind of faith to be found in the falling lines and their gesture into pattern, that the pattern might save you or make a clear reflection in which to see. Below the poets was a row of favourite novels, below that self-help, addressing the myriad qualms of body, mind and soul, *The Bates Method* for strengthening the muscles of the eye, *The Black Women's Health Book* for the blanketing afflictions of racialised gender that would apply to her, and various tomes on the practice of meditation, an activity she could never sustain for longer than a week, though Buddhism ever beckoned.

At the helm of the room, on the wall above its central manifestation as attic—a triangular recess encasing the shelves—were
three framed women in headwraps and trainers whom Melissa
had named Patience, Comfort and Mercy. She had bought them
online from Wayfair. She spoke to them sometimes and they
looked out at her with their chutzpah, their Dutch wax colour
and the empty computer pink of their backscreen. They were
the bold and silent guardians of the holy, man-free space, the
queens of this roof, beloved by its sole now gently weeping
occupant. They witnessed her moving about the room as she
stepped out of her jumpsuit and left it crumpled on the chair, as
she pulled on a gauzy black chemise, looked for a suitable track
to play, what sound? what notes can carry this night? Terry Cal-
lier, she found, scrolling, and let him flow in. The sound was a
tumble of water embraced, constantly rolling over, bending to
lift it back and fold again. His fatherly voice held the lost father
inside it and she pictured him, lifted her sheets and slid in, pictured her father walking the way he had in the last weeks when
she had visited him, that quick shuffle, the waist twitching, as
though he rushed to get somewhere that was fading before him
because of how speed had left him, or perhaps the thought that
propelled him had disappeared. With this same walk she pictured him airbound, heading for silver hills, holding his walking
stick, his clothes are too big for him, he wears a hat, the flat
tweed cap of an old northerner with the moors in his voice and
the blue in his eyes and she missed precisely the fact of those
things with a force that pressed down on her chest as he walked
away, out of the world—and again, she could not help it, she
yearned for Michael, she felt that he must know, that if it were
the other way round he would feel the same, that he would
understand the secret dimensions of it, the way David, hardly
known by comparison, a mere passer-by, never would. With
David there was no sense of a kiss so momentous it might be

named Desdemona or Angelina, there was not a universe of two, or a tower, or a palace. Nowhere else, with no one else did those things exist, and how at a time like this they gleamed.

The compulsion to contact Michael gradually abated as she lay there, sinking. She was alone, in all its power and peril and drift. She was to be her own saviour, capable of withstanding shocks, the monsters of the deep and the night terrors, the gift of which was the full possession of an entirety of thought, the quietude of the cavernous self. Lying on her back, she turned towards the skylights and registered the midnight colour. A train went by in the distance. She closed her eyes and sank further, thinking of the silver hills and how long it must take to get there, was it cold or was it warm, did the hills speak, would they welcome him when he arrived, tired from his walking? There were others too, moving that way, lifting from the high flames of Grenfell, the grey souls of the smoky children, the surprise of mothers, uncles, nephews, finding themselves out here with no way of getting back. She must go and see their tower, she felt. She must go and stand and look at it, tomorrow or the next day, in order to touch their memory and witness the crime, to be with her city as it bent. In the doorway of sleep, she felt herself rising, up the storeys of the windows, up past the praying and the shouting and the reaching, her body left behind her on the bed, a separate thing, weightless and horizontal, only a shape. She rose slowly further upwards, released from gravity. When she reached the top of the tower, with the stars and nimbus close, she believed that she might save them, that time might suspend them in life. But soon, too quickly, she began to fall. She felt the force of an angel leaving her, stepping away. There was an instant of intense fear the faster she fell, she plummeted, down and down. And then she landed, with a little waking shock, back inside her body.

4

Melissa arrived at Grenfell at the same time as Queen Elizabeth II. There she was in soft electric blue, rising from her chariot, a shiny black gleaming thing also containing the Duke of Cambridge, who by comparison sprang out the other side, smoothing his lapels, wearing the appropriate facial expression, grave sympathy undertoned by a familiar ready smile, and waving at the crowd with a certain specificity, as if he were down with it. The Queen's wave was more understated, the only wave she knew, the staid offer of the white-gloved hand, which matched the under-rim of her blue hat, which matched her coat; this was a woman of deep sartorial coordination. Sweetly shrunken in her nonagenarian circumstance, unknowingly robbed of the opportunity to present Cornelius with his card, she lingered in the forecourt of the Westway Sports Centre, talking to members of the stricken congregation.

This was no light work of a Friday 11 a.m. tour. This crowd was pissed. This crowd was composed of survivors looking for other survivors, daddies looking for their daughters, haunted women floating, people walking around holding pictures of the missing above their heads, have you seen my children? do you recognise him? them? Closer to the base of the tower was a wall full of such pictures, a three-year-old named Zainab Choucair, a twelve-year-old named Jessica Urbano Ramirez. "My niece was visiting someone there," a man who was standing behind Melissa said, "still haven't heard from her." Before that he had been berating Theresa May for not coming to visit the site ("if she can't even do that she shouldn't be running the country"), for visiting only when the death toll had risen to thirty and only the nearby fire station, while keeping her back to the aggrieved the whole time, and just last week he had voted for her to do the Brexit. In fact this crowd was so pissed with Theresa May specifically that if there had been a way of constructing an effigy of her on top of the burning tower so that she might by association feel the pith of the horror then that would be all right with them. They were annoyed with the TMO—the Kensington & Chelsea Tenant Management Organisation—for ignoring their requests to replace the tower's out-of-date fire extinguishers marked CONDEMNED with ones that worked. They were annoyed with the media who they felt sure were deliberately understating the extent of the death toll, hundreds, hundreds, surely, must be dead. And back to Theresa May they were also upset with her for trying to form a government with anti-abortionists in Northern Ireland due to her diabolical election performance and triggering Article 50 in March without so much as a plan for the Brexit, and for that matter they were not particularly impressed with the Queen either for the fact that the flag was not flying at half-mast as it would be if these were lots of British-born white people dying, and for her elitist, unerring disassociation from the politics of her country and the ordinary lives of its citizens whose taxes and historic colonial exploitation helped fund her luxury.

So there was quite a lot of pressure on those frail blue shoulders as they came into their midst. What is the point of majesty in this here situation? What can she give, one who has everything, to those who have lost everything? Yet, when the car pulled up under the Westway flyover, there was an atmosphere of deference, a hush, even a kindness towards this gesture of kindness, of seeming to give a shit. Their feelings are mixed, this furious crowd. This lady's wealth is questionable, but is it her fault that she was born onto a pile of gold culled from the destruction and theft of nations and communities, and do we have the energy, really, at this moment, to reproach her for lacking the courage at any point in her life to cast off that wealth and forge a new identity as a normal person with a proper job and obligations to HMRC? She *is* HMRC. And that aside, the tax issue aside, there was a gentleness of feeling towards her and a respect for her antiquity as she listened to the traumatised and the volunteer organisers outside the sports centre, looking up at them, peering out of her silver into the pit of another reality. Bowed and slow, she went inside with her grandson, to spend the next half an hour in the company of people whose homes had been replaced by a temporary mat on a parquet floor below a very high ceiling.

Melissa had come by tube, alighting at White City, walking northeastward through the sun-beat streets she had once trodden daily, danced along in Notting Hill Carnivals, pushed Ria along on a red and yellow tricycle and held hands along with Michael before they'd crossed the river. Their old tower was here, their palace in the sky, also run by the TMO; at night the tower block lights would wink at one another. She had come to witness, every morning this week having woken to images of flames, of Khadija Saye with her arms raised and the flames her fatal wings. Standing here in the midst of the crowd she felt part of the weight of the world's watching and its hush at the clarity of what was being shown, that the system is set wrong, life is measured below wealth ("you don't get the best materials when you're poor," someone said, "as long as it looks ok on the outside"). People were watching from the Grenfell railings. Crews of local boys with high-tops weaved through the precinct handing out bottles of water to volunteers working in the heat, sorting bags of donated clothes which would amass over the coming weeks to form disaster boutiques in the neighbourhood churches. The air smelt of ash, or the ash was a thought, a settlement. While the Queen was inside, her car and chauffeur waited outside, where a group of defeated fire fighters trailed into the clearing to a round of subdued applause. They were followed by a tall lurching black girl with some questions.

"Where's Theresa May?" she asked the chauffeur.

"I don't know," he said quietly.

"Who's in there?"

"The Queen."

"Of what? Who made her queen?"

The chauffeur was slow in responding to this, so the girl asked him instead about his gloves and why he wore gloves in the car because her mother didn't when she was driving and when she was driving she usually took off her coat as well. Eventually she wandered away, joining the other wanderers, the drifters, the watchers. Two women dressed in sleeveless black dresses sat listlessly in a government front yard before their new carcass view, trembling in the June haze. Their manor, their home turf, smoking, just across the way.

Further east, hoisted across Oxford Street on roof poles, a banner read,

LONDON EVERYONE WELCOME

(referring mainly to the West End).

Before leaving the area, Melissa joined the volunteers in the precinct helping with the clothes, and then went onwards, to Kingsbury. To the smaller, private carcass. No crowds or cordons, the keyholes are intact, you go in through the back door.

Carol was waiting for Melissa at the station and they walked together through the old manor, past the park and the trading estate, sensing themselves slipping backwards, their memories lifting from the hot pavements, of rainy drives in dark autumns and heights on the garden swings, still there, untouched. They slowed down in the driveway. They could feel it, the big hollow and the sulking rooms.

The front of the house was almost unchanged in its greyed stucco and solid, inward stare. It sat stout and tight-shouldered on its slope, the belly of its bay curved outwards at the ragged hedge and cracked stone path, at the end of which Cornelius might have waved, a ghost of him remained, an imprint in the daylight. What was different was that the windowpanes were black, and this seemed to add a human aspect, the house looked shocked, like someone who had died with open eyes. Everything that had once lived within could be felt in this black, the three little girls with their hands gripping the windowsills and the glitter of the Christmas angel with her golden circling planets. The shape of Alice sat leaning back in the bay shadows, her curtains gone, the old chandelier fallen and its crystals rolling to her slippered feet, the swish of which could still be sensed in the foundations.

Carol went in first. She waited, before pushing open the back door into the kitchen. Summertime disappeared. She stopped and put her hand to her mouth. They stood there, taking in the stunning theft of colour. That is what fire does, it erases colour in the brightness of its own and what is left is the smoke of the fight. Smoke had left its broad tongue across the ceilings and covings and banister, licked upwards past light switches and picture frames. It hung, mean and devilish, claiming the space, creating a kind of theatre. They could see themselves, running to the front door, through the hall to the back door, back and forth and out of breath. A phantom child slid down the black banister, legs swinging, and the mother drifted through with

49

her faraway wish, now the father, faster, younger and more vigorous than his final frailty.

"It feels like we're in hell," Carol said. "Oh poor Dad. I feel like I'm being swallowed up."

There was a renewed, bitter taste in Melissa's throat. It had come at every meal since the fires. Maybe it's this, she thought, maybe the smoke has got inside.

"Can you taste it?" she said.

"What?"

"The smoke. It's bitter."

"The fumes. They said that would've got him first."

"How can they know for sure?"

"Timing. Or they were just being kind when they said that."

Carol took Melissa's hand and they ventured through the kitchen, along the slip mat which made a sticking noise, into the living room where the silence and the black were deepest. This was stage-centre of the flames, the place Cornelius had returned to from the Welsh hillside except that now there was no pouffe, no straw dustbin or wooden table. At the location of the throne of patriarchy was a square-metre pit of soil, which the two sisters peered down into, not registering at first what it was, a hole at the bottom of the house, a suggestion of a tunnel, a crater.

"Wait, is that—is that where his chair was?"

"It's burnt right down," Carol said.

"No, it's there, look."

They found the chair a few feet away in the dining room, pitched crooked against the sideboard like a hulking relic of a faded reign. It was not immediately recognisable. "I didn't realise there was so much metal in it," Melissa said, "I mean, how much metal it takes to make an armchair." There he would sit, after taut and stabbing dinners, his back to the dining table which, following his retreat to the armchair, would be overtaken by wild laughter, the tension unfolding, the angry spoon gone. They would laugh and laugh, with no particular subject, in the evening freedom before deep liquor night and the booming fear.

Carol said, "Well, there's more to upholstery than most people think," and laughed despite herself, they both did, in that same delirium as if they had been transported back to their child selves. It crashed against the silence and rushed at the ash, the house could hear it, remembered it, loosened momentarily with the light sound.

Mahogany cabinets, deserted dining chairs. "See this, I can't believe the desk is still standing." There were board games fully intact in cupboards and cutlery, serviettes, place mats in the drawers, only everything was covered in a layer of dark grey and smelt of fire. Carol searched through the desk while Melissa picked through the wreckage of the living room, finding shards of ornaments and a Benin mask, a souvenir from a past visit. She went back out into the hallway, registering the cupboard under the stairs where they would be sent for misbehaving (its door was open, she slammed it shut with a certain force). On the console she found the padded winter gloves Cornelius used to wear in the garden on his icy evening walks. She picked them up, avoiding looking in the mirror, fearing that if she saw her own face here something terrible would happen and she might not be able to get out. Or she would see another face, not quite her own, and would forget how to return to herself.

Holding the gloves with both hands, she called to Carol that she was going upstairs. "On your own? Don't you want me to come with you?" But she went alone and stood before the window in her old bedroom staring out at the bright day, remembering one day in particular when Alice had told them that their father would be away for a time, in something like hospital, so that he could "get better." They hadn't quite understood it, what he had to get better from, or more precisely, that you could get better from the thing that was wrong with him in a hospital. But it didn't matter. The good thing was that he was gone. There was such an air of open joy in the house that day. The girls were singing, cartwheeling, they drank cold pineapple juice through striped straws and stayed in the garden until late.

In Cornelius's room the bed slumped sadly, wide in its loneliness, the two wardrobes fallen open. The smoke had reached this high, all the way up to the top of the house, so that the ceiling above where he lay was charred. There were three clocks in this room, one on the wall behind the bed, an alarm clock on the bedside cabinet, and a brass carriage clock on Alice's dressing table that had become Cornelius's miscellaneous place for miscellaneous things until such time as she might return. "Have you noticed?" Carol said, looking about her, she was standing out on the landing where there was the most light, coming from the window above the stairs. "Listen. The clocks. They're all silent."

No ticks. No tocks. Apart from one, the grandfather clock by the front door which had survived everything, though it no longer showed the correct hour. The time on the face said 5:20.

"I hated those clocks. All of them. I couldn't wait to get away from them."

Carol had left home at fifteen, bearing forbidden tattoos and a navel ring. She had hidden in her forbidden boyfriend's attic and eventually got a bedsit in Mill Hill. Adel was the last to leave.

"I hated them too," Melissa said. "It's weird without them, isn't it. It's too silent."

Just then, as if in response, the cuckoo in the kitchen went off, three calls in quick succession, startling them. Carol held her heart and said, "Jesus fucking Christ." Melissa grabbed on to her, her legs trembling, they laughed again in that crazed way but this time it was brief. The silence immediately following the sound was menacing, inhabited. They made their way quickly back downstairs, where Carol took the papers she'd found in the desk and said something about going through the things in the garage, not today though, they should go now. Meanwhile Melissa was looking up to where the stairs turned left, her eyes drawn there by a flicker in the white glow from the window. She could see something, an outline. It appeared, disappeared, reappeared. She was sure of it, the impression of a small girl in a pale dress the colour of dew, gazing down at her motionless, like a secret, infinite wait, her hair a flower of upward flames. The walls of the house seemed to move closer together. The girl's face was unclear, yet Melissa felt connected to her, that they knew one another.

"What's wrong?" Carol said. "You ok?"

"I need to get out of here," she said.

That evening she was sitting opposite David in a gastropub back down in the southern enclaves, East Dulwich. They were at their usual table in the corner: teal-hued, rustic woodgrain, mounted photographs of nineteenth-century farm machinery from the town's history when all this stretch of Lordship Lane eatery and artisan focaccia deli was pastoral, in the background Curtis Mayfield. David had the anxious manchild look on his face, there was something he needed from her, from the world, was frightened he wouldn't get it, too frightened to ask. He had the tense, upward-pointing shoulders of the hell-bent middle-aged jogger. Every Sunday he did 10k.

"What are you having?" he said staring at the menu.

"I'm not hungry. I'll just have something small."

"You? Not hungry?"

"Am I usually hungry?"

"Yes. You are."

"How do you know?"

"Because you usually order a big plate of something like the flat-ironed chicken or the halloumi mushroom burger or something and eat every last morsel of it as if you hadn't eaten in, like, days."

"You seem to have been watching me eat quite closely. What's it to you how I eat?"

"What's *wrong* with you today?" he said.

Melissa looked at her hand. As suspected, David was not who she wanted to be with, tonight, or possibly, she was realising, ever, but this latter revelation was too large a thing to address for the time being so she was trying to pretend it wasn't there. "Someone told me the other day I have a faint finger. What can that mean? My knuckles are hurting."

David also looked at her hand, frowning.

"Maybe you're disappearing."

"It's been a harrowing day," she said.

"Yeah, me too. Zoe had a meltdown. She was on the booze again last night, probably this morning as well. She's just like out of control. We were filming and she could hardly even hold it together for the clients. You know that producer I was telling you about, the guy from Washington? He complained about her to the publicist. It's so embarrassing."

"I've never actually understood what it feels like to be hungry. I mean, what does it feel like, in your body? What does hunger feel like?"

Now David appeared blank. He liked talking about his work and hated being interrupted. As a teenager he had stammered, so held himself in high esteem for having become a vocal coach. He worked with actors, teachers, writers, comedians, all types of people, helping them to enlarge their presence and transmit essence, which to Melissa had seemed a strange choice of career on meeting him, presenting as he did the opposite of this aspiration. He wore thin white shirts with faded jeans and round, wire-rimmed glasses of a low strength.

"I don't follow what you mean," he said.

"Just that. Tell me. Describe it to me."

"What it feels like, to be hungry?"

"Yeah."

"Well," he said slowly, patronising, "it feels like you want some food? Like you need to eat something. Your stomach grumbles. It feels like, empty?"

"But what does *emptiness* feel like? You're not answering my question, David. You're talking too generically. You could be talking about anyone or anything."

"What, you want me to tell you what it feels like when *you're* hungry? I can tell you what it feels like when *I'm* hungry. Not when—"

"I didn't—"

"Look, shall we order? I'm having the rigatoni, although I'm not sure if I'm hungry or not now. Are you hungry?"

"No! I already told you!"

"But how do you *know* that, if you don't, you know, *know*?"

The waiter came in from the beer garden, a bearded Scot named Frank. He was always here when they were, to an extent that they thought of him as their waiter, and this their place, one of the few and tenuous things that made them experience their union as something singular and coherent. They had been seeing each other for six months and all that time Melissa hadn't been sure whether she actually liked him or whether it was purely the power of him liking her and that was their faulty capsule, bound for dust. Frank towered over them holding his pad, "How're you guys doing?"

"Good, I think, thanks," David said with a hard look at Melissa. "Do you know what you're having yet?"

"I'll have some chips," she said eventually. "Sweet potato fries."

"Is that all?"

"And the rocket salad."

"Gotcha."

"If you do feel hungry," David said when Frank had gone, "you can have some of my rigatoni. You can tell me your symptoms of hunger and I can tell you if it's hunger or not."

"Stop making fun of me."

"Look, what's wrong? Tell me."

"My dad died."

"What?"

"On Tuesday, in a fire. It's fine."

"Wait, you mean *the* fire? *That* fire, the one in Portobello?"

"No. No no. Not that one."

"Oh, right." David leaned back in his chair.

"It was at his house."

"Right. God."

"It almost feels insignificant in comparison, though, which is weird. I can't stop thinking about all those people. And then I think about him."

"That's terrible. Look I'm sorry."

He took hold of her hand and said the common things, professed empathy, asked was there something he could do, anything? and finished his Peroni. A cool glaze seeped into his eyes suggesting boredom, a disappointment at such a gloomy turn in his Friday evening. This trait was something she had noticed, that he curated their times together, put careful thought into it with always the same carnal objective: they arrive at last in his sheets in the Peckham back roads, where he had bought his loft pad on the upswing of the gentrification story. Should anything obscure or threaten this outcome he sulked, though remained open in case of gaps in her fencing.

"I should've cancelled," she said. "I was going to but I didn't."

"I'm glad you didn't."

"Are you?"

"I thought you were going to tell me you'd been sacked or something."

"No, I had the day off."

She told him about the burnt house and the black carcass of the tower and the crying in the kitchen yesterday after watching Rania's prayers on Facebook, that the tears for Rania felt wider than Rania and than her father and wider even than Grenfell like a kind of waterfall of the world with all the deaths of time in it rolling, falling, mounting. "Yet we carry on. We just carry on as normal. I went back to drying lettuce with a tea towel because the kitchen towel had run out. I even felt irritated about the kitchen towel running out, you know. Why does everything always continue? Why don't we stop? We're cold, robotic beings with emotions passing through, disconnected. We're immune to external suffering."

"I don't think we're immune. We're desensitised," David said. "It's the TV news effect. The more we watch, the more we know—the more helpless we feel. So we just turn off."

Frank arrived with their food, ceramic bowls of ketchup and tahini mayonnaise and parmesan shavings on the rocket which Melissa started picking off because of her cheese intolerance. David swooped into his pasta while she, aware of a physical requirement for food, though not quite naming it hunger, ate her fries and leaves. The fries were charred at the ends. She left the charred bits. On finishing her wine she wanted to just go home and fall asleep alone in the presence of Patience, Comfort and Mercy but David suggested a walk before she get her Uber. This is how it customarily went, the Uber much later than intended, conquest on his futon, she positioned outside of the act. Sex was a foreign place, like going past someone. She rarely looked at him deeply but appreciated his desire and its power to transport. He was dynamic, sometimes brutal in his touch.

During their walk they crossed the summer night green of the Rye with its spray of poplar and blue willow and the place near his flat where a teenage boy was stabbed in the street two weeks before. "Come up for just a little while?" he said.

"I don't know," she said.

"Come on. I'll make it all go away."

And she liked the long black hairs running down his forearms, the intention in the cool grey eyes. It was enough. There might be rainbows.

But the colours dimmed and she watched from above. He had her take him this way and that way. He arranged her for maximum sensation, her legs around his skinny hips, interlocked in the diamond she made. He gazed down at her, pale as lunar, shoulders like tepees, and in her distance the hole in the floor down to the soil in the direction of the South Pacific flickered in turn with the pitched chair and the winter gloves on the console, the open cupboard door. As he drove on faster and harder, the almost-pain of it became another focus. The sense of menace she had felt on leaving her father's house backed away into the shadows, upstaged. "Am I hurting you?" he said. "No, it's fine," she said. "Ok," he said. They finished a few feet away from the futon, her head pushed up against another piece of furniture and her neck at a difficult angle.

"Didn't I make it go away?"

"Yeah, you did."

"Want some more?"

"No thanks." She extracted herself. "I'm going to have a shower."

In his windowless bathroom she bowed her head, returning to herself in the fall of the water. She hadn't thought it necessary to lock the door, until a long, dark-haired shin poked in past the plastic shower curtain, into the space of this water, like an alien object. Her hair got wet. He was pleased in their adventure. After that she got her Uber.

5

Saturday mornings are for love. Wake up sleepy not yet ready for the light and reach for him. There he is, the side of his torso and his big warm arm. His shoulder is a pool of heat. She draws close and feels him stir at her heat. Her hands across the smooth long plains of his body, along the light hair of his thighs. She crosses the intersection at first with indifference, as if it were marginal, but soon returns to that indisputable centre. This is a man whose fellatio supply is unwanting. She worships at his fountain, for in that moment she is in the throes of a holy act, she experiences the first ages of the earth, a full and satisfying usurpation of her system, it is freedom. Her domination continues as she lowers onto him, begins moving in exactly the right rhythm, exactly the right sway. He has to stop her and ease back in with a greater resolve. They stare at each other. She closes her eyes. The room is golden. She opens her eyes as always to witness him culminate, his trembling, his fear then joy, his helplessness. Now there is no doubt in her mind that he belongs to her.

Nicole had taken Michael's name. She had no complicated feelings about it. Her own surname was kept in the middle after Evelyn, her late grandmother's name, and immediately after the wedding she had changed her documents, profiles, handles and emails to Dove. As soon as she set eyes on him she knew. That way he dipped his head like a tall man does but did not stoop.

That mouth of his, everything about it, its promise, its bright stance. It was one of those boat parties on the Thames. Prosecco was flowing, tunes were rolling, he was out on deck with a couple of guys and she was climbing out from the cabin of the dancefloor twenty minutes after coming off stage (it was a very little stage, the stages had got smaller and smaller and this one was hardly even raised off the floor), all sweaty in her low-cut mesh embroidered diamante split dress. She never underdressed. She never quite overdressed. He had noticed her too, of course, watching her do her set, and actually she had first registered him mid-song, across the audience, during her cover of Sweet Love. There was a red-hot cord between them almost visible against the silver lights on the water and the loops of the bridges. She was a Christian girl and she meant to reserve her passion at least for a while, but here it was not possible. They were copular by the conclusion of date one. In the middle of the night he scrunched all her flesh up against him in pure gladness.

The wedding fourteen months later was also of water, by a cool stretch of Cotswold lake. While she had wanted a Barbados heritage-style beach wedding, this was not feasible with the amount of people she wanted to invite and the high costs of everything, so instead there was an £800 cake and a donut wall and a sit-down three-course meal, interrupted, just after the starter, by a tea-light fire at the head table in between her and Michael. He poured water over it and there was a small, weird pause, then everyone carried on eating and drinking and the dancing went on into the morning. At one point she sang for him, underscoring her vows, everyone watching. Michael's parents and children were there (without their mother, at Nicole's subtly expressed desire, which he had pre-empted anyway, thoughtful as he was), Nicole's family, work colleagues and old friends from both sides, Perry was Michael's best man, and she was relieved he hadn't chosen one of his female friends, he had

60

lots of them, she had noticed, but that was ok, she often reminded herself, because he is that kind of open-natured sensitive man that women gravitate towards for platonic connection and comfort, and after all she was not his keeper. Her maid of honour was her best friend Leona whom she had known since secondary school and went to socaerobics with on Wednesday nights. Leona, celebrity make-up artist, did her face. The dress, for this her second and last wedding, was ivory silk with lace accents.

That was two years ago. Most Saturdays since then had begun this way, this gilded enclosure, this primal union. She was a good wife. She wanted to be a good wife, liked that word, "wife." Not pertaining to the word in the traditional, burdened, utilitarian sense—mired in the domestic realm, an area that was far from her interest (their cleaner came on Fridays, the gardener once a month)—but in the sense of fulfilling his appetite, his need, which matched her own need. "Oh," she moaned, "where are you going? Don't go yet please don't," as Michael rose and turned away from her. She wanted to slumber with him and slide into repeat. She reached for his magnificent back, where the skin was luxuriantly smooth, a few tiny black moles, slowly building in middle-age, poking out here and there that she liked to map with her fingertips when he was lying on top of her.

"Almost forgot, Blake's haircut," he said standing and grabbing his shorts. The children were downstairs in Xbox/TV silence, also the stuff of Saturday mornings, which Nicole thought was a shame to interrupt. "Can't you cancel? Does it have to be today?"

"Yeah kind of. Melissa said he's been saying he wants floppy hair. He wets it in the morning before school so there's water dripping down his face and then puts gel in it."

"What's wrong with that?"

"What's wrong with that? You know what's wrong with that—don't you? It's not the gel per se, I don't care if he puts gel in his hair. It's that he's not accepting himself the way he is. Melissa said it might be good for him to go to a proper black barber."

It did not escape Nicole that the name had now been uttered twice in under a minute. Her voice assumed the dulled, impervious tone with which she met talk of Michael's former-other life.

"Can't she take him? I always took Lyle for his haircuts."

He dipped his head in feigned disappointment, smiling. When he looked at her like that she always reconfigured, felt herself widely settling like a red autumn, leaves fell.

"You know I've got them at weekends, Nic," he said.

"I know, hon, I know." She sat up in bed and arranged herself against a ramp of pillows. The room was on the top floor of their stone-front townhouse, looking out over the suburban Bromley rooftops. It was decorated to her taste in swathes of soft and classic cream, with copper lamp-ware and mirrors and Croydon-sourced designer furniture. She moved within it queen-like singing at random, the deep world of her satiny robes, her showy manicures, the lye-stretched hair wavering on the brink of going natural if she could just take that leap. Her songs, a high-winged mezzo-soprano, celebrated in 1999 with a *Blues & Soul* double-page profile but ultimately superseded by Beverley Knight, were an ongoing pursuit, never quite given up on, despite two decades working in sales to pay the bills and raise a son. She still had an agent, had a once-a-month slot at the Hideaway jazz club in Streatham, and a good relationship with a casino chain in Cyprus where she performed every year, all expenses paid. She had made two full-length albums and an EP, framed covers of which were displayed on the walls—there was one picture of her in a glossy grey shirt and pencil skirt with miniature gold stars attached to her eye make-up and cheekbone highlight, Michael's favourite photo because it captured the warm mischievousness of her gaze, her elegant hooked nose, that way she had of seeming completely devoid of vulnerability yet approachable, familiar. He had known who she was when he'd met her, remembered her brief flare from his days in pirate radio. She was on his iTunes playlist and he listened to her sometimes on his way to work. In return for being a good wife, she wanted a good husband, and she had found one. He did not play around. He bought her flowers and complimented her octave range. He did not let her down, only on Saturdays. Almost every Saturday. She couldn't quite let that drop.

"It would just be nice occasionally to do something together on Saturdays. Like go for a walk by the river. Have lunch somewhere. Go shopping."

"I hate shopping."

"I know you do."

"Anyway it's not every Saturday, is it? It's three in a month. We went to Barcelona for your birthday, remember."

"Yes, but I'm talking about just a regular weekend thing, you know, in London. The two of us alone, no kids. Nothing against your kids, my love, but, well, I want you to myself. Weekends always have to start with you missing. Most weekends."

And now Michael gave her that other, harder look, further along on the recurring theme of logistics, where he tried to get her to recall that she had known what she was getting into when she had said yes, when she had ordered the donut wall, eaten from it, put on her second and final dress. Had he ever kept a secret from her or tried to act like one of those unattached carefree weekend-gallivanters with no ex-ties or baggage or complicated co-parenting schedules? Had she not come with her own set of luggage, with scowling complicated Lyle, who'd cold-shouldered him, tried to turn Nicole against him and told her not to trust him, that he, Michael, would only hurt her, when he knew nothing about him? Lyle was at university in Birmingham now finishing a master's so her life was all hers again, she was one of the gallivanters, but was it his fault their timings were not in sync, their freedoms jagged?

Gradually she softened again, felt another pool of longing, tiny stabbings below her viscera. He said with a special warmth, "I'm not missing, am I? I'm never missing. I'm right here. I feel you on me all the day."

Their early words. He used to text her at lunchtime just that, nothing more, and she would stare at her phone until it locked.

"All the day," she returned the mantra. She watched him open his wardrobe, grab his Lakers t-shirt, no question in his beauty, it was clear to her, immediate not eventual. And he lived in this state of immediacy. It had pulled him upwards, lifted his head and drawn his shoulders back, so that when he moved, living and striding about their all-the-day space, it was a spectacle, a show of wonder. Michael was bigger, stronger than he used to be. He spent time in the gym puffing his arms and rounding his shoulders and tightening his gut, almost as a celebration of what she witnessed in him and where she travelled with his body. In the stretch of mirror at the end of the bed they were caught in an acquiescent kiss, her sumptuous roundness that he made her appreciate more for his own pleasure in it, and his rich contour and slender hands. She pulled her dressing gown around her shoulders, then picked up her phone off the bedside table and turned it on.

"Well," she said, "you do your thing. *I'm* going shopping. I need something for tonight."

"What's tonight?"

"Reloaded."

"Oh yeah."

"Tell her not to sweat it, though, about the hair. Blake, I mean. Don't make a big deal out of it. Don't pre-empt and put thoughts in his head that he might not even be having."

"Did Lyle used to say things like that?"

"Of course. I'd just tell him he was beautiful, counteract anything that told him otherwise, which was *a lot*. In the end they have to learn by themselves. Don't put too much light on it, that's all. I'm not saying that's the right way. Most of the time I was just too tired."

"He asked his mum the other day if he was black," Michael said, about to go into the en suite but lingering, seeing an opening to confide.

Nicole laughed at first. "Really? What did she say?"

"I'm not sure. She probably said something like you're black and white and brown but most of all you're you. What are you supposed to say?"

"You say of course you're fucking black, son. Not in those exact words, obviously, but tell it straight. Be clear."

"I don't know, Melissa has this thing like, she doesn't want things imposed on them—other people's ideologies, identity, all that. She's worried about his soul. She wants him to seep into being, the way—"

"Seep into being? Seep into being? You sound like a hippy. You sound like *her*. Do you think the Met will let him seep into being? What world does she think she's raising him to? He'll have enough to deal with out there without wondering if he's black, hon, you should know that. It's not something to be ashamed of, is it? If you're not clear with him you'll just *make* him ashamed, like the world tries to make him ashamed. It's your job as the parent to help him love himself."

"I thought you said don't put too much light on it."

"Yeah but he's got to get the basics? Jeez. Let me go down there now and tell him You black, child, same as Muhammad Ali, Grace Jones, Michelle Obama, Stevie Wonder, Raheem Sterling, and your hair ain't straight. Watch him ditch the gel."

Michael sighed, shaking his head, wishing nevertheless for

the freedom to seep, to have himself seeped. Of course she was right, he told her, but did not tell her that she was also right about him sounding like Melissa. Sometimes it felt as if she were inside his head, thinking for him, strands of her clinging around his bones, permanently stuck, while on the outside was Nicole, reflecting the part of him that Melissa had not fully known or understood, a part he liked and gained strength from.

"I'll take him to the barber," he said.

"Uh-huh, do your thing," she said again, staring curtly at her screen, divorced from the discourse, not her problem, almost not. Just before he closed the bathroom door and turned on the shower she remembered, prompted by a text thread, the music weekender she'd been planning on booking today and called to him, "Shall I book it then? Portugal?"

He poked his head out. "What?"

"The Algarve Soul Weekender. Next summer. I told you about it last night."

He scanned last night. A Chinese takeaway. Watching *Empire*, her thing more than his but she liked them watching something together on Friday nights while eating Häagen-Dazs. Then he remembered. Lots of people on a hot coach. All-night clubbing to soulful house and other grooves. Cocktails on the beach. Possible pool parties. Much of which he felt he was maybe too old for. "Oh, yeah." He didn't feel at this moment that he should express his complete reluctance.

"Yeah I should book?" she said.

"Um. Do you want me to come? You wouldn't have more fun with Leona?"

"She's coming too. Of course I want you to come."

"Ok . . . Is Larry going to be there?"

"It's Larry's *thing*."

"Right. Yeah you said."

"Why? You jealous?"

66

She smiled at him, not apprised of how deeply he would never be jealous of Larry, who played golf and talked too much and had issues with personal space judgement, connected to the talking too much, and wore Puma socks always pulled up as far as they could go, mid-calf. Later she would book, thinking of the beach, the music, the sea and the living of the best life. Then that night around ten she would slink into Reloaded at the Electric Brixton on her guestlist pass with her girls and shake her booty to the great tunes in her four-inch wedges. For Nicole was not a woman who was going to reach the age of fifty and stop feeling the need to party and shock out at the weekend. No. The body does not understand if it has that bombastic spark in it, this leaning towards torpor, and inertia, and homebody-behaviour. She would take the music right up until the very end, the very last beat, the final note. She was going to dance out of this life, not even knowing she was leaving.

On top of Catford, curling around a concrete beam in the direction of KFC, there is a cat, the cat. Black and white and fibreglass, erected in 1974 as a landmark, though the correlation between this cat and the matching name of its town is unconfirmed. Some say the name has more to do with cattle, of which there was much in the old days of the shepherds and the southern hills of Londinium, but these days the connection is naturally assumed, at least to newcomers. Ah there's the cat, they say, the famous cat of Catford. It reaches with its large paw maybe for a hypothetical piece of fried chicken. It watches with its pretty, dead eyes the clientele of the shopping parade below going about their economising, in Iceland, in Poundland, in the dark cash and carrys, the world-food grocers with their lychees and christophene and overpriced cans of ackee. The sales are all the time now in this era of lingering recession, nothing has quite recovered since the crash, to the extent that to buy something at full price is to overspend. You wait, for it to come down, for capitalism to experience another minute implosion. It doesn't happen with the ackee, but a bargain is always a triumph, a spray of private power.

The Best Be barber was on a corner near the railway station, a triangular room in which no cat could be swung, three heads at a time along one wall and a leather bench along another for waiting and watching: the photographs of the graded scalps of men, the armies of brushes, razors, combs and picks. Michael and Blake took a bus, the 336, through the onomatopoeic stretch of Downham, and the music of the journey was not John Legend (who he didn't listen to much these days now that he was happier in love), but Blake's talking. A music, yes, the singular pitch of a precious child, though liable to induce fatigue after half an hour of questions, observations and philosophy. "The more things that come out of your mouth that aren't true," he said as they were passing the bus station, "the more perilous the chance you can get lost." Perilous being another new word. Fumes were perilous, as was road-cycling with no helmet like that guy over there, as were cookers they could start fires like this week's terrible fire of Kingsbury that had burnt his grandfather's trousers, as well as alleyways which Melissa was always telling Ria not to go down alone. "God he's a wordy kid," Michael would say sometimes when he delivered the children back to Gipsy Hill, fleetingly relieved at the prospect of the next five days' rest, but really they were painful, those days. Five days of absence, of missed mutual mornings with a bit of dream still left, ripe for telling, *I was inside a mountain and it had a ladder up to the top that you had to climb and then* . . . Five days of small things missed, school runs, weekday dinners, and here his missing was definite and accumulated to one big thing that could not be balmed, it was a cold hard fact. He wished it were different, not least because of his heart.

Blake's heart had an extra voice. It was quiet, so quiet that the doctor who'd first heard it had held the stethoscope to his chest for an exorbitantly long time, straining to hear. A murmur, a jump in the beat where the blood flow tripped over a tiny opening through which some of the blood escaped. He got out of breath in the playing fields. Asthmatic besides, he held his chest sometimes when he was running, would have to sit out at PE and read a book instead, but it would resolve in time, they had said, eventually the opening would close by itself, though if it didn't they would have to operate. Michael thought a lot about Blake's heart especially in the absent mornings and imagined he could hear that murmur from all the way across the South Circular, along the telephone wires, the quiet perilous skip, which strangely had not been detected until he was five, the same month he'd met Nicole on the boat. He thought of it whenever Blake ran towards him crazed with joy, he would be over aware of the running while trying not to be, then pick him up and squash his little one-digit face with his hand even though Melissa via her mother was thinking inside his head that he was far too old to be picked up, he couldn't help it though, some of it was guilt, some of it was sadness, some of it a wild wish, and he wondered, had his heart always leaked, or only afterwards, after them. Had they broken it?

"You always have two choices, Daddy," he said as the cat came into view (they were sitting in the usual place up top, second from the front on the left-hand side, the town stretched out ahead in a blazing summer mass, wide-walkers with plastic bags, the traffic waiting on the road, other sizzling red bus rooftops and the round grandeur of the Broadway Theatre). "Like when you have to decide something you can just choose one thing or you can choose the other thing. Mummy calls it elimination. It's literally simple." He was holding his football cards, they were playing a game where they gave up cards on the basis of who had the higher stats. Ria was at her piano lesson and later he was taking them for pide at the Turkish place, their regular Saturday eatery. Occasionally Nicole would come with them but most times she didn't because she was getting ready for a night out or for one of her PAs on the club circuit. Ensconced in her wardrobe she would choose between outfits, the white one with the silver studs or the short red one, they were always shiny, she liked to glow, and her hair would be curled, puffed and glossed for maximum impact, out she would go to her Uber in her showbiz sheen, some black fluffy Topshop jacket around her shoulders, her lips ferociously red and her lashes extended with glue. One day not too long from now Michael expected that Nicole would retire from the stage. Her bus had passed, the boat had sailed, the stages would not grow any bigger only smaller and lower, until she would be standing on the same floor as everyone else inside the music and he would be standing next to her, applauding until the last sound. But he saw her hunger. It was still in her face, that fright that time was diminishing, her chances were slight, had she done enough, with her beauty, her voice?, what might she miss or have missed? He'd felt it that first time he saw her sing, when she'd gone on for a bit too long, one song too many, though lovely, lush as she was.

It still made him feel warm and chosen, that moment she found him, the star found her light. There he was, feeling distinctly unshiny in his dingy sea of passing one-night rafts and empty dates—once, he had even, with Perry (relentless casanova, marriage a form of torture), tried Tinder, and had ended up drunk at an S&M party in Kensington with two women, strangers, in his lap, Perry nearby in similar disposition but clearly content. He'd felt dirty. It wasn't for him, that wild way, a man in his forties. His boss Cordelia Brown had said to him that at some point in time a certain kind of man just needs to get married if he hasn't already, and that he was that kind of man.

She herself was divorced but Michael always paid attention to the things Cordelia Brown said, to him she was someone with a store of wisdom, the result of an extremity of experience (a murdered son, snatched from the world in police custody, she had set up a youth justice organisation in response and he was her deputy). He was comfortably managerial by then, slick in his suits, jeans when he felt like it but khakis were for weekends. He was living alone in a flat in Thornton Heath where some of these empty dates and one-night rafts would finish up, and for a while there had been a relationship with a woman twelve years younger than him, but it had finished badly. When he'd received the standard letter in the post from the NHS informing him that he was due for an over-40s health check, it was a clear sign that the time for dating and desperate Tinder aberrations was over. A quieter, sensible life of lasting commitment was calling. He wanted a body to hold at night, someone to share thoughts with, to return to when he was lost. He wanted someone to love him doubtlessly.

Nicole was everything Melissa was not. Not that he compared them. Not that he had been looking for her opposite, but Melissa being the other most significant love along his journey it was natural to observe the contrasts. Where Melissa had said, "You don't like me how I like me," Nicole would say, "Do you like me in this?" Melissa's "I hate it when you call me Mel" was Nicole's "I like it when you call me Nic," and "I don't feel like it" was now "Come to bed," on Saturdays, Wednesdays, Tuesdays, whenever the drive was high. With Melissa he'd sensed that physical love was her effacement, a dangerous detour or a slaying, leaving her bulleted, and somewhere angrily shattered, but with Nicole it was a requirement from her very skin, a nourishment. She took care of him, treasured and preserved him as something necessary to her own preservation. She was present, not distant. She bought him shirts, loungewear and aftershaves.

Every month she booked him a massage with Reshma Lazur in Forest Hill who used essential oils and reiki and held the yogic tree pose for five minutes at the end of the hour to emit balance and serenity, and Michael would come out of there loosened and free of work stresses, jubilant at the good fortune of his life, the glory of his wife, having forgotten about Melissa entirely, he would hardly ever think of her, in fact, if it weren't for the children, their perfect endangered creations. It was just rarely, in the still cave of a night with Nicole sleeping next to him, that he would think of her in the big ocean all that time ago in Montego Bay, walking into the waves in her black and white swimming costume, going further and further out, half a memory, half a dream, from which he would wake in the same panic he'd felt then, that she had drowned, that she was gone and would never come back and he hadn't been able to save her. What would have happened, he might allow himself to wonder in this tender state, if things had not happened the way they did, if he hadn't cheated on her with Rachel from work, and she hadn't cheated back with his friend Damian, and the house on Paradise Row had not fallen down? Would it have been blown down by something else? He didn't know where Damian was now, what path his life had taken, whether his own house was still standing, but he thought of him and remembered how well they could talk to one another, regretting that they no longer did.

"Accommodate yourself," said the barber, motioning Blake to the row of silent boys awaiting truncations, two of them eating chocolate bars. Now Blake was silent too and the music was afrobeats with the football commentary in the background.

The sides and the back, Melissa had said. Leave some height on top and the edges natural, I don't like that sharp-edged Ginuwine look. Michael explained this to the barber and he listened, but it was the fashion these days in London and at home in

Nigeria and as well in America to straight the edges and make it neat, practically every head he did was like that, almost the trimmer did it by itself without him even knowing what was happening. But he nodded and listened while Blake looked on sullenly until his turn came to take the swivel chair and the drown of the black cape around his shoulders. The barber was gruff with him but soft and respectful at the same time, recognising his sanctity, the child gift, the sanctity of the mother, any mother, simultaneously evoked, assessing nearby. He firmed the head when it slid to one side, held the crown full-palmed like a basketball when he was doing the back.

"Is it paining you?" he said in disbelief when Blake winced. He preferred his mother's haircuts. They were gentler, less public and he could watch specifically selected TV. He dared not nod, so he shrugged instead. The barber moved to the front and started broaching the edges. "Still your face," he said irritably. "There's a bit of hair in my eye," snapped Blake, trying to blink.

Meanwhile Michael was outside leaning on the Best Be ledge, concentrating not on the undesired grooming of the edges of the son but on his Twitter feed, the raging Grenfell protests, the tail of the terror attack of London Bridge, the wave of climate angst following the US's crazed withdrawal from the Paris Agreement, the ongoing outrage at the world sweep of neo fascism that he tried but failed to arrange a striking contribution to with his own particular outrage, and then exited, angrier than he was before. He moved on to some admin, changed a bank password, tried to install an update but couldn't remember his passcode. By the time he went back inside Blake's edges were straight like Ginuwine, and he experienced the same fear, like the panic of the half dream of the big sea, that he had failed her, displeased her. It was such an old and useless feeling that it made him angry again, at her, that she was so eternally residual within, that she, Melissa, must have done something irreparable to him, he was programmed in her algorithm. How long exactly would it take for her to fade, and for Nicole's algorithm to preside? How long does it take to lose what is lost? He even felt a flash of hatred.

"He looks like Drake," she said the next day, standing on her doorstep in her Sunday wrapper and vest.

"I like Drake!" said Blake.

"I said leave his edges. Didn't I say that?"

"Daddy was on his phone," and she rolled her eyes, "Course he was."

Despite her pique, there was a fragility and a rawness in her expression. She held her youth intact, a certain angelic innocence never to be punctured. She was one of the women whom time would be kindly towards and then, perhaps not long from now, would hurry towards twilight, pull harder at the lines down her face and carve an altered creature, yet the essence of her would remain, glowing out of her eyes, held firm in her small, straight neck. She had let her hair go towards grey and it met with the residual copper-brown, forming a sparkle, a magic in her crown, another area where she differed from Nicole who would never let a silver strand show. Her arms and shoulders held that same soft definition from when they used to measure their hands up against each other in the old tower and move from room to room, linked, before the children, before the river-crossing, before the current had carried her away.

"How are you?" he asked her. "How's your mum?" This made her smile a little.

"She was asking after you."

"Yeah? That's sweet. It must be rough on her."

"Yeah. It was a shock."

She looked away as if to close the subject, folding her arms awkwardly.

"Let me know when the funeral is," he said. "I'll pay my respects."

6

It does not take a crowd to make a congregation. Worship is multi-sized. A small church. That is how Alice liked it. Five, six people, three rows of chairs, those rows half empty, not necessarily a sign of the widespread disinterest in the teachings of the Lord in our modern heathen secularity (though of course this is a factor, which deeply troubles Sisters Katherine and Beatrice), but a demonstration of steady peace, of undeterred faith, of patience. Christ waits. If it takes you sixty years or six, he waits. If you have sinned or strayed into the hands of the devil he waits, be it in the magnificence of St. Paul's Cathedral, or here in this little hall on a quiet bend in Kilburn, which one day you might stumble upon, weary in your rags of impiety, might wander inside, sit down in one of the empty chairs and finally, unexpectedly, find your home.

That is how it was for Alice, some fifteen years ago, when she was fully settled in her pink-washed flat and Cornelius was far away on the other side of Blackbird Hill, trying to persuade her backwards. She was a devout disciple in the doctrine of Christianity—the Bible was by the bedside, the prayers were regular—but her impiety was that she had deserted her marriage. She had side-stepped her vows, willing, happy even, to share Wednesday meals and festive family gatherings with her husband, but no longer could she lay by him in the nights, no more the farting, the temper, the persistent critical affront of the decaying Virgo. She had needed a church, to explain herself to God and plead his sympathy, and here one Sunday morning were Sister Katherine and Sister Beatrice, welcoming her in their black habits in the vestibule, pleased at the appearance of a new addition. They had led her inside. Playing the piano was Maurice, by far the youngest member of the flock, originally from Sri Lanka, in his late-fifties, bald-crowned and fresh-faced as though recently steamed. By far the oldest was slowly approaching the pulpit, which was raised half a metre off the ground on a wooden stage flanked above by ragged Christs devoid of stained glass. A humble church, a waiting kindness. She sat down in her nicest wig and pale apricot blouse and partook.

First, the vicar, having reached the pulpit, his black shoes appearing momentarily from beneath his robes, and having secured his glasses around his ears, straightened a little, blankly surveyed the pews, and invited a hymn, How Great Thou Art, everyone stood. The rising lifted the music from the keys. Maurice's style of playing was quite a bit more frisky than the situation ever called for, Sisters Katherine and Beatrice always felt, and they regularly complained about it to each other, a bit overly flamboyant, they felt, this is worship, not cruise ship. He tapped his foot, the one that wasn't holding down the resonance pedal, causing the music to spill further outwards, to swell against the Christs, and his elbows bounced and his too-big jacket flapped around the edges of the piano seat. It was jazz, really, Sister Beatrice said once, all rebellious and hedonistic, it was hard sometimes to even *hear the singing*. But it didn't seem to bother anyone else. Apart from an occasional hard, hurt look from the vicar in the direction of the piano, the congregation dutifully joined the hymn, giving out their voices, most of them standing still.

There was one voice that rang out above the others, that first day when Alice had come, as well as today. Winifred had a forceful, deeply quivering trill, accompanied by some swaying. She knew all the lines to all the hymns without needing the book. She sang them when she was doing her washing, when she was dusting her shelves, when she was currying her goat, a sweet persistent humming when she was not singing the actual words. When Alice arrived, Winifred had turned from the front row and smiled at her, shook her hand and said good morning. She wore metal-framed glasses, a violet jumper and a patterned wool coat. In the immediate mutuality of older women born under a different sun, a warmer sun, Alice liked her, and sang along with her, her own voice much quieter and her neck making small, bird-like movements. "It's nice to see you, so nice to see you," Winifred said after the sermon was over, after the reading of the Bible, a passage from Matthew 18. "What is your name? Alice! Alice in Wonderland!" And the brightness of her, the sheer goodwill shining out of her eyes through the reflections of her glasses, which met the reflections of Alice's glasses, was a memorable boost to an otherwise lonely Sunday morning. "Well," she said, "here is like a wonderland sometimes. We never know what the Lord is going to bring and what he is going to do, but we always know he's here." Her accent was of the southeastern Caribbean island of St. Vincent, diluted by decades of England in a way that Alice's was not; she had worked for many years as a nurse at Northwick Park Hospital.

Winifred was the first to learn of Alice's bereavement, as following her absence from last Thursday's Bible meeting she had called her the next day to check if she was all right. Subsequently the Sisters had been informed, and they had shaken their heads and felt realigned in their work, all this destruction, all this fire and brimstone on earth. They had already gathered clothes, toys and food from the neighbourhood and delivered them to some of the churches in Ladbroke Grove that were operating as canteens and donation centres. They said, "So sorry for your tragic loss, Sister Alice. How devastating. What a dreadful time." They shook their heads. Sister Katherine said, "But take comfort that he has reached the house of the Lord." And Winifred said, while grasping her hand in both of hers, "Find strength in this place. You are not alone. How is your family?"

"They came last week," Alice told her, growing tearful again.

"Good. Good. They will look after you. You're not alone."

They sat down together in the front row. Maurice came and offered his condolences before returning to his piano and the vicar prayed for the safe arrival in heaven of the newly departed souls, that they would find no obstacles, that they be freed forever from the pains of this earthly state. The Sisters had organised a sympathy card which Winifred gave to Alice, signed by the congregation and meant for the whole family, the grandchildren, the wayward heathen mothers.

"Bring them soon to Sunday school. We love to see them," she said, and Alice said that she would. In fact she was always telling Melissa and Carol to bring them. Carol refused outright, saying God was a ruse of patriarchy and Clay was being raised a feminist, while Melissa was vague and non-committal about it. She didn't bother asking Adel as her children were past the age of influence.

"It's been almost five years since my husband died," Winifred said, over their tea and custard creams at the end of the service, while the Sisters, in the consistent saddening absence of Sunday school attendees, discussed the placing of the new Bibles. "But I can still feel his presence, God bless him. He watches over me through Jesus's love. Once you're married to someone the bond is never broken. There's always a connection, in some way. I know you and your husband you both weren't living in the same house anymore, but that doesn't matter."

"I still visit him sometimes," Alice said, feeling small and culpable. She could not get away from her guilt. It followed her everywhere, no matter how much she had felt forgiven these years inside the holy walls. Since the fire it had grown monstrous. There was no rationalising it. If she had been there, where she had vowed to be before the very same Lord who had supposedly forgiven her sins, there would have been no flames. Guilt was her punishment.

"Yes. Yes. You did. You were a friend to him. You mustn't blame yourself," continued Winifred. "It's not for us to claim any part in whatever happens if it is God's will. We have to just *accept*. And *trust* in it. And keep walking in the right direction." She looked off into the near distance, considering something. "Did I tell you, Alice, that my son Herbie and his wife are building a house back home in St. Vincent? They bought land. They've been worried about the way things are going over here with the government and the education, all the hostility and crime and such, it seems they're set on leaving. Well, I might even go with them, you know. Me and Felix, we had always planned to go back. And now it start to feel like the right direction, like following the path the good Lord set out for me . . . even though it is a big change, moving."

As Winifred was talking, Alice's guilt had been steadily replaced by envy. "You mean," she said, "they are doing building now?" It was not a dream, as Adel had been trying to persuade her, saying it was unrealistic and impractical. People were building houses elsewhere, on the old lands, from afar.

"It's underway, oh yes. I don't know how long it will take, maybe a year or even a few years, there's no rush. Herbie's going over soon for a site visit. I haven't been back home for about thirty years! Probably more than that, I can't even remember. Another life. Another lifetime. But now that I'm thinking about it more," Winifred took her folded tissue from under her sleeve to dab her chin and brush crumbs from her lap, "the more it feels somehow closer. I don't think it would've changed that much. I wonder if it has. When did you last go back?"

"Hm, I think," Alice tipped her head, remembering, "maybe, ten years or more. My brother died so, we went to see. All family there." They had carried him through the village. There was singing and praying, the slaughtering of a goat, the washing of the body and the lowering into the earth, which would not happen with Cornelius—he was going to be cremated, not her choice but his and stated clearly in his will: "I wish to be cremated." If it were up to her he would be buried like any normal person, back home they didn't burn a body on purpose, it was dangerous, it interferes with reincarnation (she didn't think of Cornelius as someone she would especially like to see reincarnated, probably it would be a good idea if he weren't, but that was beside the point) and it might prevent him from reaching his ancestors on the other side. All in all it posed the risk of hauntings, to which she was opposed.

Winifred said that she had never been to Africa, Alice likewise had never been to the Caribbean. She told Winifred that she too had some land and would live on it one day, in her own house that her relatives had been building, which Winifred was excited to hear about. Leaving their donations in the collection box and saying goodbye to the Sisters, Maurice and the vicar, the two women walked back along the bend to their nearby abodes, continuing their conversation, encouraging each other in reverie. The sun beat down on their court shoes and their thin legs struck down from their hems. They shared memories of when they were girls, of the first lands, the lands that had changed but also stayed the same. In the village where she grew up in Edoland, there was a goat with a long beard, Alice recalled, and she and her brothers and sisters used to play hide and seek in the moonshine with the children next door and hide behind the goat. They would walk to school, which started at eight and finished at one. There were moths in the air. It was believed that moths are future children; they fly to the light; they were not treated with animosity. Speaking of symbols of the future, Winifred remembered the farmer who lived in the house at the top of the lane and knew astrology, and she described the black sand of the volcanic Vincentian shores.

When they reached her front gate Alice offered to walk with Winifred to her front gate on the other side of the primary school but Winifred refused, saying she would be fine walking the rest of the way alone and it wasn't far, and what about when they reached *her* gate and she would want to walk Alice back again and so on and they'd never get inside, they would just keep walking back and forth from one place to the other and it was so hot, so they better say goodbye here, and they parted, laughing at themselves, their glasses glinting. Alice went inside and stood in the hallway holding her bag in both hands, before eventually setting it down on the coffee table in the living room next to her tray of coupons and pamphlets. The clock in the alcove had stopped working, like the Ansonia in the kitchen, which still said 5:20. This clock did not say 5:20. It said 4:20, which was not quite reassuring. She looked at her turquoise butterflies hanging from the curtain rail and the so many ornaments waiting for the boat, the China shoe, the Greek milkmaid, the fur donkey and the straw doll. She felt the silence of stone and cement around her. She was attached to nothing. *You are not alone.* To take her mind off her uneasiness, she sat down not in the chair where he used to sit on Wednesdays, and started leafing through the coupons.

The funeral was held at the crematorium, in the chapel there with the casket closed and the cemetery nearby where there would be no grave, nowhere to go and remember and bring flowers. In my home sometimes, Alice told Hazel, who was wearing purple velvet shoes and holding her hand, the man is buried to the east so that he can see sun coming up, and the women face west, so they can cook dinner for their husband in sunset after life. Oh, I wouldn't like that arrangement at all, Hazel said, I'd rather face east. Me too actually, Alice said, but it didn't matter anyway because he would be nowhere, nowhere to come and visit with flower, so he might be everywhere instead, she was afraid, once they scatter him.

Michael came out of propriety which Alice felt was right, his children's grandfather after all, and his presence gave her comfort, he was the kind of person who could be a house. Nicole stayed at home under his reassurance that he would stay only for the service, and he listened with the others while Carol delivered a eulogy inspired by the transcendental death wisdoms of Thich Nhat Hanh and Melissa read a poem she'd written about Cornelius on his journey to the silver hills with his walking stick and too-big suit from how he'd shrunk near the end. Afterwards they gathered at his favourite drinking hole, and then he became ornamental, contained in brushed bronze on the shelves of Pitt households across the city, starting with Adel, by an east-facing window, witnessing sunrises, transferring westwards to Kilburn for the afterlife cooking. Alice didn't like him there, dead and incinerated in her living room, it was so unnatural and barbaric, so she moved him to the bedroom which proved very bad for her sleeping and from there to the kitchen, where he was almost mistaken for sugar by Lauren, visiting one day. That was when Alice, with a cry, sent him south, Melissa drove him across the Thames, surprised at how heavy the urn was, and for just under a month he sat on a bookshelf next to his gloves which would never quite lose their sharp ash smell. Blake peered at him over dinner, "He's really, literally, *inside*? Even his vertebrae?" Ria played him nocturnes and wanted him to stay, it settled the ground of things somehow, we're all heading for a black hole, but then it was Carol's turn. She did pranayama breathing in his flat non-presence and accidentally, being prone to clumsiness, knocked him over during yoga. The time was drawing near.

"We have to send him out now to scatter," she said to Melissa on the phone in August. "It's bad for my karma." A parakeet, she said, had that morning flown, stunned and maimed itself against her kitchen window. There she was sautéing her quinoa for lunch to have after her women-only inner flow class, when a sudden violent bash had made her spin around. She found it on the ground, a brilliant, bird-green death, killed in flight: a message.

"I took it to mean that his containment has become counter-productive," she said. "He wants to be free. He wants to fly away and we're stopping that from happening by keeping him."

So they took him to the moors, all of them, Alice, Adel, Carol, Melissa, Warren and Lauren, Blake and Clay and Ria, who wanted to see him fly. It was a windy day and he flew well, in dusty cloudlike curves, over the rugged copper-streaked land, across the hills and green dales, disappearing swiftly into the air, and Alice thought how right it was that he should finally fall into this soil. For her it was a cold and barren place, caged in the chill of the North, she had only been to Dewsbury once or twice and had not felt embraced by her in-laws there, but for him it was the beginning and the end, the return, the full circle, the everywhere to which he belonged. The last of him Ria was given to hurl. She threw the old man at the north wind and set him free. They walked back to the edge of the heathery plain where it met with the road. In London by that time, the chimes of Big Ben had fallen silent for essential renovations.

★

During the process of the administration of fire the house in Kingsbury stood empty, aside from a crew of Bulgarian builders who hauled it back from smoke, stripped it, plastered, fixed the incredible armchair hole in the living room floor, drew long white rollers across the ceilings and made it habitable again, ready to be sold. But Alice did not want it to be sold. She did not believe in the selling of family houses, only building houses, which was her new religion, positioned alongside Jesus and indulged in on her churchy walks with Winifred. At home in Nigeria, she reasoned, you would never sell your house. It is the continuation of your family, the survival of your lineage, the future of your children, the stamp of your tribe. It would be like throwing yourself away.

"But who's going to live in it?" Carol asked her. "Do you want to live there?"

"I not going to live there!" Alice recoiled, imagining herself in that lonely kitchen, crowded by memories, floating among them like a lost ladle.

"Then who?"

"People. Somebody can."

These people were to be found maybe by estate agents. The people who look through the high street windows at the pictures, searching for where to put their lives inside. "So you want to be a landlady?" Carol said. "Uh-uh Mum, not me. Because you know what happens if you become a landlady? *We're* the landladies. We become the ladies, don't we. We get people calling us up at three in the morning about a pipe or a freezer or their Sky connection. You have to know the locksmiths and the water company and the plumbers. You have to be a capitalist. No way. Against my principles. Not doing it. Count me out. Sorry peeps."

Alice made the suggestion that Melissa could relocate to Kingsbury with the children, from which Melissa also recoiled.

"No thanks," she said. "I need a river between myself and my childhood."

Adel, though, was more open to the idea, believing too in the keeping of houses. She had something of her mother's sensibility, the cherishing of the land and the hugging of mortar, the stamp of a tribe in concrete. She had recently met a man in Caffè Nero who had made her question her identity, her place on the earth, her natural right to land and ownership on western soil. His name was Dr. Marcus Amankwah and he had come up to her during her lunch break while she was eating a ham and mozzarella panini and said, "We are all products of the great colonial deception, my queen. We are not what we have been led to believe. We could be so much more than this." His words had immediately stopped her in her tracks because she had been thinking overwhelmingly negative thoughts of late, not just since her father's death but before that as well, that her life would never be settled and smooth as one whole descending blanket over an even foundation, it would not happen. Adel believed in messengers, in visitations from angels of the universe who come in human form to guide us along our twisting perplexing roads. So they had got talking, she and this Dr. Amankwah. He had sat down next to her, bearded and smelling of cedarwood oil, glancing at the dirty swine in her sandwich. "We in the African diaspora have been hijacked. We built palaces and kingdoms and pyramids. It is time to reclaim our true identity, from deep within."

"You're right," she said. "You're so right. Yes, from deep within. Oh my god." She looked into his eyes and saw the materialisation of a truth, an opportunity to reset. Something had clicked. "All this time I've been waiting for myself to turn into someone else, you know, the person I think I should be, or could be—well, the person I think I *actually am,* beneath all this everyday shit—"

"Don't swear, sistren. Swearing is part of the white man's systematic poisoning of the black man and the black woman in order to demean us into fuelling their degrading colonial propaganda. You make yourself a slave."

"Sorry. Yeah. Well, what I mean is just, all that, you know that everyday . . . stuff," Adel threw up her hands in chastised lightness, "you know, the stuff that keeps you *down,* always trying to come out of the other side of something, for my original self to, sort of, resurface—only to find, now, just from sitting here talking to you, that I am *this,* only this, *this* is what I am. I'm already *here.* All I had to do is *exist,* and accept myself as I am." She laughed a crackling, tear-ambushed laugh, pumping her hands on the table so that her bar stool shook with the drama of the movement. When she confided further and told him about the possible selling of the family house, he was galvanising and grave.

"Property is reparations," he said. "If you sell it they will only steal it back from you in taxes. Surely you must realise that if you work for the DWP. Look how they're stealing from the aged. Don't give up your rightful threshold."

"I don't know any Dr. Amankwah," Carol said when Adel related this to her. "What were you doing in Caffè Nero anyway? Don't you know they practically steal their coffee from farming families and refuse to raise the ground level of their plantations to ease climate change? Fine place to preach. And anyway, if you want to keep the house so badly then *you* can live there, or *you* can manage tenants."

Adel said back, "Don't tell me where to buy my coffee. I work hard for my coffee. I can buy my coffee wherever I want. You're getting too bossy in your ecology, Carol. We don't all think the same as you."

"What, you don't believe in economic justice for all and the safety of the planet?" And so on.

The house, in any event, was going to have to be sold, containing as it did the bulk of Cornelius's estate and the inheritances laid out in the will. He had left pensions for Alice, to keep her in health and comfort until her own time came, clinging to what he saw as his husbandly duty to the very end and beyond. The three daughters were to receive equal shares from the sale and their children smaller, equal amounts to be accessed not before their eighteenth birthdays. Clocks from the garage storage were offered around; as nobody wanted the grandfather it was donated to the Clockmakers' Museum in South Kensington. The bay window, which had held so many years of effervescent Christmas tree, so many decades of trailing cigarette smoke curling upwards and the echoes of so much shouting and post-prandial tension, became an impersonal white-washed advertisement in estate agent windows around Brent. The frosted glass hiding from the street the innards of the bathroom would soon frame suggestions of other people's shower gels and hair conditioners, and the family car inching through the driveway would be that of another family, stationed here for a time, stretching forth, all traces of the previous clan wiped clean, apart from passing shadows and unexplained creaks, the invisible histories that can never be erased.

And meanwhile, what of Alice, the future of Alice? What house would house her when she could no longer live alone, a house on this shore, not a sketchy, far away house? Like Cornelius, she was shrinking in the imagining of the end. Winter was approaching and she was closer to the ground, she ate less, her forearms were thin and loose-skinned, a tinge of grey appeared in the old deep brown. It was wrong, Adel concluded, for her to keep living by herself indefinitely. They were worried about future accidents, falls or fires. They needed safety and prevention, so the most sensible thing would be for her to move to Bushey where there was a comfortable room waiting for her.

But Alice did not want to live with Adel, in a dark back room, using someone else's kitchen and someone else's ladles. Carol and Melissa tried to persuade her to cross the river, they would watch over her together, they would visit her and bring grand-children and fruit in some pleasant, sheltered retirement village, two of which they took her to see for herself, one with neat walkways and a church nearby, another, sadder place, less a vil-lage than a roadside block, with heavy fireproof doors and a desolate common room. These places made Alice feel, peering into their worlds, like a broken plastic doll, like something to be deposited and discarded, with no life of its own. She had life left. You live towards the end, all the way to the end. The whole attitude to the advance of age in this country was con-fused. The old are not debris. Their living is a gift, a tree of wisdom and experience and a key to the future. That was why so many young people were getting lost here, she and Winifred had been discussing. They didn't look after their keys.

One Sunday in late November, when the plane tree outside Alice's window was stripped to the bark and the air had steeled to cold, a summit was held in the pink parlour to try to resolve once and for all the question of this future, this after-Kilburn, the horizon of the land of the late and alone. The sisters stepped over Alice's doorway softeners—cushions the shape of gigantic worms which she had made herself to prevent slamming and were easily tripped over—and sat down among the photographs, doilies, butterflies, ornaments, coupons and candles (now two burned every evening, one for the stillborn and one for Cor-nelius). Alice was eager to hear an update on the situation with the Benin house, after the enquiries Carol had been making in the Facebook and the Nigeria building trade. More and more she dreamt of it, the more she heard of Winifred's house which by then had a roof. She pictured the rising walls as she lay in bed at night, fell asleep thinking about it, even believed in the dappled, rippling moment before full consciousness in the mornings that she was there inside it. She could almost hear the home birds, the sound of the light, the shade of it. When you know a place well, you can hear its colour.

Adel spread herself out on the sofa in her tasselled shawl, raising her feet and accepting the crochet-covered hot water bottle at her back, following her complaint of twinges. "That office you been computer for too long," Alice said. "You move about, you walk about."

"I *do* walk about, Mum. You don't need to tell me to walk about . . . Ah, that's nice. That feels good. You see, if you come to live with me *you* could look after *me* instead of the other way round."

She was drinking from a glass of white wine at one sip and sweet tea at another; Carol was on the other side of the room in the Cornelius chair, despite Alice's cryptic objections to anyone sitting there (ever since the cremation there was a kind of force around it, a throbbing, impossible to put into words but she felt strongly that he was not at rest); and Melissa was seated at the table by the window with a half-open book, which she liked to use as on-hand submersion when the tension between her sisters got too much. It had always been this way, she the youngest yet caught in the middle. There were times when they were children when they had drawn blood.

"Didn't we already rule out that idea?" Carol said in reply to Adel's coaxing.

"You might have done. I haven't. My door's always open, and I'm the only one with enough room."

"She doesn't *want* to live with you, though. We have to respect what Mum wants. She's not a child, are you Mum?" Alice was half sitting on the arm of the chair next to Carol's, near to the door, in her usual detachment. She didn't see a reason to summit. There was nothing to summit.

"I wish you'd just come south by us," said Melissa. "That place we saw was so nice, the one with the walkways? I could really see you living there. And we wouldn't have to drive all this way anymore to come and see you."

"*You* wouldn't, *I* would," Adel retorted.

But no, it was a river to cross, and she would rather cross an ocean. They didn't understand. They didn't understand that it was harder to move to the next step in the wrong direction than to the furthest step in the right direction. Alice stood her ground, regally straight in surety, her chin up. "I stay here until I go home," she told them. "I not going to where else for what, be too difficult."

It didn't matter that they could get a van, that Warren knew a man, that it would be an ideal opportunity to declutter, as Melissa tried, gesturing at her excess of cabinets, cupboards, things, trinkets, pots, straw figurines, knick-knacks and unneeded furniture. Alice was only interested in the Lagosian builder Carol had been talking to online and when he was going to start and be finishing so that the house would be ready for her when she was ready. They should just be getting on with it and stop wasting time talking. "You are cheeking me," she said, indignant. She told them about Winifred and her house, about her good son his name Herbie getting on with it. You can distance build. There is phone and computer, you communicate. She nodded, slowly and with gravity, looking downwards, declaring what was their great imperative and unnegotiable task as her living children for whom she had made sacrifices and given up the land of her birth. "When I am tired, you take me home in Africa," she said.

Now Adel became indignant. She was just not prepared to spread her middle-age sandwich geographically that far.

"Do you actually expect us to let you live out there by yourself, when you're tired?" she said, discarding the hot water bottle to the floor and sitting up. "You're going to need us more, not less. Who would look after you?"

To this a simple shrug. Somebody can. People. "Girl from family," Alice offered.

"Girl? What girl?"

For example there was her niece Imalele or her sister's friend's daughter who does housekeeping sometimes. It was easy to find people like that.

"Imalele must be my age by now. She's not a girl anymore, Mum. You have this static picture in your head of everything as it was and it's not the same. It's not *real*."

"When will you be tired?" Carol asked her.

"Yeah," Melissa chimed. "How will we *know* when you're tired?"

"Are you tired now?"

Alice turned her head and her glasses flashed. "I not very tired yet. Maybe next year or year after, I be tired."

"August maybe? February?" Adel said.

But it was clear that this was no pipedream. It must be taken in hand, seriously attended to. Melissa studied her mother, her small feet and her thin neck. If she went, there would be an empty space. There would be nowhere to go and fall down if the walls were crumbling, no one to help them remember who they were. Her absolute faith in her destination was a suggestion of how little she had lived of herself here, how little they had truly witnessed her. And it was so late, yet she was so convinced of taking what had been lost. She witnessed her mother's narrow shoulders twitching, the hampered, unknown mouth, and for a moment was awash with sadness.

The dark was drawing in through the scarlet curtains. Alice lit the candles and as she did so she thought about her boy the stillborn who was always with her, the one who had tried to come before Carol but who couldn't reach the earth. She had known he was a boy from the way he had felt in his floating. He would talk to her after Cornelius had gone to work in the mornings and keep her company. When he had stopped talking, she had heard it straight away, the terrible silence, and there was no one there who had understood, no one she could explain it to or feel together with. Everything had taken place in silence.

"Nobody know whom I am," she said, a little more kindly, perhaps mindful of the work of their task, and how they would miss her. "Any time you let me go, I like to go."

7

When Cornelius reached the gates of heaven, they wouldn't let him in. He was surprised. It was a surprise to be surprised. He had not expected consciousness at this stage. He had not expected to expect, or to have any further thoughts, observations or points to make about anything, and this he had quite strong feelings about, fear, bewilderment, irritation. Where else is there to go? What authority to complain to, what number to call, and with what apparatus? What to do next when there was not supposed to be a next?

It had been a long and upward journey, soft in nature, gradual, partly by foot, partly carried by pressing weather, across the north plains and wet moorlands, lifting and leaving, along with his walking stick which he was glad to find intact. The rest of his physical manifestation was nebulous, he might be wearing a hat but wasn't sure, there was a faint sensation of shoulders. Beyond the flames a certain transcendental interference had taken place, the body was incidental, an irrelevance, a fading shell, except for the stick. The stick felt like himself. It felt useful and transferable. Maybe there is one thing you get to keep, he pondered while he was travelling. Maybe there is a constant that passes all.

There was lots of time to ponder. The valleys being melted, the clouds expanded, into wide plates of surface that he moved across, then some marsh and some tricky mountain steps. There was no fear. There was not even any pain, which he assumed was a result of the corporeal irrelevance. Essentially he was mind and memory only, a consciousness holding on to itself, recalling a little boy riding a bike across the dales as the sun was rising, he was again that boy, swift and pure and churning in his newness. At one point he was standing still watching Sidney walking down the road and stopping to tie his shoelace, and that was followed by a speeding motion, a desire to get there quicker, to wherever he was going, that final place, so that he could see him again. He felt sure that he would be there and wondered with this looser sliding mind with its memories restored what object of himself his brother had kept, being so much younger when he'd gone, and not yet needing of a stick.

Thus sometimes floating he climbed wheeled advanced. He was moments in motion. He came to an ice-cream hut suspended between two trees. They had three flavours, lime, nectar and cotton, of which he chose nectar, for energy. Further along was a chair as tall as a house where he paused to eat the ice cream and became a part of the valleys, everything faded as it became specific, nothing was fixed or steady. The tunnel was soon after that. He had been expecting a tunnel of some kind, as one does, the tunnel with the light and the dark walls and the relatives at the end reaching out their arms. It wasn't very much like that, though. It was similar to the London Underground. Dusty, noisy and hot, a roaring, booming sound coming from the other end. No trains, however. But there were others here, the further he went the more others, moving shadows, dark around him, they all seemed alone, like him, all irrelevant to themselves. The tunnel was wide and not very long and the end was not the end, not the light or the reaching hands. Instead there was some loose ground, a falling away, a precipice, up in the distance where the booming sound was coming from. Then, at its furthest peak, a gate.

A surge of wind pushed Cornelius towards this gate, which was singularly vivid and precise, the only clear thing apart from the stick. It consisted of two panels curved at the top, and though vivid, it had no colour. Waiting on the other side of it was, at last, a pool of compelling light, a kind of luminous engulfing fog, the booming sound in its physical form. He imagined that Sidney would be waiting there for him, they would soon be together, after the world had felt so lonely without him. His father and mother, he would see them all again in the light. He was ready.

But when he got close, there came a voice.

Go back, it said. It is not your time.

It was a female voice. When he tried to object, he found that his own did not work.

Some time afterwards he was drawn away into a sea of pale flames. They were warm, not hot, and it was possible to pass through them. Far off in another sphere Christmas bells were ringing. He went in a vague, westerly direction, towards the sunset, flummoxed, newly afraid, aware that he was hungry.

TWO

8

A man steps into a bar in Paris. There's a dim blue light in it, a low ceiling. It's not far from the station. He sits down at the counter near one end—the seat by the wall, where he would rather sit, is taken by a woman, staring ahead of her into the bottles and cabinets. She watches indifferently as the man orders a Bacardi. He is stout and thickly built, with rich hair and a nervous face, a sense about him of an eternal restlessness. The woman is in her sixties and wears a shabby crimson coat. They drink inside the quiet music of a Cuban singer, whose voice blends with other voices, the few people sitting at the tables and the lone bartender. It's Wednesday in early January. Soon it will be midnight.

"Have you ever seen a fast star?" the man says, when the drink has tapped his blood. He does not expect an answer. He is speaking to a wish, an invisible companion.

The woman shrugs, maybe considering some other question, or thinking of something unrelated.

"A shooting star. Yesterday I saw one. It went across the night like that. First time."

He glances at her, then watches with a similar indifference as she orders a whisky. They are here for the medicine. The taste is their language. Eventually she says, "I don't think about the stars. They are too far away."

"Where are you from?" he asks, but there is no reply.

"Well," he continues, "it surprised me because we're in a city. Maybe the sky is clearer here." After thinking more about it, he adds, "It was a strong star."

A young couple come into the bar and order two beers, staying close to one another, his hand slipped inside her jacket. The woman has thin red hair and the man is slightly shorter than her. They smell of the weather outside, the cold on the Seine. During their exchange with the barman in French, the two strangers drinking at the counter remain silent. He is the first to speak when the couple have moved away to find a table.

"She reminded me of my wife," he says of the woman with the red hair, "ex-wife, that is—soon to be." He drinks again and stares into the cabinets. "Do you have children?"

"No," she replies.

"Ah."

"No husband no children."

"Then you're free."

"No."

And he laughs a little, she smiles also, something has opened between them. This is what he wants, to sit with someone and talk and not feel any judgement. He begins to speak more loosely.

"I have a daughter. I mean, I have two daughters and two sons. But Avril, my youngest girl, she went off somewhere, last week. I'm trying to find her. I don't know where she is."

Here the woman turns her head, for a moment taking him in, the scared look and a tremor appearing beneath his mouth. "I'll show you," Damian says taking out his phone. "I went to London, searched the streets. I had a feeling she could've got on a train and come here, but I'm not sure—look—"

A tall, long-armed girl with a slouch and a startled expression, that of a very young child, though the picture was taken this summer a few months before her sixteenth birthday. She is standing in the garden of the family home on Rally Road, wearing ripped denim shorts and a black and white tracksuit top, a shade of chestnut red in her hair like her mother's. She looks off to the left of the lens at something that could either be inside or outside of her. Her mystery, he calls it, her private universe.

"You are English?" the woman says, "from Africa?"

"Trinidad. In the Caribbean."

"Ah."

"But English, yeah. British. I was born there."

Still holding the screen, he leans closer, showing Avril to her more clearly in the blue dim. "She is a quarter Trinidadian, a quarter Italian, a quarter Irish and a quarter English."

The woman peers in and studies all the countries in the girl. She asks him what happened, why she went. Here is a story for the drowning hours and the good forgetting. In the background a song comes to an end and the voices around them become more prominent, until another song begins, low and deep, forming a cocoon in which to tell of his trouble. He is sick with it. Sometimes it comes up over him like a wave and takes him under. "She ran away?" the woman asks, "Avril?"

That was not quite right. First, she drifted away, slowly, then disappeared. "She has a difficulty, an anxiousness. Always has, since she was little. She calls it the quiet scream." Damian remembers Avril's exact words to him, that she wished for a place "where I can be peaceful inside, where the quiet scream goes still."

"I can understand that," he says. "We understood— understand—each other," and he takes another long breath, before going further into his story.

It started with panic. A big crashing wave, coming on and falling back. The time in Spain when they were holidaying with

Michael and Melissa and Avril got frightened in the villa one night. The times at school and the week before Harvey was born. Then, the silence. She would not want to talk to anyone except Jerry for days. It was a matter of ineffectual translation, of speech as betrayal. "When I speak it doesn't sound like me," she said to Stephanie, emerging from one of these episodes. She and Jerry would run around the garden in their collusion, past the tall sunflowers lining the fence like soldiers, past the garage, the log shed, again and again, and fall down in the grass laughing, while to anyone else she was mute, unyielding. She got angry with her mother for having Jerry's hair cut short when he was starting secondary school. She said she had taken away his soul and would be punished for it one day. She would say such things, with a menace in it, but in a plain and neutral tone. Other times she would explode over some perceived unfairness or slight. "She's a temper, that one," Patrick, her grandfather, would comment. "You'll need to be firm with her."

Which Stephanie tried, though Avril took heed of her father over her mother. By the time she was thirteen they had lost a certain early closeness. Stephanie was distracted with Harvey, her bright, last baby, walking away from her the way all the children do and she wanted to watch him, hold him and register every stride, every changing look. There was Summer, the eldest, a swim squad champion, busy with exams and boys and becoming; but for Avril, becoming was less straightforward, less sure—becoming who, and what, and why? She had never liked school. She didn't want to join that bouncing girl parade, headed for the future. So she and Jerry met in the middle and Damian was her confidant, the one who listened when she said, on a dark, winter afternoon in the empty house: "I don't want to grow up." She said it haltingly, with trepidation, as if expressing something forbidden.

"You don't really have to, I told her. You can stay the same inside, only outside is different. There are wonders waiting, Avy . . .

"I was never sure I was telling her the right things, though. She said she was scared of getting lost."

"Well. I know," the woman now says to him, accepting another whisky, this time with some ice to soften it. They have not exchanged names but will remain anonymous to each other. A deep red has spread across her face, into her temples and tousled grey hair; there is a flicker in her eyes of the pleasure of recognition. "I can remember this same feeling when I was young. Look at what the world is. The children some will be sad. They see. They can see the world is hard, the clouds ahead, so many."

"I wanted to give her more than that," Damian says. "More than clouds."

"So because of this, she went away? Tell me."

That was the thing that haunted him most. He hasn't said these words to anyone before.

"She went, I think, because I went."

It had come to that in the end, like a train finally pulling in to a destination that has always been waiting, sensed beyond the present. The new baby brought his golden magic. He held him, lost in his flawless oblivion, and for a time the youngest held the family, they were washed by birth, fervently complete. Four years went by, five. The flush of pregnancy and expectation were history and Damian and Stephanie had returned to a tame and housy partnership more regimental than before, there were more lists (shopping, schedules), more yearly collages of photographs. He learnt that a long feeling is always right. A feeling is a demand for action, cannot be quashed, and if it is continually ignored it grows bigger and bigger until you are consumed in it. You become its antibody and its containment, and therefore exist in a state of impossibility. You become a kind of monster, feeding on itself.

"Something was happening to me. It was so frightening. I

couldn't stop it or put it right." He can remember the sensation clearly, the confusion. "You start to lie inside your own mind, so that you can get through the days without feeling the lie. Then, because of this, your thoughts start to change. You don't think the thoughts you thought you would think. You think unlike yourself. You start to behave and speak unlike yourself, because you're living wrong, and it gets to the point where you don't know who you are anymore. It's hard to make decisions, even the smallest decisions. You're literally losing your mind. That's when I had to go. It was stay, or madness."

The black-kohled eyes of his listener widen. She says, "I have been mad. Three times."

"Three? What was it like?"

But she doesn't want to speak of it, except that twice she was in the hospital and once she tried to leave the earth for good. She waves these facts away with a jerk of her hand, seeming suddenly perplexed and under threat.

"Did you know why?" he says. A foolish question.

"Madness does not know why. That is the quality. The why is no more. If you know why, then you cannot be mad."

Damian thinks about this for a while, frowning, his knuckles pressing against his mouth. "I'm not sure. No," he says, "I'm not sure I agree with that."

"Sometimes there is no reason." Almost in a whisper, the woman adds, "You fall into the dark."

Last year in August it happened. He was working in the planning and regeneration department at the local council headquarters by then, no longer commuting to London and back. One day in the stirrings of a capricious storm when the winds were going higher and the muddy clouds were bulging low he was on the train coming home from a meeting in Croydon and he looked out across the fields and saw through the big raindrops building on the window an image of himself on the other side. He was standing faintly there, a shadow, a ghost, pitched slightly forward. The other possibility, the other man. They watched each other, he and this other self, this more courageous, truer self, and he felt with a terrifying closeness his approaching disintegration, a crumbling away, down to his biology, the fall and set of his face. Was it too late? he wondered. Had this weakness gone too far, for too long?

When he arrived home, Avril and the two boys were in the living room watching TV. He pictured them without him. He would still be near. Avril had developed a worrying distraction at the edge of her eyes which would come and go, but that day her face was open, in fact she was the clearest thing, secretly she was his favourite child. By contrast, on seeing Stephanie, her head appearing above the stairs as she leaned over the banister and called a greeting, he found it difficult to look at her. It was as though she existed in another sphere, far apart from him and unknown. He must tell her, that night, the important thing, the most fundamental thing, those words he had recently started to hear in his head at random moments, out of nowhere: You must change your life.

"You ok?" Stephanie said. "You look a bit strange."

"Yeah. Good," he said.

"Ok. Can you check Jerry's homework, once you're settled?"

In his greatest drawing down of courage, igniting simultaneously the greatest guilt, the greatest sense of failure, he sat her down in the night's cold moon. Not in the bedroom; the kitchen, at the table. He smoked first in the back letting the rain wet his shoulders and didn't mind the nicotine on his breath, everything was past. The homework was checked. He would keep checking it, he told her. Anything she wanted he would do it. He was only trying to save himself, so that he could continue, continue to—

"To what?" she said.

"To function. To manage. Be a person, a father—to be myself."

"Which is all you've ever really thought about."

She was set hard and pushed back tears. It had come to this, the shaking broken place. Over these several years she had sensed it would come. Only she had not expected to feel so belittled, like an expended piece of machinery.

"There's no one else. It's not that."

"And that makes it all right? I'm not going to make this easy for you . . . How absurd—'to be a father . . .' "

She made him tell the children by himself, in the living room while she sat at the bottom of the stairs, a ready harbour, awaiting exits. The air in the house was cracked and leaden. Avril stood and walked out of the room, through the kitchen, into the garden, and for the next four days did not speak to anyone except Jerry, and that was only once, to ask him for a charger.

When Damian left, he lost his name. He was "their father," "your dad," referred to by common noun, the one who had abandoned, ditched, vacated, who was allowed access fortnightly at weekends. Now it was called access. There were official terms. There was mediation. There were lawyers. He had hoped it would be simpler, that they would talk it through without strangers involved, make amicable arrangements, and that Stephanie would understand that he had done the rational thing, the right thing. Now, in his mind, the children would have two complete and mentally well human beings for parents. The fact that they no longer lived in the same house was much less important (and maybe even, who knew?, perhaps they might again, maybe a sabbatical was all he needed, a reassembling in retreat . . .).

Stephanie saw it differently. What is over is done. "Men," said her mother, "they leave. That's what they do." "Dad never left," Stephanie said. "Well, we had the business. A family-run business can keep a family together." "Are you saying you and

Dad have only been together all this time because of some plants and cane furniture for sale along the A24?" Verena shrugged and shook her head kindly as if tickled by the naivety of the young, though by then Stephanie is well into her forties, in that turning season when mothers are relieved of any private envy of youth in their daughters, watching closely the infiltration of age into hair and skin texture and under-eye tissue, the interesting parallel drying out of their mutual flesh. "Love," said Verena, in a profound declaration that Stephanie would keep with her, "is not adequate as an adhesive. Money is better. I love your father, don't doubt it, but what does that matter? He stayed. We both stayed." A pause for contemplation, then, "It's quite a few plants. There's hundreds of them."

Patrick was more vociferous and accusatory in his leanings. "I knew he was a shitter. I knew this day would come, deserting my princess" (Stephanie did not feel "deserted," not personally, that was not quite the right word), "abandoning his littl'ns" (well they were not that little anymore, nor was she very princessy, come to think of it), "that coward, that wasteman" (Patrick had become aware of the phraseology of Stormzy and found it useful sometimes), "that, that" (he was about to say "whoreson" but thought this might be too much), "*scumbag*," he decided instead, "who never was capable, it's clear to us all now, but I always saw it, of carrying a family on his shoulders" (Stephanie did not think "carrying" was the right word), "of putting his wife and children before his own disturbed compulsions. A child, that's what he is, a big baby. A *man* would sit down and talk about it. There's Relate. Did you ever try couples' therapy? It works for a lot of people: Ben and Angela, on the brink of divorce and then a second honeymoon! It's *possible*, but it takes adults, two adults, talking through their problems and putting what's most important first. Now, I know he was a melancholic—" (he had swiftly taken to referring to Damian in the past tense), "I could've strung him up sometimes having to look at that long face. And I know he smoked, Steph, and it wasn't just tobacco. He was on the skunk, wasn't he. I smelt it on him more than once. He was a Caribbean?" "Dad, he's from Stockwell, in South London?" "Well he had the genes. The Caribbeans all like the silly smoke, don't they . . ." "Dad, I don't think there's any such thing as 'a Caribbean'?" "Well aren't I a European?" "Not for much longer, thanks to you," Stephanie said. "Oh not this again," said Patrick. And now there was a sure possibility of Stephanie and her father entering into another annoying debate about the EU referendum which was the spiky thing that popped up in all kinds of family discussions in this epoch, from pending divorces to the availability of seasonal farm produce to the career aspirations of the young. One of the reasons Stephanie had voted remain was that Summer wanted to go to Budapest for her gap year, and because it had seemed like common sense.

The first thing Damian did, at this cataclysmic ending, this discombobulation of habitat, of fixed ground, was get a place. His long-held plan of getting some kind of studio apartment in a tree-lit, bohemian and familiar part of London—maybe Brixton, maybe Peckham, not too far from the children, though, so he was prepared to consider Erith, or Charlton, one of those places the estate agents were trying to tell people were a "village" but actually were scruffy towns skirted by the large tarmac intersections of motorways—was quickly dispelled by money, by basic logistics. If he wanted to see the children and have them over to stay, which of course he did, because he was not going to be one of those fathers who didn't contribute, who just disappeared like dust, like Beck Tull in *Dinner at the Homesick Restaurant,* he was going to need a studio with more than one bedroom, which did not technically exist, he soon discovered on Rightmove: a studio is a one-space place (how far marriage had taken him from the culture, the diction of single life!). Stephanie told him firmly, "I'm not having them staying in some pigsty crawling with germs and drug-dealers standing outside." If he wanted them nights, any night, it had to be "decent," a proper home, with proper bedrooms.

So he found a maisonette, in Merstham. Not in London, because it transpired that if he wanted anything with two or more bedrooms in London he would have to be an aristocrat, an investment banker, a television executive or a lottery winner, the city was swamped with oligarchs and tycoons, empty buildings in the centre while the homeless mounted on the streets outside, new luxury apartment blocks at the edges for people who could no longer afford the centre but were still somewhat minted—and the people in between, the people who owned it in their hearts, scrambling for what was left, the council buys, the rare find with a hole in the roof or the nicest bit of a pigsty. London was a ghost with pockets full of gold and Merstham was a slim departure from Dorking, only twenty minutes away, a not so energising place for an inspired divorcee but affordable, as well as practical, the maisonette was near a Safestore repository facility, the A23 was in hearing distance. He had two bedrooms and a sofa-bed, so all four of the children could stay over at once, which they never did. Summer had left for university and was anyway cool towards him. Stephanie kept Harvey close and rarely released him overnight. So it was just Avril and Jerry, with their iPads, increasing fights and their requests for lasagne, the one dish Damian cooked with confidence. He tried to put colours in the flat to break up its beiges and whites—a red sofa, a Basquiat print and a house plant—but it maintained an air of bland, motel-style transience. This was not it, the destination. He was still off the A–Z, misplaced, possibly more so. Yet there were new, smaller freedoms. The drifting alone into a day, no hard looks if he bought own-brand pesto or the wrong size baguette. A major infringement of family life on his adult experience had been the inability to have Crunchy Nut Cornflakes at hand in his kitchen, so he ate a lot of those, sometimes had them for dinner, twice, one bowl after another like in the advert (his waistband responding accordingly). He often thought of Michael in this new existence, whether it had been like this for him when he and Melissa had split, the loneliness, the melancholia. He wanted to call him up and talk about it, like old times, but had used up all his courage—until last week, that is, when he'd called him to see if he knew anything or had seen her, perhaps Ria had seen her, were they still in touch?

Avril's silences became more private. Her voice became quieter, she spoke as though she wanted to keep a bit of herself inside. Stephanie encouraged social interaction such as more extra-curricular activities and park hang-outs with her friends but Avril was dismissive, and took to spending most of her time alone in her room. "She looks at me as if she hates me," Stephanie said to Damian. "Hostile. That's it. Looking out from darkness. Exactly the way you used to look at me. Says I'm trying to control her life, to mind my own business. She never used to talk to me like that. Says I can't make her eat her dinner, go to school, turn off her screen. It's true I can't physically but she's *got* to, doesn't she, she's got her mocks coming up. Great timing by the way, Damian, just amazing. Who is the parent? I asked her, Tell me, who is the parent?"

"She's just anxious," he said. "You've got to be gentle with her."

"Thank you but I don't feel an urge to take any advice from you."

"A depressive, you mean? Wouldn't I know something about it?"

They lay down, he and Avril, in one of the lonely rooms of Merstham, their heads hanging off the edge of the bed, the late spring light swinging butter-gold into the evening. "Share a thought," he said.

"Ok. Dragons are real."

In a particular alignment of circumstance, an open space in time, he could catch her like this. She would descend into his oxygen as if he had just cast her into the air above him and waited. They could talk, the way they always could, about almost anything.

"Your turn."

"All right. I'm scared of heights. Didn't used to be."

"That's boring," she said.

It was an old game, they would go back and forth. Her thoughts were glittering, otherworldly things. "Your turn."

"Let me think."

"You're not supposed to think."

"I don't like mirrors."

"Why?"

"You're not allowed to ask why."

"Sorry. I forgot."

"Now you."

"I can't think."

"You're not *supposed* to," she scolded, and they laughed. "Shall I take your turn?"

"Yeah go on," he said.

"I've had an idea."

"Ok, what?"

"That all the sadness of the world should be thrown upwards, by everyone, so the load for all of us is lighter."

"That's a good idea," he said.

"I know."

After a meal sometimes she would disappear into the bath-room, returning a while later with red in her eyes and a slow way of moving, a hesitation. The school reports were worried and uncomplimentary, which made Stephanie watch her harder while simultaneously reaching for gentleness, patience—but when Avril announced in September that she wanted to leave school, to not take her GCSEs, to get away somewhere different, that she was sixteen soon and no one could stop her, the air between them exploded; Stephanie became autocratic, Avril, as a result, obstinate, decided. Christmas was strained with the weight of it all, and two days before New Year's Eve, she left, on a Friday, the same day her father had left, but she did not go to him, she did not go anywhere anyone would think to look, not to the library, not to any of the school friends Stephanie called, not to Ria in London who told her they hadn't been in touch lately, and not, apparently, into any of the Christmas-lit streets, nooks and alleyways of Dorking, where Patrick and Damian went searching in Patrick's company van.

"I want you to know," his father-in-law said, with the Scandinavian palms rustling in the back, "that I blame all of this on you. Everything. That's all I'll say. May this mark remain on your conscience forever hereafter."

The police had been called. Stephanie, standing in the hallway, unsure of where she should be, what window to look out from, fixated by an image of her daughter walking towards the house in her navy-check uniform and knee-high socks, past the final sessile oak, caught in its green shower of late-afternoon light, turning in through the front gate.

"Her passport's gone . . . No, she wasn't in any trouble . . ."

At 2 a.m., Damian and his drinking companion left the bar and he walked in the direction of the hotel he had booked for the night. "Avril will come back to you," the woman said with a curious certainty. He remembered again the shooting star, the auspicious speed of it, and took hope in her surety. She mocked his offer to walk her to where she lived, and he wondered, as she turned unsteadily into a side street clutching her crimson coat about her neck, whether she had a place at all. He had not slept in two days. Last night and all day he had walked around Paris looking, along the boulevards, through the parks and squares and the noon violins. Now he would go and sleep and begin again tomorrow. He felt vaguely foolish in his seeking, but could not shake off the sensation that she was here somewhere, it was almost a telepathy, a fatedness, and the woman in the bar seemed part of it.

The hotel was a cheap place with a cramped reception area and a bar leading off it. The bar was closed, but that was all right, he had a small bottle of rum to set him down. He put the bottle on the table next to the bed which took up most of the room. After taking a shot he slept for a few minutes, with his jacket still on, and dreamt that Avril was draped over his back like a coat, holding on to him in an expression of need, a request for understanding, the edge of her thin face just visible. He woke feverishly, still feeling the clutch of her hands around his.

A little more rum did its work. He took off his jacket and laid it across the chair in the corner, realising then that his phone needed charging, so he plugged it in and settled back on the bed, this time half upright with his head against the pillows, a swirl of dots shooting across the abyss behind his eyes when he leaned back too far. When he opened his eyes again, the phone had lit up.

A message. Stephanie. Three words: "She's been found."

9

So far in drafting her email to Donald Trump, Ria had only got as far as writing "You suck." She couldn't think of anything else pressing she wanted to say to him ("you make me want to vomit," "justice will be served in the fullness of time"?), and wanting a forceful message, she decided to pause the effort and see if the right words would come through music. They often did. Pieces of a geography essay or an analysis of *Lord of the Flies,* sometimes chemistry equations. Donald Trump was not an attractive port from which to sail out into melody but she quickly forgot him, that was the point, you leave a thing behind in the wonder of the sound and outlined in luminescence it might return to you with ribbons, useful and afloat, precisely captured. In the song, a bold, hurtling piece with bright lines, mounting in crescendo, he did not; instead a delicious breathlessness and an appreciation of the ability to transcend the ugly world in this way—and a phone vibrate, an undelivered message, she had been trying to text Avril.

Occasionally they would wave at each other across the stratosphere, a short exchange, a holler from afar. Avril would say, "Ria!," always with the exclamation mark, and then disappear, to reappear some time later with the same shout. They were distant comrades in the matter of growing. One summer they had taken a kayaking course on a lake in Bexley and capsized together; Ria could still remember the slippery green gloom of the water and how quickly fear had flicked by them, passing onwards in the freedom they'd felt. Since then they had drifted as their parents, the adults who'd linked them, had drifted and disbanded, the couples now decoupled, no longer gathering for dinners, drinks or holidays. Yet they were important, these shouts out of the blue. It took Ria back to the cool green water. They shared a certain understanding about life, she and Avril, that it was large and engulfing and quite befuddling and you have to stay close to your boat. She had not heard anything more from Stephanie since her worried phone call last week.

The time was eight forty-five on a Saturday night in January, a time when Ria would normally be weekending at her father's but she was staying home to get a break from Blake and his requests for definition ("What does flounce mean?" "What's austerity?" "What exactly is a courtyard?"), as well as his lack of respect for privacy and personal space—using her approaching mocks as an excuse. In the bathroom next door Melissa was getting ready to go out while playing her serotonin selection on the Boss speaker (Rihanna, Method Man, the Designer song about the panda). Ria knocked on the wall, implying that should she wish to visit, her door would be open. She soon came into view in a fluster of garment crisis, tight-jeaned and puff-haired. "I'm going. I'm just going to go now but there's a hole in my top but so what it's only Hazel. Will you be all right without me?"

"Yeah I'll be fine."

"Calvin's downstairs."

In the spotlight blare of Ria's ceiling her mother was rendered paler of face and somewhat coated, her eyebrows overly straight. Above the jeans she had on a loose purple shiny thing with slits in the arms. Ria didn't like arm-slits, or skirt-slits, only jean rips, and made this known. "Wait you've got white stuff under your eyes, is that meant to be there?"

115

"It's concealer uplift."

"I have no idea what that is. Your eyes look better with the grey circles."

"Wow. Thanks, dearest," this was followed by some rushed dabbing back in the bathroom mirror, further checking of chin-shine and afro shape, while Ria chastised through the wall, "You shouldn't be obsessed with appearance."

"I'm not *obsessed*. I just want to look *nice*. It seems to be getting harder."

"Well," she said. "Well. You should accept."

"Anyway when're you going to start wearing make-up and piercing your lips and stealing things from New Look?" Melissa said returning. She had long been braced for the teenage blitz. She was ready for rebellion and hedonism, the famous friction between clutching and departure. So far there was little sign of it.

"Do you *want* me to get piercings and steal things from New Look? I don't even like New Look."

"Ok, a preferred retail outlet. Don't you want to go clubbing or something? The church of the young? Go to a disco?"

"A disco!" Ria scoffed. "Mummy, you are so wack."

"That's more like it."

"Nightclubs are dirty and sweaty and full of drunk people."

"Yes. Drunk people having fun. Sometimes fun is necessary."

"I know. You do deserve a night out."

"We're just going for a drink."

There was a notion in Melissa during such conversations with her daughter that they could be transposed, the younger was older in wisdom due to less living, that living stripped knowledge rather than added to it. She had no real perception yet of her own beauty which could catch a girl too soon. Instead she seemed to cling to a purer beginning, the child straining within to hold on to childhood, asking not to be demanded too much of, while the mother looked on with fascination at what could no longer be contained, its nature standing in judgement.

"I'm staying here," the girl said, turning back to her piano keys, "Music is my church," and her fingers sank into its yellowed sound. Calvin's wife had been a music teacher and the piano had belonged to her, he played a little himself, had taught Ria the basics. Eventually he'd donated the instrument to her on account of her "gift," he would even go so far as to say "her future."

"I'm proud of you," Melissa said, moved by her melody. "You can be anything you want to be. You're impressive."

"Thanks . . . Don't all parents say that to their children?"

She paused to think. "No. My parents never said anything like that to me."

"Oh, ok. Well don't get drunk and don't be back too late," Ria said as Melissa was pulling on her jacket, fumbling with a useless-looking cord-string bag with a silly loveheart on it.

"Try telling that to Hazel. She's the wild one."

"You're both wild. You wild women."

"Make sure you leave your phone and iPad in the kitchen when you go to sleep."

"It's not an iPad. It's a tablet."

℮

"So hear what, yeah. My man's telling me he can't make it to the appointment because he's got to shoot Beyoncé. This is the one time he's gonna get to shoot her and she's in town only for like ten minutes so basically that's more important than my fanny. I get it. It's Beyoncé. I get that it's a pinnacle of his career and she's the queen of the fucking solar system and we could reschedule with the gyny but we've *already* rescheduled. Rescheduling is his second name. Bruce Reschedule Wiley. I'll tell him we've got an appointment for an ultrasound on Friday afternoon and on

117

Thursday night he's like oh, I have to go to Japan tomorrow morning for *Vogue*. I say don't forget the clinic next week, I'll put a reminder on the fridge, a post-it in his sock drawer, another on his bedside table and same day, *same day* you know, oh, my agent just called I have to go to New York, like, now. Well, *fuck* New York. Fuck Beyoncé. Can't *she* reschedule? Might she not find it in her heart being a mother of what now *three* to prioritise the struggling ovary of a middle-aged childless woman? Or just can't someone *else* do it? My time is short! These are my last days! The man lets me *down*, man. I told him, I'm not putting up with it anymore, I've had enough, I'm not dealing with this dysfunction and habitual side-lining anymore. Sometimes you have to make a choice and this time it's me or her, I don't care who the fuck she is, this is what it's finally come down to so now it's on *him*. I'm going to just go about my business and he can be there or not be there, he's not indispensable, I have money, I can buy seed, his dick ain't no prerequisite. Men are becoming superfluous anyway."

"But you love men."

"So? What's love got to do with it?"

And quite in the spirit of Tina she walked, a vodka-heated Hazel, skinny jeans, freebie Gucci, French freckles, along a cobbled backstreet in Croydon leading to The Granaries nightspot, a stalwart of low-calibre post-pub clubbing in the area. The eyes of men were watching, layers of them from through the ages, left over in the bricks, in the damp and drainpipes, in the interchangeable bouncers, up and down they swept.

"Don't talk to me about love. That's not even on my agenda these days, if we fuck it's functional. I'm friendly with him, that's all. I refuse to sleep with him when there's bad feeling between us. Unlike him. He's not bothered if there's an atmosphere. He'll come step to me twenty minutes after an argument and think he's getting pussy. I say listen to me, fucker, there's no way you're getting up inside this juice while we've still got beef.

Not happening. You obviously lack the emotional intelligence to communicate honestly and clear the air with the person you intend to ejaculate towards but I'm a sentient being. My lubrication is connected to my mood. I'm human. I'm not a slab of meat."

Speaking of which, incidentally, The Granaries, as far as clubs go, falls into the category of what is commonly known as "meat market." Bachelors and sweaty divorcees come here from all over southeast London and beyond, from nearby Selhurst, from the Siberias of Coulsdon and Biggin Hill, in search not of love exactly but more the physicality, the branding, of love, some fineness standing by a speaker, some deftly moving figure who just might not mind a sudden hardness against the rear in the thick of a mighty tune, say a Sanchez or Tony Rebel or a Dennis Brown. There are two floors of reggae, one rough one soft, and a ground floor of R&B, hip hop and rare grooves. The higher you go the more brazen the come-ons. Few women last long at the top without a chaperone or spouse to fend them off. Melissa and Hazel lasted twelve minutes (they were blending Lauryn Hill into the Stalag riddim track) after which they barged their way out and went down a floor. There were frowsty patterned carpets on the stairs, the kind found in airports. "Jesus when was this place last decorated? It's a *dive*. Why did you bring me here?" Hazel said.

"It's not that bad. And this was your idea, remember. I would've been quite happy to go back to mine but you wanted to go clubbing."

"At least the music's good."

"Plus it's cheap."

Ladies were free before ten and five pounds before midnight. Buy one get one free on rum punch. The dress code was no hats, hoods, air bubbles or white soles. There were occasional Caucasians, generally reggae heads, pub litter or sturdy Croydon women partnered with immigrant black men. In a corner by the sofa was a married couple apparently in their sixties, frantically dancing. You could tell they were married from the way they were dancing. It was contractual, between each other and between them and the music. I need to dance to stay alive and you are my husband so you must bring me to the dance on Saturdays, this curly-weaved black woman seemed to say, facing her twilight, feeling its encroaching weight against her daily onward motion. And without you I am half a thing, said her gentleman, dapper like a Linton, creases down his slacks, holding a Guinness stout, Come spin with me, come we go swing. They would stay until the moment she announced that she was ready to go. They swayed on their wavelength, perspiring from their foreheads, lurching and skanking and using the sofa for rest when a lesser tune came on, except that now they had to share it during some such intervals with Melissa and Hazel, who watched them, discreetly. She wondered if they had children. She wondered what a woman who has had children looks like later in life, whether she herself looked like a woman who has not had children, might not ever have children, and Melissa looked like one who has.

"That boy has destroyed my life," she said sometimes of Blake, of how he had caught her, turned her head away from the road and made her meander, the cataclysm of a second child.

Or she complained—complained! "Here I am in the woodland, collecting berries to make jam. Do I want to make jam? No! I have no desire whatsoever to make jam. But I'm trying to give them *experiences,* to think of interesting adventures for them. It's relentless. I can't keep up with it all, their timetables, their asthmas, their peak flows, their water bottles, their *injuries . . .*"

Hazel would quite like to make jam with a little sticky-handed fun-thirsting human she had made herself, actually. She would quite like to know how it feels to be destroyed by the most sublime and consuming love, to be changed by it. *She* would walk into it, open, giving, turned. These women who don't know what they have.

Bruce and Hazel had been married for six years. It had happened quickly, once she had realised that here was a man who could set her on fire, was an outstanding cook (when he cooked), had an exciting lifestyle, intelligence, success, was crazy about her, presumably wanted children—this had not been checked, per se, beforehand, but there had been conversations, ruminations. After some time trying for a baby she'd had them both investigated and the outcome was that his parts were working fine and hers were not, with which information the yearning increased, for the sticky-handed ones, the floppy dribbling bundle, the huge crying. She did have her two nieces and her godmother responsibilities towards Blake, and she was now aunt-in-law and co-godmother to Bruce's brother Gabriele's brood, including a newborn, but these proximities, these small hands in her life that sometimes she was required to help wash if they couldn't reach a sink, or hold when crossing a road, they only made it worse. She could smell it, everywhere, the primal youth, the joy and disarming, destroying power. Maybe not in Granaries so much but in most other places. It made her want to weep with hopelessness.

So she drank her cheap punch. Accepted an offer of another drink from a passing bachelor called Wayne who seemed half decent, not rampant. They all danced together, he and his friend Sherwin and Hazel and Melissa and the married couple and the sturdy Croydon women, to a Luciano then a Gregory Isaacs highlight, top of the night, the room jumped and whirled, it was righteous, a light drizzle gathering at the windows and condensation in the misty panes from the heat. Wayne and Sherwin were helpful in that they formed a moral barricade around Hazel who was prone to advances, the pull of her aesthetic, the tumbling black curls and the valleys in her shape, no others came forward for a while, no other reaching boys or damp divorcees. Continuing on the subject of Bruce which was the pressing issue of the night, talking as they danced, the dancing slowly becoming secondary, a mere leaning and shallow bounce near the wall, Melissa said that the urgency of the situation was not real for him in the way it was for her. The physical aspect of it was purely notional. The dream of a child was different between men and women.

"He can wait, even though he knows you can't wait. He's being selfish. He does want to be a father, does he?"

"Oh yeah he says so, he says oh baby let's make a baby I worship you I want to come into your womb and make a someone, all that. But really I'm not so sure anymore. I used to be sure. This time though, there's more pressure and it seems like he's trying to run away from it. They run away! They're children themselves! He fixates on his pictures instead and his work. Maybe he even makes these things up. Maybe there's no Beyoncé at all. Maybe when he gets one of those calls it's really just Gabriele and he's arranged it with him to get him off the hook. Brother tricks. They've done that kind of thing before, pretending to be each other's voices."

"So juvenile," Melissa said.

"When we were living in Paris, I didn't mind as much if he was unreliable. It was exciting. We had that amazing apartment in Montmartre. I used to go out and get croissants and warm bread in the mornings—it was like a movie. Ok he's got that wayward eye of his but I had it too, the place is overflowing with fineness, man, and one thing I do know at least is that Bruce has never cheated on me. He knows that's my mudflats zone. That's where I get off." She reached over to put another empty cup of punch on the windowsill and carried on, wistfully, "He was always buying me roses. We'd hang out with his trendy fashion friends and go to the galleries. We could be whatever we wanted to be over there, there was no shape for us to fit ourselves into. But since we've been back—well, it's not *just* about that, obviously—but things just feel . . . difficult. This country feels like a cage. It makes us smaller. Everything feels *smaller*—"

"Hm, I know."

"—and whenever we try and have a proper conversation about it, whenever I try and address things *properly,* he just says what he thinks I want to hear instead of what he really thinks. I wish he'd be honest with me. It's like he's divided into sections and can only operate through one section at a time. It's so annoying. He thinks sex can solve everything. Well it can't."

"I think it's such a shame sometimes how there always has to be a man at the end of a penis," Melissa said.

"Tell me about it. Remember Pete? Amount of times I had that fool in my mouth. What a waste of suction." At this Melissa needed to cough, choking momentarily on her drink.

By now they were sitting next to each other on the sofa, the dancing bodies before them, the married couple entwined in a lover's rock song. Wayne and Sherwin had accepted that there would be no further developments from their drinks-buying and name-exchanging and had moved on to other prospects. Old sensations of new rapture flickered across Hazel's memory, she had met him like this, in the music and the gathering, before all this labour, this absence of labour, how they had danced that first time in the wings of the lunar eclipse, how they had soared and flown. No doubt he was her one, the one, as she had always hoped there would be. "Look, I love my husband, the selfish fuck," she said. "I don't know why. He doesn't deserve it but he does, he does, I love him. And that's the thing to remember. It's so easy to forget. You're lucky, Lis. You have your kids. Don't forget how lucky you are to have them. You're on one road with them, you and Michael, even though you're not together anymore, you're together in *them,* you're connected. It's strange—yes, I know this annoys you when I say this—but my mind just won't accept you've split with him for good. I'd lose my faith." She gestured at the happy marriage grinding against the wall and laughed. "They remind me of you two. What could still be."

Melissa looked at them too and shook her head, "No, we didn't have that joy. We didn't dance like that."

"Yes you did. You've forgotten."

"And you've forgotten he's married."

"To the wrong person."

"Don't say that, I wish him well. I want him to be happy."

"Me too. And does this David guy make you happy?"

"You always call him David guy. That's not his surname, you know, guy."

Hazel nudged her, harder than intended due to the two-for-one punch getting to her spatial and impact awareness. "Why are white men always called David anyhow?" she blurted. "There's two of them at work as well. I don't know a single black David."

"Oh shut up!" Melissa found herself nevertheless trying to think of black men who were called David and started naming some, David Harewood, David Oyelowo, David Olusoga . . .

"You're avoiding the question, about David guy."

"Does he make me happy? What, like Bruce makes *you* happy?"

"Bruce is Bruce," Hazel waved him away with her hand. "That's another thing. My concern is you and your unseemly tangent. You're working against the flow with this one, I can tell. Michael was nice and wholesome. Not one of these weird types you like—Damian and whoever."

"Damian doesn't count."

"He did at the time. He practically split you up!"

"No he didn't, he was just a symptom, of other things."

"He definitely factored, though, didn't he? I know you liked him. You two had this weird vibe going on, I couldn't understand it personally, same thing with that other one as well from back in the day, the one with the high-waisted trousers who looked like James Dean and never spoke, I think he had a small willy? I don't like strange men. They're like grapes. They can't be trusted."

"He wasn't strange, he was just—troubled. Aren't we all troubled?"

"Yeah but leave the troubled ones alone, hon, we've got enough trouble of our own. And this David guy, he does seem like a slight moron to me I'm afraid."

"Is there such a thing as a slight moron?" Melissa wondered. "He wants me to go to Rome with him soon for the weekend. I don't know if I will, though. We've never been abroad together. I think it would feel too intimate, somehow, sitting next to him on a plane, which is kind of bizarre isn't it. The thing is, we're not really 'together' in that way. We're both just *there*, if you see what I mean."

"No hon, I don't."

She decided not to mention anything else about David, his occasional roughness of touch and the odd relief she found in it. He closed doors in her that were trying to slide open, those hazy pictures from the underworld of yesterday, their creeping menace. Sometimes in the middle of the night she woke in an icy sweat, and thought she could see an outline of a figure standing at the end of the bed, a suggestion of flames around it. She would have to turn on the lamp, convince herself she was alone, watch and wait for dawn coming in through the skylights and the sound of the pigeons walking on the roof. David made everything blank for a while, she could be empty, unfeeling, none of which she could explain to Hazel. Instead she reminded her, before they went downstairs to the house of R&B and rare grooves, of Michael's own dalliance, preceding the mistake with Damian, and surely far greater in impact if they were talking about reasons for the end of Paradise. But this Hazel also tossed away, declaring, "You and Michael are like the sea. You just need the right land to hug." Melissa said "Oh, poetry now," yet felt the lost sublimity of it, that good shore, that it was too late, it was gone.

On the stairs a passing casanova leaned in with "w'happen baby" and made her feel a sharp homesickness, there came more of them, these salivating creatures, leering at the bar where Hazel spilled her vodka over her jeans. The DJ played a slow Jodeci, bringing new dance requests, "beg a dance shortie," "want a drink baby?," which escalated into a mounting tide of men reaching out their hands and circling, until Melissa said around one thirty, "Ok, I need to get out of here." Hazel agreed and anyway needed to smoke, a habit she had acquired late in life though since exploring IVF reserved for socialising. She smoked on the cobbles outside with the other smokers, by now used to this evicted practice, left behind together in a lonely mist only they understood. The voyeurs in the brickwork watched the two deserters leave in the small-hour damp, wayward-footed, clutching one another, shivering at the cold and bound for Gipsy Hill, after necessary chips. Far out on the horizon of Penge the sky was Eiffels wrapped in reams of night. Hazel stayed over. They talked into the dawn and listened to Meshell Ndegeocello and Joan Armatrading's *Walk Under Ladders*. They talked about when they were girls, the things they had seen and suffered, they knew the clouds in each other, they felt the echoes. "If you can't rationalise the things that happened to you in your childhood, you will be insane," Hazel said, and when she was very drunk, her voice slurred and melted, "I could never fade away from you, Lis. We'll always see each other in the dark." She was found in the morning by early-riser Ria lying half on and half off the sofa, her mascara collected under her lash-line and an empty wine glass nearby.

"Erm, Aunty? . . . Shall I wake her, or anything? I mean, shall I leave her like that?"

e∽

On Monday morning Melissa put on her tights, culottes and ankle boots and walked Blake to school before going to work. He was wearing his Monday socks. He told her that the dark patches on the moon are old seas of lava and it has no atmosphere. He told her his five Fs: football, food, family, friends and freedom, freedom meaning being able to do whatever he likes without anyone stopping him because of his colour, to which Melissa reminded him he was a king and felt her heart crack. They edged around the subject of a girl. He was shy about it. He wouldn't say her name.

"What does she look like?"

"She's very, very white."

Worried, Melissa said, "Is that why you like her?"

"No. She finds *everything* funny."

"Oh, that's nice. What colour is her hair—brown, black, red, blonde?"

"It's blonde. It's very, very light."

Worried, Melissa tried to think of brown girls in his class. "Do you like Sangita?"

"*No.*"

"Why not?" she said, worried.

"Because she's rude. She's rude. She calls Martin an idiot and stupid, even though we call each other that as well but she won't let other people use her pencil case. She uses other people's pencil cases but she doesn't let people touch hers."

Melissa defended Sangita's pencil case behaviour in a conflicted clueless way. They went along the path by the little green furnished with benches and an outdoor gym. They turned right at the edge of the playing fields as Blake was asking for a Victorian costume to wear on dressing-up day, he didn't want something home-assembled like last time, he wanted one of those proper ones from a shop. "They're too expensive. For you to use for just one day? You've already dressed up as a Victorian. How long are they going to teach you about those people?"

"I don't know. Please, I won't just wear it once. I'll wear it other times."

"That's very unlikely."

"And I don't want to be a chimney sweep."

"I'll think about it. Maybe ask your dad," she said as they were parting. "Don't swear, spit or slouch."

"I won't."

"Don't forget to take your inhaler before PE."

"I won't."

"Remember."

"I will I will, don't worry. You should be positive, Mummy. Self-care is health-care. That's what you're always telling me."

"How many puffs?" she said.

"Two."

"Ok."

He shoulder-touched a classmate and forgot about her. She walked away, looking back repeatedly until he was out of sight, struck by his existence, his furthering separateness, the fragile yet solid moving picture he made. On the train she tried to read a book but ended up on the internet, and by the time she reached the office was riddled with bullet holes of paranoid parental anguish exacerbated by Google—anguish for his seeping, anguish at the ancestral strains of the Middle Passage that might be in his soul, anger at the education system for omissions of the truth and lazy regurgitations of Victorians and Tudors. Pushing open the door to the building she had a call from a plumbing company about a repair to her mother's bath leak, and a long-winded text from Carol about rising cement costs in Nigeria due to the economic downturn and the resulting devaluation of the naira and could she help her look into suppliers to check the contractor wasn't trying to fleece them? She slumped down in front of her desktop opposite Carlie, trainee sub. The dentists were already upstairs scraping and readying their x-ray machines, a bliss of pure bright purpose above. "I think I should train to become a dental nurse. I think it would be soothing," she said.

"You? Hah. You can't even stand the sight of blood."

"Dentists rank among the highest suicide rates in the professions," said Pedro, two desks along, pony-tailed, from Cincinnati and wearer of colourful shirts. All the subs worked together in the production section, next to Features, where through the arched window there was a distant view of the Shard.

"Really? I don't believe it. All the dentists I've ever known seem content."

Carlie and Pedro thought back on their own encounters with dentists while the sound of drilling and footsteps filtered through the ceiling. "You seem stressed," Carlie said. "Are you stressed?"

"Yes, I am. My mum wants to go to Africa to die and we've got to build a house. I'm worried about the souls of the children. You don't know what they're putting into their minds. They're drilling my boy with one-sided information that erases him, plus I can't keep up with the school admin. My printer's not working and I have to print out all the emails from their schools, otherwise I won't remember what I have to do."

"Don't do that," the features editor Jean said, overhearing. She was standing near Pedro's chair, equine of mouth, gangly and rocket-like, a fierce observer of the pyramid journalism rule while eating usually Minstrels, and she did everything fast as if to a deadline, including speaking. "Don't print them out. Ignore them," she said. "Every time you print out one of those things you're fastening yourself more fatally to patriarchy and female domestic submission. Don't join the PTA. Don't do the raffles, the uniform sales, the donut days, none of it."

"But he'll miss things. And what about my civic duty?"

"Civic duty what. Aren't you raising the kids by yourself, child?"

"God help me." She related the five Fs while Carlie, wide-eyed, ate her belVita biscuits. She had the kind of mind whose walls were of an oily, shiny substance so that dark and heavy things didn't stick and this is one of the reasons Melissa liked her.

"Oh my god," she said. "What did you say to him?"

"What are you supposed to say? I told him he's a king."

"You can't protect them, can you."

"Hey we should do a column about this stuff," said Pedro, empathic and fascinated, he was ever strident on the issue of diversity, it was full of good copy. "Victorians and Vikings. The imbalance in the education curriculum and the espousal of the colonial code. It's a kind of brainwashing, really, allowing children to grow up with a hole in their historical knowledge. It's criminal."

"It *is* criminal," said Carlie.

"But then, does the truth hurt them more? That's what I worry about. When should you tell them the truth? What if he knows too much already?"

"Melissa, I think you should write this," Jean said. "It's fresh for you. A column on black twenty-first-century parenting. The pains and joys. It's been done before but you can make it your own—there's always more to say."

"That doesn't really sound like my thing, Jean."

"Why not?"

"*You* write it if you want. I'm not going to be that black

person everyone goes to for the word. I don't want to be a race star. I want to live a quiet life in lower case. I'm in the struggle. I *am* the struggle."

Jean was appalled. "Malcolm X was a race star! Angela! Nelson! Claudia Jones!"

"Does that mean I have to be one too? Part of the problem is expecting all black people to soldier the fight as if it's only our fight, while everyone else gets let off the hook. I don't see why I should provide an account of something people might read as an anthropological text, or an agony page. Let me keep my agony to myself, thanks." She switched on her computer to look at her emails. "I don't even want to write a column—I've done enough of those in my time. I think I'm going to try a poetry workshop."

"Poetry? The poets are *crazy,*" Pedro said.

"They definitely have a high suicide rate," said Jean.

"Yet when we're all expired and people aren't even reading magazines or newspapers anymore, there will be poets. The poets are immortal. They're the wisdom of the ages. They will have the final word."

"It's true. A few decades from now we'll all be gone. This place will be desolate." Pedro looked around him at the partitions, the shelves, the layouts of the magazine covers on the walls. "People don't actually read much anymore, you know. They look at phones and watch Netflix."

"That's crap," Jean said, and went back to her article on the diamond mines in the DRC.

"You should come and have a pedicure with me after work," Carlie said to Melissa. "It'll chill you out."

"I can't. I can't stand people touching my feet."

"Ok then a manicure."

Melissa considered her hands, their nascent wrinkles and jagged cuticles and leathery knuckles and occasional senior pain in the little shakes of the wrist. "Maybe," she said. But in the end it didn't happen. The day rushed by. She had to stay late for a cover story deadline and was the last to leave the building, along with one of the dentists, whose hands by comparison were large and bony and he had startled grey eyes as if he'd never grown up and a sweet and comforting wholesomeness about him that made her want to lie down on his dental chair and rest.

10

The house that Nicole grew up in had five bedrooms and a portico porch and long clean windows and a haloed front room with plastic-covered sofas reserved for adults. There was a record player in the other front room, the back room, where the other sofa was, the one with no plastic on it meant for children, where they could sit and hang or dance around without fear of spoiling or being shooed away, but when her parents were out at church Nicole and her siblings preferred to listen to music in the real front room, with the glass things in it, the theatrical ceiling rose and the air of the forbidden. Their mother could tell they had been playing devil's music—Prince, Freddy Jackson, The Pointer Sisters, Earth, Wind and Fire—yet turned a blind eye as long as it wasn't a Sunday (she went to church six days a week). Nicole's father played the trombone. He could also sing, a sweet, mesmerising growl that disarmed his wife, but which was kept from the world by his shyness and stage fright. He just couldn't do it, hold the song in front of an audience, remember the words and make himself theatre. The trombone was where he was comfortable, in a corner at the back of the band, sending out the brass sound, with someone else in the spotlight. His voice was private—a waste, people who knew him said, such a gift to be kept inside.

Except that some essence of it, some guttural flair, had leaked into his progeny, the youngest boy, also shy, but Nicole wasn't shy, not a bit. She could stand up in front of anyone and shout, recite, croon, any amount of people in any situation, and come across whole and unmuffled as if she were at home in her kitchen. She had played the Virgin Mary twice, Cinderella, five narrators, and the innkeeper (a frustrating role for her as it was too peripheral). She *liked* being on stage, right at the front. She liked it more than not being on stage because up there she was captured in an optimum coherence where all her energy and magnanimous feeling gathered and became a kind of firework. She was the most she could possibly be, whereas off-stage she was less, which she found dreary and disorientating. Her family became accustomed to her talent, her father was glad to see it, at least the waste was mended, but whenever she sang in public, at church, at the Wandsworth talent contest when she was fourteen, it caused something of a sensation. She appeared in the local paper that year in white jeans and afro puffs, holding her trophy to her chest, a bold smile denoting her absolute certainty that the prize was meant for her, no doubt, no competition. At seventeen she was approached by an A&R man looking for demo material and a grim shade passed over her mother's face at the thought of her daughter cavorting with Satan—she was fine with her singing gospel and a little harmless soul, but that edgy Prince style, the funky house and such like, she felt that Nicole was too young to get involved in that wildness in a professional way.

The house was not far from here, that is, from the Hideaway jazz club in Streatham where she was performing her monthly slot. She was dressed in a black leather mini jumpsuit and four-inch emerald-green heels with straps up the ankles. Her look was fashioned partly on Tina Turner, partly on Donna Summer in her heyday, with the big flowing hair acquired from Pak Cosmetics on Peckham High Street. Just before her slot one of her eyelashes had fallen off en route from the communal dressing room and she'd had to search around for it on the floor and reapply it. She could feel it dislodging again and hoped to make it to the end of the set without an embarrassment. It was not a lucky night, not a smash, not one to remember like the Charing Cross Road Astoria in the summer of 1999, the Shepherd's Bush Empire the year after, and even here at the Hideaway more recently when the audience, composed of stalwart fans, local people, thirty-something ravers, had formed an amber-lit huddle close to the stage during her encore, almost religious, it had felt, singing along with her and sometimes alone while she held out the mic through repeated choruses of her most famous song, Call Me (When She's Gone) after the management had turned on the main lights and closed the bar. Tonight the audience was rather sparse and not especially attentive—they were chatting among themselves, getting up for drinks, a few of them were dancing, like the two women at the table to her right who got up at the start of Call Me with an excited urgency and started jigging by their chairs. Overall the energy was low—was it the weather? it was gloomy and wet outside, the usual February desert before Valentine's—or perhaps the Hideaway itself was losing momentum. It bothered her how close she was to where she'd grown up. She and this gift of hers had not travelled far at all, it seemed.

Larry had got her this slot, long-time DJ and events manager, entrepreneur of soul, lovers and funky house. They went way back. He knew Nicole when she was starting out, before she changed her name from Nicola Bridges to Nicole Gold, was there at the beginning when she burst through on the underground garage scene and ended up a cover girl in a caramel kaftan and china bumps, the photograph taken by the legendary Bruce Wiley early in his career, before he became the UK's preeminent black photographer—she was his first cover shoot.

Eventually her mother came round to the idea of her working and fraternising with these people, once she saw that she was getting somewhere, the TV appearances, the record deal, the hearing her daughter's *voice* on the *radio* while she was frying her *callaloo*. Nicole didn't blame her much for trying to thwart her at the outset, and if it hadn't been for her mother there would've been no way for her to carry on touring once Lyle came along, that soft pearl of life, adored and felt in every song of her absence. It was true what they said: it does get harder. Babies are light, simple, they need love, food, warmth and shelter. With growth their needs broaden: school books and stories in the evening and ground rules and firm consistent discipline—the way she was raised, in one house, with a porch and a garden and a front room. "See those houses there," she would say to Lyle as they were walking through the finer streets of the neighbourhood and he had just asked her for a Ninjago Lego set, a PlayStation or Air Jordans, "How much do you think they cost?" "I dunno," he'd say, "two hundred pounds?" "Think more a million. And what do you think it takes to get a house like that? Tell me, Lyle, what have I taught you?" And he would say with a set mouth, "Hard work." "Yes, hard work. Nothing comes free. No one's going to give you something just because you want it. So if I give you things just because you want them, how is that going to help you when you have to fend for yourself in the world and go out and get yours? I'm teaching you early, Lyle. You'll thank me one day, you will. Believe."

That was when they were living in a flat above a pharmacy in Crofton Park, sharing a bedroom with a curtain affixed down the middle for privacy; before she came to the painful realisation that if she was ever going to manifest this house aspiration, this dream of portico porch and pretty garden etc., she would have to give up a few things herself. She went and got a full-time job, and stayed, in one office or another, for fifteen years. She bought the house, moved to another, more suburban one with a bigger garden when Lyle was past the age to delight in it—the house she lived in now with Michael—and performed and made music when she could. Lyle's father, a dub producer named Taurus, was a willing if irregular presence, but they had different ideas on the making of a man. "I couldn't raise him the way I wanted to with him," she'd told Michael when they were getting to know each other. "We were always arguing. He didn't care about how Lyle spoke or how he carried himself, about his posture, his manners, things like that—or at least he didn't accept he should have a role in shaping any of it. Those things were important to me." Now Lyle worked for Microsoft, a tech role straight out of university, and he bought her flowers sometimes which always made her cry at the reminder that her sacrifice had been worth it, as well as forgetful of how, when she had made that sacrifice, her star had perhaps already been on the descent.

She finished her set to a wave of mostly polite applause not warranting an encore, but encores were part of the act these days so she went back on, her eyelash still holding out. The two women at the table to the right clapped hard, one said, "Call Me! Do it again, again!" It was ever ready, the band knew it backwards and sideways so she let them have it a second time. The thing about that song was that it had an infallibly bright pitch and skip to it, the melody walked by itself and she could sing it almost without a spirit, emptily. Her agent, Rob, who was sitting at the bar in an Adidas tracksuit, he dropped in on her gigs sometimes, announced afterwards, "I think it might have finally had its day, that song. What's your feeling?" It dismayed Nicole that he could sense it too, but she demurred, "People still seem to love it," at which point, as if summoned, the two excited women approached, cowering in her presence, oily-cheeked like her from the late hour and the stuffy air and the long-past absorption of matting powder.

"Nicole?" one said, the taller, in headwrap and slacks with a belt, "Do you mind if I call you Nicole? Sorry. Thank you. I mean, I just have to say *thank you*—for *that*, for everything! We've been fans from *time*, innit Grace?" Grace agreed. They had been there at the Astoria, they had all her CDs, even a few songs on vinyl so that the growl, the sweet womanly growl inherited from her father, was fully audible and preserved. They asked her when she would be releasing new material. Could they have her autograph?, and while Nicole was signing with uncertain curlicue, for she was out of practice, a folded sleeve of her Call Me single, they whispered among themselves. When she handed the sleeve back, Marcia ventured, "Um, can we ask—I mean, you probably don't even do things like this, you're probably too busy—but we're doing this, thing?, a joint birthday event—"

"It's in a marquee—" Grace said.

"For our fiftieths—"

"Big one! Major!"

"Us two and another friend of ours, Priscilla—she couldn't make it tonight but she *loves* you, we all do! So, April time, mid-April? We haven't booked it yet but we're thinking Kent somewhere, one of those golf clubs with lots of space—"

"Parking, all that—"

"We'd pay you of course," Marcia said. "We don't expect freeness. Obviously though it's not gonna be O2 rate but still, you work you get paid." Grace was looking at Marcia with scepticism as if she were going about it the wrong way. Rob was looking at all of them with—what? Compassion? Detachment. Yes, that was it.

"This is my agent, by the way—Rob." He raised his drink at them. "He deals with that side of things mostly," though as Nicole was saying this it occurred to her that maybe that was part of the problem, all these years with him being in control, the intermediary between her and her deliverance. Look at him. He didn't even make an effort with his appearance. He should either just shave or not shave. Larry would probably be a better agent than him even though it wasn't his area, but at least he looked strong and dynamic. This man looked tired.

"We would so love it if you could come and sing for us," Grace said cutting to the chase.

"We would," said Marcia.

"It would just make our night, our year, our half a century!"

"It would!"

Nicole was feeling tired herself from their high-octane attention and said she would think about it, "Let me take your number and I'll let you know." Whereas normally she would leave such admin to Rob, tonight she didn't want to. "Really? Oh wow," Grace and Marcia made a shambolic diving into their bags for phones, pens, paper; paper seemed old-fashioned but more appropriate (would she actually want *us* as *contacts* in her *phone*?), but the phone was more practical (what if she *lost* the piece of paper with their numbers on it!). When she took out her phone, deciding the issue, she tapped in both their numbers to settle it faster. They hugged her and went to gather their coats from the backs of their chairs, waving and looking back at her as they left, leaving her with an inexplicably deepened melancholia.

"Well, Rob," she said, taking a bar stool next to him, hooking her emerald heels behind the foot rail and gesturing for her usual, a lime drop martini, "when *am* I going to be releasing some new material? It's been a long time. When's this deal coming then?"

"We had a deal but you didn't want it, remember," Rob said.

"No. I mean a *proper* deal. Not one where I'm going to get exploited, underpaid, overworked and then not even sound like me. Those people are crooks, you know they are. They just wanted to steal from us—from me, that is." What exactly was he doing for his 15 per cent cut anyway? Wasn't he supposed to stand for her, find her a home, a stable, understand what she wanted, what she deserved?

"They weren't crooks, Nicole," he was saying, observing her with a certain unkindness, a bad faith. Rob had once worked for Sony and had struck out alone, with Nicole as one of his premier singers, but they had been together long enough to lose spark, were paling, fading together before the beautiful fever of the new young fireworks. "I don't work with crooks, thank you very much," he said. "The industry is changing. No one sounds like themselves anymore, that's not what it's about. I mean look at Ed Sheeran—"

"Oh please—"

"I'm just using him as an example, all right?, of someone who shapeshifts, who can move into different sounds. He's different every time, every collaboration is—"

"No he's not! He sounds *exactly* the same, on every song, no matter whose song it is, no matter what genre it is, he throws a great big ball of Ed Sheeranness on top of it and kills any scrap of originality so that it's absolutely bland. I *hate* Ed Sheeran."

"But you said it yourself there—it's exactly *his* voice. Distinct."

"Yeah. Unmistakable," she said.

"A different surrounding, is what I mean."

Rob ran his hand irritably through his lank hair, the colour of raw umber heading for grey. Over on the stage the tech crew were moving the lead microphone back, gathering the wires and unplugging the amplifiers. Nicole preferred a real set of drums over the digitised kits but she had got used to it, considered herself adaptable, easy to work with, not clinging to the past the way some artists did when things changed. The main lights were up. A few people were talking near the exit, among them the bass guitarist who took every opportunity after a gig to find someone to go home with. He gave Nicole a high salute and blew a kiss as he was stepping out the door.

"I'll tell you what we have got, though," Rob said more positively, there was a reason for his visit. "I think you're going to like this. Something to keep you working in the meantime, keep your face out there, your name up in lights—how does that grab you?" He slapped his small hands on the counter quite suddenly and said, "Musical theatre. Yes, sweetheart, now that's what I'm talking about. It's solid, regular work. Pretty well paid too. A chance of touring—listen, it's a good gig."

"What, you mean, West End?" Nicole said, a smile appearing.

"Well, no. Eventually maybe. I don't see why not—once you got started."

"Where then?"

"Catford Broadway. They want you for the *Wizard of Oz* next year."

"Oh. *The Wizard of Oz*. Oh. You mean, a pantomime? The Catford pantomime?"

"Right, that's the one."

"Panto."

"Technically it's classed as musical theatre."

Nicole's parents used to take her to the Broadway pantomime every Christmas. They would stuff their faces with popcorn in the messy plastic pews. They would do the call and response chant. They would laugh at someone in a green wig, someone in a gaudy dress, someone getting sprayed with water pistols or slapped in the face with a wet pie. You didn't actually have to be able to sing to be in a pantomime.

With the realisation of what was being proposed to her, Nicole stood up, straightening the thigh hems of her jumpsuit, and grabbed the neck of the martini glass in her fist. When she had drained it, she slammed it back down on the counter causing a hairline split. She said, "Rob, let me tell you something, sweetheart, so that we understand each other. This is my time now. It's my time, you hear? I'm not done yet, and I have no intention of taking anything less than I deserve—which, apparently, includes you. Panto! Is that really all you've got for me? *Really*? Hmph, I'll take my jewels elsewhere, thank you. There are higher places I can go. I *know* there are higher places."

And she was so certain of it. Certain as she stormed back to the dressing room. Almost as certain when she caught herself in the mirror in the empty room with only one eyelash, the large surrounding hair, dry-looking and possibly dated, and the thinned unlorded mouth. Still just as convinced, she was—for what then? what then?—as she emerged out into the shimmer of Streatham High Road and the end of another rain.

❧

"This country has a superiority complex. It's been sold a lie. The lie that said they're better than them out there, and so have some divine right to steal, murder and exploit for their own comfort, because that's the way it was meant to be, the way God willed it. Religion has been useful. It keeps us in chains. It keeps them believing in their purity, their supremacy. Everything is angled in favour of the lie and we still live wrapped inside it, our houses are built on it, the streets we walk on are made of it, it continues to breed meanness, distrust and hatred of others. Look at us, we're a diverse, well-resourced country, the sixth richest country in the world. We have more than enough of everything we need, yet we spend so much time and energy pitting ourselves against each other. And that's the most corrupt thing imaginable. We don't *have* to like each other, but surely our values could be shared, couldn't they? a sense of right and wrong, of human compassion? Instead you have people thinking, Why are those black people getting more than me? or Why should *those* people have access to *our* resources? Being stoked by the *Daily Mail* and the right-wing media into a state of panic and xenophobia—shame on them. It doesn't have to be like this. It shouldn't be like this. Britain needs to be attached to something larger than itself in order to see itself clearly, to remember the importance of connection. You know, I was driving through London the other day and I saw something. Can I tell you what I saw?"

"Tell us. Please," said Femi Boafo, Talk FM evening radio host.

"A youth club. Remember that? Remember those places? I was shocked for a minute because I hadn't seen one for such a long time, just passing by like that. Our infrastructure, our social provision has been so *depleted,* so destroyed by the Tories and austerity and this evil culture of self-centredness that the things we used to take for granted, that used to be a part of our reality, are becoming *fossils,* relics on the cityscape, passing reminders of when we lived in a more caring society and our young people at least had somewhere to go." Here Michael held the words in his palms, closing them together and over one another in his customary priestly way, as if to protect their sanctity. He said, "And we wonder why there's so much trouble on the streets. Lawlessness. Cowboys, liars and thieves. If there's lawlessness at the top, there will be lawlessness at the bottom."

"Indeed. Indeed," Femi said, his use of this word inspired by the character of Omar Little in *The Wire*. "But wait, is that really the case, that we live in a less caring society? I mean, as things stand on the ground, is it any worse for young people now than it used to be? What do you think, Mrs. Brown. Was it easier for your kids when they were coming up? Obviously—it wasn't. We know it wasn't easy, for your son, especially—"

"I have two daughters as well," Cordelia Brown said, straight-backed and rigid, seated opposite Femi across the circle of microphones with Michael to her right.

"Your daughters too, yes, indeed. Was it very different for them? And how did you prepare them, if I may ask, for stepping out into the world? Was there anything you'd say to them to help them deal with the barriers and obstacles they might face?"

"Well," she shifted in her seat, giving Femi a straight, sharp stare that people often found unnerving, "I told them the same things you would tell your children now. I tried to instil strength, resilience: keep your head up and walk tall, be respectful. I never singled them out as black kids. I didn't tell them they were going to have to deal with this and that and stop and search and those things—it wasn't like that. I made sure they knew their history, yes. But I wouldn't put ideas and thoughts into their heads about what their lives are going to be like or who their enemies are. I believe that's wrong. They have the right to be who they are, the person I birthed. That's their birthright. The trouble is it gets taken away from them, doesn't it. It gets beaten out of them over time. But I refused to contribute to that."

As usual with these interviewers, Femi made a comment about Cordelia's calmness and her exemplary sturdy resolve, to which she shrugged, haughty and humble at the same time. Several times a day someone called her a pillar or a rock. They didn't see the wells of churning unease beneath, the big fog obscuring her vision on a morning, making it difficult to rise from the bed.

The atmosphere in the studio was tinged with an air of familiar loss, of absence. There was an opening, Femi held it that way, for her to talk about her son, the one who had died in custody. They always wanted her to talk about it even when she was there to talk about something else, like today she was here to talk about the Race Disparity Audit. She was an emblem, a cipher, and Michael, tall and wide-shouldered, protective, in his slim dark jacket and jeans, was her barrier between them and her. She had come to a point where she couldn't do without him. It was his great kindness and a certain deep light in him that had softened her and made her want him alongside her. Whenever she was asked to speak on a panel or talk to the broadcasters he was close by, increasingly, of late, more vocal, manoeuvring the discussion in such a way that she felt herself incubated against undue rubbing of the wound, difficult in this work of perpetual recall but it was work she believed in, even as it kept her anchored in the past. Michael took up the rein of Femi's next question, broadening the theme outwards, away from the personal. He was good at that expansive, pulpit kind of talk. Better than she was. Cordelia was not one for a speech. She was just a quiet woman with a loud imperative.

Michael, on the other hand, had found that he was suited to such speech-making and public debate. He had a natural meander to a line of argument making it not always clear where he was headed but absorbing nevertheless, he would put on his radio voice (hadn't he always known he was meant for radio? even Nicole said he had "a voice," "you could sing lovers, you could've been the Wayne Wonder that never was"), he would scribble down a list of points he wanted to make in preparation, and dip into some favourite passage from James Baldwin to rouse his passion and steer his focus. He liked being Cordelia's chaperone, virtual bodyguard and confidant. It was a welcome antidote to the more unfulfilling aspects of his job, the fundraising and report-writing, the commission boards and meetings with hollow government officials. The combination of all of these things, though, brought him a sustained satisfaction that he had never managed to achieve before. Perhaps for the first time in his working life, he was satisfied, imbued with purpose, engaged, he felt, in the wheel of change. They—the people out there, editors, makers of opinion—cared about what he thought. He stood more centrally now, with less shyness, less skirting of the periphery, at those stuffy corporate functions, and he left the house in the mornings with enthusiasm rather than sloth, not arriving back sometimes until long after his official hours.

When the interview was over Femi pranced round and moved Cordelia's chair back to ease her slower rising, she was a full foot smaller than Michael, whose hand she accepted at her elbow. They went through a warren of dim studio corridors and five floors down in the lift to the courtesy car waiting for them on Cleveland Street. Once inside, Cordelia took long sighs, leaning back and looking out of the window at the rainy city going by, the wind-tossed trees, the approaching Trafalgar expanse and the rooftop domes. They were going south.

"You were excellent, as usual. I didn't like him very much. He made me feel on edge."

"Oh, Femi's all right. He can be a little careless, I guess."

"Maybe it's me. Maybe I'm just tired of it. I get this hostile feeling, like they're trying to catch me out or they want to accuse me of something."

"Accuse you? Of what?"

Cordelia didn't reply, but closed her eyes as they started across the river. She liked to imagine the water more than see it. She opened her eyes some way over the bridge and saw the silver beauty around her, the ever-glowing lights, and felt a new wave of sorrow at all that he had missed, how much had been taken from her. She was discovering, in these mounting waves and surges, that the more time passes the more profound the grief, because you are looking backwards at where the beloved stopped, while the chasm between there and where you go on, every day, is widening, so full in its emptiness. She felt that she could fall into it and drown.

"I think it's time for me to go inside, Michael," she said. "I've been out here for so long, I can't breathe. I don't sleep well. I can hear him talking to me."

Michael knew that she was talking about her son. He was

ever-present, in the direction of her hours and the texture of her voice. It was rare that she veered into this ghostly evocation of him. When she talked like this, he felt that he was being exposed to something too private and so remained quiet, listening and trying not to intrude with his listening. He didn't ask a question or treat it as a conversation. It was as if she were talking in her sleep, completely vulnerable and endangered, and he were sitting a way off in the shade of her quiet room.

The bridge was behind them now and they were taking the Oval curve towards Kennington.

"Whenever I was tired, Robert used to tell me to rest. He'd tell me to go and lie down. He was the only person who could persuade me. Lie down, Mum, *right now*. I don't know if it's me or him saying it. I don't know where he ends and I begin."

Was she crying? Michael wasn't sure. He had never seen her cry in six years working with her.

"Hey, you ok?" he said. "Is there something I can do?"

"Yes," she said. "Yes, there is something you can do for me, Michael."

Cordelia Brown took another long breath. There was a terrible thirst at the back of her throat, like parts of herself were separating, could not reach one another. "I've been thinking about this for a while. I think it's approaching the time now. I want you to step in for me—will you, please? I want you to take over. You're the only one who'll do it right. I trust you. There's some people who want to take us in a different direction and I know you wouldn't do that."

Her tone had regained some of the stark professionalism and aloofness with which she usually carried herself around colleagues. To Michael's initial reaction that he was not in a position to replace her, did not have the credentials, she was dismissive. "Managing director is just a title, that's all. It doesn't mean that much. All it means is that you know everything about how the

147

organisation works, which you do, and therefore you know the best way to manage it, more than everyone else, which you do."

"It's yours, though. I mean, it's yours, and his."

"I'm ready to let him go."

A wash of relief, a heave of regret as the car sped on, along the A202 and these streets his old shadow walked. That was what he meant, she could hear it clearly. That she must lie down, because he wanted to lie down. He was tired of walking. And what could she say this walking had achieved when the menace was rising up again, coming out unashamed into the open— monkey chants, swastikas in the street? Cordelia had become used to being threatened by people who wanted her to be silent and swallow the wrong that had been done, but the looks she saw in some of the faces these days, the murderous anger and hatred, just passing by if you were on an errand to buy bread or salt, it made her want to run out of the country for good, until she remembered that the country was hers and she had wanted to make it better for the young ones coming up. For the first time in front of Michael, she did weep, unable to pretend all the tears had been cried. There were so many more. She had not known there would be so many more on the other side. She let him wrap his arms around her and leaned into his thick coat. When they reached her house, he helped her out, so heavy she felt as they walked to the door. He hugged her in that engulfing way he did. You could put a hug like that in a packet and sell it as comfort.

"Lie down, Mrs. Brown," he said. "You go in now and lie down."

She did so. And she slept better that night than she had slept in months.

Michael also slept well, after staying up for a while waiting to share his news and the doubts he was feeling. He wanted to call his mother and ask her what she thought but didn't want to wake her. He had never been a leader of something, had never imagined he could do it. Nicole arrived back just before one and lay down next to him in her ivory chemise. She buried her face in his back, drawing the comfort, ruminating on her own future, until the worry of it leaked away, running clear. Deep in the night all was still, and they woke and shifted, he wrapped himself around her from behind with his knees in the backs of her knees and her shoulders inside his shoulders. At some point she opened her eyes and noted the deep perfection of things, then closed them again. By the morning they were facing away from each other, back to back, crushed into the pillows with tiny frowns, a new light slowly glowing around the edges of the window, like a visit from another world.

11

Alice refused, she *refused* to take Ria's room with its proper bed. Melissa's room was too much stair, Blake's was a box. The sofa was the place. This is where she would lay her cloth to lie down on, her dressing gown over one arm, her night hat and her faded handkerchief. This little table next to it was fine to set her Nivea, her stress-buster, her water bottle, her crocheted coaster and her vapour rub. She would not listen to Melissa's solicitations towards the bedrooms, fuelled by basic propriety: when your mother, a woman in her seventh decade, a Nigerian from the village, the journey through her life long and confounding, comes to stay with you for a while after recently becoming an estranged widow, possibly a haunted one, you give her the best bed in the place, as indeed it would be in the village. She sleeps sumptuously on your pillow, makes your space her space etc. It felt wrong to have her camping out like this in the communal area, her travel bag next to the sofa serving as a temporary wardrobe, in the mornings the cloth and night hat stored away out of sight. Even Ria tried to persuade her—"There's planets on my ceiling! I've got this cool night light from Ikea so the dark's kind of blue?"—but she remained adamant. She was not interested in looking at planets on a ceiling (what if she was struck by a falling Neptune in the middle of the night?), and she did not really agree that Ria's bed, with

150

its metal scaffolding and various decoration and paraphernalia of youth, was a proper one.

As if she were moving to another country, perhaps because she had moved to another country, she came with some luggage, not just the personal items required to simulate home in any place, on any sofa, but enough food to allay hunger in the event of disaster, sudden poverty or unexpected company. Having hauled the bags, the polka-dot trolley, the bin liner of particular essential cloths, with Calvin's help, up the stairs onto Melissa's landing, quite a long time was spent there with Alice explaining the identity and function of each food stuff as she fished it out, this five-kilogram bag of basmati which Melissa was incapable of cooking, not understanding the spirit of basmati, this raw chicken "for freezer or you put in fridge," some corn on the cob on a tin plate, some cooked beans, an apple pie, fried akara, "chin chin for children," a bottle of Nigerian salted peanuts, five kilograms of gari for eba which Melissa was once and for all going to learn how to make as her duty and obligation both motherly and daughterly, "I show you." She had been cooking for days, she told her. She had also brought gifts from the church, things hard to fathom yet meant in kindness and reminder of Christ, such as a hardback of children's stories in Italian and a miniature gold-bound excerpt from the Book of Mark, this too in Italian. Finally there was a plant. In the village, the guest has their own obligation: you do not come empty-handed.

At long last, Alice had agreed to come and stay for a little while, as refuge. Though she generally felt out of her depth outside Kilburn—it was either Kilburn or Nigeria, a void in between—she had accepted that time away might do her good. But only for a few days, "You take me home on Tuesday." It was the Ansonia clock that had allowed her to be persuaded. The batteries had been replaced twice, still it ground to a halt at 5:20, and three times now the phone had rung at 5:20, one of those in the morning, and when she'd answered there was silence, with a presence inside it. "Is punishment," she said, weeping gently; she wept often in this aftermath, her voice would fall into it without event. She was convinced that, somehow, from the next place, Cornelius was trying to communicate with her. Maybe he wanted a Wednesday dinner. He wanted to come and sit, one last time. It was not over. He was stuck. It happened, when the soul was in shock, or if it was too heavy for heaven or if it had been cremated instead of buried like it was supposed to be, maybe he couldn't pass through. "Mum, it's probably a marketing call," Melissa persisted. "Someone's trying to sell you something, that's all." Alice listened to this explanation, wanting to believe it, folding one of her cloths on her lap and slowly shaking her head. She did look smaller out here, away from her pink walls. She would not say yes to the removing of the Ansonia clock and replacing it with another, in case it made things worse, but was employing her own trusted methods of exorcism involving the use of plantain skin and potent vegetables.

Blake was excited by this visit. It could be the king of Spain, a gas engineer, an aunty, a father, a fisherman, a relative from the north—any outer being in the home was an opportunity for interesting times and literary exhibition. "Shall I read you my story? It's about a dragon slayer." At school they had been working on paired adjectives. He read, Alice seated on her sofa, expectant and characteristically dreamy, bathing in the light high voice of a little son: "Carefully, the dragon slayer strolled along the rusty, uncomfortable road with mixed emotions. On one hand he was happy that he saved three jubilant, baby dragons, but on the other hand he was sad that he shouldn't be called the dragon slayer anymore because he hadn't slayed them. He left them in his small, ancient garage then he sauntered out to get some vegetables for them (mostly carrots) and left them joyfully eating their crunchy, delicious carrots . . ."

"It's not finished yet," he said when he'd come to a stop.

"You should finish it," said Ria, leaning on a sofa arm. "You always start them and don't finish."

"I *will* finish. The people are going to find out and then the dragon slayer loses his powers and—"

"And you shouldn't tell everyone what's in the story until you've written it because it might run away from you into the bushes and never come out."

"Shut up."

Alice rubbed Ria's back randomly with a low laugh. She rubbed the backs of her children and grandchildren whenever they were close, in appeasement, comfort, companionship, appreciation, acknowledgement, or just simple co-existence in a story, an expression of being linked by blood on the earth. When Ria was younger she had felt distant from her grandmother's ways, her cryptic talk, her detachment from a room while being physically present in it, her mundane silence, yet this regular reaching out in natural ownership. She was a paradox of adoration and disconnection, love and indifference. In the course of things, Ria had come to understand this mode of being, and to contain some of the same qualities herself, the reluctance to commit her whole presence to a place, wanting always to remain somewhat singular, so deeply rooted in the self for the safety it gave, the ability to see clearly and assess. They clapped for Blake, recognising his yearning for praise, the praise itself providing a satisfying conclusion to the story which, as a result, might now indeed never be finished. He stood for a flourish and a courtly bow.

"What of his heart?" Alice asked later. She was scared about the murmur, an inheritance, she was sure, from Cornelius, who had not been able to fight in the Second World War because of it (hence the ambulance duty). She did not want Blake to fight in the army but she also did not want him to murmur.

Melissa told her he was fine apart from getting tired in the fields sometimes. She omitted the bit about the recent intensification of the tiredness, the worsening of the asthma and the visit to the doctor, so as not to worry her when she was already worried, about the stopping of clocks and intrusions from the next world and such.

"Be sure you mash and medicate. You make him lie down in hot water."

"I will."

"Be sure you never wash hair before sleep," which too could cause ill-health—colds, fevers, affronts to murmurs.

"I won't."

"What of Michael?"

"What about him?"

"Where he is?"

"Probably at home with his wife, Mum."

"I know." A brief, pissed-off shake of the head. A shrug of long-serving capitulation. "He live near?"

"He lives in Bromley. It's not far."

"He bought another house?"

Everyone now who had any affiliation with a house, any possibility of buying, building or currently living in one, was of interest to Alice. Where, how did they buy land? Who did they pay? How much money? She had asked Carol to play the lottery on her behalf to raise money for her house and when Carol had refused on the grounds of not wanting to participate in the individualist fuelling of monetary greed and social disparity in the UK and the spiritually starving West as a whole, as purported by Buddhism, she had asked Adel, who now bought Alice's ticket on Saturdays and phoned her with the numbers. She watched the draw every Saturday evening without fail. With a few millions she could easily pay the builders Carol had found to finish the house. They were going to start work soon. They did not know how long it would take but the main thing was that they were in place. It was very expensive, making rooms and roofs and doorways to other rooms to hold the air. Alice had told Adel to send them more money from the savings account, to help them with getting on with it. Soon, when it was finished, maybe with her millions but if she did not win lottery she could use what Cornelius had left her, it must be enough, she would go and see. She would take the plane and land in Lagos and they would go to Benin to see it finish, God be praise.

With some reticence, Melissa answered, "He lives with his wife. I'm not sure if they bought the place together or what. It's not my business." She was uncomfortable, sensitive to the details of Michael's life. It would be easier not to know any of these things, his direction and changing circumstances, for him to have disappeared from her awareness, only to be thought of fleetingly in wondering where he was or what he was doing. It would be straightforward, easier, too, for Alice to accept, if there were no children to share, to bind them all together this way. "She's a singer," she added incidentally, picturing—this fixed, halcyon image she held of his life with Nicole—a dulcet, serenaded atmosphere, musical footprints through the house and acoustic showers of revolving private love songs, written personally for him, maybe even vice versa.

"Is she?" Alice said, though this was not news, and she said it a little hopelessly as if well then there was no chance of getting him back, Melissa being less exciting in her work. "In church?" She was imagining someone Aretha Franklin–like in a wonderful gown and an accompanying choir. While on the subject of church, it being Sunday tomorrow, an approaching question was whether the children were ever being taken there to the holy house, to receive the Lord and the grace of His guidance. "You read Bible with them sometimes?" Melissa said no. "They need it," she nodded sternly, holding her night cloth and look-ing out at the lunar show, a high far silver in the dark, halved and trembling. God is in that moon, she thought. God gave it to us, and soon, towards eleven, she lay down in its shadow in her white dress that let breathe her thinned and papery arms, the scaled stalks of her legs and her tiny lifted feet, while the hea-then young slept around and above her in the air-holding rooms.

In the morning they did go to church, to make Alice happy and her Sunday duly holy, a local evangelical branch with on-stage percussion and pastors in jeans, *jeans,* which Alice was not impressed by, doubting the sanctity of their sermons. She had woken early and sat up looking out, so far out it circled back inwards, to memories and inner visions. She was a slower life, waiting, not for death, only for the next moment and the next, absorbing the waiting. Melissa came down in her jogging clothes—half-length leggings, a Lauryn Hill t-shirt and zip-up track top—mystifying to Alice in her demonstration of the reality of outdoor jogging in the world, those people showing their leg and body movements in undignified way in public road, sweating and panting. "Are you going to run about?" she said with scepticism.

"Yeah, wanna come?"

At this she laughed; it was good to see her laugh from the belly. To Brandy's On Top of the World and Jazzman Olofin's Shake Something Melissa ran upwards across the bumpy green and down past the petrol station to Missy Elliot, then right at the roundabout taking the great hill to the Crystal Palace tower on the Parade where the ice wind picked up and a disc of grey winter cloud was gathering around the peak. When she was running the thoughts under the music settled into a lake of manageable rippling pictures, unanswered questions lost their urgency and unmade decisions were allowed to coast.

She did not have to understand, for example, why it was that she could not end the thing with David, despite wanting such closure. He was bad for her, there was little tenderness, it bordered on the clinical, was even edging toward cruelty the way he charged through her, pressing her up against a wall or down beneath him on the sheets, hardly aware of her. The blankness she'd felt was no longer rescuing, the last time she'd left him she had driven around for hours in the dark, subsumed in a miasma of confusion and self-reproach, trying to recollect a once-reliable centre. She was treading water, the current below was building, with a quiet consistent panic that she was in imminent danger. There was no need, also, to answer the question of how it was that she had found herself, a week after that long drive, lying semi-clothed on a disused dental chair at two in the morning with the bony boy-like junior orthodontist above her in his clean blue cotton, his skin against her skin and his eyes wide with a fresh wonder. Was it the emanation of intense hygiene, the desire to be made pure? Was it a running away from what was ugly to what was smooth and bright and could be made straight? His mouth was cool and became warm. It had provoked another long drive. She had dreamt that night of Paradise Row, of walking in through the back door and finding vines hanging from the ceiling, boards over the windows.

She rested for a while on the Parade, watching the traffic go by and the sail of a yellow morning kite. When she got back Alice was in the kitchen wearing an apron she had brought with her, having remembered while packing that Melissa did not believe in aprons, refused to wear them, that crazy feminism, all it was was that Alice didn't like getting dirty when she was cooking, it didn't have to mean that she was weak or that a man had told her to put it on. Carol was the same, worse. "The apron is the language of control, the cloth of imprisonment." A useful thing, that was all. She moved from sink to fridge to balcony, her Achilles heel pronounced above her swishing slippers, that oceanic sound which Cornelius could still hear from behind his gauze of purgatory, a sound broken when she stopped at the counter to stir or chop or add, or when she was talking to Calvin down in his garden about the ongoing problem with her bitter leaf. They had already discussed his coriander and the general benefits of tomato feed but the bitter leaf was the main issue. She had tried Baby Bio, different windows, repotting, "Nothing coming up!"

"Could be the soil maybe," said Calvin, hand on hip, rubbing his neck. "Some plants need a special kind of soil. I have some ericaceous, wait let me get it." He went into his shed and came out again.

"It different from the other one?"

"Different nutrients."

"Did you plant it at an angle not straight?" Melissa remembered this advice from her cousin Ose in Lagos the last time they'd been in Nigeria, standing outside Murtala Muhammed airport as he'd drawn the plant from the boot of his car. If you plant it straight it won't work out, he'd said.

Alice was adamant that she had done as instructed. She'd potted it crooked and put it on the windowsill in much light and air.

"What's this about not straight?" asked Calvin.

When Melissa explained it to him he said he'd never heard that before but it made sense. In the car on the way to church Alice had lots of questions about Calvin, his place of origin and marital history, house ownership details, whether he played lottery. Why not Calvin, speaking of gaps in husbandry, forever a spectral concern in the fact of the two fatherless children in the back seat? After all they were practically living together, it was just like a marriage, landlord husband same thing. "But he's like my *uncle*," Melissa said, which wasn't considered much of an objection, he was strong and good at gardening, his plants so green. Melissa gradually fell silent and turned up the radio.

The pastor in jeans, the percussion, the overhead screen showing the words of the hymns, and so many people in a large room devoid of surrounding Christs and under such bright lights, this evangelism was something to see, Alice would tell Winifred next week. They sat towards the back, among rows of people waving their arms and humming and swaying in the peaks of the songs, Alice diminutive in the midst of it, pitched a little to the left, herself at an angle not straight. Ria was bored, Blake was restless, relieved to be taken away to another room for the infiltration of the young which included sweets. The last church they had been to was Alice's, on a recent visit to Kilburn when she had persuaded them all to come along. Sister Katherine and Sister Beatrice had been pleased at the sight of an actual teenager in the vestibule, clinging to her headphones yes but they would be prized off her soon enough, Sister Katherine bending and peering down at her once seated and suggesting she let God's goodness flow into her ears without hindrance. Throughout the service Ria's face had been fixed in an expression of misery, as it was now while the pastor told a questionable story about God's miraculous intervention into a parking ticket penalty waiver that had reinforced his faith, and facilitated a silly game involving an over-sized rubber balloon being batted around the room as a demonstration of comradeship and collective responsibility. Following this, though, there was a serene, half-prayed sermon from another pastor, marble-haired and commanding by comparison, who talked about the walk of final days and the entrance into paradise. "And you know you are coming to the end of your life," he said, while the singers hummed in the background, "and you are walking, walking towards the vantage point, upwards and onwards . . . And you can hear a faint music playing, the worship, it is only quiet but you can hear it, and you keep going, closer and closer . . . And when you arrive, there are billions of people surrounding the Father, who is a burning light, and the songs are booming all around you . . ." For a moment, inside this beguiling silver voice, Melissa believed. There was a sweet lift that had come into the atmosphere, as if everything had been washed and left to float.

Later Alice gave her eba lesson, advising on stew development and mashing. She was specific without being bossy. "Put pepper," "Put Magi." Calvin was invited up to try some and he ate it seriously, shadowing the bowl with his big shoulders. He ate it like a person tasting something they had forgotten or missed out on for a long time, in a hushed way. It wasn't clear whether he liked it or not because his mouth at points suggested sourness. Melissa secretly hoped that he didn't, so that Alice wouldn't be able to make up another far-fetched reason for his husband suitability.

"Now that is food," he said when he had almost finished. "That is what I call home food. Thank you, Mama."

"She's not your mama," Blake said.

"Well, she's not your mama either."

"She's Mama's mama," said Ria, and they laughed and ate.

"I like having you here," Melissa said when they were alone together. There was a stillness over the rooms, a passing train in the distance. Alice was sitting in the lamplight in her place on the sofa wearing her nightdress and a turquoise sleeveless cardigan, looking smaller than ever. She was someone to be silent with. Her presence was a comfort. It was solid ground when the ground was unstable. "I wish you'd cross the river, Mum, come and live nearby."

She smiled her easy non-committal smile.

"It's too much for me to move twice. From here I go home," she said.

"But we'll worry about you all that way away. You should be around family when you're old. Adel's right, you'll need us more, not less."

"Adel make fuss every time."

"Maybe because she's scared you'll get sick and we won't be able to take care of you."

"I be fine. When I go at last I don't want you to bring me back here."

It was no use. Any effort to persuade her returned to the same resolve, and for the first time Melissa felt annoyed by her mother's insistence on something she would not be able to achieve without their help. The travelling back and forth, the building, the tedious considerations of insulation and sheathing and cladding that Carol had been talking about on the phone last week, and the complicated financial arrangements. Why did she appear to assume it was nothing for her to exit from their lives, as if Cornelius had been her only reason to remain, as if she had no weight for them without him? It seemed a blindly selfish and uncaring proposition.

"Don't you want to see your grandkids grow up? Won't you miss them when you're there? They need you too, you know. I don't know why you think we don't need you or want you around."

Alice looked at Melissa now with displeasure. It was brief and chilling. You have no idea, it seemed to say. You are a moth, flittering in the light. You don't understand anything. She said only, "Be sure you read Bible to them sometimes and take them to church. I not very tired yet."

"Ria doesn't like church. I'm not going to force her to go the way Dad did when we were kids. I hated going."

"Don't say that."

"I did. It was all lies. Listening to those stories about sin and salvation, then going back home to him, a hypocrite. He never went himself. He's the one who needed to. We needed salvation from him, not from our own souls."

"Sit on chair, Omo," Alice said sharply.

"No. I like sitting on the floor."

A turn of the head and a sniff of her vapour rub. There was nothing she could do about any of this anymore, if they wanted to sit on their leg and squash them, if they wanted to throw away the Lord, say no to their parent, send away their husband, it was all their life and not hers. That was how they didn't need her. Mother love is instruction. It never ends, it is the longest love in the world. She could watch them through the skies from her window in Benin and God would pass them her love through his words and his house. "Is right to praise," she said, moving out into her distance, but Melissa wouldn't let her go. There was something she wanted to ask her, about the flashes, the current, the rising panic.

"Remember that cupboard, Mum, under the stairs at home," she said. "We used to get sent there when we were in trouble. We used to have to stand in the dark for an hour. If he caught us sitting down he'd start one of the clocks again, do you remember? Well, it keeps coming into my head, lately." She paused, before continuing in a lowered tone. "I'm standing inside it. There's a shadow close to me, coming closer—I'm frightened, I don't know what's going to happen—and then, then it just, disappears. Everything goes blank. It's as if I've stepped into outer space."

Alice was looking past Melissa's face, towards the window, giving the impression that she was half listening, that the parameters around what she was willing or able to hear were close to being reached. There were parameters too around what Melissa could articulate. The words, the avenues, could not be found. It

162

was too far back in her formation. There are places in the history of the mind to which the voice doesn't travel and can therefore bring nothing back, nothing clear enough, and we are alone in the raw nerve feeling. In trying to communicate to Alice what she could only sense, she was reminded of their natural alienation from each other. As a child she had thought of them all as one body, one female body against one male monster. But her mother had harboured more power than that, and had failed to use it.

"I understand now why I was never afraid of things when I was young," she went on. "It's because there was a missing piece. Something was taken from us. Nothing was dangerous because we'd never been safe. Did you know how unsafe we were? Did you know?" She moved closer on the rug to where her mother was sitting and waited for her to speak. Alice remained silent for a time, with her gaze turned down, remembering her own fear that had never left her, her own missing piece, arriving at the airport in the autumn, Cornelius waiting for her in a blue suit, the way his hand sprang up when he'd caught sight of her, the utter fright she had felt at the reality of her new habitat. She was leaving everything behind, and that leaving could still be felt in the backs of her shoulders, leaving her sisters and brothers and parents, leaving the life she'd imagined for herself in Benin City, an upward kind of life of owning a shop or having a good job in trading or administration. She had been studying for her college certificate, having left her father's compound in the village. In London she hoped that she might uphold these dreams of inhabiting beyond the home, of participating in the city. But the home had weakened her. Her voice imploded, disallowing a translation of herself. She could still feel the leaving in the backs of her shoulders. She began to unfurl a string of thoughts that clung to her mind like webs.

"Without him I reach nowhere. I cannot manage on my own.

I stay and brought family up. Otherwise my life is nothing. We have to feel strong, we have to feel strong . . ." She carried on talking until she trailed off, out in her universe, unreachable. In the corner of the room on a shelf by the window a candle was burning. The flame dipped and shrank and swelled again. Cornelius passed through it in his walking, unable yet to rest. The fire through which he travelled was both exterior and interior, with the power to both burn and save. There would be no more from her mother along this line, Melissa saw. Alice was closed. She would give nothing further, and how cruel it felt, how lonely. Men hurt women. That was something they both knew. That was what they had learnt.

12

London has changed. Coming in on the Eurostar at St. Pancras, it is not immediately apparent, this change, but a growing sensation beyond the sheen and shimmer of the shopping strip. Go past LK Bennett and Dune, in the upward drifting of the public piano which Ria once played shyly. And go by the glassy eateries selling, judging by their price, the sandwiches of kings and queens. High up on a billboard near departures is written, "Get ready for Brexit," and this six-letter word, recently created, instils silos of passion in people walking by, the ones who want to forget, the ones who cannot wait, and the ones who can't accept. The passions choke the atmosphere as you go through passport control, thinking more deeply about your passport and its future, when it will change colour, how you will relate to one another, how it might be used against you; and then you are in King's Cross, the real place, the St. Pancras concourse only its shiny face, and it has changed. The poverty is louder, fuller. There is anger in the skies over the red-brick steeples.

Damian had come in from Paris, in the first week of the new year, after hearing word of Avril. Her face in his mind was a feature of the landscape speeding by. She was in the streets, in the corners, in the young figures wrapped in sleeping bags in the station alcoves and dirty walkways. It was freezing outside, the evening birds very faint. He took another train, manoeuvring through the throng with his rucksack and the early stages of a beard settling over his cheeks, aware all the time of this great tension around him, as if something grave and final were about to happen that would change the accustomed positionings. It was a foolish word, he had thought, the first time he'd heard it. The naming of it was a tribal act, insidious. First it was named—a proposition, a dream, an army—and then appeared its enemy. A new place was laid for fighting. A hook was there to hang old hates.

Here he was, a man of forty-six, a father of four, arriving back in his life. He went to Merstham first to set down his things and gather himself—Stephanie had given him a specific time, twelve o'clock on Saturday, "you don't get to just turn up." The flat had a remote and finite air. He had an eroding sensation as he went inside that he was seeing it for the first time, the smudges of bicycle dirt on the wall in the hallway and the soulless brown-beige kitchen. A letter had arrived about late rent. He was out of step with himself, was losing favour at work, had failed to notify them before going off. That night he took down the Christmas tree which looked barren and lacklustre in its corner, then had a drink to soften his nerves. A whole day to wait before he could see her.

"Have a nice trip did we?" Stephanie said as she stepped out of the house. She wanted to say a few things before he came in. "A tonne of good that did, you going a-hunting. Did you get to see some sights?"

Her appetite for sarcasm had intensified since they'd separated, was never far from her countenance towards him. She looked tired and harried, an agitation had settled permanently into her face, a state of alarm. He'd hoped for a softer reception in light of shared relief but could see he remained the culprit, for any distressing or unwanted eventuality.

"Don't give me a hard time, Steph, I just want—"

166

"Stephanie."

He sighed. "Can I see my daughter?"

"In a minute. First I want to make sure you're not going to say anything to her that's going to send her off again or confuse her. She's staying with me. None of this going back and forth anymore, she needs to be in one place. She needs her mum and I'm going to look after her, all right?"

"Are you taking away access? She needs me too."

It saddened him the default to business terms. He felt another avalanche of internal blame that it was all his doing, yet when he glimpsed again the bygone alternative he still could not see another outcome.

"For a while I want her to stay put," Stephanie said. "Her bed, her room, her home. Do you understand the importance of that? It's not about what you want, it's about what she needs, and if that means restricting access I don't care. And don't give her the third degree, ok? She's had that from everyone else. Turns out she did go to Paris, but you must've missed each other. My mum's taken away her passport. She wants her to have a pregnancy test."

"A what?"

"A pregnancy test. She thinks that—"

"Is she pregnant?"

"*No*," Avril said. "*No*, Dad, I'm not *pregnant*. Mum, can you *stop*?"

Damian pushed open the door as Stephanie instinctively moved out of the way for him, and then she was in his arms, a lanky resurrection of bones and beloved flesh, in dark red tracksuit bottoms, shrinking away from him perhaps because he was holding her too tightly, she let out a cough and he loosened his grip, his eyes flooding with tears. "I thought—god Avy, I thought—"

"It's cool, Dad. I'm all right," she said. He recaptured her image. She was thinner. Her closed-in shoulders, her glaring look with its meekness and rebellion. How strange children appear after such a scare. Her movements seemed clumsy and inchoate, as if something unknown to them had damaged her. "Where *were* you?" he couldn't help asking, causing a reproach from Stephanie. "But were you by yourself? Were you alone?"

"I was with a friend, ok?"

"Avril, a waiter in the Gare du Nord is not a friend."

"I only stayed with him for one night!"

"A *waiter*? You stayed with a *waiter*? What?"

"Lucky for us he wasn't a psychopath."

The waiter had let her sleep on his sofa, Stephanie would inform him, having found her sitting on the floor outside the station restaurant at closing time with no idea of where she was going to stay. After that she'd spent a couple of nights in a youth hostel. The mother of a girl Avril had known in primary school had called Stephanie on Wednesday telling her Avril was with them, had turned up on their doorstep, afraid to go home. She must have angels protecting her, Damian thought, remembering what the woman in the bar in Paris had said to him with such surety, *she will come back to you*. So she had. She had found her way back.

He sat down with her in the living room, the same room with the sessile oak through the window and the old pictures, though the ones of him had been taken away. A fire was going in the wood burner. She didn't want to talk much, it was as if her presence here was an incredible task, but it was enough for him to simply inhabit the same space as her. "Just remember we're all still one," he said, "even though things are different. We're all part of each other." At this her mouth scrunched up sideways and she looked as if she would cry. She said, "It's good to see you, Dad," and rested her head on his shoulder.

★

That was January. Now he worked in retail. A mutual parting of ways from the council headquarters. He needed something fast and empty. A two-floor chain store in a retail park, selling furniture—enormous beds, glass dining tables and highbrow European sideboards. Families came in on Saturdays and tried out the suites. He wore a shirt and tie, employee rules. The children took warm cookies from the refreshment stand and spilled hot chocolate, but the manager said the chocolate was key, it was sweet, it made people buy, this small touch, whole corner sofas and divans, there was an economic science to chocolate. It is not enough, this manager said, to sell a sofa, or a sideboard or the thing originally intended, the thing the customer came in here for in the first place. No. You must offer more than what they thought they wanted. We must make them remember what they will soon want or what they have forgotten that they wanted. Do you need a coffee table, an ottoman? What about a designer lamp, to read or scroll by its light, while sitting luxuriantly on your new sofa?

Damian did what he could for this modus of aspiration. How are you? he was told to ask the customer. Have you found everything you were looking for today? Would you like to save ten per cent by opening an account at Fabric?

Just the table, thanks, they said, or No, I only need a bed, I came in here for a bed. And he agreed with their occasional brisk tone. Why, if a person decides they want to sell suites, why can they not just sell the suites and be really good at selling them? Why do they then decide they must also sell mirrors, curtain poles, vases and tiles? I do not have the capital soul, Damian said to himself, before and after these transactions. All he wanted was a simple pay packet and a steady line to follow, one foot in front of the other. Something that had happened since returning to single life was that he had no ambition left, none at all, no more than to survive and be here for his children. He was coming to recognise that all yearning comes from obstruction. We are released, and we cease to yearn.

Stephanie had a new man, a friend of a school-run bestie. Apparently he was a driving instructor, according to Jerry, who was a high-spirited, open-natured boy, the one who seemed to hold the least animosity towards his father for leaving. This information, delivered in the park playing ball, did not quite cause jealousy in Damian, but there was a modicum of regret. He thought of the red shoes that she had walked through London in when they were sweethearts. A wish, for an instant, that they could be tapped together to send them both spinning backwards to that time, when everything lay before them. That day in January when he saw Avril at the house and Stephanie came out to speak to him, he had first glanced past her into the hallway, into their yesterdays, and seen a ghost of Jerry running across, a girl coming watchfully down the stairs. It had once all been enough.

"I needed less than you," Stephanie said to him when the divorce came through. He'd asked her whether she had been content with him, really content. She said, "It's wanting that makes you unhappy. You want too much. You always did. I'm glad I don't have to deal with that anymore."

The problem with being home, though, was that here is where the quiet scream started. It started in a supermoon, she remembered, a total lunar eclipse, the world went dark, she was very young, just six or seven years old, and it began in a high pitch which sounded like anything she had ever been scared of was gathered together in song, and when the light came back and the moon passed over, it was still there, very quiet, very low. Avril was not completely sure of this, the exact time and location, it was difficult to retrieve, but she remembered that she had been frightened, incredibly frightened, so much so that a kind of beating tremor skittered up inside her and she was sure she was going to be pushed out of her body. If she didn't speak, it would have to let her stay.

Jerry made her laugh so much. She was pleased to be with him again. She loved the place they were together. His drama was so funny, that he found injustice in small things and freely complained. She never wanted him to grow up, despite his big flat feet lengthening and the school shirt getting short for him. There was always some mud on his trousers.

"Don't do that again," he said. "I was worried about you."

"I won't. Don't worry your little head."

Only Jerry was allowed in her room for long periods. They sat on her bed and ate jelly beans. She was secretly counting her chewing which was a habit she had developed. With Jerry it was easy because whenever they had sweets they always counted how many each of them had, so it was part of it. The quantity of the chewing of each sweet must be double the total number she was having which was eight. It was quite terrifying, actually, as her mother kept saying she was too thin and making her eat too much, and what would become of all that later, all over her? She didn't think she was thin.

During the day Jerry and Harvey were at school and Avril spent her time job hunting and exercising. Sometimes when her mother was at work her grandmother would come, to keep an eye on her, she knew, and they might go for a walk around the neighbourhood or out to the shops. She was quite glamorous, her grandmother, careful of her face and highly rouged, always a bit tense. Avril felt that there was a huge canyon between them and that she must get away. She thought about going to stay with her father. There was that night, she had never forgotten it, in the middle of the night, when she had seen him in his room taking clothes out of the drawers and shoving them into a bag, and there was the distressed look on his face when he'd realised he was found out and that he must after all stay, because of her. She had ever since carried a certain burden because of that look. Was it the same thing he had felt then, that she was feeling now, this loud pressure and closing in, the desire to smash away the walls, to push all experience outwards? Jerry made it light. When Jerry was around everything was clearer.

"Mum wants you to go back to school," he said chewing his jelly beans without counting.

"I'm not going back."

"What're you going to do instead?"

Stephanie's neat vision of the future: her graduate brood framed and smiling in black cloaks and tasselled hats on the dining room sideboard. The marriage unravelled and the family disfigured, she still could not take this new prospect of additional collapse. All her hard work, all these years. Yes, Avril would follow Summer, into the rolling campus greens and the lecture theatres and the student union bar. Summer whom Avril could never match up to, who always did everything she was told.

"I'll find something. I might work in a factory."

"A factory? A factory!" Stephanie shouted when she heard of this idea.

"Or I could get some kind of apprenticeship, or something," Avril replied to calm her down.

"You need your GCSEs! It's not negotiable. You're getting your qualifications and that's final."

Never, never had Stephanie imagined that she would say such a thing, in such a way, that she would be the sort of mother who laid down the law. The tragedy of child-rearing is that one day you find yourself yelling at your daughter about qualifications and obligations to fulfil her potential on account of everything that has been poured into her by her parents' hard work, and she is regarding you with a look of resignation,

172

stoicism and accusation making you realise that you have embodied exactly the thing you promised yourself that you would not.

"But Mum, I don't *want* to study anymore," Avril said angrily, the fight was playing out all over again. "I don't *want* to go to uni. Why should I? I'll just be in debt for like, forever."

"You won't be. It's only when you're earning enough money you have to pay it back."

"Oh yeah so great, study for three years, no, *six* more years when I hate studying, then get a job I hate that eventually will pay me enough money to pay for the studying I hated. Some life *that* will be."

"*Why* are you so *negative*? You sound just like—" Stephanie stopped.

"Go on, say it. Like Dad."

"Avril."

"There's a reason he's like that."

Look. They are walking away from you, as soon as they can walk. The painting on the wall of the pier going into the misty sea that Stephanie woke to every morning, she could almost see Avril standing there, the ocean all thrown out and wild for her, a girl, throbbing with naivety. And it is also true that it gets heavier, this work of raising, not lighter, for you come to carry the entire possibility of a great fall of what was born and fed so carefully, you come to see how brittle it remains, perhaps at some fault of your many forgotten mistakes, and now your power is limited, yet so necessary. One day you set a boat to sail and you have no idea of the existence, location or likelihood of another shore.

Avril had a book, from her father, one of the many he had given her. It was called *Tigers Are Better-Looking,* and had a picture on the front of a woman wearing a wide-brimmed hat and staring dark-eyed at a single point. She had taken it with her when

173

she'd gone, as a last thought, because she liked the expression on the face, how determined and withholding she looked. She'd read it on the trains and in the cold stations, lured by its Parisian mood. The pages were old and yellow. Her adventure was bigger than herself and when she'd got anxious the words were comforting, they seemed to know the truth. People don't know what to do with themselves, she thought. We don't know where to go. We don't know whether to turn away from the world or towards it.

ᶜ↬

She got a job in an Italian café in Dorking town centre as a waitress and cycled there on her bike. She had four shifts a week of walking about taking orders, delivering orders, clearing away empty plates, she liked how active the work was. She would much rather do this than sit at a desk all day typing, and Ria during their text conversations agreed that working in an office was brutal. Do you get free food? she asked. Yh, Avril replied, greasy tho. She hardly ate any of it because all she could think about was the slime swilling around the spaghetti, the butter soaking in the garlic bread, the oil at loose in the meat. Resisting it made her feel powerful, that she didn't have to surrender to it. Stephanie was not aware of her distaste. As far as she knew this is what Avril was having for dinner at the end of her shifts instead of eating at home—delicious calzones, fresh Bolognese.

Lots of kids take a gap year during their education, Stephanie did her best to reassure herself. Not everyone wants to hurtle on to the next thing straight away. Some need to take a step back and think about what the next step is. She was sure Avril would discover it soon, she told herself and the mothers of ex-classmates she ran into in the street or at the adventure playground with Harvey. All part of her resolve to be more open, understanding and laid back, so that she wouldn't lose her again.

What a feeling it was, riding through the evening as light as a bird. How charged and translucent Avril felt pushing her bike up the driveway after a shift and drinking a long glass of water or even pineapple juice if she felt deserving, if she had done enough walking about, and then going to bed. In the morning she could eat a proper breakfast because she would be doing more cycling and had started going to the gym twice a week as well because she could afford a membership. She liked being so independent. Once, when she was at school, a girl had come up to her and said, "You're quite overweight, aren't you." She hadn't known what overweight meant yet and had thought it meant she'd been waiting too long. Now she knew what it meant. That was why she didn't like looking in the mirror sometimes, especially after eating one of her mother's insistent dinners, the pasta, the carbohydrate. "Avril, are you eating properly?"

She came into the furniture shop one afternoon on her day off while Damian was serving a customer. He was disturbed by how thin she was getting. She was wearing a pair of narrow jeans with one of Jerry's tops. There were patches of shade around her eyes and she made clumsy, angular shapes when she moved. When she sat down on a flame-red fabric suite, the colour billowed outwards from her like a desert. "This one's nice," she said. "Are you eating properly?" he said. "Yeah." "Have you eaten today?" "Yeah, I just had lunch." "What did you have?" "A sandwich." "What was in it?" "Ham, cheese, mustard and lettuce." "Are you eating three meals a day? You need to eat three meals a day, you know. Especially as you're still growing." He asked her if she wanted a warm cookie, and when she declined he said please would she have it because it would make him feel better. He watched her eat it. She looked like a girl in a magazine, those bony figures, displayed as beauty. He noticed the veins of her hands protruding through her skin.

By this time she was beginning to hear a voice. She did what the voice said: no sugar, breads, potatoes, rice, cheeses, butter. There was no longer a quiet scream or a feeling of wanting to escape. Only a single, steady voice.

In April, Stephanie took her to the doctor. It had been such a cold start to the spring; blossom travelled over the gardens, believing itself to be snow. While Avril sat on the chair next to the doctor's desk moving her toes up and down in her shoes, because movement was power and stillness was surrender, she was asked intrusive, inconvenient questions about her lifestyle which she didn't appreciate. It emerged that they could have been making it worse, despite their attempts not to, the frantic trawling for information and remedy. They weren't supposed to comment on her appearance either positively or negatively, because it could cause a self-negating reaction. A plan of sustenance and assessment was introduced. She found it difficult to accept.

"Share a thought," Damian said.

"I want to come and live with you," she said.

"You know that can't happen, Avy."

"Your turn."

"Ok. All the sadness of the world should be thrown upwards, so the load for everyone will be lighter. It will fall off our shoulders like rain. But you've got to throw it up first. You've got to throw it."

"I will," she said. "I am. It's ok, Dad."

13

Dear Sisters

The builders I found in Lagos have pulled out so I found another one,
in Benin which is better anyhow. References are good. They're going
to do a site visit of Mum's house soon and said they'd send pics. I've
told Mum we have to pay an upfront fee for them to buy materials and
she's fine with that. Adel, is it ok if I put them in touch with you so
that you can do the transfer? If all goes well they'll be able to start
work in the next couple of months, finally! Fingers crossed. I'll keep
you posted.

Carol x

Melissa received this email coming out of Camden tube station on her way to the Thursday evening meeting of the Regents
Poetry Circle, her first time. She was dry-throated at the thought
of sharing her stanzas with strangers, and Camden felt like a long
way to go in the dank spring cold and intermittent drizzle, which
was made worse at the thought of Alice's materialising house, the
hole it would leave in Kilburn, the fathomless hole it would leave
in England. The meeting was held in a college classroom with
metal-legged tables. She had sent poems in advance to the group's
chairperson, Allard Botcherby, which he had distributed to the
other participants. They were all supposed to come with important, constructive things to say about each other's "work."

Allard had a cereal-bowl haircut and a bulbous, monastic face. There was a thespian flair to his voice and gestures, while opposite him was a commanding Japanese woman dressed in hot pink with matching lipstick, her eyes bright and scrupulous. Jan next to her was white and wan and shawled and translucent, holding an old-fashioned stopwatch which she used to keep time on the critiques. The oldest in the room was a tall, anoraked veteran with nicotine fingers who was writing about the Falklands War and his travels through Italy. They greeted Melissa with serious smiles or nods. They were searching, complex, mature, interested, interest*ing* poets, not just your average amateur clique, they meant to convey.

"Each person gets twenty minutes of feedback," Allard said, explaining their procedure. "One person at a time can speak, to a maximum of five minutes, then we move on to the next critique." Jan was ready. She was forceful and exacting. When the speaker reached the end of their fourth minute, no matter the profundity or sensitivity of the point being made, such as Allard's own dramatic take on the dichotomous treatment of trees in Zoe's excerpt, she would push her face towards them with a raised index finger and say, "You have one minute." Her face was moist, her eyes wild. Melissa kept her observations short to avoid her temporal wrath, realising in any case that she was not well versed in deconstructing verse, she just liked the flow and pattern, the pictures in the lines.

"Stilled and sliced on the shattered shore," Zoe recited the opening of the Falkland man's third stanza. "It's such a striking image. It made me think of butchered meat. It's about the cost of war on living things, and I could really *feel* that. I think it's really, really, so powerful, Greg. One thing I want to say, though, is that there're too many exclamation marks. Four in this one verse."

"Is that too many?" said Greg.

"I think so. They're coarse." She turned her head. "I never use them."

"What, never?"

"Never."

"But what about when there's a shout or a big moment, you know?"

"You have one minute," Jan said.

"I mean personally, for myself, I don't think you need to have such a heavy recurring thing in the punctuation. They're sort of military, in a way, aren't they, like soldiers standing at attention, which is appropriate for your subject matter but I still think it's too much. And another thing is that then the next verse we're in Naples—it seems like too much of a jump."

Further along, Allard said, "There's such a brilliant pathos in the impact of just that one word that ricochets through the entire piece," speaking of Melissa's poem about friendship, "and I'm wondering if that effect might be achieved in an even *deeper* way if it were *repeated*, perhaps in the final verse."

"You mean repeat the word mordant?"

"Or, or even use *another* word. It could be a word like verdant, or mandate."

"I'm not sure I want it to rhyme," she said.

"Well, those are just examples off the top of my head but what I'm getting at is the ex—"

"You have one minute."

"—the expansion of existing meaning that could take the poem *beyond* its own scope, in a kind of circumterrestrial journey. I remember reading this kind of thing in a Dylan Thomas poem and it struck me as a good way of maximising the potential of an image."

"I didn't think it worked, that one word in the middle," Greg said when his turn came.

There was a pause before he elaborated.

"I don't like it when poems are so broken up. I'm always distrustful of experimentation for the sake of it. There has to be a good reason for it."

"The reason was to——"

"You're not really supposed to go into explanations when you're receiving feedback?" said Jan.

"I forgot to mention that but yes," said Allard.

"Unless you're specifically asked a question in order to clarify something in the feedback."

"*Was* there a reason?" Zoe asked.

"Um, it was to emphasise the sense of loneliness in——"

"Anyway I'm not interested in the reason. The reason is not the reader's business, is it? The reader's business is the impact and when you have words floating around on the page like that it's just distracting, I think, in my personal opinion."

"Excuse me but is it fair to impose your own preferences for traditionalism on someone else's style?" Zoe interjected again, annoyed with Greg, which was a common occurrence.

"You're not allowed to interrupt during feedback, you can comment afterwards by raising your pen. Sorry but we have to stick to the rules otherwise it's a fiasco."

Greg shot forward in his chair, pointing his pen at Zoe. "Do you know who uses exclamation marks *all the time*? Coleridge. Heard of him? *And*—William Blake!"

Hi Carol

I'm concerned. How do you know we can trust these builders? Have you met any of them in person? Presumably you haven't. I'm not happy with sending money to them when we don't even know whose hands it will actually end up in. I still think it's dangerous to keep filling Mum with ideas about going back home. We should be trying to persuade her to let go of it and accept staying here. It won't do her any good in the end.

Can't we all sing from the same hymn sheet? I thought we'd dropped this idea and it feels like you've been going behind our backs.
Adel x

Hi both
Adel, you call it going behind your backs (can't believe you'd think that!) but I call it getting on with it. Last year when I was trying to start looking into this and was emailing you details you didn't seem interested or helpful in any way, so I stopped sharing and decided just to send updates when needed. Mum wants to return home. Those are her wishes. Does that mean anything to you? Is she a grown woman or a child with no choices of her own? If there is a hymn sheet that we should all sing from it should be hers, not yours, or even ours.

I'll send the exact figure they need for the materials once I have it and we have a contract in place. The contractor's name is Austin, if it makes you feel better, Bini Build. Remember, it's for Mum to decide what she does with her money.
C

M
Do you know what her problem is?? It's beginning to feel like she's deliberately standing in the way.

But I could be wrong. Off-key is all I'm saying. Will try to remain calm.
Cxx

These emails were read on the train from London Bridge to Gipsy Hill with the drizzle insisting at the windows, on the way back from the Regents Poetry Circle. Those people were not her tribe, Melissa sensed. She would never see them again, Allard, Jan, Zoe and Greg. It was David who suggested she try the spoken word scene instead. You speak the lines. It doesn't matter where they sit. No one will tell you mordant is in the wrong place or

181

verdant is missing or you should have a comma in place of a colon, because they can't see it. You get to keep the poem in its body, he said. It's still yours. Which was one of the most useful and promising things he had said to her. It made her think differently of him.

"The only problem with that, though, is that it involves standing up in front of people and reciting," she said. They were at his flat the following weekend. He was pouring some vegetable chips into a bowl at the kitchen counter as an hors d'oeuvre to Deliveroo.

"Yeah, you can do that," he coaxed.

"No I can't. I'm too shy."

"Oh, come on. Didn't you used to do it in school? The secret is not to think of it as performance but a square of the present. Don't try. Be."

"What do you mean by that—a square of the present?"

"I mean," he sat down next to her, the cord string of his hoodie brushing the top of the wine bottle, "you capture yourself in a moment of transference from within. Like, the whole concept of the performance is shaved away into a single square and you just concentrate on that, on the square. It's a reversal of your own façade, if you like. Instead of being looked *at*, you're looking outwards, at them. So you cancel their power over you."

"Hm. You're good."

"I know I am."

"Maybe you should give me some sessions."

"Freeness. Comes with a price."

"Oh not *now*, what about Deliveroo, aren't you hungry?"

"I'm not sure. Are *you* hungry?"

"You can't just grab at me like that when I'm eating crisps, David. Where's your sense of nuance and delicacy?" Melissa moved away from him.

"You're like an avocado," he said bitterly. "You refuse to ripen if prematurely opened, out of spite."

It had happened first, the opening, on Peckham Rye, in the drunken mid-spring dark, a week after they'd met. They wriggled in the grass like teens, the willows swayed over, she shone like a gift in the leafy dim. This had set a fevered tone that reality did not live up to and he felt an escalating disappointment in her, that their drives did not match, she had teased him, he felt, at a time in his life when he was braced for a crescendo.

"Gosh," she said, "that must be the pinnacle of your flattery towards me. If I'm an avocado, what does that make you? A passion fruit?"

"We only touch when you want to."

"Yes."

"What about when *I* want to? You're cold, cold."

"Oh, that's what they always say about me."

And she mildly hated him again. The hatred brought them closer. He manoeuvred over her with the lampglow ghostly on the tips of his shoulders. When she looked at their two bodies together she experienced the habitual dislocation, they were atoms passing one another, she a supernova, dying and exploding, occupying a vast space, and in this way she could disappear even from herself. It was the same thing she'd experienced in Rome in the narrow hotel after an episode of phantasmagorical panic. They had been travelling on the metro in the evening. She was engulfed by pressing darkness, which had receded as they came up the stairs into the open air of the piazza, but intensified again when the lift doors in the hotel lobby closed. Back in their room, she had sat down on the bed to catch her breath. He came towards her, and she blankly accepted his body, disappearing into it until she was another place. "You know, you're strange," he had said. "I can't tell if you're feeling anything. It's like you've gone somewhere."

★

Hello sisters

Sorry for delay. Sounds like things are starting to move. Exciting for Mum but I agree we should be careful with transfers. If the references are good and they're personally recommended it's probably fine. Look forward to more updates!

Btw pls put post in the right sections of the filing cabinet (spent ages organising it).
Mx

Hi C

Yes stay calm. I have no idea what the problem is but I'm staying out of it—better that way. Life is brief.

Wanna try a Vikram class with me? Never done it before.
Mxx

She found a spoken word event for black women at a bar in Clapham and imagined it could be a safe place to attempt a recital, so she went to watch the poets in flow. They were nervous, daring, staring, intense, strong, dreamy, prolix, depressive, at times brightly, in braids and beads, or other hair stories. One read a love poem told in colours. Another sang her final stanza. There were cascades of warm applause at the truth, the feeling. Mustering bravery, reaching perhaps for a former innocence when she had walked the lanes of the university campus clutching hardback Alice Walkers and Rita Doves, just materialising, Melissa decided to employ David's expertise. Insights were gained into the secrets of his work. He filmed her at arbitrary moments to help her forget herself and downplay the concept of being watched. He would say, in the middle of a conversation, "When you're unsure about something you turn away, expecting to find the answer written on a wall or hanging in the air." Or he would say, "Most people think too much about their own reception, their impact. Don't try to be impactful. Concentrate on the present in a square shape."

"I still don't follow what you mean by that but never mind."

"It will dawn on you."

He filmed her reading a poem standing on a chair facing the window. She was monotonal, thin-based, flat and unrhythmical. "I'm not a real poet," she said, "it's just thoughts I write down in a list."

"Don't worry about all that," he said.

She tried again, became worse, philosophical. "My deep flaw is that I care too much what people think of me. I'm worried that whatever I say or do will be inferior. It's annoying, such self-doubt."

"I know. I understand."

"Like always preparing for a disaster that never happens and when it doesn't happen it's a relief. You're forever exhaling while holding your breath."

"Have you ever thought of changing your name?" he said offhandedly.

"What for? What's wrong with my name?"

"Well, it's, sort of—sunken. Pitt. It's a downward name. What about Rich, or Schmidt—Melia Schmidt. That's a good name."

"My first name as well? I'm not trying to become someone else here, David."

"But you *are*, in a way, that's the whole point," he said. "You can't go on stage as *you*. It's a *different* you. A higher, bigger version. Look, let's try it again. Let's try it with me introducing you as Melia Schmidt, just as an exercise, and see what difference it makes."

This experiment also proved ineffective. "I hate this," she said as he was leading her to his futon, his hands about her neck. "I'm not supposed to be in the spotlight. I'm better behind the scenes. I've always been that way—better on paper than in person, better in person than on a screen. I'm a series of dissolving possibilities. In the end there's nothing, only silence . . ."

"Yes," he said, "yes . . ."

He started calling her Melia sometimes in sensual jest. One night she saw him take something in his hand, a cloth of some kind, a blindfold. "I want you to only feel me, not see me," he said. She let him cover her eyes. The next time she let him cover her eyes and tie her wrists together. It released a strange unsavoury pleasure. He loved her roughly, harder than ever before. The pain was no longer almost.

"It doesn't interfere with my life," she told Hazel on the phone, when asked whether she had dumped him yet. "He'll never have to be accepted by the children because I don't think of him as my boyfriend."

"What is he then?"

"He's a, a fuck buddy. Like you said."

"That was last year, hon, those things aren't supposed to run on like this."

"Ok. He's a—guy."

"Precisely."

They had met him once, the children. They'd had crepes together in Herne Hill one Saturday afternoon at the place under the bridge opposite Brockwell Park.

"I don't trust him," Ria had said.

"I don't like his voice."

"What about his voice?"

"It's, sort of, spiky. I prefer Daddy's voice," Blake had expanded. For Daddy remained the sky, preferable to a sandwich, a crepe, a tennis racket, a ferry, a football stadium. Any tall thing. Daddy was even better than a tree. He could be climbed, hidden in, sheltered under. No one smiled like him. No one had a lower-face boomerang like him that threw out at you and then came back so that you both were smiling the same smile. He let them eat Haribos between meals and told them not to tell their mother. Blake thought he said "your mum" in a special-sounding way. He bought ice cream at random moments, was simply a superior being to "that spiky-talking man"—whose kiss, it must be noted, and Melissa had long noted it, had no trace of a Desdemona, no higher seraph in sight.

There was a particular memory Melissa held of Michael from Paradise Row. He was standing in the garden. She had called him out there to look at the summer moon which was shaped in a lazy crescent, like a comma. He looked up at it, splay-footed, bear-like, hands in pockets, less interested in this comma than she was but willing to follow her wonder. That was what love looked like now from her lower vantage point, an ascent to witness the transcendent wish of another, while fully occupying your own self, and neither one is lost.

A few days before the intended poetry reading she came across Michael by surprise while watching the news; he was discussing Tory MP Amber Rudd's treatment of members of the Windrush generation. He had on a navy suit and dark-grey shirt, was wearing glasses that complimented him. He spoke eloquently of the implicit discrimination in Home Office policy and the British justice system. What am I doing with this David guy when I used to be with him? Melissa wondered, was still wondering later that evening over drinks at Patchwork when she and David got into a disagreement about her colleague Luander who'd been passed over for promotion to senior lecturer again. She wanted to take it to a tribunal but was scared of being sacked or ridiculed.

"Is she the one who has cancer?" David said.

"Yeah. It's cleared now."

"Maybe that's why they didn't promote her."

"Well, that's still not a *reason,* is it? They're not allowed to discriminate." Melissa disliked having to explain to him how intimidating an appeal process could be when you knew you would be in a minority, that you might not be listened to or trusted.

"If you approach it in that way, though, that's how it's going to seem," he said.

"What d'you mean?"

"I mean like, if you go in there with that in your mind, all that about being the minority, then that's what it becomes about, whatever the outcome. It's a paranoia. It just gets in the way."

"Of course it gets in the way. That's the problem," she said sharply.

"I know."

"No I don't think you do know."

"What?"

"That there's a problem, because it doesn't affect you, so you can't see it, even though it's all around you. You know my nephew Warren?"

"What about him?"

"He came round the other night—I made him dinner. I asked him, just out of interest as we were talking, how many times he's been stopped and searched by police, and you know what?, he couldn't count them, he couldn't remember, there's been so many. He *shrugged.* It was heartbreaking the way he shrugged, as if, you know, that's just life. It made me so angry. It's probably the same for my other nephew Clay and he's only fourteen. *Blake* is going to have to deal with that shit. Michael is having to give him *special advice,* for what to do when—not if—it happens. Have you ever been stopped and searched? Can you imagine how it might make you feel paranoid or that something's in the way?"

"How's tricks, guys?" Frank, their regular Patchwork waiter, towered over the table. "Haven't seen you in a while." David had tensed to the state of a prune. "Everything ok?"

"Um, yeah, ok, er, d'you want another drink?"

"No."

"I think we're fine. Thanks, Frank."

"Do you realise how heavily the world is arranged in your favour?" Melissa continued when he'd gone. "The luxury you have, of nothing standing in your way, of not even having to consider the possibility that someone might take one look at you and make a negative judgement that has the power to restrict your life. Michael couldn't get a job for years when he left university. He'd turn up at interviews and he'd know straight away he wasn't getting the job from the way they looked at him. Would you call that paranoia? That's what racism does. It makes you paranoid. You can't relax."

"*Okay,* will *you* relax? God. Why're you having a go at me?" David said.

"It annoys me, that's all. You should check your privilege."

"Hmph. My privilege."

"Yes."

"So there's nothing standing in my way, ever. No one will look at me and make a judgement."

"It's not comparable."

At around 2 a.m. that night she left his flat and drove through the dark lanes and steep hills around Biggin Hill going out towards the countryside, wishing she had ended the evening after that conversation. They had sat there for a while longer. He apologised for being insensitive and she apologised for overreacting. As they walked by the Rye the same pattern unfolded, but this time there was no pleasure in his cruelty, not even from her customary distance. Her hands were tied behind her. Her eyes were covered. At some point he put his hand on her neck, and it was then, the pressure onto her throat and his thumb in her collarbone, that she felt a rising panic, that shadow coming closer and closer, a desire to scream. She asked him to stop. He didn't stop right away because it required a hauling back of himself from a place near his rhapsody.

When he did, she struggled upright, coughing. He went to get her a glass of water. She showered with the bathroom door locked. She drove the steeps and lanes for two hours.

On mounting the stairs to her floor, the door to Calvin's flat opened and he appeared, wearing his dressing gown. "You all right, Melissa?" he said.

"Yeah. I'm fine. Why?"

"You don't look fine to me." He stared at her with a strange combination of compassion and desire, his thick weathered shoulders, the shiny top of his head. She felt a willingness to be enfolded by him, in a reliable safety, yet at the same time disgusted. "I'm fine, Calvin," she said. Something was transgressed and settled between them. He looked after her as she climbed the rest of the way up, his door clicking softly closed once she was inside.

Hello again both
See here the pics of Mum's house. As you can see there's lots of work to do on the structure and grounds (much more than I expected tbh). The electricity supply is already in place though which is good. Next week they're going to be withdrawing the funds to buy materials. Adel please transfer by Thursday to give it time to go through and I still need you to add my name to the account to make things easier.
C

Hi Carol
You have to go through Mum to add your name.
Have you shown the pics to her and is she aware of how much this is all going to cost? I haven't even seen the builder references yet.
Adel

Melissa replied also, surprised at how far Carol had got, how real it was becoming. The images showed a shallow rectangular building on a stretch of red-brown earth. A tree leaning to the right and the beginnings of a roof, piles of bricks and rubble around the edges. She could imagine Alice looking out from one of the windows at the crooked tree, but it still seemed an unlikely prospect, her permanent residence there, so far away. Eventually, she still hoped, her mother would move to a place nearby and they would watch over her as she neared the final eclipse—the house, if it was ever finished, would be somewhere to stay when they were visiting Nigeria. She put down her phone and carried on getting ready for the poetry jam. There was a certain look she wanted to achieve for her recital: a little boho, rootsy, bookish. She chose Dr. Martens and a maxi-dress, all the while as she was changing wishing she hadn't allowed David to come along as it would affect her confidence, why was she still with him, why? She ended up overthinking her head-wrap because of it. She had to tie it four times before the shape was right.

He was waiting for her outside the venue in his usual apparel, white shirt, jeans and Converse. She allowed him to kiss her on the side of the mouth, after which he brushed something from her forehead. Inside there were poets, other chaperones, the curious, drinkers, locals arriving, heading to the bar and gathering around the tables and cushioned stools. There was a stage with a single standing mic, to one side of which the women were gathered, holding their pamphlets, skimming their print-outs, talking and helping themselves to the light bready refreshments.

"Have you read Ocean Vuong?" one said to another. "Oh, he's ending my life."

They talked of Warsan Shire and Audre Lorde and Raymond Antrobus's expected first collection.

"I can't eat before I read, I can only drink, a lot, so it's like I'm *almost* drunk."

"I like your dress," a woman said to Melissa, she herself wearing a green and orange African Dutch wax number, flared and dramatic of collar, tailored in Dalston. Many had complimented her on it already, whomever she spoke to, whichever sandwich tray she visited.

"Thanks. I like yours too."

"*Thank* you. I'm trying to decolonise my wardrobe."

"Have you seen they do these prints in places like Primark now? I got one last summer."

"Yes. Cashing in as usual," she soured, brushing crumbs from the bodice.

Another woman arrived dressed all in sky-blue. She had long braids wrapped into a pile on her crown from neat, hexagonal partings, and she greeted everyone with a radiating magnanimous warmth, you could feel it from metres away, like a heater. Breezing onto the stage to open the line-up, she set a warm, energetic tone for the waiting poets, all of whom, Melissa felt, read fluently, with presence and persuasion. When her turn came she was accosted by nerves, read too quietly and her hands shook, there was sweat running down the backs of her knees. David had said, just before she went up, "Break a leg, Melia," which had thrown her, and made her see with a violent clarity that it must come to an end, tonight. He obfuscated her wavelength, he obliterated her core, brought shame and disorientation, he was a bad road and she must once and for all turn off. She sat back down next to him but didn't look at him. He whispered something into her ear which she didn't hear or ask him to repeat.

"Are you ready to go?" he said after the final reading, the woman in the Dutch wax.

"No, I think I'll stay for a while."

"I thought we were going to eat."

"I'm not hungry."

He laughed. "Come on, we'll go to Frank's. You'll be hungry by the time we get there. If you're not I'll explain it."

"I said I'm not coming," she said.

"Listen, I've just sat through a hundred minutes of broken word slush and that's not a hundred minutes I'm ever getting back. Are you going to come and have dinner with me or are you going to stay here with your gang talking about sonnets?"

"They're not my gang. I don't even know them. I've only just met them."

"Well exactly, so come on."

He took her by the hand and led her in the direction of the exit but she stopped near the bar. It was important to stay on this side of the exit door because on the other side she might lose resolve. The woman in the sky-blue, her name was Shona, and two of the other poets were ordering drinks. They glanced over. David's face tried to change into a smoother expression. "Are you staying for a drink?" Shona said, addressing Melissa. David told her they had a dinner reservation. "Oh you could cancel, right? I loved what you read, by the way. We're doing this anthology project—we should talk about it."

Shona continued to regard only Melissa as she took up her drinks. There was a note of threat in her voice. "We're all sitting over there," an emphasis on the "all." "I'll see you in a minute."

"Come on babe, it's me," he said. "Let's just go and have a chat somewhere. We don't even have to eat. We'll go to mine, ok?"

"I don't wanna come to your place anymore, David. I'm staying here and then I'm going home. Something's not right with us—with me. I need to stop. It has to stop."

"Please. You've *got* to."

He came towards her. The women at the table looked. A great emptiness opened and she walked past him towards the door where she kept to the right side of it while he reminded her of why he believed she must come with him, how good it was, how she'd miss him, how he needed her and vice versa, he even mentioned some compromising pictures he had of her, which made him appear so small and nutty that she pushed him, leading to his grabbing of the back of her head just above the nape and holding her there, in an apparent embrace.

"You're a fucking cold bitch," he sneered. "You're cold as ice."

Shona was walking to the door like sky. Melissa's legs were trembling.

"That's what they say when they can't have what they want."

14

Of all the women seated at the round table by the window overlooking the street in Nicole's living room this Saturday afternoon, Vida was the one who believed most firmly that Meghan Markle was a turning point in the public perception and relevance of the royal family, purely on account of its imminent racification. Janice, though, sitting next to Vida, in a knitted burgundy top, a long, tumultuous mound of Nunhead weave foaming down her back, felt that this was a misguided projection, that she would have no power or impact at all in the strangling whiteness of the aristocracy and would eventually disappear inside it, be swallowed and crushed like Diana, because the monarchy was fundamentally an unchanging, immovable and insidious structure. But then Leona, Nicole's best friend, pictured with Nicole among the framed photographs on one of the glass-topped side tables nearby, was adamant that this was a different time that we are living in now and this wedding was something to celebrate, the grand union of colour—brown, black, white, ginger, beige—and she is not the first black person to be joining the royal family anyway, nor the first actress. Technically she was though because Edward had abdicated and gone to America to marry his love so it was different, said someone else, and we should focus on these two people who have found each other instead of all the politics, said Vida and

Leona together, in different sentences amounting to the same sentiment.

There were fourteen women in the room so far, chatting also on the sofa, on the patio beyond the open French doors and in the kitchen, but mainly in view of the big fifty-five-inch TV above the fireplace whose screen contained flashes of a promenading Oprah. Serena Williams too, the Beckhams, the Clooneys, all of them wading showily through the noon May Windsor heat in their fashions as if it were the premiere of a movie, which in a way it was, or a Hollywood festival, which in a way it was. Every so often the conversations in the room lapsed, when there was a notable spectacle to pause at, such as Idris Elba chatting to Oprah or an interview with someone interesting, and there was a certain indignant pride in the air as the perception of indigenousness snuggled into a new kind of expensive cushioning. They discussed the outfits, the hats, the suits, the clustering, the commentary, while eating cashews and drinking from their cocktails, which Nicole went to the kitchen to replenish at intervals, finding space on the counter amidst trays of chicken and macaroni cheese covered with clingfilm. As more women arrived she called out greetings, took hugs, laughed loudly, her shoulders and arms bare and smooth in her bright green dress, her hair in a natural twist-out and an eternal dewy wafting perfume. This was one of her frequent random shebangs, a women-centred event which was something she had been wanting to do for a while, and what better reason than a wedding such as this, a woman of the diaspora in the palace, the cathedral, her dreadlocked yoga-teaching mother becoming fellow in-law to the Queen, who seems a little bit sweeter and more ownable in this light, even possibly harbouring of some faint, far back African blood herself ("I met her once. Close up you can see it"). And then there would be Sheku Kanneh-Mason on his cello, and the African-American preacher, the choir. Why would you not invite people to come and eat and drink and watch, make an occasion of the occasion?

The festivities were ensuing in living rooms, cribs and yards across the world. It was like a FIFA cup final or the inauguration of Obama, millions in the watching. From the system in the corner music was playing, some nineties lovers rock and echoey swingbeat, and the occasional DJ popped in to drop some tunes or equipment for the sounds or to have a discussion with Nicole about an event. Another reason for this gathering of her ladies was that Lyle, Nicole's son, was coming by and she always liked to show him off. When he arrived, with two of his friends, the sound pitch increased. Women said, "Hey look at you dressed to impress," or "Come hug me up handsome bwoy, but when he get so fine?" and Lyle, wide-faced and healthy-looking, smiled with a little dip at his knees and said things like "What's happening Aunty V?" "You're looking well," and "Mum, I like that scent." He was perfectly mannered, sculpted by hard work and hard discipline, enriched by a plethora of sub-sidised extra-curricular activities during his school years includ-ing karate, hockey, trumpet-playing, the Duke of Edinburgh's Award scheme and Christian hiking trips in Chesham and Petts Wood. Everything Nicole had poured into him had settled in the right way. She held his face for a moment in the passage, studying it, as if checking all was as she'd left it, and said she was going to fix them each a plate, "you best be hungry yeah."

Upstairs in the same house, aware of the commotion around the entrance of the beloved, Michael was holding the inside door handle of Lyle's old bedroom which he sometimes used as an office, while in the other hand holding his phone to his ear in an automated conversation to do with trying to unlock his Govern-ment Gateway account. The voice announced that he had been sent a six-digit code that needed to be tapped into his keypad, so he segued into his text messages to get it, mouthing it to himself to try and remember it. The noise from downstairs, which he was about to descend into with some reservation, not being in the mood for a party after a heavy week at work, distracted him, and he tapped the code in wrong so had to start the process again. He then needed to call the bank because one of his cards had expired and he hadn't been sent a new one yet, plus there was a text from Melissa about Blake's doctor appointment next week. He went down fifteen minutes later into the volume, saw ladies slanted about, leaning in doorframes, languishing across the furniture, the sofa, where he really just wanted to sit quietly and watch basketball, in fact believed it his worker's right, to slope around unshaven in his house clothes and socks on a Saturday and let the week wriggle out of him with its uncomfortable staffing disputes, tricky differences in consciousness, tiring historical denials and misled guilty kindnesses. "Oh *there* you are, Michael," Leona said, tipsy and ruby-lipped, "I thought you weren't at *home*." "No, I'm here," he said, accepting her arms flung around his neck before moving on, to Sandy, and Mandy, and Natalie. They were everywhere. Everywhere he went there was a weave or a cleavage, and why were they all so dressed up to come round and watch TV? It wasn't as if they weren't here often enough in their sprays and shimmer and dancing clothes. Michael had thought, when he was marrying Nicole, that he was marrying only Nicole, not the rare groove funky house raving communities of South London. She was never at home on a New Year's Eve unless there were a hundred people in her house. It was the same with birthdays (recently her fiftieth, still vibrating in the walls), Valentine's Day, Easter. Sometimes he wanted to say "Girl, you have too many people in your house!" He wanted to say that now, to ask her wasn't she capable of being alone? Was she ever exhausted by her continual efforts to destroy the natural stillness of life? Wasn't he enough for her anymore? Plus he didn't like this music. He did not like nineties swingbeat.

All of this was going through his mind as he was giving Lyle and his friends dap. Lyle said he looked tired. They had a brief conversation about Michael's new job and how much extra work it was, Lyle said he'd heard him talking politics on the radio, but beyond that there was little to say in his current mood, he felt he was being pushed further inwards rather than surfacing outwards, and wondered tangentially whether this was another trait left over from Melissa. She who had never been a morning greeter or speaker, had needed the settling, the inner waking and travelling out towards the world and that included the people you lived with. It used to irritate him, this insistence on matutinal sacredness, he'd thought it pretentious, earnest, western, sanctimonious, selfish, self-important, impractical, pseudo-buddhist and yogic, but now he could see her logic. You have to be able to be a person, he reflected, pausing at the crowded kitchen. You have to be able to exist, with nothing, except for maybe your phone.

"Hon, you're with us, at last! Want something to eat?" Nicole came to him and they delicately hugged. She looked him up and down in a way that made him feel disappointing. He was wearing tracksuit bottoms and a sleeveless hoodie with a washed-out sports top underneath.

"Nah, I'm fine. I'll get something in a bit," he said.

"Watching the wedding with us?"

To this he shrugged, "I might. I've got a little work to do."

"It's Saturday you know."

"Yeah."

Nicole shifted her focus to opening a container of pasta. It was becoming a point of contention she had with him, in return, that there was no end to his work. As the rare groove society was always with Nicole, work, it seemed, was always with Michael. He spoke in the words of the office, phrases such as "the long and short of it," "in terms of" and "as previously established." He talked about his work colleagues as if she should be interested in them and their private lives, motives and philosophies. She would be sitting on the sofa or at the table having brunch while reading *Vogue,* and he would be pacing up and down the living room with his phone attached to his head and say something like, "I think with the internal recruitment we definitely need to prioritise Glasgow." Or they would be talking about a film she wanted to see or a possible holiday, for example the postponed Portugal trip, and he would start talking about his desire to do a degree in criminology. Nicole was moved and inspired by her husband's commitment to the peoples, that he wanted to try and change the world, dismantle capitalism, overthrow racism, obliterate toryism. His fervour and substance had made him all the more exciting to her because she had never been with someone like him, who believed so strongly in personal political power. But a question had been emerging slowly over these recent months since his promotion to managing director that troubled her: Was Michael boring? Was it the situation here that she had married someone who perhaps did not appreciate or share in her high entertainment requirements? Did her assessment of him as steady, courteous, sexy, nice (these latter two occurring together a rare find, she had thought), responsible, intellectual and mellow, actually compute to dull, inert, avuncular, darkened, and by association darken*ing*? She wondered, moving back into the living room with Lyle's plate and a tray of baklava, whether this was becoming a situation that she should begin to worry about, that the man in her house might be an outsider, was maybe not "one of us."

"Look at Doria. Look at her! Oh my god. The man is opening the door for her. Look. Look at her dreads!" said Vida.

The room was in a state of mass captivation. Rastafarian follicular custom in the vicinity of the British monarchy. Never before seen on Earth, at least at this level of surface parity.

"I like the way she's only wearing a little bit of make-up. Hasn't overdone it," was said of Meghan's face.

"Look at the way they're looking at each other!"

Then there was Bishop Michael Curry's speech which floored them, especially the bit about the slaves and the antebellum South. The women were crying.

"He's talking about the slaves, the slaves!"

"I don't like Camilla, you know."

"They don't even understand what he's talking about."

"Look at Philip though."

Michael peered in, hovered non-committally, took refuge in the emptied kitchen and made himself a chicken bagel. He got the gist of the descent down the steps and the waving carriage ride. He didn't feel the need to watch the commentary after-wards. What he was more concerned about were the obscene cost of it all and the hiding of the homeless in Windsor to make it easier on the celebrity eye. Where had they taken them? Were they being held underground somewhere, or in vacant office buildings, to be poured back out onto the streets when it was over? Did anyone in this building realise that rough sleeping in England had reached the highest level since records began? Did any of them not see the sheer ugliness and parasitism of the monarchy as a reason not to feel enthusiasm? But wary of damp-ening the atmosphere, he kept such reservations to himself and eventually drifted back upstairs, this was not his party, it was her party, so there was no obligation for him to stay. This was not even his house, it was her house, and if she wanted to treat it like a music and entertainment venue then he had no say in the matter. He had moved into her universe and lived by its flashing, strip-lit orbit. He must seek suitable places for himself, to do admin, to be quiet, to watch the Chicago Bulls versus the Los Angeles Lakers in peace.

★

She found him upstairs, fast asleep. He was lying across the bed with his knees folded up, the door had been closed behind him, the TV screen had returned to menu, a stretch of naked indigo night was pressing at the window. The sight of him like that made her feel tender inside, the stark vulnerability of a grown, unconscious man, yet she stopped short of lying down next to him as she normally might. He was, for an instant when she had opened the door, an alien presence, an intruder. She sat down on the edge of the bed and considered him for a few minutes, thinking about their own wedding, the rightness of it, that joy that she had found the one she wanted, the one she'd been waiting for, which made her reach out to touch the warmth of his back.

"Hey, hon? Everyone's left. They've gone."

He was slowly waking and turned his face into the pillow. He always did that before opening his eyes, as if refusing something underneath his life.

"Lyle said bye."

"Lyle's gone? You should've called me."

"They've gone out raving, don't worry. We didn't want to disturb you. He thought maybe you were ill, actually. Have you been asleep for all this time?"

She smelt of cherry brandy and the remnant of her perfume. She still had on the green Ted Baker dress, the very specific, noisy green she'd been looking for and had found in Bluewater Shopping Centre. He wanted to travel inside its fabric and graze and kiss her dampened dimpled skin, it was a primal, waking impulse.

"I was reading for a while—then," pulling towards her, "I guess I was waiting for you."

"You should've come down and got me."

"Nah, you're with your friends, man. Can't drag you away like that when you're having fun."

"But I like it when you're with us."

"I like it when I'm with you."

He persuaded her down over him though she was pensive, resisting at first in his manoeuvring around her legs to make her straddle him. She allowed some brief grazing in her verdant bodice. He paused, looking up at her, sensing a requirement to check. "How are you?" he said.

"Hm, ok."

"What is it?"

"I'm more than me, though. I'm not just me."

"What do you mean?"

"I mean my friends, my people. All of that's me. So if you're with me, you're with those other things too." (So he *was* with Sandy and Mandy and Leona? He had married all of them?) He continued watching her, close into her face, with a calm and friendly smile. "That's what's on my mind right now," she said. "Don't look at me like that, I'm serious."

"Are you annoyed at me for not coming down?"

"I'm not annoyed."

"You seem annoyed."

"I'm not, I'm just—" She didn't finish. She moved away and started to stand. "I'm gonna go clear up. Don't fancy doing it in the morning. Anyway it's not like we have plans for tonight."

"Tonight? Is there more tonight?" he said as she left the room. And to himself, in the new silence, a moment ago so full of intimate promise, "Well, *I* had a plan. There it goes."

He understood now that there were obligations, to quell her stony grouch, to refresh their harmony, he must go and be with her in her displeasure and draw her back to him through the swamp. He could hear things in the kitchen being moved around. When he found her again she was in the living room collecting dessert plates—each woman had received a personalised cake, made by Nicole's caterer friend who'd worn a dress the same colour as the icing. "You don't have to help. It's not your stuff," she said, underlining her point. But he picked up glasses and stray napkins and followed her back into the kitchen, where they engaged in some one-sided small talk in which the loading of the dishwasher took more of her concentration than ever before.

"We don't have to do everything together, Nic," he said in low-key defiance. "We're two people."

"Yes, I do realise that. But we are together, aren't we? We're sharing our lives. We share experiences. At least that was my understanding of it."

"I don't really think of a royal wedding as an 'experience,'" he said.

"The wedding was just an excuse, Michael. The point was bringing people together, spending time, having some jokes. *Lyle* was here. You didn't even really chat to him much."

He fought the urge to contest her claim that the wedding itself didn't matter to her as he didn't want to veer into a political debate that might annoy her more, as it would involve some possible denouncing of her latent royalism. Sticking to the path of absolution, he replied, "I'm sorry. I didn't know I was gonna fall asleep like that. I meant to catch up with him, I did."

"It doesn't matter, it's what it is," she said, and there was a long pause full of mutual umbrage during which they carried on wiping and clearing and washing, the running tap, the opening and closing of the fridge, the securing of clingfilm around serving bowls. He resented his concession to apologise, without quite wishing he hadn't, but wanted not to have a small remorse forced on him like this in his home, in his innocent, work-tired slumber, leading him to crave a place, a structure, that was truly, wholly his in its origin, somewhere that he had chosen and found and claimed for himself: a refuge in the world. What does it mean to be married to someone? he wanted to ask her. Does it mean that you must like what the other person likes and live as they live? Or does it mean that you accept what the other person likes and grant them the space to live? What is partnership—reflection, or co-existence? But he couldn't form the right tone, the right articulation of this question, he felt, without undermining her entire perception of their unity.

She, meanwhile, had not fully let go of another "moment" from last month, when he had come to pick her up from her live PA at Grace and Marcia's fiftieth birthday event in the marquee in Kent. They had treated her well, those girls. She'd liked their sharp, professional efficiency and the sunny seriousness with which they took their joy, they went to great lengths, they prioritised their pleasure. It may not have been one of her most prestigious stages (once, Nicole had sung at the Royal Albert Hall!) but it was, overall, one of her recent favourites; the comedian had made her laugh and the audience was affectionate. In the car on the way home she had mentioned to Michael that she was reconsidering accepting the pantomime role—it was relatively well paid, a lead character part, lots of other artists appear in pantomimes and it might even be fun, a chance as well to expand her skills to acting. He was dubious. "You sure you wanna do that? It's not really acting, is it," he'd said, and he had sounded old and cynical. A shower of soot-speckled grey had fallen over her optimism, making her waver again, making her worry that she was not thinking about it with her own mind anymore but with some of his mind. Is this marriage? Or *this* marriage? If it was right, this mental merging, surely it should not feel uncomfortable or unlike yourself. The stain of that moment was merging tonight with a new fall of soot, bringing her to announce: "Sometimes I feel like you're a different kind of person to me, Michael."

She turned around, leaned against the counter with the olive-green kitchen blind over the window behind her. Why couldn't he then just walk towards her and sink at her feet, all of this atmosphere disappear? None of it mattered.

"Do you even want to come to Portugal with me this time? Whenever I mention it you change the subject."

"No I don't."

"Yes you do."

"Do I? I don't even remember when you mentioned it."

"Yeah, because you changed the subject."

He started to ramble about what she might have misinterpreted as his avoidance of the subject of the forthcoming Algarve Soul Weekender, dropping some transparent plastic spoons on the floor as he was talking, but she interrupted him coolly, folding her arms, touching her hair behind her neck at her right shoulder then folding her arms again. "Anyway it's not that, specifically. I just have this general feeling that you don't want to participate in my life—our life. You don't want to share in things, and that's ok, if that's how you feel. I don't want to be the person to force you to do things you don't want to do. We're all different. We're all on our own journey—'I don't know where the journey will end but I know where to start'—Aloe Blacc. But as for me and *my* journey, well, I need excitement. Did I ever tell you I went to see a stone-reader once and she told me, she said these exact words to me, 'If you don't dance in the light you will sink beneath the sand and die?' That's what she said. I've never forgotten it. Sink beneath the sand. I won't let it happen. So just tell me what it is I'm dealing with here, hon. Is this all too much for you? Do you want me to stop trying to include you in things and leave you alone in your quiet place? I mean I really don't wanna be a nuisance—"

"You're not a nuisance. Stop talking like this." He went to her and caressed down the backs of her arms. And how could he make it known, in this invitation for honesty, that he did not really want to go on the Algarve Soul Weekender, had never been interested in visiting the Algarve, would rather go to Brazil or Cape Verde, did not like pool parties, had no desire to party while wet? He couldn't swim. He didn't look especially amazing in trunks. He didn't even like trunks. He didn't want to participate in a spectacle of almost-naked adults throwing balls and drinking cocktails and swimming between each other's legs. He was not a beach-basker or bather, more of a city-stepper, a cerebral retreater within clean, unwild environments. Michael did not feel he could say any of these things to Nicole, such frank, simple truths about himself. Instead he said, "I do want to come."

"Really? You're sure now?"

"Yes."

"Because you know what, I'm not ready to settle into my embalming outfit just yet please. I am not going to waste away while there's a whole great juicy world out there to be enjoyed, and—"

"You look so gorgeous in that green," he said. "You look like a field of grass. I could lie down in you right now and stay there, for hours."

"Could you? How many hours?"

It was past midnight. A soft breeze circled the house, the lowest city stars miles over the dark flat chimneys. He said when she was angry with him it made him love her deeper and she said again that she wasn't angry with him, she just wanted to know him clearly, so that she could love him with the right intricacy. They moved presently into the living room, after finding their peak there at the kitchen window, and their knees had weakened with the loosening in their veins. Supine she stayed open and hungry for his mouth. No other mouth over her half century had known the things he knew, where to find her, how finely to call her. Twice, another peak, another. Mid-heights, she registered an interior shift that maybe she could slow and settle in his land, if these were its fruits, if this its wild vegetation and old and surging rivers. "I love you, Michael," she said, "more than anyone else. There's no one else like you," and he was reminded afresh of how his body had become needful of her music, how richly she had rescued him from emptiness.

They dozed in the gleam of the copper lamps. Approaching three, they went back upstairs, the house silent except for the bamboo rustling along the back fence. He followed her onto the landing, she closed the bedroom blind. His phone was where he had left it on the bed and he picked it up to check messages. His body stilled for a few seconds. He was no longer with her. He breathed in deeply, and out again with the same intensity, though faster. It was a breath taken on behalf of his son. He had flown into his ribcage through the night and across the A205, and where his small lungs were failing him, he applied the power of his own paternal strength, the reserves of it that are saved for such times of emergency, of freakish wheezing, of brown and blue inhalers that were sometimes not enough. They were going to operate on his heart. If they left it until much later, Blake might run out of breath. She could feel it in the room, taking him away.

15

The mist is on the river. It curls upwards in a white, morning whisper, across the expanse of Waterloo. The old theatre is held in it and the bridges over the water, the great wheel and the blue-tree banks. Through the haze a pale gold of street lights endures from the night to make shivering liquid glows along the pavements, empty and beginning to wake. The trains are pulling in to the station, its vast atrium unfurling. They pull in and draw out, into many dimensions of days, the forgettable and the shattering, the ones from which there may be no return. Near the station is the square geometry of the children's hospital with its panels of light, the ceilings of the silent wards are still dim, the mist a ghostly magic, hanging at the windows.

A man, a woman and a child emerge from the station and walk along the main road before turning right down a cobbled market lane. She is holding on to the child's hand and sometimes the man puts his arm around him, so that during those moments the man and the woman are physically linked. Their faces have a serious set to them, even when the three of them laugh together, the faces of the father and mother return to a difficult focus, while the boy gazes gently ahead. They disappear into the mist and it travels with them beneath the flyovers. They emerge again crossing the road to the entrance of the hospital, the man's long stride with a tiny skip in it, the woman's small straight figure fervent yet careful, and close to the boy, their hands are almost the same size. The doors slide swiftly open. It's warm and inviting inside, but thick with the gravity of saving, a sense of foreboding sleeps.

On the third floor they exit the lift and are directed to their ward, where the boy's bed is waiting on the right-hand side, second from the window. He knows little about his heart, does not quite understand its fault—a problem with his veins and the flow of blood, and sometimes he cannot breathe—yet he claims the bed, walks to it and sits down, marvelling at the personal TV overhead on its mechanical arm, the sheer luck of this mid-week Thursday adventure, the classroom is far away, the playing fields waiting in the future. They are going to fix the extra voice of his heart and help him jump and breathe. He does not know, as his mother and father know, that there is a chance of failure. There is a very small chance of haemorrhage, stroke, heart attack, kidney damage, allergic reaction to medications, and in extreme circumstances death. A form has been signed confirming awareness of these risks, discarding liability. They want to get him out of this place as fast as possible.

Melissa unpacks items from his night bag onto the bedside table, a packet of tissues, a book he is reading and some playing cards. She smooths his pillows and hangs her scarf and poncho over the back of the chair next to the bed. Every time she looks at him she can see thirst in his face; it is pale and patchy, thinned from the fasting of the night, the doctors have instructed no food or water in the lead-up to the procedure. On the other side of the bed, Michael stands alert, a little stooped at the shoulders, also watching Blake in a relishing way, as if soon he might disappear.

"You're all set," he says to him. "Want to sleep for a while? You can, it's still early."

"Can I watch TV?"

"In a while," Melissa says. "The lights are still down. People are only just starting to wake up." He leans back, thirst and hunger falling over him, and idly plays with the cards, swapping them from one hand to another. There is a play area at the end of the ward which Michael says they could go and see as long as they stay quiet.

On the opposite side of the room, lying in an identical bed beneath a red blanket, is another boy, smaller than Blake, five or six years old, with curls of black hair and full, bluish lips. A woman, his mother—she has the same precise pale colour and dark mouth, and she trembles slightly, for he is quite sick—is on her feet next to him wearing a black coat that she will keep on throughout the day. Her eyes are brave and hurt and full of waiting. As the boy whimpers, complaining of hunger, she tells him it's ok, it won't be long now. She rubs his head and kisses him, her every movement in care of him, arranging his things, deliberating where to put his slippers and folding and re-folding his clothes with an air of busyness. There is a kind of fierce protection about her, simultaneously cowering and defiant, as though locked in a fight that has already delivered lethal blows.

The two women are acutely aware of each other's presence, their identical restlessness and high worry, as they fold, and wait, and watch, but there is a reserve between them, placed there by the wide and distant past that has rendered them natural opponents, yet sisters. On this soil they have been brought to think of themselves as marginal, in which context their reflections in one another are a reminder of their vulnerability, they can no longer pretend, they will be found out, how much they must lie and veil. Soon the barrier fades, here stripped down to the pumping hearts of boys from the womb. They are on the same road and approaching a junction, comments begin to pass between them, about the hunger, the fear, about how long last night felt and the bleak dawn.

"Don't worry about your boy," the woman says, holding her son's anorak in both hands. "He will be fine. He'll be up and out of here in no time, you watch."

Melissa confesses to her, "It seems impossible, what they're going to do"—the insertion of a tube into his body, directed towards the organ, all while he is unconscious. "I just can't picture it."

"Please," she says, "I promise you, they're so good here. My son's had three surgeries and always comes through. This is his last one." There are tears in her eyes. She is opening her palms in a beseeching way. Perhaps any lack of faith will shake her own, increase risk. "I owe them everything, everything. They love the children. They treat them like family. We're in safe hands. It's amazing how the body repairs itself," and she picks up the green coat again which she had laid on the edge of the bed, looks down at the weak child beneath the blanket and seems to glare at him for a second. When Blake returns he watches from his own bed, assessing the boy for play, but he is not interested in anything around him.

The woman tells Melissa he was born with a hole in his heart. The doctors kept trying to fix the hole but it kept growing bigger, new veins sprouting around it, an octopus heart, ever multiplying, a mutant, a freak of a heart. But today it will all be over. "He's been through so much. I can't refuse him anything. Whatever he wants I give it to him, I let him have it. I never tell him no. What would you like, sweetheart, after it's all over? We'll go home and get your favourite things, anything you want. Just tell me and I'll get it for you . . ."

More and more lights are coming on across the ward. The children are waking, eating breakfast, taking medications, nurses walking by in pale greens with brisk, stoic expressions. On the walls there are dark pictures of abstract landscapes in maroon and navy. The smell of coffee wafts out from the kitchen, where relatives wander in and out, held in their waiting. It is coming up to eight thirty by the time the sick little boy is taken away. His mother marches along behind, her shoulders powerful and drawn back beneath the coat. She has retreated from all awareness besides the particulars of this moment, this passage through a series of doors and the arrival in a bright metallic place. She has made herself ready.

"One thing. I don't mean to scare you," she said, before they came for him. Her ringed and cloudy eyes went hollow and her tone deepened. "Prepare yourself for when they put him to sleep. He'll go heavy in your arms. They'll put a mask over his face and his head will roll down. He might shake. It's the worst part."

So began a season of waiting. After the boy was gone, a subtle link was broken between Melissa and his mother, she returned shadowed in her fear, determinedly aloof and avoiding eye contact. She tidied, walked up and down, smoothed and folded the red blanket. Her lips were fixed together and she no longer spoke to anyone except the nurses, conferring with them whenever they appeared in a private, familiar, yet business-like mode. Blake eventually drifted into sleep to the sound of his parents' sporadic talking. They were sitting across from one another on opposite sides of the bed. He imagined as he fell that they were one house and he was inside it.

The conversation at first sustained a routine distance, as of the Sunday exchanges of children, school meetings, or one of Ria's piano recitals. Melissa was leaning forward onto the bed with her chin in the heel of her palm, half turned towards Blake. She felt the presence of a familiar reassurance, sitting here with Michael, that everything was correctly positioned and the day would after all be well, despite the anxiety swirling in her stomach. The woman on the other side of the ward had sat down and was staring at some yellow papers in her hand. She suddenly stood up and went towards the kitchen. Michael shifted in his chair.

"What about you?" he said, wanting to keep talking, he'd never liked the silence of hospitals. Melissa had been asking after his brother who lived in Barcelona. "How are things with your sisters?"

"Hm," she looked down, "well, I wouldn't say we're getting calmer with each other. I'd say we're getting the opposite, actually. There's more between us now, not less."

"Like what?" he asked.

"Oh, you know, my mum, my dad. Even though he's not here anymore. He's still here, threaded through us. We never really get away from our parents, I don't think." At which, as if the ether were listening, Melissa's phone vibrated on the bedside. It was Adel, calling from Alice's parlour. "Mum wants to speak to you," she said. "Omo, how is *he*?" cried Alice, a hysteria in her voice, a dubiousness of heart procedures.

"He's fine, Mum, he's sleeping. He hasn't gone in yet."

"Make sure you mash him after with that rub."

"Ok, I will."

"Don't give him bath straight away, be too dangerous."

"I won't, don't worry."

"She's worried," Adel said when Alice had handed the phone back to her. "I keep telling her it will be fine but she won't listen to me. Make sure you call her when it's over, all right? I'm going in a minute, I was just popping in."

It was the first time Melissa had spoken to Adel in weeks, and it occurred to her how rarely they ever spoke to each other on the phone, how little she knew of her daily life. The house in Benin, she told Michael, was the main thing that was coming between them all. The builders had started work. Beams and lintels were being fixed in place, doorframes, pipework constructed, but Adel still wanted to abandon the project and she and Carol were now barely speaking to one another. Melissa as usual was caught in the middle, the neutraliser, until yesterday morning when Carol had sent her another longwinded text chastising her for her lack of involvement, for leaving her to manage it all by herself and failing to offer any support to the fulfilment of Alice's wish, and that in refusing to take either side she was being spineless. "All of this was in a text," Melissa said, "a whole essay." She was glinting with the upset of it. Michael remembered how she would glint like that when flustered by something.

"You'll miss her, won't you, if she goes?" he said.

"You know I will. She's the ground."

For there she was, standing at her door, that bent shawled figure in the terraces of Kilburn, waiting for her children. Alice was how they perceived and understood themselves. She had given rescue. The idea of an Aliceless England was a distressing, untethering thought. Yet how long must she wait?

"I think, in a way, she's already gone," Melissa went on. "She's not fully here anymore. She doesn't make me eba when I go and visit. She makes pancakes instead. She's almost like a shell, just waiting to go."

"Then you've got to make it happen," Michael said.

"Yeah, we do."

"Without ending up hating each other."

"And now I see how that can happen, how things can get that far. We're fracturing. We're coming undone. The whole thing's falling apart. Do you remember how I used to say I feel erased around my family, that they don't really know who I am?"

"You've always felt like that."

"I know." She paused to consider. "Maybe it's because we're too familiar to each other. They know too much. And that knowledge is essential to your life. I've been thinking about this, how other people can carry parts of you through the world and you only get to live those parts of yourself when you're with those people. My sisters, when we were growing up, we made each other, each in our own different way. We saved each other. They're the foundation. That must be why it feels like the earth is shaking beneath me."

Blake sighed in his sleep and Melissa stood, touching his hair with its path of sunlight in it and the side of his face which felt dry and cool. It had been two hours since the little boy had been taken in. His mother re-entered the ward via the lift and had a short exchange with one of the nurses, who could be heard saying, "We can't interrupt them, you see." She returned to the empty bed and neatened the sheets again, preparing for him. She took items of food out of the night bag and put them back in as if ruminating on what to give him to eat first. It seemed impossible for her to keep still. Melissa ventured to ask her if he was all right, whether they had told her anything.

"It takes a bit longer sometimes, that's all," she said. "He'll be coming out soon. I'm just thinking about your poor boy! He must be starving."

Awake now and lying on his front, Blake was staring up at the TV where animated creatures were flicking and darting across the screen. He remained that way for another hour, by which time the woman opposite was alternating between simply standing, very still, at the foot of her son's bed with her hand clenched on the sheet, and pacing the area between the bed and the kitchen. Would she know, Melissa wondered, if her boy was in that instant being taken by the gods? If his blood stopped running, his face went limp, does a mother know? And would she have someone there to take care of her, to walk her through this crack in the earth? She went out once more towards the lift and did not return. A slow sceptre of terror skulked through the ward, licking the ceiling, the paintings, the silver door handles. But then there was a rush and a flutter of movement, a sweep of voices coming closer, a high freeing in the air. Here she was returning, like a sea change, out of breath, with her son and two of the nurses, wheeling him back towards the bed and, once there, transferring him from the stretcher. She flapped around him like a great descending eagle. He was limp, groggy, surrendered to her care. The red blanket was drawn onto him. She wept as the tail of the fright passed over, her hand on her hip and her head down. Outside the river dipped, the sky was grey and still over Waterloo, hardly a movement up there. Clouds hung motionless against the light tapping rain.

When Blake was taken in, it was just as she had described it. The mask went over his face and his head fell. He went weak, boneless, the muscles collapsed. A cluster of staff crowded over him in his thin hospital gown while the mother and father walked away, out of the double doors into a corridor, through another set of doors, finally into a large atrium overlooking the river via a wall of glass. Along the walls framing the glass there were cushioned chairs, two vending machines and the corridors to the wards leading off. They waited. They bought sandwiches from the kiosk on the ground floor and ate them in view of the water. One hour passed, another.

"He's going to be all right, isn't he?"

It came naturally to him, ordinarily, to hold faith in something wished for. The image of Blake's head rolling forward kept playing in her mind. There was a loud, freakish dread within that it could be the last picture and she tried to suppress it. All Michael said was, "I hope so," and these words felt dangerous to him.

"A long time ago you would've said yes, he'll be fine."

"When?"

"Before."

"Maybe I've changed since then."

"I'm sorry," she said. "I can't stand this waiting."

He walked over to the glass wall and laid his palms on the rail. He wore loose jeans and a navy fleece, the customary white-soled trainers, and held a stiffness in his shoulders that she wanted to smooth down. He would go home to his wife when it was over. Melissa saw him like this, from a distance, and was compelled by the idea of who he was with Nicole. Did he manifest differently, was he made a different man by her? Was Nicole aware of his facility for preserving hope, enough for two people, or did she have enough of her own? It struck her how much of ourselves might be entirely dependent—given life, a kind of puppetry—by the gaps, desires and needs in someone else, and she experienced a fleeting sorrow that she and Michael would never grow old together as she had once envisaged, they would not look back on looking out on the river at Greenwich post-wedding, she in electric blue and he in white. He would have been an easy soul to go there with.

"I don't want to tempt fate, that's all," he said. "I haven't really changed much." He delivered this in a defensive way, because secretly he wanted to remain, at least in her eyes, the same as before, so as not to lose completely the country they had been. It troubled him more and more that she still had an effect on him, could pull strings in him with her proximity. There was a frightening idea that possibly he had not quite moved into himself through his marriage to Nicole, had not found the place, and she, Melissa, might forever bar him from it simply with who she was; she could be his Genevieve, another old love standing in the way. His life had been dominated by women. He would like to stand alone again within the mountain hut of himself and feel its atmosphere. Would it reveal to him some essential piece of information that would make his thoughts clearer, his present path more certain?

"People don't change," she said, "I mean, on a fundamental level. I saw my old friend the other day—do you remember

Elly? We hadn't seen each other in about fifteen years. We went for a walk in Hyde Park. I don't know why but I was so nervous meeting her, I thought we must've drifted apart, that she'd be different, or I'd be different and we wouldn't know what to say to each other. But she was just the same, almost exactly the same. In fact she was more intensely herself than ever, more extreme in who she is. I think people move closer to themselves as they get older, not further out, like those boats over there. We're cyclical creatures. No, you haven't changed. You're more yourself now. I took you away from that. I know I did. I hid you from yourself because I was suffocating. I was suffocating in that house."

She had come to stand next to him at the window. They had never spoken frankly like this about the wounds they had applied to one another, and here, in the sharp waiting with that note of subtle apology in her voice, it disarmed him. He felt that they could topple back into Paradise, another house, a different structure, and go on. They could lift up their boy and strengthen him.

"I probably did the same to you," he said, "hid you, I mean. There are lots of things that take us away from ourselves."

"Yes. That's true." Melissa paused, then said more quietly, "It can happen very early. Right at the beginning of your life."

From the edge of his vision, Michael caught something passing across her face, a bitter mystery. It alarmed him as it reminded him so clearly of an expression she would assume sometimes when they were together, a shut away look, he would feel that he was far above her and she had exited her body while he was part of it. Her special power to disappear. There was a reason for it, which might have kept her from him all that time. "Is that how it was for you?" he asked gently, looking at her with new possibility, a sense of dismay.

She shrugged. "I don't know . . . I have, flashes, pictures.

They're not quite memories. I can't remember. Only, that I lost something, early on."

Over the city bridges the traffic was passing to the north, to the past. The big Parliament clock on the other side of the water was still covered in a white sheath and time withheld underneath. They watched the river in silence, the space between them altered, decreased. A yellow crane struck long and crooked through the bird-streaked air.

"Let's go back to the ward now," she said. "They haven't called us yet but he must be coming out soon. I'm starting to panic." He comforted her with his embracing arms and she leaned up into the slant of his body, the long reassuring warmth of it. Her voice was muffled, but it spun ribbons in him. He heard her say, "There's a way that you complete me, Michael. I wish it wasn't so. I know you think I didn't love you, but I did. I still do. I liked who I was with you. Sometimes I wish I could have her back."

When they returned to the ward, the other boy was lying asleep beneath his blanket and his mother was napping in the chair beside him, finally at peace. They had swapped positions, she and Melissa. Now it was she who could not keep still. She went through Blake's bag of clothes, moved objects around on the bedside table, arranged the pillows. She asked the nurse passing the kitchen door if there was any news. The nurse had a flat, sober look, attuned to tragedy, and seemed to hesitate before she spoke.

"No news is usually good news," she said. "Sit tight. You'll hear something soon."

So she went back to the bed and waited. She tried to read a book but couldn't concentrate, the words fell from her mind unstudied. In the vortex of her thoughts she assembled the very worst thing that could happen. The mind couldn't hold it. A thousand spears were leaking down quickly through her blood.

She wanted his small body here directly before her breathing and in motion. "Why is it taking so long?" she said to Michael, sunken in his chair, his head supported by his palm. She saw Ria in his face and the opposite of Ria, his singular, future twilight, his gentle inching towards it. The fear felt more manageable if she remained close to him.

The woman opposite was standing watching them. She smiled severely at Melissa.

"Your boy will be fine. He'll be just fine."

With a sudden force, Michael stood up, his chair making a scraping noise across the floor.

"I'm gonna find out what's happening."

16

They are coming through the trees, the women. Summer in bright blue shoes. Verena in black and veiled, pale-faced, linking her arm. Stephanie, also in black, hugs the tradition of the darkest colour as a place to fall into. They are coming through the woodland towards the path that leads to the chapel. They have seen where she will lie, receiving rain and blossom and snowfall above, and now they walk into the gathering, holding on to one other with their shivering limbs and their demolition. She is never coming back. Her childhood will never be her history; it is her whole life, her absence.

Inside the entrance to the chapel Damian has positioned himself. Here he can withstand condolences, the strange and earnest pleasantries of funerals, the careful apologies and the staring. Teenagers walk by crying through their mascara. There are voices all around him but a larger hush of disbelief. Here he can be transient and outside of talking while appearing to function in the proper manner, the shaking of hands and a stability of expression. The difficult thing is walking to the front to sit down with the others, his sons, his ex-wife and her father, to whom he is a murderer.

Patrick cannot look at him. Not when he is at the lectern speaking too quietly about how much she was to him and the sweetness of her company, finding it hard to use the past tense so veering into the present. Nor when Summer steps valiantly up, bewildered and lessened of a sister, not yet understanding how to live in that way. She wants them to know what she was like, this specific thing about Avril: "Whenever people were talking, saying bad things about someone or criticising them or whatever, she never would join in. She always put herself in the place of that person. She would say, There could be a reason they behave like they do, or it might have taken a lot for them to sing that song and they might have been really scared singing it." Jerry and Harvey cried after this sentence, because Summer was crying and they hardly ever saw her cry. "I told you we shouldn't let them come," Verena said to Stephanie.

The casket was topped with lilies. This was another place to position himself, as the congregation returned into the blue October day, next to her, like a defunct security guard who does not know where to go next. They held their stomachs as they went by, imagining her young closed face. The body was too much for Patrick, how many times he had carried it and held its hand along a street. He was struck by the rational implausibility of the situation, the burial of grandchild by grandparent. Only then could he look at Damian. They were eye to eye with each other, his hands in weak and notional fists. In a splutter of rage, he said incorrectly, "My daughter is a widow, before her mother. It's not right!"

He waited there with her until the room was empty but for its priest.

Stephanie: She had thought she was getting better. She had thought they were slowly winning. How lacerating it was. Sometimes she wanted to smash the food down her throat. Sometimes she wanted to strap her to a chair in the dining room and haul it into her mouth. If she put a plate on the table in front of Avril and Avril cleared some of the food off it before

223

conceding to eat, she wanted to pick it up and break the plate over her head. How dare you treat the vessel that carried you this way? She said to her once, "Your body belongs to me. You have to treat it properly." Avril gave a black-eyed glare and shut the door in her face.

She wondered, Are you in the trees now? Do you remember when we used to walk in the woods and I would tell you their names? White-bark beech. Orange maple. Did you climb up to the top to see heaven? No it's not right. Your mother is destroyed. She wept with the dew-brushed willows. She woke up every morning in a mesh of sharp bushes and pulled on threads of memory to get her back, because the world couldn't be without her. When did it happen? she wondered. When did we walk away from each other to the edges of the earth? What did you see there? What did I neglect to tell you?

She had come to temper this desire to smash and feed. She followed all the advice and listened to the nurses when they told her she must let Avril feel she had some control. She cannot feel that you are in charge of her body, they said. She is in conflict with it, there is a kind of monster in her mind behind where her eyes look out at herself and that is really who she is fighting with. You have to let her win by herself while standing alongside her against the storm. She came out of the hospital. You had begun to see her bones moving inside her clothes and when you held her it was like holding a bird that had flown into her place and become trapped. In the middle of the nights you were breathless. When it rained, Avril was every raindrop.

Red cedar. Great oak. Remember the meadow of blue in the spring at Box Hill. That time when Harvey was only just walking. Avril and Jerry ran into the violet land and found their sticks as they always found a stick, as if God were waiting to hand one to them. Stephanie had thought, those times, that nothing would take her away as long as there is this, that they would always be able to find their sphere of wild peace. The voice of the woods, of the trees, would save her. They would speak to her of the beginning of time and help her recollect our priceless insignificance. We do not matter, only to each other.

The call came in the afternoon. A small cardiovascular failure as she was riding her bike. The doctors tried but couldn't. One day you lose something important to you, Stephanie thought when she was calmer, and you find it again, but that you lost it is a warning that you will soon lose it forever. So it was. She found her and lost her, lost her twice, this time forever. In her ghosted bedroom in the evenings she tapped her iPad search history, looked through her scribblings, the little notes to self: "you are strong, healthy and happy," "you will be well." There was a stick drawing in a Zap book of her and Jerry with a caption underneath that read "us running through the funny fancy bluebells." When Stephanie read this line she crumpled like a dishrag onto the red foam sofa with the feeling that all the veins inside her body had burst open.

The day after the funeral, she gets up early and goes to the woods. It is just her alone. She walks the path they walked together many times. Across the long green meadow and up the track, along the dandelion path in a low wind. She imagines that she sees Avril some way up ahead in her black and white tracksuit top. She walks faster to keep up with her, faster and faster, loses sight of her, sees her again flitting through the trees, then she disappears completely and she calls out her name. I'm here, she says, into the silence, and there she is, standing on top of the mound where they used to stop and look at the view of Guildford. There is a sense of surety and irrefutable belonging in her, her arms outstretched in the air, and Stephanie has a feeling of being in awe, of being humbled by her possibility. Wait for me, she says. You're going too fast. Sorry Mum, I wanted to run, she says. It's very freeing.

Grey birch. Cherry blossom. This is where Stephanie goes when it gets too hard.

Jerry: He took the Zap book with him in his school bag and round about. There were other things in it like cartoon strips and games of noughts and crosses they'd played. He remembered precisely the time of that particular game when they were waiting at the doctor's surgery for their mum to come out from her appointment. It was in the dark afternoon of a new winter when night is confused. Avril liked the cold. She liked snow and candyfloss. During his lunch hour, a month after the funeral, he took out the Zap book sitting on a bench in the corridor and read the bluebell caption again. It was painful, that the voice of the ink would not speak to him anymore, only the ink itself. And where exactly would he find her and how? She was a friend to his life, the one who knows him better. He wished he would have been able to fell the monster and bring her back. Oh, it's so beautiful here, she had said by the lake in August when a quiet steady flash had come into her eyes. I wish things were always like this. He had wanted her to see with him the crooked swaying world and feel its irresistible energy charging through.

Damian: You tell yourself it has happened, the thing you couldn't bear. That you are still breathing and you are still here. A part of you even believes that you have survived it. You see that you will continue. You do continue—the days go on, the planet moves. But it emerges over time that the breaking happens gradually; you have not survived. The thing you couldn't bear is exactly that.

Have you found everything you were looking for today? Would you like to save ten per cent by opening an account at Fabric?

A final, feeble conviction went out of these questions. If they did not want to buy a purple corner suite, he would not encourage them to buy the purple corner suite. Or the faux-gilt mirror, or the bow-legged onyx dining table. The tables and the mirrors and footstools and grey leather recliners were afloat about the floor, some higher, some lower. His influence over their saleability was seen by management as negative, that rugged, distracted one with his repeated shirt and spiritless pitch. They were empathetic to the notion of family bereavement but in practice steered by the bottom line. "Use the work, use it," a fellow furniture retail assistant said. "Throw yourself into it and distract."

Have you seen our range of armchair lamps to compliment your purchase?

They listened out for his phrasing and intonation while undertaking a gentle empathetic assessment of his low commission score. The floor manager, the one in charge of staff training, arranged for him to receive refresher sessions over two weekends in November, when the bridges were being blocked over the Thames by the eco rebels. He watched them on the news, sitting on the tarmac in the cold, and thought that that must be the only way to live now, exposed to the elements and feeling the hard ground. Around him in his flat there were nervous flickering corners. The walls were too straight and the ceiling too close. He often could not sleep in the bedroom so would move to the sofa and wake up there after two hours with the morning charging through the window slamming him into another day. On the second weekend of refresher training he skipped the Sunday session and was given a kind though firm talk by the manager on Tuesday, when he went back in after his day off.

This business of the floating furniture, it ventured outwards from the shop floor, out into the roads, the skies, they drifted, armchairs, sideboards. In the bedroom one night after a bottle of Merlot he opened his eyes to find the bedside table high over him and a figure of his lost girl trying to open the drawer to get something she had left there. Her red-flecked hair was knotted in clumps around her, her shoulders draped in rags and sharp-boned, there were feathers behind her as if she had wings. He rose, needing to escape, and returned to the sofa where he tried to read a book, but the words themselves floated, they gave him no meaning or comfort, so he had more wine instead from his supply in the cardboard box next to the fridge.

We're a bit concerned that shop floor might be too much of a challenge for you at the moment, Damian. What do you think?

Tanya, fellow retail attendant, new staff member, had herself experienced loss. She reached out and hugged him to the wool of her pistachio jumper at the discovery of whom he mourned, how profoundly he must suffer, as they were standing at the back entrance to the warehouse smoking. She was overcome. "Sometimes you just cry," she said. "Sometimes it just surges up inside you all the agony and unfairness of everything and you just cry and cry and can't stop. You poor thing. I'm so sorry." She was widowed four years earlier by a car accident. Her presence helped him for a while, no more visions and visitations in the night, the sound of another living breath by his side and her dense, clammy scent. The only thing they had in common was sorrow and Fabric, which initially was enough, they could venture some way to a place of forgetting. When they got back, though, they didn't know who each other was and felt lonely. They ate breakfast together, unconvinced.

Jerry and Harvey were not allowed to stay another night in his home. They were allowed a few hours with him every other Sunday, and if Patrick had anything to do with it this would either be reduced or stopped. Sweet-natured Jerry, pretending to believe it wasn't his father's fault despite Patrick's regular infiltrations and comments to the contrary. And Harvey asking for her, "Is she going to come back?"

"She's not coming back," Damian said.

"But Jerry said she was waiting for us at the bluebells. So did Mummy."

This led to a disagreement over the phone: "You need to tell him the truth so we can help him deal with it."

"I'm handling it the way I think's best," Stephanie said, "It's none of your business."

"None of my business?" How can that be, that little boy and his big brother running through the park for the ball, their flesh of his flesh, their future the single meaning of his present? Is it possible that they could forget him, the way he virtually forgot his own mother when he was a boy?, and he has a fierce, unaccustomed yearning for her then, to have known her well, it might have saved him somehow from this, the children drawing away from him, disappearing into an embrace of trees.

He stayed nights with Tanya in her cul-de-sac house where she had lived with her husband. There were pictures of him on the walls, a pair of his shoes was still in the hallway positioned neatly next to the shoe rack, not inside it, a half-acceptance, half-expectation. Yet it was an easier place. Whenever he returned to his flat he wanted to walk back out the door or smash through the walls with his fists. The rooms lay in wait, thick with gloom. Dust and gossamer accumulated on the surfaces and in the terrible complex corners and with this the floating lamps, the night visions, formed a barricade at the door, daring him to come inside. The day he walked out of Fabric for the last time, two-thirds through his shift, without informing management and leaving behind his coat and mug, the barricade had become so solid that his entrance into the hallway required a physical strength. The long magnolia walls skulked. The objects, the fixtures of his life, seemed unwarranted. Stepping towards the bedroom, he had meant to lie down, but he realised that this would not be possible, no kind of settlement or rest here. He had to get out. He simply had to go. Behind him as he plunged some things into a bag there was the memory of Avril watching him the night he had tried and failed to leave all those years before, her worried face, her private discernment. This time he would go. There was nothing left to keep him. Yes Daddy, go, she whispered.

Perhaps there is a place where the dead gather beneath the stars. You can reach it, you can see it, with the combination of the night and a dangerous freedom. They shine down on the wave-peaks of the river and make silver speak. They lift the air as you are walking, pulling towards the north and laying a particular light on the ground, when you find yourself inside it, enveloped in the glory of its moving, and so you move closer to them. They have not left. It is that they have ascended and we who live on the ground cannot see them, only sense them, on the edge of ourselves, beyond the walls. Out here, he felt her closer. No solid structure around him or overhead surface. No compartment of sleeping, eating or dressing. The answer to unbearable loss is extraction, and in this way, for days at a time, Damian began to take to the streets for the long haul, walking like Dickens, crossing the bridges of his childhood, the squares and the old greens of Camberwell and Hyde Park Corner. He walked until he was tired and would sit down on a bench or in a doorway to rest and a shadow of her would sit with him. One night he went through China Town and stood in the red light looking up at one of the restaurant windows, from which he, Avril and Summer had once watched the New Year dragons down in the street below. He remembered his daughters' sand-coloured palms against the glass, their wonder at the city's unrolling treasure, all the shaking red and gold, the lanterns. He remembered, walking on, coming across her in the dining room making her toffee ship when she was six, the wafer she was holding, the rust-brown liquid she was dipping it into. We're going to eat it! she said, the whole family! He walked. Onwards he walked.

"At that time," Damian would say to a good friend some years from now, "I had no sense of who I could be anymore, in the world. It was like that. I didn't count. I had no value to anyone. So I followed the known shadows. I followed her wherever I could sense her, or thought I could sense her." Through the town and the town parks and the thoroughfares. Across Marble Arch he went, down Oxford Street with the Christmas lights above him and the drink inside him from his stops along the way. Outside Forever 21 she was see-through, her face momentarily fluorescent. He sat down there in a shop doorway, and once he sat down he found that he couldn't get up again, so he stayed there, and he came to see, in the amber fog of his mind, that there is really not much of a gap between walking past someone lying in a shop doorway on Oxford Street, and lying in a shop doorway on Oxford Street.

ॐ

"Do you ever think about death? About what it's like?" Michael said.

"You mean apart from today?" she said.

"Yeah, apart from today."

"Today—yesterday—I was trying so hard not to think about it, but I couldn't help it."

"Me too."

"Generally, though, yes, it's been on my mind. The moment of death. How hard it must be. How you cope with it."

"What do you mean, how you cope with it?" he said.

"Well, I mean, the fear. It must be terrifying, crossing over from consciousness, into oblivion. Not knowing what's going to happen. How you cope with that terror. Doesn't it frighten you?"

"But you won't be aware of it. You won't be conscious anymore, when you cross."

"What about before you lose consciousness, when you have to face the fact that you're going to die? I think about Khadija Saye and her mother a lot. Especially them, their terror, try and hold it in my mind, I don't know, maybe as a kind of homage to them. They were together right at the end, mother and child. What was that like? We have to at least think about it because it stops us from being blind, from going blindly through this world." She faced him again on the pillow. "Why?" she said. "Do you think about death?"

"Of course."

"A lot?"

He still carried it with him, an expectation of leaving. "I'm surprised I'm still here. I'm thinking maybe seven more years."

"Seven years?"

"Maybe a little more than that, until the kids are grown."

"But don't you think they'll need you," she said, "the way you need your parents, your mum? Why do you think that? I don't understand."

"I don't know. I've always felt like something's going to get me."

"What, like bad police or something?"

"Not just that. Living here, in this society. Always having to close myself in and compromise. I have so much rage and frustration inside me because of it, and it takes so much energy, to be dodging all the time, downplaying, pretending it's fine. It's wearing me out. One day I think I'm going to plain just run out of energy. And if that doesn't get me, something else will."

He could not say these things to Nicole. She would think him morbid and defeatist. At the time of this conversation Nicole had been in Cyprus singing at the casino. Melissa held him closer. The queens of her roof, Patience, Comfort and Mercy, looked out from their backscreen with sympathy.

"It shouldn't be like that. You shouldn't feel like that." In a firmer, determined voice, she said, "You have to be defiant."

His breathing was deepening and his body becoming heavier where it covered hers.

"Is that why you're not afraid?"

"I guess so, yeah."

She stroked him, the graded scalp and shoulders and the cotton vest across his skin. There is a belief in a sacred book, she had told him, that when two bodies have moved inside one another their souls have touched and the door stays open. They can lie side by side and it will have no negative moral weight. "Lie down with me, just to be close," she'd said, and the relief was pure and expansive, the return of her little body to him, its soft and clutching shape. Blake was now sleeping in the room below. The patch of sun on the back of his head had saved him, was her theory, leaked gold into his heart. Ria was sleeping next door to him in her room, underneath her planets. Outside on the hills the towers were haloed in cloud.

"You can rest here," she said, "in our house near the water. I'll watch you from the window and protect you. All your labours will be done. We'll go into the garden. Late in our lives, we'll go into the garden and sleep."

THREE

17

The basement of the Nigeria High Commission, Northumberland Ave, Nigerians in transit. Alice among them in her mac and copper-streaked wig, her handbag and her lucky chain to still her somersaulting heart. Carol next to her with the essential documents and some extra cash to slip to a useful chancer, one with a fast-track promise, say, some red-tape-disappearing magic or a VIP contact in the Home Office. The rows of chairs go all the way back to the photocopiers, full of people waiting and waiting, perusing the offline content of their phones or managing their children or wiping their foreheads and necks with damp pieces of material. Every so often at the sounding of a buzzer someone will get up and head tunnel-visioned to a front counter, where the embassy staff will either facilitate or obfuscate their next touchdown at Murtala Muhammed Airport. The air is tense, tempers braced.

The journey here began a month ago at the end of January, in preparation for one such wished-for touchdown, when Carol put in an online application to renew Alice's soon-to-expire British passport so that she could go home in the spring and survey the developments on her house. Her other passport, the Nigerian one, had expired in 1995. Her young face looked out from its fuzzy sepia history, her expression upwards, clear-eyed and mild. It failed to convince the processing office of Alice's right to dual citizenship, and they wrote explaining that in order to renew her British passport, she would have to either renew or renounce the Nigerian. The only way to renounce was in person, they said unhelpfully from the immigration office in Abuja, and anyway Alice did not want to renounce. Renounce her land? her blessed Edo soil in which were buried the bones of her parents and their parents and maybe soon as well her own? Cut herself away from the thick Naija air and the compounds and sounds of her people? No, she said to Carol, and Carol had agreed, no. But no one ever answered the phone at Northumberland Ave. The website was cryptic, the appointment system unclear. All of which was irrelevant to the nonchalant, Welsh male voice in the technical department of the Processing Centre of Her Majesty's Passport Office to whom Carol had been referred for some human-to-human discussion on the matter: no renewal there, no renewal here.

During this time Alice had been passing her days in a state of anguish. She waited, drained and fraught, in her newly tenuous pink room, for good phone calls that didn't come. Would the room now be taken away by the housing association? Would she be taken away from the room and deposited in one of the immigration centres she had heard about where they unload the person, the person they have decided is illegal, out of the back of the immigration van and throw them in a cell? She had seen them, these vans, driving around the neighbourhood. She had seen one on West End Lane with its dark windows and what looked like the outline of a cage inside and she had imagined her own face behind the cage. They were sending people back to the islands. They were pulling them out of their houses in the middle of the night and asking for their documents, their *passports*. They were halting them at the immigration desks in the airports and stopping them from returning and getting them sacked from their jobs and making them homeless so that they were forced to live in bin sheds, derelict buildings, industrial units and night buses. She had heard about it from Winifred. It was all in the news since last year. They were willing the ships backwards. They were sending home the help, erasing lives of service to the NHS and regular tax payments to HMRC. The lands of origin had once been useful to them but now they found the people of the lands inconvenient. What would she do if they knocked on her door in the middle of the night? What could she say to them that they would listen to her? It was so frightening. She felt that she was drifting above the earth with no ground to step on, about to fall.

As a rule, Alice did not communicate directly with the State, the State being any external or unknown body, the people from the council, the gas and electricity companies, the kitchen refurbishment admin team, they were all basically the government and they did not follow her sentences. The only ones she had any time for were the Jehovah's Witnesses because she approved of their leaflets and their good work of calling the flock; God's voice has no language. "You talk to them," she would say to whichever visiting daughter if coaxed to the phone, "They never understand me." Thus such dialogue, any kind of official communication or transaction about her life, fell to the children. Isn't that what they are there for when you no longer look after them but they would look after you, when you are getting tired? At home in the village when she was a child there used to be no such thing as an old people's home. There was only one home, the family home. The old, the young, the middle, all would live together, in mutual care. The State does not care. They do not know whom you are! Only the children know after looking at you from the very beginning and following your voice.

Carol had managed, finally, to decipher the way to get a renewal appointment at the embassy, which involved applying via the Abuja office and the algorithms circling back through to

London. She picked Alice up from her flat and they took the Bakerloo line into town. In Trafalgar Square a man was making music out of a two-wheeled cart of glass bottles, by blowing across their tops, the sound rose high with the flights of the fountain pigeons. It soothed Alice momentarily, but the fear intensified again as they approached the building. Her eyes were red and moist from the worry of weeks. She had lost weight from worrying too much to eat. Even the Nigerian faces and voices inside did not comfort her at first because they all could be sent away like her, they were all in the same black boat, the same basement, sitting underneath the government and waiting for the knock at the door in the night.

After fifteen minutes, a young man in a blue shirt and brown slacks called Alice and Carol forward, directing them not to one of the counters but to a desk off to the side.

"Good day, ma," he said, deferential in the presence of an elder, eager to bid her to sit down opposite him on one of the two chairs. "Now, you want to renew your Nigerian passport."

Alice confirmed this was so, Carol leaned forward, ready with her documents and backstory and prepared beseechings and bribe cash. She told him about the conundrum, the unwant-ing to renounce and lose Nigeria, that they only wanted to take Alice back home for a visit but she would come back and then maybe go again when she was tired unless she changed her mind. That was all they wanted. That was all they were trying to do.

He listened patiently. Carol was expecting him to say some-thing convoluting or obstructive, that would require them to go to another office, call some other department in another build-ing, wait a few more weeks, move the trip from spring to later in the year. But it didn't come. "Don't worry, ma," he said sim-ply, "it is ok. You are getting fast-track service today—we will not make you wait. You have the former passport?"

Carol handed it to him in delayed surprise. No cash would be needed apart from the official payment. The clerk issued the new passport and stamped it here and there, while asking them about their plans for their visit, would they be seeing family? what part of Edo State was Alice from? he himself was from Aba in Abia State but he had a friend who lived in Benin City. When they stood to leave, Alice was on the brink of weeping, hiding it in her throat. She felt like an old woman and not an animal in a cage.

"Safe travel home," the man said as he showed them to the door.

"Thank you. Good boy," she said, and pushed a Werther's Original into his hand from the packet she always carried in her bag.

Afterwards she and Carol were in such high spirits that they decided to go and look at paintings in the National Gallery, light and leisurely as now the day seemed. They wandered through the great parquet halls, among the pearly alabaster figures from the anterior centuries. Carol took a picture of Alice standing in front of Raphael's *Madonna and Child* in its gilded frame, her lucky chain bright white against her black jumper, her winter scarf loosened about her neck, her eyes still a little swollen, amidst the smooth anthroposophy of her face.

With almost as many suitcases with which she had left Cornelius, they went. Warren went with them, having arranged time off from What!!! because he wanted to see the motherland, walk the soil, put his forehead on it and introduce his Nigerian portion to its origin, plus they all agreed it was a good idea to have a man in the party. During the flight he drank three whisky and cokes and slumbered against the window, while Alice, in the middle, anticipated her destination, the almost finished home, ready in the field for her to walk inside and live in when she was tired enough. The next time she did this flight would be her last. There would be even more suitcases, full of every final thing she needed, all her pots and pans and ornaments and the crochet, the three-vase set, the fur donkey, the jewellery trinket of Cornelius's rings he had given her, towels, rags, hats . . .

"Do you remember Frances, Mum?" came Carol's voice softly, emerging through the quiet night dim of airbound dozing strangers somewhere over the Atlantic.

"Yes," she said. "I remember."

"I was just thinking about her, when we were all at Bantem Street. Where is she now? Did she go back to Ireland in the end?"

"I think so. She send me postcard sometimes."

Frances had been on the same floor as Alice and Carol at the Bantem Street house. She had thick, coily, reed-coloured hair and freckles and was always biting her nails. She had taken a liking to Alice, would sit with her in the evenings reading a book or trying crochet. It must be a comfort to you, she would say, having your daughter living here with you. Carol had moved in the year before, as an alternative to living at home, and when Alice decided she also wanted to leave, she had again been her communication with a state body.

"Do you remember the market we used to go to on Saturday mornings? Frances went with you sometimes."

"We buy cloth, we buy everything," Alice laughed.

"You were good friends," Carol said.

One day Frances had bought Alice a radio for her windowsill and tuned it to the pirates operating in the vicinity of Elephant and Castle. They would buy suya from the hut and eat it on the bus. At Bantem Street there was not a man anywhere in sight and Frances used to say it was paradise. No man lurking in the bedroom. No man brandishing a poison drink or waiting with his fist. Just us women and our own lives. And it was true, Alice could once more feel the outline of herself, she felt herself returning to something long buried that had not been crushed after all, but had preserved itself through the storms of marriage, with a secret primal power. They were a ship of women off the Old Kent Road, with ropes and masts and wide nets for gathering strength. While they were there, Frances came to know what Alice knew, about the children who don't in the end arrive, the pain of it. She carried a child for two months, during which Alice made her eat three meals a day and looked after her, until one day she felt a weakness, a subtle leaving, and the heartbeat fell away, it changed its mind. "That happen to me too," she told Frances in the grieving violet dusk. "He live only for ten minute." This was the first time she had revealed this small piece of information to anyone. "In the evening I light candle. I talk to him sometimes."

"If you go and live in Nigeria for good," Carol said, "she won't know where you live, Frances, if she wanted to visit you."

This Alice considered, settling deeper into her seat. The plane blanket was over her knees. An air steward went by and slapped shut an overhead compartment with the heel of his hand. She didn't much like being sky high like this and was looking forward to landing, to seeing the runway coming closer at Murtala.

"Maybe she can send me postcard there. You tell her where I am," she said.

Lately Carol had taken to jogging Alice's memory like this, following a series of routine tests that had noted short-term recall-infringement. She asked her questions about the past. She got her to talk about the tapestry classes she used to do at the adult education centre, the long drives to Devon when they went on holiday, early memories she had of her parents and siblings. Surging over the Atlantic, Carol formed a picture in her mind of her mother at home, years from now, older than now,

243

sitting in her Benin house and reading her postcards, her family letters, with her ornaments and her last things around her. She was hoping that on this visit she might change her mind about leaving. She might feel her distance from her dream and see that home was more than simply land, but the threads you have spun in your life, the ties you have made with your blood and company. She hoped that she would wheel around and say, on the soils of Benin, I cannot leave my children, my grandchildren! That it might just take this journey through the clouds towards the Delta and the mangrove swamps to realise it.

But she was not sure it would go that way. They might well lose her, as Melissa so feared, as Adel so adamantly opposed. Yet she must give her the choice. She took Alice's hand and held it.

Alice had left Nigeria at the ascent of the Biafran War. She never saw her little brother Abraham again. He died in an airstrike during the capture of Enugu. It was something that had bonded her to Cornelius, that they both lost brothers this way, they had a same-shape void. She cried for weeks through the freezing English winter. She cried for him again when the baby died after ten minutes, because she was sure that it was Abraham returning to her then changing his mind, he did not want to stay in this bleak and alien place. Her older brother, Rufus, survived. He later set up an import-export business and went on to have three sons and two daughters from two wives. One of the wives was swarve and regal and the other was rough and fat. They disliked but tolerated each other. Alice often thought that she would like it if Cornelius had another wife, she would have no problem with it at all. It made sense. A man can be a burden to share.

Of Rufus's five children, two went to Canada, another to America. One daughter was killed in a bus accident, which caused the second wife's hair to grey overnight and she never dyed it.

244

The middle son, Ose, moved to Lagos and set up a bakery that developed into a café and restaurant serving all kinds of food—burgers, rice, banana milkshakes, yogurts—though the area of specialism remained with flour-based products, the most popular orders being the New York bagels and spicy suya baguettes. Sometimes if business was bad his father would help him out with a cash injection, but this was not possible anymore after Rufus fell ill and had high hospital bills to pay. Then there were the funeral costs, the outstanding bills and creditors. Bouquet of Flour (the name was the idea of Ose's wife Sabrina) managed to stay afloat on its own by adjusting to market changes and expanding its menu, even if the menus themselves did become worn, and the outside of the café required some unaffordable updating partly due to occasional flooding from the street. There was still a large demand for the baguettes at lunchtimes from local office workers and staffers.

Generally Ose did not like to present himself in his uniform when he wasn't at the café. He found it demeaning, in a way, as he was after all the CEO, but often he had to serve the food himself to the customers together with Sabrina and their waiter when it was very busy. It was so busy this morning that he'd had to rush out to the airport to meet his aunt without changing first—luckily he had the smarter jacket that he kept in the boot of his Nissan, which he put on and buttoned at the front even though it made him sweat more in the twenty-eight-degree heat. Alice did not recognise him for an instant because he had put on weight, and he did not immediately recognise her either because she had lost weight. She was a smaller, much older woman, her step very light and hesitating. Her skin had taken on a strange grey hue. Yet the smile, it was the fabulous family smile, still the same. Carol and Warren hugged him too and they all busied with the luggage towards the car, which bore the company logo along one side. He had never met Warren before and one of the first things he said to Ose during traffic conversation on Airport Road amidst the exhaust fumes and the tuk tuks and the oxide-stained bicycles was that he wanted to visit Fela Kuti's shrine. To begin with, Ose took them to Bouquet of Flour for lunch.

"Aunty, you must eat more. Please now, finish your baguette."

"It's too much," Alice said. "I eat again later."

Warren finished it for her followed by a milkshake. The next day Ose and Sabrina did take them to the New Afrika Shrine, reluctantly, keeping to the edges of the place, close to the exit, uncomfortable in the weedy vapours and the lazy daytime apathy. "These people, all these boys here wasting their time," Ose bemoaned, "just sitting around. It's so unhealthy. They have no direction." He also showed them the Nigerian National Museum, Tafawa Balewa Square and the Red Door Gallery in Victoria Island, partly with the help of a trusted cab driver friend named Daniel who charged them the correct price instead of using their conspicuous oyibo foreignness to rip them off. Everywhere they went Warren took pictures on his iPhone, of the waters of the Lagoon and the fishermen's huts on stilts from the Third Mainland Bridge, the bukas emitting wafts of pepper sauce, amala and assorted meats, the hawkers weaving through the cars and the dusty drape of market scenes and distant tenement facades, even a row of dead bugs lying flat-winged on the blue stairs leading to Ose's NEPA generator. "I can't believe I'm here," he kept saying, staring at women walking by with heroic hairstyles, boys playing out street, and he kept saying thank you again and again to Ose and Sabrina for any small event or experience, such as when she put in front of him some egusi stew and pounded yam cooked by their house-help on their last evening staying with them. They did not eat the baguettes much at home. None of them, including their two children, twins, a girl and a boy, could really stand the sight of that long French loaf in their kitchen.

Ose left it until the latest available opportunity to approach Alice with his proposition. He did not want to appear calculating, presumptuous, desperate, or lacking in class; he was none of those things. And he was well aware of how people's relatives in Nigeria could come across during visits like these, asking for computers and phones and money, as if the person who had moved to the West must be rich. What he wanted was only to offer her an investment opportunity, to give her the chance to see some of her late husband's money grow in an honest and sturdy Nigerian business. Maybe they would expand beyond just one café. Maybe they would become a brand, recognisable across the world like Five Guys or Pret a Manger, there was no telling what could happen. In the morning before driving them to the bus park for the journey to Benin City, he broached the subject, inviting Alice and Carol to sit down for a minute in the living room. Here, too, Carol represented for her mother, treating the conversation almost as an official exchange.

"I don't think this is something we can think about right now, hey Mum? We're here to see about the house. We should focus on that. Maybe in the future . . ."

Ose looked at Alice, wanting confirmation. He had noticed how Carol often spoke for her mother or answered a question for her as if she couldn't speak for herself. She had been in England for too long, where levels of familial ranking were all mixed up.

"You would have a thirty per cent share," he said, "which is very generous, I must say that. Above all your funds will be safe. We have a solid foundation, a strong business, only needing some new investors to build up more. Aunty, please consider it."

Alice told him that she would. "Maybe as we said in future. We think about it."

As Carol was beginning to get up, Ose said, trying another angle of persuasion, "My father invested as well, you know.

Your brother, your uncle," indicating to them each in turn. "He knew we have a solid business in Bouquet of Flour because it is family-run. I'm sure he would be approving if his sister took up the baton now of the occasional injection to keep everything running."

"I didn't know Uncle Rufus had money to invest in business," Carol said offhandedly, with a glance towards Alice. Ose was about to say something in return but decided not to. He was worried he might say the wrong thing, or had already revealed something that he shouldn't have. "Anyway, we better go now," she said, "we mustn't miss the bus." They packed the remaining luggage in the car—some items had already been given as gifts to their hosts, then there were more gifts for the relatives in Benin, Alice's younger sister Nancy, her niece and nephews and their own children. At the station they hugged Ose goodbye and thanked him for his hospitality. He stayed amidst the throng of travellers, traders, pickpockets and area boys, brooding and dabbing his forehead with the cloth from his pocket, until the shuttle pulled out onto the outbound road, heading east.

The journey took four hours, slowed by checkpoints. They went through Ondo State and into Edo State. Off the hot roads dust lifted in their wake. Alice thought about Winifred as they were travelling, and whether she had felt the same as this when she went back to St. Vincent to visit. Did she have the same feeling that everything had changed and remained as it was? That it is possible to slip back inside the place of your birth and continue as if these decades of absence had not happened? So much time had passed. There was a sorrow that she had somehow missed her life, but a determination to take the rest of it.

When they arrived at Nancy's house in the northern part of Benin City—it had green-painted window frames and a grill across the front porch—Alice found that her sister mirrored this quality of having changed yet not changed. The wide cheeks and pretty smile, worthy of movie stars; close-cropped black hair, dyed, and a fuller figure. Alice could hear the similarity of her voice to her own and it made her mind clear, all at once. What it is like is that you have been walking in a mist for so long that it has become invisible to you, when suddenly you pass out of it and realise not only that you had forgotten it was there, but that you were invisible inside it. They clutched each other and spoke in Edo. Nancy embraced Carol and Warren and commented on how handsome he was. She was not impressed, though, that his father was not a Nigerian. He must try and make sure that when he himself married, his wife was one from among them. "Alice, my sister," she said. "You did not teach them to speak our tongue?" When questioning Carol on her own circumstances, children and relationship status, she was told matter-of-factly about her new girlfriend in London who was half Swedish.

They stayed with Nancy for a week, using her daughter's old bedroom and her lumpy leather sofa, meeting more relatives eager to assess them. The dawns came in wearing buttery gowns and laid their elbows on the windowsills. Warren would open his eyes and watch the mounting light, enjoying the sensation within of a rare kind of peace. There was an absence here of being distrusted, disfigured, questioned. Everyone was the same surface and he was part of it, and when he stepped outside to walk around the district, to go and buy milk or agege bread from the nearby stall, he did not feel threatened by his ascribed positioning as a threat, or trapped in the stain of past mistakes. His shoulders became looser. He was more inside his body because he was certain it fully belonged to him and would not be stolen, so he spread out in it. On Wednesday it rained, an aspect of the season, and he watched it, the way it darkened in the afternoon as if the earth were turning in on itself, into a huge silence. It showered for a few minutes, leaving the air close and warm and hollow; then, after half an hour, it truly, viciously rained. He stood outside by the cashew tree in Nancy's yard and let it soak him through, watched by a group of people sheltering under a canopy further along the street.

The next day they went to see the house. The contractor, Austin, was meeting them there, Nancy accompanied them, having her own gate key to the plot which she kept on a ring with her other keys, for security. Her son-in-law Joseph drove them in his sedan and he and Nancy chatted loudly on the way, Alice interjecting in Edo or laughing in places, Carol could not remember when she had last seen her so animated and excited, and it quashed any remaining hope that this trip might change her mind. She had dressed for the occasion in a blouse and favourite wrapper with the bob-style wig, as if she were going to a festive church service or a birthday party rather than to a construction site. They passed rows of shops, a leisure resort, a photo studio with a placard outside. "We will soon be there," Nancy said as they were turning off the main road. "There is work to do yet, but you will see it now."

The fields by the teaching hospital had shrunk with the years, new houses had been built, neighbourhoods spread out. It was still visible in the distance as they neared the site, in the gaps between the compounds and other dwellings, some with high gates at the front topped with circular wiring, some with low rain-stained boundary walls. Joseph beeped at a group of children who were playing near the road and drove on further, before turning left into a street with a block of flats on the corner and a bar and food stall opposite. He pulled up next to an unfinished building surrounded by metal fencing, with piles of sand outside it and some strewn rubble. The gate was open, beyond it some rough shrub-land and deep puddles of water reddened from the rain. Then, the

250

dream itself. Its roof trusses were naked of sheathing. Its windows were wanting of their panes.

"Is it here?" Alice said uncertainly.

"Yes, it is here," Nancy said.

They stared. They looked around. Nancy got out of the car and stretched. Warren offered his arm to Alice as she followed.

"I thought things would be further on than this," Carol said.

"It is coming along. I believe they are waiting for more funds to finish, but when they receive it I'm sure they will do it quickly."

"More funds? They have the funds. We sent it through."

"Come. Come and see inside, my daughter. Look now, here is Austin."

A hefty man got out of a truck that had pulled up behind Joseph's car. He strode in through the gate with his hand outstretched, greeting Joseph and Warren first, saying "Good day, Madam" to Alice who had to tip her head back to get a proper look at him, he wore sunglasses and big black leather shoes covered in dust. Carol mentioned straight away that she had expected things to have progressed further, for the roof to be completed at least, to which Austin said that they had run into difficulty acquiring materials, everything was doubling in price, the plywood, cladding, insulation. "Many projects are getting stuck or slowing down. People want to build quickly and finish, but right now it's not possible," he shrugged. "Don't worry, we are in second stage. Even it's better sometimes to build much slowly, not rush. Come, Madam."

He and Nancy went ahead towards the plastic sheeting over the area of the porch and front door, avoiding a particularly cavernous puddle on the way. Inside they stood together in a notional parlour, with the sun beaming down on their heads, Alice kept looking up, disturbed by the chasm between her expectation and reality. She could not imagine, in this room, not yet, the comfortable silence of evenings, sitting within it the way she could sit in her room in Kilburn with all her things around her and her pictures and hanging butterflies. The atmosphere felt strangely unknown.

"This very one is sitting-room—parlour," Austin said, then indicating through another opening, "This one dining. You can enter by the kitchen." He led them through the whole configuration of spaces, along a corridor to the bedrooms, three of them, "This one master, en suite, this be second room," and to a passage at one end. "That very one veranda . . . yes, to outside. Veranda will be in back, porch in front." When the tour was over he clasped together his thick palms and said, "Madam, by the special grace of God you are happy."

Alice looked upwards again at the open sky. She looked out of a paneless window at the shrub-land where she meant to grow her bitter leaf. "I wish you finish roof quickly," she said, "rain getting in everywhere. Floor must come last. So much to do—it's not ready yet," and she flicked her shoulders in distaste, her mouth downturned, a flash of her glasses. She wasn't sure whether she trusted Austin or not. It seemed it would be so long before they could put in furniture and kitchen sink and proper bed, let alone smaller important things, maybe longer than by the time she was ready to come and live. It was not yet a house, far from a home.

"We must have patience o, please," Austin said, repeating his point that slowly was sometimes more favourable, and addressing primarily the men present, as if they were better listeners, or better at understanding. Carol interrupted him.

"There's all the plastering to do still. The windows as well? It was supposed to be a six-month time-span. We sent you all the payments." She was trying to measure her tone as Nancy was observing her sternly, arms folded, and had already marked her out as a trouble-maker judging from the way she talked across her sometimes and cut her eye in her presence. Carol did not want to appear disrespectful to Austin or to her mother's sister, but something was wrong here, there was some accusation she did not feel she could express.

"I am not sure. You must check your bank in London," Austin told her. Then Nancy said something clandestine to him, Joseph and Alice which made them all smile, while Warren went and waited outside, watching the street beyond the gate.

It was later that evening that Carol approached her aunt about the matter of the delayed funds. She had not been made aware before now that the builders had not received everything. She and Adel had both sent payments and Austin had said in his last email to her before they came to Nigeria that he had bought granite and scaffolding. "Please," said Nancy, "you will discuss everything with your contractor. I am not in charge."

"But who is handling the finances at this end? As far as I was aware the contractor was being paid directly, but have I got that wrong?"

The more questions Carol asked, the more resistant Nancy seemed, until she stood up from her chair in her terracotta-coloured kitchen and said to Alice, "Tell this your daughter to watch her words to me. You are treating me as if I have stolen from you. You are here in my house, I give you hospitality, but you suspect *me*." She wiped her hands one against the other, her face set in an offended smirk with her bottom lip pushed up towards her nose, and said definitively before leaving the room, "I am not a thief."

Before they left, Alice dreamt of it. How it might be. Night birds settled in the house. They knew the future was unknown and unformed. They made nests, carried grass, bred children. Roaches crawled through the gaps in the rough and mottled walls. Soon she would be tired. She wanted her body to be carried through the paths on the arms of the men of her country, to be lowered into the ground at the end of her long journey, down into the old red earth. But perhaps it was too much to want, too much to make possible. Perhaps her death, as well as her life, would be a disagreement of place, and once you have left you can never really go back. Everything changes. The great doors close. That child she once was who began here, maybe they would never be allowed to meet each other again, as wrong as it seemed to her. And maybe it mattered less.

18

But it's *raining*. And there are no walls, no ceilings, no en suites? The bathroom is through the trees, over the bridge and across the field, over there, in the rain? And if it is the middle of the night you mean I have to torch-walk through the rural spook, in my onesie, having donned dirty wellies while half asleep in a low-fabric hovel with a zip for a door? And when I go back to the hovel I might trip over a tent rope and fall on my face on the dark damp ground glistening with long wild worms and harrowing slugs?

Hazel had various problems with camping (no wardrobe space, the proximity of insect life) and had overcome her reservations for Melissa who'd suggested some time in nature, but the downpour that exploded over the A273 as she was nearing the campsite was discouraging. Her big white Range Rover came tentatively down the lane into the cluster of the trees, which stretched tall and rustled at height, their sound often mistaken for rain, deep at night, a calling from strange and earthy sleeps, sheltered in nylon.

Melissa met her at the car window and noted the expression on her face. "It's just a shower, it will stop soon." She was wearing waterproofs. Her tent was already up and she was hopeful of a restorative bucolic retreat in the pastures of Sussex.

"This is not a shower, babe, let's be straight."

It was June. In the wet grey drifts beyond, children were edging the fields, out on green voyages, jumping over brooks and testing the pond for algae thickness and temperature. Over in the area of civilisation were the bathrooms, fridges and the campsite shop, popular with the young for its sweets; queues and gangs of them formed, grateful for the parental leniency that came with this heavenly place, that let them be wild in the wild, let them consume and roam lawlessly, holding sticks, climbing the lower trees and making dens out of twigs and fallen leaves. Ria was a kind of piratic leader, along with cousin Clay, striding around with one such curved stick that she had found in a glade. The younger children followed while maintaining their attitude of lawlessness, there was Blake and his two new campsite friends Simon and Mark, and a little girl, Min, who belonged to Melissa and Hazel's old schoolfriend Nila, her husband was here too, they camped yearly. The rain did not bother them, these miniature musketeers. It only added another, squelching dimension to the experience, leading them gradually to the big greenhouse opposite the shop where there were board games and wicker chairs and a translucent ceiling spattered with planetary debris. Here they would rest and allow themselves to dry.

This particular fixture is where Hazel would spend much of the next three days during the "showers," sitting in her Mexican blanket with her hair tied up, sans make-up. Ria and Clay helped her erect her tent. "I went to Halfords," she told them. "I bought an extra gas cylinder in case I run out. Bought a flask as well." "Aunty, you shouldn't have brought white trainers, they'll get all muddy," Ria said. "They look new as well," said Clay. "They're only Tesco. I didn't want to get my other ones dirty." "Decadence. Excess," scolded Ria. Soon Hazel's hovel was a final shape in the commune among the trees, four tents spaced out around a central fire-pit, the heart of the matter, where the marshmallow-melting happened and guitar-playing and the talking into the bare pitch of night. The fire was tended mostly by Nila and Max—he was a quiet, rustic type, short and strong and easy company—they poked it, blew on it, added logs at the right angle, conferring with one another and overseeing the softening of foiled potatoes baking in the hot corners. Melissa watched them amidst the music in their orange light and admired, envied too, their bonded certainty, their singular married path, a path that was becoming more inviting to her as she approached her mid-century, she saw how they could relax and rest in one another. She watched them and then looked beyond them, into the flames, until drawn back by Hazel topping up her mug of wine or a fine tune from Clay's eclectic playlist coming from the speaker hoisted in a nook between two branches.

Hazel did not bring Bruce with her. No, Bruce did not camp, she explained. He had told her with extreme finality, "Sleeping on the ground in the cold you must be mad. Later." And actually it was good that he did not—the two of them in a trembling zip-up cave, tossing and seeking comfort, Bruce straining all night against his sleeping bag, in the morning waking up to his pastoral trauma which would deepen her own, among the ants and hanging spiders. It was better he stayed home and she have some time away from him to think. She had brought her hormone shots with her for the second round of IVF, the second expenditure of hope. Where would it end? How long could she keep yearning for these drugs and needles to make life? She longed for a wish-free place, where there was nothing she spiritually needed in order to register a beautiful sky and be moved by it, that peace, that acceptance of everything as it is. But even out here, in the gift of a rainbow, the damp, crystal blue of dusk behind a faint and golden tree, it was difficult to find. The children, all their lift and purity, how they merged into one another, their elf-like claiming of the land and their inner magic ever

257

outward, they made her yearn harder. She wanted to devote to one of their kind, and a dark foreboding was spreading out inside her that it would never be so.

"Come for a walk with me," Ria whispered through the nylon door, early in the morning, the dew on the grass, the new light pearly thin.

"What time is it?" Hazel said.

"Oh, sixish half fiveish."

"Jesus Christ what are you trying to do to me?"

"Come on it'll be fun."

Anoraks over onesies they went up the lane towards the grazing cows and watched them for a while, their clarifying indifference. From there they walked along the circular path edging the fields, when Hazel complained of ongoing earliness Ria said, "Don't you like the air, being inside the weather?" The truth was that Hazel would go anywhere with this child, this daughter who was almost her own. She had watched her and held her through the years, she saw the many different versions of her when she looked at her, Ria at five, Ria at nine, now the quirky melody-making girl on the cusp of adulthood who still clung to a clearer beginning; sometimes a sheer, higher note would creep into her voice, the child within straining to hold on to dominance, asking not to be demanded too much of, let me stay in my world, it is all I own. The countryside suited her.

"You may have noticed I'm more of a city girl," she told her. "I like city air, city weather, petrol fumes. I even like city rain."

"Yeah. But it's so much *bigger* out here. Everything's *open*, and *wide*. Are you coming canoeing with us later?"

"I can't swim."

"It doesn't matter. If you capsize it's not that deep so."

"Have you capsized before?"

"Yeah once. Ages ago."

"I might just stay in the greenhouse and play a game."

"Oh," Ria said, pretending to sulk. They entered the woods, where the dens were built, where the rope swings swung over the deep muddy ditch. "I wish my dad was here. He can't swim either. He could sit with you in the greenhouse while we're gone. I don't like how everything always has to be separate instead of all of us in one place at the same time."

"Does he like camping? I can't imagine him camping."

"No, he's like you quite a lot actually—city. He'd bring the wrong shoes like you did."

"Hey I got those shoes especially for the mud!"

"Exactly," Ria laughed.

"Do you still miss him? I mean even though you see him often?"

"I miss them both together."

"Yeah. I know. It's not the same."

"Look, here's the den we made—it has a window."

"Wow. Sturdy. It reminds me of a shieling I saw once in Scotland, this little shepherd's hut on a hillside, miles away from anyone."

"I'd like to live somewhere like that one day when I'm older."

"So you've finally accepted you're going to be an adult."

Ria pushed her shoulder lightly. She thought of Avril to whom it would not happen. She had found out from Stephanie a few months ago (she had been unable to call and break the news to people who weren't in regular contact with Avril) and still couldn't believe she wasn't here anymore, it seemed impossible, too unreal. She kept expecting to see her walking along a street or riding a bus, or appearing here among these trees and joining their trail through the woods. They came out the other side of the thicket and followed the path towards the pond. There were reeds standing through the water and a silver film on the surface. Yesterday Min had ventured into the outskirts in her wetsuit, delighted, watched by a song of frogs liming on the lily pads.

Other children had followed, returning to the tents soaked and searching for dwindling stocks of dry clothes.

"Maybe you could all go away together some time," Hazel said, resuming the conversation. "Your parents are still friends. It's not horrid and acrimonious, thank god. I knew a couple once who'd broken up but still took their kids on holidays together."

"I don't know if Nicole would really be into that," Ria said.

"Why not? She's all right isn't she? I mean, I don't know her. Do you like her?"

"Yeah she's ok. She's not my stepmum though. I don't see her like that."

"Ok."

"She's just a woman he married."

"Ha, I don't think you should let your dad hear you say that."

"Well, she *is*. No offence to her. She's not my *family*."

"Families are complicated things. In every family there's a sacrifice."

"Is that why you don't have kids? Because it makes things too complicated? I'm definitely not having any."

"Don't say that! You might want them one day."

"I won't."

"I used to think that and I changed my mind."

"Why haven't you got them then?"

"It just hasn't—happened for me yet."

"Are you too old now?"

"Who knows? Maybe I am. Maybe that's the problem."

At this juncture, Hazel sat down in front of the silent spectacle of the reeds, for her legs had melted beneath her, an outright need to sink, right there, and look at the water and consider the possible unbearable reality that there would be no Min or Blake ever given to her by the angels, no Ria of her own that she could be with in this way, early in the morning, her young voice unhindered by the world, by propriety or tact or the hard things life puts inside us, a reminder of how to be free.

"Oh, did I upset you? Are you ok?"

She could not reply for the time being. She put her face down into the crook of her arm and stayed that way, nodding her head once or twice to try and send a message of reassurance. Ria sat down next to her looking solemn and worried, waiting.

"I'm sorry."

"It's not you, you didn't do anything."

Another tumult ensued, wracking her shoulders.

"God I can't bear it."

Then the frogs began to sing. A guttural orchestra on the lilies at the edge of the pond, and Hazel suddenly laughed at the funny sound of it before knowing what it was, a choked and suffering laugh that fell away again into sobbing.

"Aunty, do you want me to go and get my mum?" Ria said.

"No, don't go. I'd rather be with you. I'll be ok in a minute. Sorry. You must think I'm mad."

"Um, yeah, of course you are."

Hazel put her arm around her and Ria reciprocated, staring at her because she had returned to laughing. She thought that maybe she was going mad in a bad way and was fascinated alongside her concern. Her relationship with Hazel had always been loose like this, she was akin to an older sister, there were no rules or orders, but she had never seen her in this dashed unfolding state, she was always strong and supreme, like a disco ball.

"Is it really that bad you don't have any babies?"

Calmer, Hazel said yes, it was. "I feel like I'm not complete."

"Why?"

"Why? Look at you. Why wouldn't I want a you?"

"But you wouldn't get a me. You don't know what you'd get. You could get a murderer or a dictator or something. A high school shooter."

"That's true, I guess."

"And anyway, you have me. I'm already here."

An epiphany. So she was. A complete thing, whole and in progress, and the earth is turning on its axis, the frogs are ugly and harmonious. How sharply the view on the horizon can change.

"Ah. Yes," Hazel said. "I do."

"You have to make peace with it, Aunty. None of us knows how long we'll be here for. Not everyone makes it."

Melissa's suggestion of spending time in nature had been prompted by a CBT therapist she was seeing, Debbie Petronsky, to address her recent panics. She operated from a square blue room at the GP surgery, which had caused some initial shyness, sitting in the reception area until she was called in for her mind, but Debbie went about things in an unexpectedly prosaic way. "I didn't feel like I was going to die, exactly. It was just this whirling, out-of-control feeling, like something horrible was about to happen, or it already was happening but I didn't know what it was . . ."

"Rome, you say you were, when this happened, last year?" Debbie said. Melissa confirmed this was correct. "And how long were you there for? I love Rome."

They talked about the piazzas and the crowds at the Colosseum, a park she liked where people took their dogs. Returning to the point, Melissa described the freak-out on the metro, the weird clanging noises and David's seduction in the hotel room afterwards. "Why did I feel I had no power? Why did I feel responsible, like I owed him something?" she said, tracing back through her time with him, trying to work out why she had stayed with him for so long. "I'm always too worried about confrontation or hurting someone's feelings, so I end up going blank and submitting to things with men that I don't want."

"What floor was this hotel room on?"

"The sixth, I think."

Debbie noted this down and took off her glasses. The lenses were so thick that without them she looked fish-like and abandoned. She cleaned them with a floppy lens cloth, while commenting on the narrowness and claustrophobia of some of those hotels in the old buildings. Melissa came to hear of her early European travels when she had first left South Africa, her love of the Lake District where she canoed annually on Ullswater with her husband Ruben, and the death of her cat. She couldn't tell whether she was skiving on the job or creating a chatty framework for psychological dissection; sometimes she veered, maybe by accident, into the sage and absolute.

"You had a breakdown," she surmised from the account of the fall of Paradise, when they discussed the end of the relationship with Michael.

"Hm, I don't think of it entirely like that."

"What was it about that house that made you feel like that? So smothered and possessed."

"It was—narrow. I didn't like being inside it. I've never liked houses very much, actually."

"All houses?"

"Mainly the conventional ones."

"Did you grow up in a house?"

"Yes."

"A conventional one? What do you mean by conventional?"

"You know, with the stairs going up on the left or right— ours were on the right—and the kitchen ahead of you. Sometimes a bay window at the front. A cupboard under the stairs."

"A cupboard under the stairs."

"Hm."

"Your voice just changed when you said that."

"What?"

"About the cupboard."

"Did it?"

"Yes. Didn't you feel it?"

Among the practical "exercises" Debbie prescribed was to enjoy the great outdoors (this is where she got on to talking about Ullswater), and to take notice of how she felt in it, whether it helped with the underlying anxiety. It was a fail-safe remedy for any kind of malaise, in her experience, and Melissa did enjoy the being in the weather, waking to the cool unbridled touch of the elements. The immediacy of birdsong took precedence over a voice that sometimes met her at the door to consciousness, that said *no, not yet, not yet,* a voice that she could not explain to Hazel or anyone else because it was cryptic and inchoate. She had begun to feel that she carried a mild insanity which was a result of searching too far into the back of her mind for questions that were inherently ambiguous, perhaps not meant to be answered. Debbie herself had said that as we get older we lose our defences against our own neuroses and we *become* them, they take over, all we can do is ride along in the backseat. The moment, the final straw that had sent Melissa to Debbie seemed suggestive of this: a couple of months after Blake's operation, when he had come to her at the end of a long day with the pressing complaint that his leg and arm were hurting, and she had burst out at him, "Just self-soothe, will you! You hurt your foot, your neck hurts, your head hurts, I'm not *interested* in your so many *hurts,* Blake. How much time do you think I have for every scrape and ache and crisis? I have my own crisis to attend to, do you ever think about that? That I might have my own hurt, one that can't be fixed with a plaster or a bandage but could take years of psychiatry? years of silent retreats and positive affirmations and meditation, and even then you're still not fixed? you're just a damaged thing in a high-maintenance container, always climbing uphill . . ." Blake had left the room, lonely and defeated in his pyjamas; when she'd tried to reach for him he'd moved away and said, "It's ok I'll just, self-soothe, or whatever." It had made her feel terrible.

The same thing, this overtaking by neurosis, the building craze, might be happening, Melissa sensed, to Hazel, too, or something similar. They could not hide from each other out here in the drizzly ether, nor could they evade the barrier emerging between them which compelled them to pretend that everything was fine. After the long walk with Ria, Hazel blamed her swollen eyes on the grasses. Admittedly the fire-pit was a public area, crowded with breakfast gatherers around Nila and Max's professional-level camping kitchenette as they disseminated fried eggs with a giant spatula. Everyone had the haggard look of sleeping in the wild, the rough skin, the creased clothes, the creases on the faces of the adults, the mud on the elbows of the children. Melissa was en route to the showers with a flat afro and her toilet bag.

"I didn't know you got hayfever. There's some antihistamines in the side pocket of my rucksack if you want some," she said.

"I'm all right thanks."

They came across one another at the kettle station, the washing up shelter. Hazel did not share with Melissa her solitary contemplations in the greenhouse while applying a taupe gloss gel to her toenails: it occurred to her, with a fleeting brightness, that she could put her mothering out there, into the world, in a pure form, unhampered and undrained by direct responsibility, like that situation earlier on when a squabble had broken out between Blake and Simon and she had diplomatically appeased them to perform reluctant apologies. She could guide and mash the young, from a serener distance, and the possibility had emerged that that could almost be enough. It was a relief, this shift in perspective. She had been keeping her barren sadness inside because it had grown too heavy to reveal without a

265

peeling away of necessary armour, and now it had lightened, was a little easier to carry.

In the evening they went with Ria and Clay to watch the sunset over the cow field as it burned red at the lowest point. Further away the land spread out, stretching green and sunflower yellow through the days, with intervals of violet and dense brown. The air was shimmering with rain. Clouds hung in white curls and moved slowly onward towards the east in shadowy dusks. Later, as they were falling asleep in their tents, a stream beneath a faint bridge could be heard sliding by, and the swish of traffic on the dark roads sounded higher, overhead, as if they were lying in the core of the earth. Waking in the small hours, Melissa thought of her father and wondered if he had made it, or was he drifting close by, unable to find the place, and that was his whispering in the trees and moaning in the wind on the far hills. She listened instead to the breathing of the children through the tent's nylon partition, the foundational wealth of that sound.

"It seems there's a lot to discuss," Debbie said. "The panics started not long after your father died, a few months? What was he like, your father? Was he good?"

"He was good at DIY."

"Oh, I've always wished Ruben was good at that. But it doesn't matter. I've come to accept it. And otherwise?"

"I wouldn't say he was good. There were times when he was nice—many, in fact. When he was being extra nice it was usually to make up for being bad. He called us names."

"What kind of names?"

"He used the word 'louse' a lot."

A wingless insect—Debbie checked the definition on her phone which was not switched off—that lives on other creatures, with a flat body, and short legs. Related to "lice," a person worthy of contempt.

"Anything else?"

"He used to say we'd amount to nothing and would end up as scrap."

"Hm. Nice. What did you used to think when he'd say such things? Did you believe him?"

"Not on the surface. Deep down maybe I did. I pitied him. He was so tormented, I didn't know whether he deserved to be so tormented and unhappy. But I also hated him. I think it's a kind of divine justice the way he died. We gave him more love than he deserved."

Debbie was thinking. She had an ability to throw a gaze both piercing and detached.

"Children," she said, "will believe the things we tell them, because they know nothing of the world. They are born with self-worth in the face of everything, which comes from the natural instinct to survive, but it can easily get knocked out of them. Children who have suffered and survived are often very self-possessed, as they've had to fight within to maintain their humanity. They'll often, not always, have a high moral sense, know right from wrong in an extreme way, they're compassionate. The myriad feelings you have towards your father point to this. When you've grown up being told you're a louse, a part of you will unavoidably feel like an insect. But you survived, didn't you? You didn't let him crush you."

A memory came to Melissa then, in the office just off the GP reception area on a Friday afternoon, of Cornelius lying on the kitchen floor one summer morning when it was time to go to school. It leaked into her awareness with a cold sliver of sweat and made another adjustment to her voice, which Debbie again noted. She wanted to know if lying on the kitchen floor was something he did very often and whether they'd had tiles or linoleum, tiles being more uncomfortable for sleeping.

"We had lino, I think. It was striped, I think. At first I thought he was dead."

"Yes?"

"My sister said we should get to school but I didn't want to go. I wanted to wait for him to wake up. He was lying on his front. All the downstairs of the house smelt of alcohol so I opened the windows. My mum was upstairs. I stayed down-stairs in the hallway waiting and waiting, and eventually I went—I went and waited, in the, in the cupboard."

"Ah. The one under the stairs, you mean?"

"Yeah."

"You waited there. How long for?"

"I don't remember."

"Was it all day?"

"I can't remember. No, I don't think so."

"And did he wake up, eventually?"

The fire was started early that evening to gather warmth as the air cooled after the end of the rains. Max made hot chocolate for the kids, Ria and Clay had sweet ciders and the adults wine, beers and chased spirits. Marshmallow sugar dipped into the flames, emerging black-skinned and brokenly moist, while Ria strummed her guitar joined by random drink-fuelled singing. Hazel, Melissa and Nila went on a swaying expedition to the bathrooms through the darkness with their torches, their voices loud, disturbing the dragonflies and long spiders glued to the corners of the cubicles. On the way back they missed the turning over the wooden bridge, being deep in conversation about the past, the present and the future, Nila was sharing a revelation, "All this striving and scrambling," she was saying, "where does it actually lead us to, ladies? We spend our whole lives wanting things and being told we should have them, driving ourselves round the bend, trying to get them—and then one day, right, you're walking through Marks & Spencer when you're, like, fifty, and you're fucking mash-up, and you realise it doesn't even *matter*. None of it. It don't mean piss. Hah! It's hilarious when you think about it. I wish I'd known sooner." Hazel said, "Oh, I always feel like that when I'm walking through Marks & Spencer." Then Melissa shared her own awakening, revealed to her by Debbie when they'd been talking about her desire to go to Peru and how it hadn't happened yet (Debbie had never been to Peru either but she'd been to Bolivia and Colombia), she had said: "It goes away, you know, all that fire and puff. All that tortured yearning. It evaporates. Puff." At the time, Melissa had been convinced that she was wrong, yearning is direction, is energy, but there was no denying the fact that she wanted to go to Peru less.

They found themselves in the woods on the track that led to the dens. Twigs were breaking beneath their feet, gossamer broke finely on their faces. "Look at this," Hazel said, "the kids made it. Shall we go inside? It's big enough." "We might break it," Melissa said. "No we won't. It's big enough." Hazel went in and sat down and Nila tried to squeeze in next to her but there wasn't enough room. "Come in, Lis, you're smaller, you'll fit." The cold panic feeling was stirring and slithering around Melissa's ankles. She could feel the shadow again, coming closer. She looked through the trees and saw a silver unmoving light. Hazel was holding out her hand, Nila giggled as she stumbled backwards in the leaves.

"I don't want to talk about this. I'd better stop talking about this."

"Why?" Debbie said.

"I don't remember."

"The body remembers."

"What?"

"Sometimes only the body remembers."

There was a silence.

"Are you aware of this, that you talk to me about your life as if you were talking about someone else?"

"Do I?"

"Yes, you do. There is something called disassociation, where

269

you extract yourself from experience. It's a way of carrying unwanted matter, where you posit yourself, subconsciously, outside reality. The effect can be a feeling of blankness, or alienation, or that you are not in your body. Does any of this sound applicable, or familiar to you?"

Another, longer silence. She was trying to see inside. Slowly she began to speak again.

"I heard him waking up."

"Ok . . ."

"He sounded like an animal, not a human being. I think he pulled the kitchen table down when he was struggling to get up because I remember it was on its side—there was a crash. I wanted to get out and run out of the house. I heard him moving around, getting closer . . . I could see parts of him, through the slats. He bent towards me . . . he, he was all crooked, and jerky . . ."

"What are you doing in there?" he said.

He seemed surprised, pleased and deranged.

"What's wrong?" said Hazel. "It's ok it's not going to break, it's strong."

"Let's go back to the fire now."

"Your hands are *freezing*."

"Please, I'm cold."

"My mum used to say we all have a den inside us," Nila said as they were leaving the clearing, "and it's situated below your ribs but above your belly button. It's always quiet there, even if everything else around you is stormy and chaotic. It's the one place we can all go to for peace."

Hazel said, "I like that. I'm gonna try and remember that one."

She had her arm wrapped tightly around Melissa to keep her warm and because there was a new unsettled silence in her that she recognised from when they were girls. Hazel had always walked a stubborn yellow road, covered with confetti and tinsel, so that she was a magnificently adorned vessel, any wreckage far below the surface. Her full bold being was an anchor that Melissa cherished. She held on to her. "Don't lose me," she said, and Hazel said back, "I could never lose you. Remember, I'll always see you in the dark."

They came in sight of the greenhouse and crossed the wooden bridge into the towering trees where the low fire was burning in the pit. They could hear voices and the guitar, beyond that night birds in the sylvan hush. "Hear that, Max?" Nila said, creeping up behind him to drape herself curtain-like over his shoulders, "Would you follow me to the ends of the earth, like Bruce would follow Hazel? She was just saying she's thinking of leaving London and moving to the pastures. I can't see that ever happening, though." "Me neither," said Ria. "The only place I'm moving to right now is my fisherman's sack," Max said, "I'm trashed," and he struggled up from the ditch of his chair to make a drunken weaving journey to a nylon sleep, where Min and Blake already harboured, to be followed a little later by Clay and Ria, "Night, Mummy," she said, her gentle hands brushing her coat. The three women were left, near midnight, watching the fire. Melissa said, "You're not really thinking of leaving, are you?" to which Hazel replied only, "Stranger things." She was like a landmark or a river scene. All the pictures she'd made: Brixton High Road in an aqua coat, Hoxton in ballet pumps and indigo denim.

"She ain't going nowhere," Nila said lighting up a Lambert. Hazel took one. They blew up at the visible stars, one of which miraculously shot across, causing amazement and a sense of cosmic witness.

"I've never seen one before," Hazel said. "It means something. It's like we were saying, where does it lead us, the yearning? Nothing matters. Everything evaporates. Puff. Why not just change your life completely?"

Here Melissa was reminded of Debbie's parting observation, just before the end of their last session. Having returned to the concept of the bad house, Melissa had said that the years had passed, so many years of her life had passed, and she had lived in different places and different rooms, yet in some way, she felt that she was still living in that house, her father's house, and it in turn was living inside her, directing her thoughts, actions and responses. It had her in its grip. Debbie had said to this, in her sagest moment of all, after a long pause for thought and glasses-cleaning: "You could be something else, you know, Melissa. Have you ever thought about that? You could be something different. You don't have to be the thing your suffering has deemed you to become. You have power over yourself. You have power."

She pushed the cupboard door open. The fire lifted and the smoke went high, concocting magic shapes, joining with the Lambert smoke dancing long-armed from the embers. In the distance music was playing, and a memory surfaced of a little girl, holding her dress in a semicircle before sailing down the stairs. The fire was caught in her hair. There was a hot orange sweep by her neck. And that was where the body remembered. His breath on her neck, in the dark of a summer day. It flashed through her and set her head on fire. She saw herself in the centre of the flames coming from the pit, the eyes staring, the hands burnt. There came a buzzing sound. It was difficult to keep standing. Something comes up, out of the deep, and flattens you. Her legs weakened beneath her and she slumped down onto the grass.

19

Larry prepared his swing. Feet parallel, forearms plunged, booty pert. The gold meridian sun was beating on the fairway. He fixed his aim, scanned his position one last time and hauled it back. "Each hole is unique," he said, "like the player is unique," then more quietly, "Claim the terrain." He swung it through with a pretty flex of the left hip and a bend of the right knee, holding high in the aftermath like a gladiator in his arena, the surrounding green crisp and clean against his ankle-length white slacks and matching smile. He had small, very white teeth, straightened by a mid-level practitioner after he had won his house in Littlehampton. His eyes were set close together amidst a knife-sharp, haughty, even wicked kind of handsomeness intensifying in middle-age. He wore a polo-shirt of soft brushed cotton, and the Puma socks.

"Yeah," he said, "find a joy, brother. That's what I'm talking about. Now you take the next one."

They continued walking, heading for the seventh putt. Michael did not yet understand the appeal of golf and was observing so far that if he was going to walk such a long way he'd rather it was through terrain more interesting. But he preferred to be here than by the pool, where the party was, the lunchtime public nudity, the volleyball and nineties swingbeat. "My game's always been basketball," he said.

"You play it much?"

"Watch mostly."

"Find a local club. Get involved, don't wait."

The note of goodtime sanctimony in Larry's demeanour was starting to grate on Michael though he was doing his best not to let it bother him. It was only day one. There were three more days after this one. It was all for Nicole, he told himself.

"You don't know what's around the corner. When I hit the big four-five I had to sit back and reassess. I said Larry, are you happy in your work? Are you spending your days in the way you want to spend your days or are you grafting for the man? Where do you want to put your energy, into what you need, or into what you want? Is your health and happiness *worthy* of your energy? That's what you have to ask yourself."

"I'd say I'm happy in my work. It's tiring, but it means something."

"So many people say that. It's tiring. It's tiring but important. It's tiring but it's changing the fucking world. We just accept being tired as if it's our duty, like we owe *them* something, instead of the other way round. So I realised, see, I don't wanna be tired anymore, man. I got my house. That day was holy, man. I streamlined the business so it's just the events, no more slinging music and promoting for other people. Got divorced the same year, remarried six months later."

"What's it like living in Littlehampton? You got kids?"

"One. Lives with her mum. Best way innit."

"Mm, not always." They arrived at the putt and Larry twisted his paunchy torso each way in a health-conscious loosening exercise, perusing the clubs, seemingly half listening. "I still wish my kids lived with both their parents, but it didn't work out in the end. Ideally I'd want them in one house, one family, not going back and forth like they do."

"Oh, no no no no no no no," Larry said. "You don't raise the

274

pickney with the same woman you have the second life with, no. Too much luggage, too much irateness under the bridge. Can you imagine if you'd raised your kids with Nicole? You think you'd be together today, a lightning queen like that? Nah my friend, you done it the right way round. Got her all to yourself. I bet she's even sweeter now than she was before—respect due. She's kept herself in top form, man. Need to treat that one *nice*."

This reference to Larry and Nicole's fleeting bygone entanglement was uncomfortable, they had strayed too far from small talk, and Larry was only good for small talk even if Michael did find his brand of it jarring. He resented the hint of ownership, or at least lasting guardianship, in the way he was referring to his wife, as if Larry had an instruction manual to her inner workings. He drew out a club sword-like in the calm Atlantic breeze and took position, concentrating on the ground. He said, cold and firm, loud enough to pierce him, "I treat her good."

"Course you do, bro. She wouldn't be with you if you didn't. Ok keep your fingers strong. Look out there. See the blue flag? Register . . . register it. Ok, it's yours."

Michael swung, enjoying the violence of the hard whack against the hard white ball. It went far off over the lime and shining undulations, he didn't know where, whether it went anywhere near the hole, only that it was the first time he'd hurled it clear off the tee without stubbing it or missing. Larry patted him on the back. "*Now* you're getting the drift. You're feeling it, aren't you, I can tell."

"I think I had the focus more that time. Did it land? I didn't see it."

"Far far. To the trees but still. Get the swing right and the rest will follow."

They headed onwards and as they walked Larry returned to the subject of Littlehampton, the small-town Sussex mode, the terrain he liked best at Brighton Head where he played with the same crew. They played twice, sometimes three times a week. It was respite from marriages as well as good exercise, better than you'd expect, and cheaper than having a yacht. "I don't even like sailing," he said, "but I like golf, and I like fishing as well. I like that feeling of waiting for the fish when it's hooked on and it can't get away, then all you have to do is roll it in, roll it in easy, slowly. That's my favourite part. The part when everything is inevitable, everything is yours. Know what I'm saying?"

At this point Michael didn't know whether Larry was talking about Nicole or the fish, but either way he hated him.

The Valentine Hotel was a six-minute drive from the golf course, down on the Portimao coast. Even at two in the afternoon the thump and buzz of the night scene shimmered from its aqua vista, from the big blue curving pool where there was always music playing, the straw parasols shading hangovers on Praia da Rocha beach, and the palm-lined stretch of strobe-lit tarmac leading to reception. Along this final strip of road the coach had come last night on its journey from Faro, full of enthusiastic partakers in this the fourth Algarve Soul Weekender, a gift from Larry to groovers who preferred classic sounds, the nostalgic ones who rebuffed all this over-complicated beat-annihilated trap and drill and what have you and just wanted to dance to a pure soul intention, music with some melody in it, like Blackstreet or Usher or The Fugees, the nineties and noughties tunes which would be played for them by DJs who still remembered handling vinyl and the twelve inch and even the Pass the Dutchie seven inch. There would also be some soulful house and reggae—DJ Gussey was flying in from Belgium, Axel Washington and Janet Kay were doing PAs, Coco D was coming from the USA along with Randy Gee and DJ Pappy from Jamaica. Nicole and Leona had bubbled with excitement in their seat two rows back from the driver, drinking portable rum and cokes while their hairstyles gleamed fresh, Nicole's reach for natural had been abandoned the previous month. She had new blonde highlights and a Mary J fringe. She would not be doing an appearance at this extravaganza, was here strictly for pleasure.

Michael expected to see her amid the poolside social when he was eventually allowed back into the complex without his wristband. He didn't want to wear the wristband, he felt it was infantilising and herd-like, but without it, they had told him at reception, he would not have access to any of the facilities—the spa the gym etc.—or the food or drinks. He would not be able to have the barbeque lunch, the smell of it adrift in the surrounding air, or any of the happy hour cocktails at the beach bar when he was parched from the rays. So he headed up to the hotel room to get it, passing the pool area on the way. He saw Leona in the lunch queue in sunglasses and sarong, standing with another woman who'd been sitting near them on the coach, he recognised her from one of Nicole's parties, long synthetic ponytail and orange lipstick. Larry, who did not need a wristband, was already lying back on a sunbed between someone's thighs, not his wife's because she wasn't here, and there were people playing volley in the water to the beat of Shalamar. He found Nicole coming down the white stone stairs from their floor adjusting the strap of her hip bag, wearing a red wraparound and a bikini highlighting the dunes of her shoulders. "Oh hi, how was golf?" she said as they hugged.

"Hm, different."

"I thought you'd like it," she said.

"No I did like it, the space, fresh air, all that. Where're you off to?"

"I'm gonna eat, you coming? Just needed to freshen up."

"I have to get my wristband, wait for me."

"I told you to just keep it on, Mic," she called as he dashed up the stairs.

The room was clean and sedate with the light from the Atlantic falling in and a balcony beyond the patio doors. He would have liked to stay there for a while, to sit out and read his book about the history of the Black Panther Party or lie on the albeit hard bed and relax, but she was waiting for him, so he grabbed the wristband, used a spritz and went back down into the action. Michael was perennially aware, during this twice-postponed trip, of the fact that these were not his people, these ravers and extroverts with their clubby clothes and melting mojitos. He was a different creature, the cerebral species that lived its life on levels and needed full use of the pitch and volume dials. He was equally aware, though, that it would be good for his current life if he could *appear* to feel one with this crowd, as Nicole was. For he could feel her creeping doubt of his rightness. The way she looked at him sometimes as if he were far away from her. He wanted to get rid of that look this weekend and return to Bromley gelled and fixed and fervent, he would be better, better for her, even if it meant a fractional slipping away of his gene type. What did it matter if he didn't read when he felt like reading because he should go and have public barbeque instead? Anyway he was hungry.

Eating coleslaw, he stood near the buffet table holding his plate, in his khakis and NBA top, while Nicole chatted nearby with some of Larry's friends. They were trying to persuade her to do a duet with Janet Kay and she was cheerfully refusing, he heard her say that she was branching out into musicals. "Ohhh," one said, "you're gonna be in the West End! Wah." "Well, not straight away," she said, "maybe one day." The other asked who she was here with and Nicole turned, searching for him, and drew Michael into the conversation, then there were two conversations, one about Janet Kay's back catalogue and the other

278

about the doomful cloud of Boris Johnson, the underlying permanence of British racism, and radio host Danny Baker's recent pictorial assault on the bi-racial royal baby.

"What gets me is he'll just turn up somewhere else in a couple of weeks, on some other station. These people will always have a platform."

"Yep. They're not seen as a threat, that's why, even though they're aiding far-right terrorism. If the media called it out for what it is they wouldn't be able to get away with this stuff," Michael said, glad to be talking to someone who seemed interested in the accumulative world crisis. He was a little man named Krish with a stud in his ear and a way of frowning at the ground while listening.

"Whereas if you or I called Kate's baby an elf, say, we'd get arrested for it," a machine-gunning laugh, and he illustrated, "Quick! Stop him! Catch that insulting person! Throw him in the dungeons!"

"You know. Watch that," Michael agreed.

Lunch was followed by sunbathing and preparations for raving. The venue for the night's entertainment was NoSoloÁgua on the beach strip. Nicole, Leona, Vida and Sandy swept down in their get-ups, noise-making heels and Aunt Jackie's Curl Custard: their fingers played music with their rings, they were sprayed, blushed, moisturised and puffed, their shinbones oiled, their bare heels smoothed with cracked heel cream, the collar bones and insides of wrists dabbed with Fenty and other favoured scents. The men came likewise groomed in fitted shirts, muscle-kissing vests and Levis. They had sculpted their facial hair, some had applied eyeliner, the hairlines were correct and socks clean in case of one-night stands. With the bars being open practically all day there was a general air of drunkenness running through the chlorinated waters, the sea waters, through the UV rays sweeping over the bay and up the white stairways with the doors and corridors leading off into private weather systems. The cocktails ran into afternoon siesta into dinner and beyond, Michael trod water along this cascading stream, past the lapping beach, across the plaza in his own evening shirt that he suspected might not be shiny enough, and into the nightclub where DJ Gussey was spinning the sounds: "Good gosh! Somebody call the cops!" he cried, which brought more people frisking and shimmying to the floor to the beat of Sean Paul and Blu Cantrell. "Nuff vibes go out to the lady like Nicole," he said among his shout-outs, "Oh boy this thing is gonna get *sweet*!"

At the mention of her name, Nicole raised her arms and did flicking motions with her fingers in some cliquey sorority code. When DJ Gussey played the We Are Family classic they were all hugging each other and swaying their flashy polyester torsos in a circular quartet. By this point Michael was sitting back at their table in the VIP section, scrolling his phone and drinking the prosecco on ice, after having spent episodes at the edge of the dancefloor feeling that he did not know how to enter their circle. Every so often Nicole had come to him and they would two-step together and smooch, the lights making fast red circles on their faces, but soon she would sashay back to her friends, sensing more fun in that direction, more communal sonic euphoria. Now she stepped to him again for more prosecco. "Come and dance, come and dance, you never dance!" she said. "I *was* dancing," he yelled over the music, "*we* were dancing!"

"Shout out to all my connoisseurs of music," said DJ Gussey. "I'm telling you man I'm telling you! Who sings this version?"

"Five minutes. Be ready for me yeah hon? Ohhhh no!" A raver friend pranced up and got Nicole in a headlock. She waved a flamboyant farewell as she was being moseyed away somewhere, to another grotto of amusement, leaving Michael to himself doubting she would be back in five minutes. He looked at some of the news about the proroguing of parliament in

London which made him fume, then to calm himself down he looked at old pictures of the kids, found some really old ones in his photo gallery from when Ria was a baby, another life, another time. With the bottle finished he went to the bar to replenish and ran into Krish next to the smoking area—the bar was outdoor, covered by a canopy, the VIP section leading directly onto the beach. From Praia da Rocha you could walk all the way to Praia da Vau and see the rock formations on the way, Krish said. He was thinking about moving out to Portugal soon, maybe Lisbon, "Have you been there?" Michael said he hadn't but would like to.

"You've got the right idea, man. I feel like doing the same thing."

"Yeah, lots of people are leaving our little island aren't they. Mass exodus. Let's see what happens when we start to need a visa to go to Marbella. It's gonna be carnage."

"The whole thing is lies," Michael burst out, the rage of the proroguing flooding back. "I still can't believe how many votes there were for this shit. Have you heard what they're trying to do now—stop parliament? Shut everything down so they can do what they want?"

"I know," Krish said. "Democracy is broken. It's done. The political process is now just a way of effacing and opposing identities for selfish gain, instead of actually achieving anything worthwhile for society." Again that funny machine-gun laugh. "I think we should all govern ourselves, take over. Revolution! Seize Downing Street!"

"We should, but we won't," Michael replied. "There's too much complacency. We always assume the left has a moral advantage and common sense will prevail, but it ain't like that. We have to keep naming and speaking it. One thing the right can never be accused of is laziness. We can't rely on goodness or decency as a default."

"And what's *really* scary," Krish said wide-eyed, "is that because the default is shifting, the left is being accused of radicalism and the right is becoming centre-field, the *perceived* centre-field. I saw a far-right news channel the other day being described in a headline as 'conservative,' as if conservatism and fascism are the same thing!"

From the edge of his vision Michael glimpsed the white-trousered, canvas-shoed figure of Larry lurching over. Krish returned to his earlier point about opposing identities, adding that the dwindling of nuance caused by ideological polarisation is a dangerous thing, and Larry with a bleached displeased smile said, "Man, what are you lot talking about? Don't tell me you're doing that lame thing where you come to the jam and stand outside talking politics. Come on now." He laughed, and Michael felt embarrassed.

"We're just chewing the fat," he said.

"Your wife's in there getting all kinds of love from the punters."

"What—she's on stage?"

"Nah, she'd probably fall off it."

Back inside the crowd swung this way and the crowd swung that way to the floor jerker that was It Takes Two. The dancing went on until four. Coco D did his set. So did Janet Kay. The music pumped and thumped over the parasols and beyond to the curling waves. While Nicole partied with her homies until the lights came on, Michael did, finally, retire to the sedate and peaceful room, and spent time on the balcony watching the ocean. He always thought of Melissa in front of an ocean, he couldn't help it, the brown arms turning, the black and white swimming costume, the fear that she'd left the world before he could know her. An understanding had settled between them since the time of Blake's operation last year, that they could be friends who had shared something special, the feelings they might still have for each other were acceptable, yet not to be enacted. He sent an under considered text, checking the kids were ok, and assumed she wouldn't get it until many hours later. She replied straight away with an under considered kiss at the end, the friendly kind, as in, here we both are in the stratosphere, bump. He replied back, also with the same kind of kiss, and they went back and forth for a bit without kisses because they would have been superfluous. He left the phone on the bed and had a blissful Jacuzzi bath, thinking Nicole might get back before he went to sleep, and when she didn't he went to sleep alone still in a state of blissful relaxation, in the background the fading sounds of people laughing and shouting above the music. At one point he thought he heard her voice specifically, calling over the others, but it could've been someone else. Everything quietened as darkness began to thin, the surface of the pool, the thick leaves of the beachside palms, the tassels of the parasols casting shifting shadows on the sand.

Redemptive hopes for the harmonising effect of the Algarve Soul Weekender came under attack two days later when Nicole and Michael had a fight, their first altercation that could correctly be termed "fight," about not one specific thing but a few, each one leading calamitously on from the last. It was the day after the boat trip to the Benagil Caves, which Nicole had weathered with no hint of a hangover from her 7 a.m.–1 p.m. post-rave crash, and Michael had weathered with stoic tolerance of Larry's gropy lady-circling proximity. The evening's events were calmer, some drinks and a comedy show, then in the morning Nicole got up early to go to the gym. When she went to the gym she mainly used the treadmill, working on her thighs. She would choose a machine, take her time getting settled— straightening the waistband of her leggings, placing her towel at hand, unravelling her earphones—until she was ready to programme in her speed and incline. She used an elasticated resistance band from Decathlon which she stepped into and pulled up her legs. She would start walking, using the pressure of the band against her thigh muscles to maximise the toning. She didn't ever run, only walked, for about thirty minutes. The effect was proven and considerable.

When she got back to the hotel room Michael was on the balcony talking on the phone and didn't see her head into the shower. Afterwards she sat on the bed in her complimentary bath robe going through her make-up bag to assemble the day's look, she wanted something gingerish, speckled, ivory under the outer brow. Soon he slid open the patio door, "Hey where you been?" She could tell he was distracted because he started walking up and down the room while she was talking. There was some media crisis going on at work. One of his staff had messed up. "Hon, I can't listen to what you're saying when you're walking up and down like that, can you stand still and speak?" "Sorry," he said, a word she felt he used too often, and it went on, the exact nature of the mess-up, the document that was sent in the wrong iteration and how it was all going to fall on him because he was the face and the top.

"But you're on holiday, darling. You can't be the face and the top right now. Just tell them you'll deal with it on Tuesday."

"I can't do that."

"Yes you can, you need to chill out. Why don't you go to the gym?"

This was not a reference to his lately waning musculature commitment, but it was a reference to his lately waning musculature commitment.

"I might go later," he said.

"I saw Larry in there." She chuckled softly. "He was telling me about you and Krish talking politics the other night outside the jam."

"Yeah what's funny about that?"

"Nothing, really, it's just, you know, not in the spirit of things."

"What am I supposed to talk about? Is there a chart of the things we're allowed to talk about on this Algarve Soul Weekender, along with the wristbands? Can you ask Larry to pass me a copy of it so I don't have any more of the wrong conversations?"

"Oh all right calm down. You didn't *have* to come with me, you know, if you really didn't want to."

And now he wanted to strongly disagree and say yes he did, yes he did have to come, but he couldn't say that because then she'd know he'd been faking any modicum of enthusiasm she had ever detected from him about the Algarve Soul Weekender and that would make it worse. The point was that they had to have a nice time, no matter what, at least until Tuesday, so that she wouldn't be led to hold this Weekender in her memory as something he had spoiled for her. On the TV opposite the bed a make-over show was transforming a girl into Jada Pinkett Smith by changing her clothes, her hair and her face, after which she gave cries of joy and gratitude at her new electric blue eyes, squealed when her two friends turned up, all of them crying and hugging at the success of this smothering of realness.

"Look, I'm sorry," he said again, irritating her again.

"Stop saying sorry."

"Sorry . . . Sorry. I do want to be here, ok?"

"But you don't seem to want to *do* anything. You don't wanna dance, you don't wanna swim, you don't wanna play. What *do* you want to do, Michael, apart from work? I mean look at where we *are*—look at the *ocean*, it's *glittering,* in the *sun,* and you're stressing out about work as usual. Don't you *want* to have a proper break?"

"Of *course* I do," he raised his voice, there were bags under his eyes and he looked greasy and exhausted. "D'you think I want all this stress on me all the time?" he said. "I wanna rest, I wanna go and live in a hut in the middle of nowhere and sleep and have sex and eat from the land. I want to get away from all the passwords, the barriers, from always having to break through something. Why do I always have to break through something, when people around me can just cruise along? They can fuck up all they want and they carry on cruising, while I'm here taking a hundred tonnes of flack because I'm the one society decided to shit on. And I'm not allowed to say anything about it, am I? No, I have to stay calm and not get angry, not go on the defensive. Do you realise how difficult it is to hold it down like that all the time? I've had enough. It's too much pressure."

"Exactly," she said rising. "So leave it at home." Nicole was taken aback by this tirade and preferred not to look at him, standing there in his dull tracksuit and socks, his shoulders rigid and drawn up, it was having a usurping effect on her. She gathered the items of make-up from the bed and moved them to the dressing table. He watched her looking through her clothes, wanting her to say something empathetic. She didn't. "Please don't come here and bring all your stress with us—I don't wanna think about any of that when I'm on holiday," she said with her hands full of beachwear and dangling straps, feeling herself getting more and more upset. "I'm trying to clear my head, ok? to just forget about everything and have some fun—and it feels like, it feels like, you're *dumping* on my *joy*. I mean, it's not like I don't support you or I'm not there for you—I show an interest in your work, I listen to you, I engage—but it's like, *you* don't move to *me*. *You* don't step into *my* space, the way *I* step into *your* space."

By this point Michael was over aware of her italics, her voice was higher, on the verge of tears, she was breathing deeply with the effort of saying something she had been keeping in for a long time. He went towards her, holding out his hand, careful not to say sorry. "Come," he said. "Come here." She took his hand reluctantly and let him lead her to the bed, where once seated he told her how bad it was for him to dump on her joy and how he hated that it felt like that. Had he done that to Melissa, he wondered? Had he dumped on her joy? He felt loathsome. "It's the job," he said. "I didn't realise how much it was gonna take out of me. It feels bigger than me."

"Just try not to think about it. Put it out of your head."

"It's so consuming, I want to keep Cordelia's vision in place and—"

"I know, let's not talk about it anymore."

"Sorry."

"Look, just, just don't, talk—don't talk just, hold me. It's all right."

Temporarily, it was all right, pressed together in the sunlight with the air between them clearer and laced by a sexy honesty. They could say anything they wanted, any extra thought they wanted to add, like promising to be open to one another not closed, to consider the other's feelings more, "And I'm not going to apologise anymore, Michael, when I'm not sorry for something," she said pulling away for a moment. "Too much sorrying is bad for self-esteem."

"You don't need to apologise."

"I know."

"Are you all right, generally I mean?"

"Yeah, I'm ok."

"Are you worried about work?"

"Not really. Well, I'm trying not to be."

"I'm here if you wanna talk."

She hesitated. "No, I'm gonna get changed," but remained seated, then sighed deeply before deciding to confide in him. "I keep thinking I shouldn't have accepted the panto. It's the end of the line, like you said. It's like doing *Big Brother*. It means it's over, doesn't it?"

"Not necessarily," he said, employing delicacy in this delicate moment.

"That's not what you said before. Let's be honest, Rob shouldn't even be trying to get me work in that area. I've never told him I want to work in that area."

"Maybe he's just trying to get you something. Instead of nothing."

Nicole looked down at the bikini straps curling over her hands like worms, garish relics of yesterday's glory. They belonged to another sphere, perhaps one she no longer had access to. She felt like a woman at the end of her beauty. The world did not see her anymore. Something, or someone, was sailing out of her. She said with uncharacteristic gloom, "Maybe I am nothing. I'm practically invisible at this stage." And that was enough for her, expressing this hideous bleak thought. It was enough to just sit there with it with her husband's arms around her and the knowledge that he would love her anyway, when everyone had forgotten her name and her beauty. If only he hadn't said what he said next.

"You're not invisible. People still see you. Whether you do panto or not, you've still got that position where you're established. They know your name, your voice."

Which did not solve the issue of the ending of beauty and women's enslavement to its fascism. His habitual return to the positive default flustered her. It took the comfort away.

"Yes I know that," she said, shrugging his arm off her. "I was just telling you. I was expressing myself. You don't have to solve it, ok? It's not even really a problem. I wasn't asking for your help. I'm just telling you something. Why do you think you have to make it better?"

Michael was becoming re-flustered. "I'm listening to you, that's all. I was responding to what you said?"

"No but you're *not* listening. You're doing—not being. God, I can understand where that word 'dickhead' comes from. Men always seem to approach everything from one place, the place of intervention and conquer. It's so annoying."

"Did you just call me a dickhead?"

"No! I'm just stating a fact."

"So you are calling me a dickhead."

"I'm not."

"You just did."

"That's not what I meant! Oh, look, forget it. Forget it," she was moving around, bundling up clothes, make-up, beach items, "I was just thinking aloud and you start throwing your weight around in my thinking, and now I'm just fucking vex."

Michael was standing watching her with his hands at his sides, baffled. "I don't understand what's happening here. I don't understand what you want."

"Nothing. I don't want anything."

"I was *trying* to help."

"Oh, go away!" she said, and went into the bathroom, slamming the door behind her.

Following this there was a remote period of avoidance and inner searching in which Michael tried to work out what had gone wrong and realign himself on the hopeful redemptive path. While Nicole went to the beach to sunbathe, he did the long coastal walk to Praia da Vau alone and was calmed by the smooth grey curvature of the rock formations, their constancy and antiquity in the face of water and weather. That was marriage, a firm location, immovable at its foundation yet evolving, the way the rocks had changed colour with the passing of the centuries. He and Nicole may not always understand each other, but they were rooted in their vows and were a refuge from the storms. He returned to the hotel invigorated by this alchemical reminder of their bond, determined anew to make their time together a success and not upset her or sit on joy. He remained determined even at the sight of Larry's arm flopped around her on their approach to the bar for a post-meridian cocktail as Michael arrived on the beach, looking for her. Behind them the sea was an aqua dream, frills of waves combed by August breeze. Larry was wearing a horrible string vest that gave Michael confidence. He claimed her, his lovely wife, and asked her would she like to walk with him along the shore and maybe sit down in the water and let the waves lap around them. She would. She herself was calm. The sun, plummeting into her skin, had heated away the ice, and she liked the sharpened manliness of his behaviour combined with the tenderness in his beautiful eyes.

For the rest of the day they did everything together, they sat by the pool, they played pool, had more cocktails, queued up together in the banqueting hall at dinner, becoming apprised of the incredible sensuality that a fight, once passed over, can bring to the health of the couple. He wanted to take off her clothes. She wanted to slam him down on his back and mouth him centrally, then sit on him and take joy. And the waiting, the waiting and watching, waiting while she licked the last spoonful of tiramisu from her dessert bowl, watching as he asked at reception about breakfast room service with such manly command and style, taking her hand then and leading her up the stairs, waiting for her to emerge from the bathroom, her outer clothes already removed, and by the time they touched each other there was such a fury of desire between them that their bodies were almost not enough, in kissing her he wanted to kiss everything at once, in working her hands she wanted more hands, more breath, they were running out of breath. But something happened. It was connected in some way to her earlier calling of him a dickhead and the line that had been crossed even though, as he (kind of) accepted, she hadn't technically called him one. It impinged nevertheless, floated within him that awful confusing moment, and once apparent it became impossible to quash, affecting his ability to maintain the solidity of his love. Less than half a minute into her rhythm, he softened, with a slow yet definite truth, filling her with a raging shock of frustration that must however be tempered with sensitivity, she couldn't help but ask, "huh, what's wrong?," to which his forced, confounded reply was, "nothing, it's cool." Was it cool? she thought. For whom was it cool? Then he said, "sorry," and she in turn was confounded, by the combination of the requirement for this word at this time, her hatred of it coming from his lips, and its resulting inadequacy, like the boy who cried wolf. She sank and laid her breasts over his breastplate, and when this felt suddenly, tragically, over intimate, slid onto her side, their juices unmet, their peaks unreached.

In the middle of the night he had a dream. It was about Melissa and the sea. He was standing at the shore and she had swum out and they were the only people left in the world. He waited and waited, wishing for her warmth next to him in the loneliness. Come back, he called when the sea did not deliver her. He called louder, Come back, come back.

"What?" Nicole said, looking over at him in the semi-dark in her night-slip and satin bonnet.

"Hm?" he murmured; his eyes opened, closed again.

"You just said, 'Come back.'"

"Hm, did I?"

"Yeah. You did."

"Hm," a sigh, with a little grumbling noise at the end of it, and he plunged back to sleep, into profound blankness, while Nicole continued to regard his long body in the gloom, lying on its front with the feet off the end of the bed, like a dead giant. A flicker of light to the left of her vision made her turn her head to his bedside table. The culprit: his phone, on silent but active, the action being a message from Melissa with a kiss at the end of it.

She didn't get to read the whole thing clearly before the notification timed out, but all she needed to see was that felonious x in this solitary, covert hour of the night.

The next morning Michael assumed a cheerful demeanour above his anxiety about the failure of his genitals and was hopeful that the last day of the Algarve Soul Weekender would at least be pleasant. She seemed distant, which he anxiously put down to the non-performance. He went to the gym (Google said exercise was crucial). He played some music and during Beyoncé's Love on Top, when he commented, "She changes octaves four times in that song," she merely glanced up at the speaker, disinterested, and he worried he'd accidentally rubbed salt into her panto wound. It was a day full of worry. Leona and Nicole talking seriously on a sunbed. Larry and Nicole in the pool together behaving like an item, which bothered him more today than yesterday because he had lost some of yesterday's determination, this holiday was just not going to be a marital highpoint for them. "What are you doing?" he asked her when she came out of the pool. He felt like a schmuck, sitting there under a parasol waiting for her to stop shaming him. "What do you mean what am I doing?" she said. "With Larry." "Larry? Nothing. What are you doing?" He was confused again. "Is there something going on here that I've missed?" "No. Is there something going on that *I've* missed?" It went on like this, she kept saying "he's *Larry*, he's just *Larry*, he's harmless," until Larry himself came up and flopped his arm on her making him want to hit him. "Hey big man," he had the audacity to say. "Me and Larry go back a long way, don't we," Nicole said gazing up at him. "He discovered me." "I didn't discover you, darlin', I just got you connected. The rest was plain sailing." "Would you mind taking your arm off my wife for a minute, Larry?" Michael said. He obliged, raising his hands in the air and walking backwards to the rim of the pool, then did a clownish show of falling in as if he hadn't known it was there, which made Nicole laugh.

The thing that was going on that Michael didn't know about lurked in their midst through the evening and came to a head during a second, deeper fight which began when they were getting ready for dinner. Nicole had saved her most spectacular outfit for the last night, a gold fishtail dress with camisole straps, a Topshop choker, lace-up heels, and Michael said she did look spectacular, though she was wearing too much make-up which he made sure not to mention. He had learnt through Nicole what a primer and contour were without understanding what they were, only that you have to let the layers of application set, after applying mist, for moisture, then powder, for matting, one on top of the other. Her layers and her eyelashes were taking over her face and the clouds were taking over the dusk, advancing with the wind in the waves so that the temperature felt cooler. As he was putting on his jacket, Nicole mentioned that they'd be sitting with Leona and Larry at dinner and he couldn't hide his disappointment. "There was me thinking I'd have you all to myself, finally."

"You had me to yourself last night."

"I know"—was that a dig?—"it's just, you know," he shrugged. "Is Krish gonna be there?"

"No, why would he be?"

"I like Krish, he's interesting. He's got a lot to say."

"Well, you can sit with Krish if you like."

Michael was tired by now of the thing he didn't know about and the way it was making her behave so curtly towards him, he was running low on patience and looking forward to going home. "Don't worry about it," he said. "I'll just hang with you lot and try not to talk about anything that means anything like politics or the unequal distribution of wealth or any of that stuff." As soon as he said it he wished he hadn't.

"Oh why does everything have to *mean* something?" she cried. "And what do you *mean* by that anyway? Isn't there ever a time when you want to just let go of the world and all its problems?"

"I was joking, Nic."

"No you weren't, you *weren't* joking. You've been looking down your nose the whole weekend, acting like this snooty intellectual type who's too sophisticated to descend to our level, like we're beneath you."

"No no no—"

"You have. You think you're the only one who knows what's going on and has something important to say about it. Apart from Krish, that is. We didn't come here to have a summit. Just because people wanna chill out and have a good time it doesn't mean they don't pay attention to issues."

"Ok Nic."

"Like I know you think I don't register things, but I do. When Choice FM got swallowed up by Capital Radio like that and they started calling it Capital Xtra? You think I don't care about that? Why not keep calling it Choice? They *stole* it. They appropriated it. When I'm looking to play Capital Xtra now on my phone I still search for Choice—there's a void there. Anyway I'm just using that as an example. It pisses me off how you always assume you know more than everyone else, whether it's about politics or race or whatever. I *live* that stuff, remember? It affects me every day. Do you think I don't realise that?"

"Nic, let's go to dinner."

"*Wait.* I want to talk about this now. The other day when we were having that conversation about Obama. And you were being all negative as usual, not letting me say positive things about him, going on about the drones—see, there you go again. Don't smirk at me like that."

"We are allowed to say nice things about Obama, but he did allow mass drone killings in Pakistan and other places and he did fail on his promises to end the war in Afghanistan and close Guantánamo Bay. He wasn't a messiah. It's fine if you like him. I like him too. I'd rather have him than Boris any day."

"I quite like Boris, actually, in a way."

Michael swung round, he had turned to get his wallet off the bedside. "*What*?"

"I didn't say I'd vote for him. I just think he has some qualities."

"You *like* Boris? Qualities?"

"And what if I did vote for him? Would that make me a traitor? Are all of us supposed to do and think the same? If I wanted to vote Tory I would."

"I bet Larry votes Tory."

"Larry again."

"Yes. Larry who won a fucking house and plays golf and drives a—I don't know what he drives. I don't care what he drives."

"What do you have against Larry?"

"Oh, apart from the fact that he can't keep his hands off you right in front of my face? What do you *see* in him? He's so *fake*. He doesn't have a genuine bone in his body. He's selfish and empty. He's one of those people who accepts the limits of their allowance at humanness and adjusts themselves around it. They're like sheep, compliant. They try and dodge the fight by pretending it's not there, that they're already complete. And they think they can do that with money. They think if they acquire enough of it it will place them beyond everything, beyond reproach, community, everything. I despise people like that. How can you have any respect for someone like that?"

"I'm getting out of here," Nicole said. She had bent to adjust her shoe, leaning on the door handle. Her gold purse dropped to the floor and she picked it up. "You're going to be full of bitterness, you know that? You know what you sound like? You sound like one of those old people complaining about the price of inflation. You know that scene at the beginning of the Thatcher biopic where she goes to buy a pint of milk and can't believe it's 40p, then goes home to complain to Denis about it? That's what you remind me of."

"Another Tory reference," he said coldly.

"I'm gonna go have fun with my mates. You can do what you want. You can stay here and text your ex, I don't give a shit. I'm going to *take* my joy, and *you* are not going to *shit* on it, *anymore,* you hear me? You're a coward, Michael. You never really left her. You just thought you did."

As she tore open the door, it dawned on Michael that the innocent late-night texting with Melissa might be at the root of her hostility. Had she been checking his phone? "Have you been checking my phone?" he said, but she was gone. He went after her and side-skipped down the stairs trying to keep pace, "If you've been checking my phone you shouldn't be, first of all. And if this is about me texting Melissa—which is allowed, by the way, we're friends—isn't it just a little bit hypocritical of you to be acting like this?"

"Friends don't chat in the middle of the night. Friends don't call each other's names in their asleep."

"I was just seeing if the kids were ok! Aren't I—"

They were walking through the hexagonal arrangement of palm trees between the rooms and the restaurant and it accentuated her tallness. She stopped to face him.

"Listen. I didn't want to go into this before we got back home because I didn't want it to ruin my time, but it's already ruined, almost, so I might as well just say it." She gathered herself and straightened, focusing in on him for the announcement of her ultimate grievance. "There are three of us here, in this marriage," she said. "You, me, and her. Same as Diana, Charles and Camilla. It's been like that from the beginning. I can *see* the way you love her. I *see* it. She's here, the ghost between us, and that's why it's never going to work. So I think you should just, go back to her, if she'll have you. You can talk about issues together. You can give her lectures on democracy and economic exploitation. That's all I'll say for now. I don't want another mention of it while we're here, ok? I'm gonna find my mates. Don't wait up."

Then she walked off. He was too stunned to go after her, by the frightening resolve in her voice and by the possibility that he had lost her, their foundation had crumbled. He couldn't bear the thought of another love crumbling. No it could not happen. It must not happen. And with this opposing resolve in mind, yet drained of the energy to act on it, he wandered away, found a beer at one of the bars along the strip, feeling a grim misanthropy to everyone he came across, the groups of people lounging in the booths, the happy couples strolling along the promenade and the ravers heading to the dancefloors for more hours of pulsing music that he would have no part in, nor the raucous midnight pool party, nor the impromptu dawn breakfast on the beach. He sloped away onto the shadowy sand and sat down on the end of a sunbed with his head hanging, one hand on the back of his neck. He was so tired and dismayed. All his hopes for the weekend were crushed. They would not be returning to London gelled or fixed or bonded. They would not even be speaking to each another. The whole thing was a disaster.

20

Adel did not know how old her mother was. Nobody knew for sure. Maybe seventy-six, maybe seventy-four. The date of birth on her passport was notional; her actual birth date was a lost memory, measured of the village crops and unrecorded. But the birthday they were celebrating was in official terms her seventy-fifth, this frosty Saturday in early December, with Storm Dennis coming across from the north and the smoke from the cars drifting up from lines of traffic on the city roads. And they were not going to celebrate in her parlour as usual. Instead Carol had booked a Nigerian restaurant in Harrow Road which had taken some persuading, Alice not believing in the concept of restaurants. Why pay to eat food in another building when you can cook it for yourself? Who cooked the food? Did they do it properly? Where did they buy the ingredients? Did they not just buy in Tesco and cook it wrong way then charge you more? You throw away your money. Carol had explained about atmosphere and occasion and pointed out the restaurant's conscientious vegan options, adding simply, "We want to take you out for a change."

Are you picking up Mum? she messaged Adel at three, I'm coming by tube so can't. Adel told her Melissa was picking her up on her way from the south, which was followed by a curt Ok, so she added that she had to wait for Lauren and Warren to

298

meet her at home first and was currently out (she was in Watford shopping centre looking for a gift). Adel sometimes thought that Carol's refusal to own a car was a sneaky way of shirking her responsibilities. She was always ready to order people around in her righteous ecologising tone, but when it came to carrying out concrete tasks herself her load was relatively light, she glided on convenience, could not do pick-ups, couldn't cover that dentist appointment or this MRI scan because she had glued herself to a building. All she had managed to do for their mother over the past two and a half years was rekindle a senseless yearning for a house that would never be finished, a dream that should stay in the mind, a life that could not be retrieved. The more Adel thought about it, this idea of the Benin death, the last horizon on the motherland, the more ridiculous it seemed. She and Carol had argued about it again on the phone last month and the air had not cooled. Why did she have to insist on complicating things? Why couldn't she just accept, and therefore help their mother accept, the most practical, manageable option for everyone? She was a boat-rocker, a troublemaker, a lover of drama. Adel did not like drama.

She ambled along the scarf aisle of TK Maxx trying to remember what she had bought for Alice last year, probably a scarf. She bought her scarves, perfume, gloves, another scarf. If she asked her what she wanted she would say nothing, I don't need anything, I not going anywhere, but still they bought her scarves, things, the gifts amassed, at times Alice would give one of them something that had been given to her having forgotten it was a gift, and in this way a wagon-crowd of objects went back and forth between sideboards, dressing tables, cupboards and accessory drawers. But here was a nice purple one with leopard print. She could see Alice wearing it with her short brown wig and a cardigan, and feeling the material with her fingertips she saw that it was soft enough yet warm, so she gathered it up and went to find wrapping paper, the corners of her mouth turning downwards and stiffening as often happened when she was buying something for her mother. The obligation she felt, a shaft of resentment. It had been the same with Cornelius. She was sure they did not deserve her sweet gestures and sacrifices, the way she deserved them from her own children.

Warren was almost thirty now and he remembered his childhood clearly. They would talk about it, particular memories and pictures. He remembered the time he broke Alice's vase when he was four and she asked him why he'd broken it and he had felt dismayed, and he remembered the day at the West Midland Safari Park when the giraffe was standing in the road. Adel, on the other hand, had only disjointed recollections of her childhood, short lines of movement, there were no yesterdays or tomorrows in her memories, no sequence of time. Warren, for example, remembered the day after the giraffe: we drove home in a thunderstorm, it had been hot for days and the sky opened, in the morning we ate crumpets and jam, there were towels hanging over the doors, everything damp. He had told her this sitting across from her in the visiting room at the young offenders institute in Feltham when he was nineteen. It was a strange place to talk about things like that, but during that time they'd talked more than ever, perhaps because he had all that time to think. She had told him that she was lonely when she was young, that her sisters were very close, and while her loneliness was a cage their closeness made them free.

Whenever Adel was in a shop, considering what to buy, whether to buy it, walking to the cash desks, she was excessively aware of the possibility of theft. It would be possible for her, with this purple leopard print scarf, to make her silent way to the door, to remove the security tag, slip the thing into her bag and go home with it. She wanted to do it, to test the boundary, put herself there where he had been and see what he had felt like. She had always had a desire to feel exactly what her children felt, to inhabit them, to feel it for them so that she could be with them if it hurt. When Warren had been served six months for aiding and abetting a robbery, she had wanted to be right inside his ribs and his legs and his shoulders so that they could carry his fear together. If he behaved well he might get out sooner, they'd said. He'd served four months. She was there when he came out, a new age in his face despite the sunny disposition, a scar underneath his right eye. There he was, her boy. Coming out of the bars, the future unknown.

She didn't tell anyone. It is surprisingly easy in a city to pretend someone is here when they are not. Luckily the term did not touch a Christmas, so at Clay's fifth birthday party Warren was away with friends, at Easter he was working, and so on. If people asked her how is your son, she would say he was fine and give few details. It was not quite shame that made the secret. It was protection, for him; for her, a refusal of judgement, a drawing in. They would not be able to say—her mother and her sisters, the world—that she had raised him drastically, rocked him badly or let him stray. No one would put him into another cage. When he was free he would be free of the weight of their perception. It was a glitch, a moment of bad judgement, a stumbling into the wrong company, that was all. He was a good child, from whom too little was expected and too much was punitive.

She gave him some money to help him out, and when whatever she could spare ran out she used credit cards and asked her father for help. Jobs did not come easily now that he had a criminal record. He went from one brief stint to another, couldn't seem to settle on any one thing, he needed a place of his own, clothes, leisure money. She gave him everything she could, running herself into debt, so determined was she that he surpass this hurdle. "You're in a fix," she'd say, "A fix can be fixed," and she would laugh to make him feel light. She knew that eventually she would have to let him fall and build upwards by himself, but your children always need you, she had come to realise, no matter how old they are, be it money, or some advice, or shelter, or a lift to Harrow Road. She reached the front of the queue and put the scarf and giftwrap on the counter. The cashier was a young man like Warren and he asked her if she wanted a 10p carrier bag. She said yes, but that she wanted the receipt in her hand not in the bag, so that she could put it straight into her wallet instead of having to fish around in the bag to find it first, which she felt was a lazy reduction in quality of service in the retail industry and completely unnecessary, "I mean," she said, "is it really that much trouble for you to just pass it to me?" The cashier sighed under his breath, relegating her to the difficult customer category. Then he made the mistake of asking for her email address. "No you cannot have my email address," Adel said. "You don't need my email address. Why would I give you my email address? It's invasion of privacy. All you're going to do with it is send me junk. And don't try and tell me you need my email address so that you can send me an electronic receipt. I don't want an electronic receipt. I want a hardcopy receipt, in my hand, to put in my wallet, thank you very much. I know my rights. I know how this all works." At which she strode away with her paid-for goods, returning her wallet to her handbag, glad to have got that particular grievance off her chest, while the boy looked after her shaking his head.

"See that man over there?" Melissa said driving through Vauxhall in the Vauxhall. She was referring to the person bending down on the pavement with their head between their knees and one arm stuck bent in the sleeve of his jacket. He jerked back upright, scuttled forwards a few paces and bent down again. "That is what happens to you when you take drugs. Ok?"

The children looked, studied this sad parade of dishevelment. "Ok," they said.

And while they were on the subject of future avoidance of self-annihilating vices, she said to Blake especially, as at ten he was of gang-recruiting age, "If someone comes and asks you to do something for them in exchange for sweets or money, like take this package to that person or that place, you just walk away, all right?"

"What if they say I'll kill you if you don't do it?" he said.

Melissa thought about this.

"Run."

"What if they have really good aim?"

"Dodge," said Ria, and carried on eating, they were having yogurt bars in the backseat.

Blake pictured himself dodging a flying bullet administered by a sweet-giving gangster and decided that the next time they were in Toys R Us he would like to get a bow and arrow. But then he remembered the recent closing down of Toys R Us and felt sorrow. Where had all those toys gone? Why had they gone? What did "administration" even mean? All that space, given to ham and rice and vegetables. Aldi! What a waste.

"And another thing," Melissa said over the Thames, "you know if you wear your trousers like that with the waistband down over your buttocks it won't look the same on you as it does on Stormzy?"

"Yeah. You don't have enough bum," Ria said laughing.

"I've seen people wearing them like that when they don't have a bum."

"Technically you don't need one."

This discussion continued along Bayswater onwards through Notting Hill. They became solemn by the high green Grenfell heart, looming over Latimer Road, the imagined sound of the flames in the air, the outlines of the ghosts of the flames lashed with green. It put a cry in the sky. There was a disgrace in the tourist slant of Ladbroke Grove. "We must never forget what happened here," Melissa said. They went over the junction, up the carnival way. "It was a massacre. All those people *died*. Families, whole families, obliterated. And there's still no justice. We can't forget them." The heart stayed in sight through the gaps between other towers and the lesser rooftops, until it receded into the invisible distance.

They were dressed in African Dutch wax: Ria androgynous in a red and black caftan and jeans, Blake in an agbada, Melissa in a dress she'd bought from Deptford Market last year. Alice was pleased at the sight of them in traditional fashions, that they all matched, she in her long wrapper and top, covered with necklaces, she had put on one after another, about five of them in total, so rarely did she wear them she thought they needed some use. In the parlour there were gifts from the church. A card from Winifred said, "Dear Sis, may God bless you always and make every birthday the happiest of days," a joint one from Sisters Katherine and Beatrice, "For Alice, birthday greetings from the family of our Lord," as for the gifts, she had only opened a few of them so far, an ornamental olive oil and balsamic vinegar duo, a giant Toblerone and a luxury bathing set. They were left on the dining table by the window that looked out on the quiet bend of the church. Winifred had been away for the past two Sundays. She was back in St. Vincent staying in the finished house, on a trial basis, she had said.

"You look nice, Nena," Blake commented as they were walking her to the car. They were almost the same height. Her years were pulling her down towards the ground, that's what it seemed like to him, that when you are growing up you are pulled away from the ground into the air and the weather, to take part in everything, and when you are growing old you are sucked back in to the beginning, like a jack in the box but slowly.

"Where would you like to sit?" said Ria, "in the back or in the front?"

"In back," she said, and let sink her little frame crookedly behind the driver's seat. Blake sat next to her. She asked him if his mother was putting vapour rub on his chest every night to make sure it heal properly, to which he knew to answer yes.

"I like your hair," he said.

"Thank you," she touched her head and smiled. "Carol bought it."

"It makes you look younger. How old *are* you, Nena?"

She replied to this with laughter, pointing in front of her at Melissa whom she still regularly chastised for her expanding grey streaks. "I keep on reminding her about that dye you buy in shop. She doesn't listen."

"A woman's power is her age," Melissa said, and drove on through the urban definition to navigate the traffic-clogged advance into Harrow Road.

Through the dusty window of Naija Taste on the dusty high street, beneath the banner featuring pictures of its food, Carol could be seen standing at the counter near the entrance to the kitchen in conversation with a member of staff. Her own grey crown, a hive of electric silver, was achieved by wrapping the locks in a binding swirl on top, which she had offset with a blue and white dress fabric, Tibetan earrings, glittered turquoise eye shadow and tens of bangles. There was no one else in the restaurant because most of its business was takeaway, hence the row of buffet trays next to the till, so she had been invited when she'd arrived to take any of the tables along the glowy wood-panelled walls lined with vinyl seating. Alice would sit in the middle, of course. Three of the tables had been pushed together and serving utensils lain out. She was explaining to the owner that the vegan egusi she had ordered must be completely free of animal extract, not even a spec of crayfish must be in it, and the puff puff should be fried in non-meated oil. She had made the order in advance over the phone and knew exactly what everyone was having.

On their approach along the high street past the nail salon and the betting shop and the internet café, Melissa's party ran into Clay who was coming from his Saturday job. He fell in step with Ria and Blake, in his parka and woolly hat, telling them about his weird journey on the bus from Victoria, and pulled open the door when he saw his mother walking towards it from within, with bountiful authority, as if she owned the place. "You're only ten minutes late," she said, "impressive. How was the traffic?" Melissa hugged her amidst the scramble of familial hugging and said it was always Park Lane that did it, then Carol took Alice's coat, she was looking around her, up into people's faces, dwarfed by this unusual foray into the catering experience. Blake's was the nearest back to rub in comfort and co-existence so she rubbed that, until she was led to her central seat which took time to take, requiring her to slide along the upholstery to reach it. Discourse followed on where everyone else should sit, and it was decided eventually that second generation be at one end and third at the other, it was more fun for them that way.

"Your hair's getting so long," Carol said to Melissa when they were seated opposite each other, Carol next to Alice.

"I know. I've been putting Jamaican black castor oil in it with peppermint and rosemary essential oils, and a little bit of lemongrass."

"That make it grow?"

"Yeah."

"You give me some."

"Me too."

"Ok, we'll do some mixes for Christmas. Ria knows how to do it."

"How's school, Ria?"

"It's good. I've started my A levels."

"In what?"

"Chemistry, music and English Language."

"Hm, interesting combination. What's your favourite?" Carol asked.

"I think music. But I really like chemistry as well."

The owner came out of the kitchen in her blue plastic hat and red lipstick and asked about the drinks situation, should she bring out wine now? They had reserved two bottles; soft drinks would be ordered as and when. "Is there Fanta?" asked Blake, hankering for that wondrous fizzy of Nigeria. They ordered five of them and Carol requested one of the bottles of wine to have while they were waiting for the others, followed by one portion of the puff puff as people were getting hungry. "I knew Adel would be late," she said. "Why can't she just be on time for once? She's always late when there's something important happening." When she finally arrived, flush-cheeked and harried, trailing behind a gust of wintry air, Carol could not hold down her pique. "Why are you late? You were supposed to be here at five thirty. And where's Lauren?"

"She can't make it now. She said to say sorry everyone but she had to go and see about a friend. I dropped her there first. Do you know how far it is to drive all this way from Bushey? Then we got stuck in Harlesden on that stupid one-way system?"

"What d'you mean Lauren can't make it? How can she not make it?"

"It's *ok,* Aunty, *we're* here—everyone's here!" Warren went around doing the familial embracing, after hugging Alice vigorously he added a birthday card to her pile of presents, another mound waiting for unwrapping. He took a seat on the third generation end and grabbed Blake's forehead with its unstraight edges, touched Clay's shoulder, took off his Superdry coat. "Nena, aren't you going to open them?" Ria said, referring to the gifts. Slowly, at her pace, Alice started to inspect the pile, hovering over an object with her hand, an expression on her face suggesting harassment and obligation. None of these things were relevant or necessary, the red beaded gloves from Clay, the salad spoons from Carol who had become increasingly practical in her gift choices, everything must have a utilitarian stamp. "Do you like it?" Adel said as Alice unfolded the scarf, "Beautiful," was her routine response, while Adel looked on from her end of the table with a tense and dutiful smile. The largest object was from Melissa and the children, a musical instrument which she and Ria had come upon while shopping for a capo, and the reason for Ria's eagerness for the unwrapping. It was pink. It came in a large, quadrilateral-shaped box. "What is this?" Alice asked, when she had finally managed to open it amidst all the wrapping paper and tableware spread out before her.

"It's a ukulele!" said Ria. "It's almost the same colour as your living room. Do you like it? You could play it in the evenings or when you're bored. Do you like it?"

Alice took a longer look at it. She strummed it, releasing a stringy echo. Under her breath she started to hum one of her church hymns, her head tipped back and her glasses reflecting the ceiling lights. She was imagining that she was sitting in her parlour in Benin and she was singing to the Lord near the end of her life while the world outside was peaceful and indifferent. "Ah, she likes it!" said Melissa. "It suits you, doesn't it Ria?"

"Yeah, it's just the right size, nice and small."

"You can take it with you when you go home," Carol suggested. At this Adel raised her eyes and pursed her lips with the effort to hold in her pique.

"I wish you'd stop going on about that all the time, Carol, will you just drop it for once?" she snapped.

"What? Why?" Carol said, surprised. "What d'you mean 'going on about it'? I'm not always going on about it."

"Yes you are. And the more you go on about it the more unhelpful you're being."

"Why is it unhelpful? *You're* the one who's unhelpful, not *me. I'm* the one who's been trying to get things done all this time!"

"Exactly. And it's still not done. It's never going to be done. It's just wasted energy, wasted time and money."

"Ok look, we are not going to argue about this now, today," Carol said, gathering bunches of wrapping paper in her hands. "We are not going to ruin Mum's birthday." But a thought occurred to her then that she had never had before, never considered, and it seemed absurd that she hadn't. There was something too profoundly insistent in Adel's objections to the Benin house. It was a personal objection, to do with her own circumstances and conscience. How difficult it had been to get her to do bank transfers. How long it had taken her to share access to Alice's account.

"Puff puff?" The owner's edge-controlled teenage daughter appeared tentatively at the table with another portion, along with the beef suya. "Put it here," Carol pointed to the third generation section, where they proceeded to demolish the puff puff. The owner herself came out and asked if they were ready for the mains. "What am I having again, Mum?" said Clay.

"You're having the hot stew with pounded yam."

"Is that eba?"

"No," the owner said, and explained that you can have it with eba instead, if you want, or if you want you can have it with jollof or white rice, some people like to have the hot stew with rice. "It is extra hot—you know that, right? Even for me it's too hot. I want to make sure you are aware. And if you find it too hot it's best not to drink water but something like milk to cool down, that helps."

"It's a bit late to change the order, Clay," said Carol.

"Don't worry, I can accommodate small changes like this."

"You know what, I'll stick with the yam."

It made his eyes water, the stew. The heat consumed the meat. It ended up floating around the table along with the crayfish moi moi and plantain as a communal dish, remaining mostly unconquered though, while cousins shared their jollof mounds and their milder portions of chicken with him. Alice ate only a modicum of her enormous plate. Although regularly reminded by one or other member of her spawn to eat three meals a day, she found that two were more than enough, maybe some bread and warmed ham in the morning, a little fruit during the day, later on rice or potato. She was chewing on a piece of plantain when Carol next to her rose, tapping the edge of a wine glass with a fork. "A toast, everyone," she said, "to Mum." Fantas, wines and waters were raised. "Happy Birthday," they chimed, "Happy Birthday, Nena." Then Carol expanded, in a longer salute, "You'll always be among us, even if you're far away. We don't know how many more times like this there'll be in the future, when we're all together like this. It's special. Let's enjoy it while we can." They all drank. "Love you, Nena," Warren said. "Love you," said Blake. Melissa looked at Adel to see if she was going to say anything tetchy. Alice thought that this would be a good time to make her announcement.

"Speech! Speech!" they said.

The table quietened to make way for her quietness. Utensils paused. The sounds in the kitchen lulled, Harrow Road was slow motion beyond.

Alice looked ahead of her. She twitched her neck and nodded at her pace. Since returning from Nigeria in the spring, that doubt she had entertained there about the feasibility of the circle of her life being completed due to the sloth and difficulty of the building project, well, it had vanished, completely. For a while it had propelled her into deeper involvement in Winifred's church-led community initiative to improve infrastructure for the elderly in Kilburn—they organised bench-to-bench walks, met up in cafés, campaigned for longer countdown times at pedestrian crossings and the fixing of uneven pavement slabs. They also made soft toys for children affected by the Grenfell fire, Alice was most active in this area, crocheting and sewing miniature outfits and stuffing the casings with foam. Her essential wish, though, to return home, had been steadily refuelled by the British months. Every time she stuffed one of those teddies she thought of the pain of those families and the negligence with which they had been treated. There was a cold, greedy machine at the centre of the nation. She wanted to be in her country that knew her well. It didn't matter less anymore. It mattered more than ever, for the time was drawing near.

"My children," she said, and looked around indistinctly at their faces. "By God grace, I am getting tired. It be time soon. I want you my children to take me home in Africa."

For a few moments, no one spoke.

Melissa said, "When?"

"I am ready now."

"Now? What, right now?" said Adel. "You want us to go and pack up your stuff and send you out there now on a plane, to live by yourself?"

"That *is* the general plan, Adel," said Carol.

"It's *not* the plan," she threw down her napkin, cheeks flushing. "It's a ridiculous plan—and you, Carol, are careless and irresponsible to keep letting her entertain it. I am *sick* of this *refusal* to face reality. It's just fundamentally *reckless*. Who's supposed to look after her out there?"

"Oh for god's sake, we've discussed this so many times. We'll *find* someone."

"But *who* someone? Do you know them? Has any one of us

ever met this person? We didn't discuss any of this, not really, they're just vague ideas you throw around—"

"Can you keep your voice down, please, we're in a restaurant," Melissa said.

"—you throw around without thinking them through properly. The house isn't even finished. Is it ready to live in if Mum arrived there with her bags and this stranger person who's going to take her to the dentist? And what about the memory test? They said to keep an eye on her, yet you're still happy to send her away—it's *madness*! Mum, you're coming to live with me in Bushey. If no one else is going to take this situation in hand and be sensible about it, then I'll take care of it myself."

Carol was appalled by such throwing around of weight, such brazen infantilising. She looked from Adel to Alice and back again. "Hang on a minute—you're talking about a grown woman here, not a child," she said. "Who do you think you are ordering her around like that? It's her *life*. It's not your life it's *her* life. It's up to her where she lives."

Meanwhile Alice was nodding in a distressed way, muttering to herself, "Is my life, my only life . . ."

"Just because it's not *convenient* for you if she wants to go and live in Nigeria, that doesn't make it wrong. *You're* the one who's wrong. It's *you*. Why did it take you all that time to send the money for the house? It should've been finished years ago anyway. What was happening to all that money Dad was sending to Uncle Rufus?"

"I told you we couldn't trust them with it," Adel said.

"Maybe it's you we can't trust."

"Aunty, don't say that," Warren interjected.

"Yeah, watch what you're accusing me of, Carol. You don't know what you're talking about."

"Well why don't you *tell* me what I'm talking about."

The silence around the table had reached a sombre intensity, at the despoiling of this rare and special dinner, the younger cousins looking on with strained politeness, scared of saying anything yet sensing they should not be privy to such a scene. With a scrape of her chair, Adel laid her hands on the table and stood up. The owner's daughter approached and sheepishly took away fewer plates than she had planned to, before retreating.

"Well?" Carol said.

"He is watching," Alice muttered, "watching watching everything."

"I'm not gonna stay here and let you accuse me of things you don't understand, ok?" Adel was wrapping her crimson scarf around her neck and bent down to get her bag from under the table. "None of you realise the sacrifices I've made for this family. None of you knows how much has been taken from me, and what I deserve because of it."

"Where are you going, you can't leave? It's Mum's dinner. You always do this, doesn't she, Melissa—she always has to make everything about *her*."

"There you go again. The two of you ganging up on me."

"We're not ganging up on you!"

"Clay," Melissa said, "maybe you kids should go for a walk around the block."

The cousins immediately stood up apart from Warren, who felt he should stay and support his mother. When Melissa encouraged him to go with them Adel said, "No, let him stay. There's nothing I've got to say that he can't hear."

"Around here, though? On a Saturday night, by themselves?"

"It's ok, I know this area," said Clay. "I'm dependable innit. We'll be fine." He headed for the door with Ria and Blake, who ran back to grab a Fanta bottle to take with him. The Naija Taste door chime rang with their exit.

"Sit down, child," Alice said to Adel, but she refused and remained standing. "No, Mum, I'm not staying. I need to go.

I've had it with this family. It's like this suffocating container trapping me in and I can't breathe. None of you *see* me. None of you knows how lonely I've been, always." She glared at her sisters, both sitting there, looking up at her without seeing her. "It was you two together all the time when we were kids, excluding me, letting me carry everything, all of his dirt, and your *darkness,* Mum. *I* was the one who carried the darkness. It was like I was covered in dust wherever I went and I couldn't get rid of it. Even now I can't get rid of it. It follows me everywhere, this old, old cloud with no voice," she glanced towards the door, as if anticipating her way out. "So, I think the only thing to do is to just step away from the source of it and find my own culture, my own container. I need to stop living in the structure he made. This, this place, this meal—it's all part of the structure that I have to escape. There's nothing reassuring or especially amazing about us all gathering here, not for me. It's all a pretence. The only amazing thing about this family is its ability to lie."

"Do you see what I mean about making everything about her?" said Carol. "You haven't answered my question about the money yet."

"He *owed* me. That's what I'm telling you! He crushed me, the core of me."

"He crushed *all* of us, it wasn't just you," Carol retorted. "We come from the same place, Adel. He was a tyrant and a monster and we all carry scars. We can't get away from the thing we come from—it's not possible. But we can learn to live beside it. We can make our own destiny."

"Oh, that's very easy for you to say from where you're standing. No we don't come from the same place. You were his favourite. Mum as well. They favoured you. You left me alone, Mum. You let me get crushed by his rage and I will never forgive you for that. And yes, I took a little bit of that money to help with my debts. I'm sure I'm not the only one, and it was a small portion compared to what I deserve. I looked after him. I did my duty by him, despite everything. Now it's over—and I don't *understand* why you can't just leave it alone and accept that this is where you *are,* Mum. You made us and you belong with us, no matter what. It's our duty to look after you, the way I looked after him, and it's your duty to stay. You don't get to just fly away and leave us all behind. I am *not* sending you away."

"Calm down, sister," Melissa said softly, with tears in her eyes. "It's all right, it's all right."

With that Adel shrivelled down into her chair sobbing. Alice too was emotional, shaking her head in the private universe of her mistakes. She wished she could start again from the beginning and do it right, but then she thought that even if she could she still would do it wrong. The soil here had made her weak. The enclosure he had put her in had held her for decades and she had never made it out, only in the house of the Lord. That was why she wanted her own house, to make herself strong again, even just for the leaving. "He take my life," she said. "I blame myself for stay with him, I didn't know, I didn't know where else but be with you children." Taking her napkin, she wiped it roughly across her face and eyes, then screwed it up in her hand. "I try to feel strong . . . it's misfortune, my life is still here . . ."

"You used to look at me sometimes with such hatred," Adel told her. "I used to think *everything* was my fault, everything, even the cold outside, the ugliness. I was so young I didn't understand it wasn't supposed to be like that."

But Alice had retreated into herself, hardly listening anymore. She stuck out her bottom lip with a cruel uncrushed pride. She was going to take whatever she could, whatever she had left. "You bring me home," she said. "It supposed to be. I blame myself only. I'm sorry."

"Haven't you heard what I've said? It's not happening, Mum! I'm going to take care of it. You're coming in with me."

"Don't *talk* to her like that," Carol rose again from her seat.

"Look, will everyone just calm down, calm *down*!"

"And Melissa, I'm sick of you sitting on the fence all the time," Carol said turning on her. "Why don't you ever say what you think? You always just drift along not stepping up to either option, as if it's got nothing to do with you."

"Why are you starting on me? I'm supposed to be on one side or the other? It's not black and white like that."

"How is it not? You either support me on this or you don't."

"Ok," Melissa now ventured, gathering the strands of an impression she had become aware of in recent months, a fragility in her eldest sister that spoke to her own. "I think you should have more empathy. That's what I think."

"I *do* have empathy," Carol replied. "That's why I—"

It was at this point that Warren cut in. From the third generation corner, having watched this escalation build, he said: "I'll take her."

"What?" Adel turned to him.

"I'll take Nena home."

"No."

"Why not?"

"No. That's not it. No."

"I can. I'd like to."

"You take me home?" Alice said.

"He's not going anywhere."

"Adel, I think that's up to him."

"I like it there. I like the way I feel there."

"No."

And with this no hanging in the air, over the table, over the shiny curls of stray wrapping paper, the ukulele, the half-empty glasses and the remains of the crayfish moi moi, the door chime rang. A rush of icy air came in from the high street and the three Pitt cousins came traipsing back into the egusi-smelling ambience, having explored some gritty west London terrain. "Are we having pudding?" Blake said.

☙

The Good Witch of the South was adorned in baby pink, bell-shaped in her skirts, wings erupting from her shoulders, on her head a tall crown from which hung her pressed Kolkata weave. She held a wand of impressive length whose star was repeated over the top netting of the dress making her sparkling multiple, but beneath the bodice the heart was wilted in its keenness. She was aware, Nicole, every night of this rendition, every time she uttered the words, "Follow the yellow brick road," that she had entered a phase beyond feasible album success. There would be no member of the A&R sector arriving at her dressing room door amped by her performance or wishing to get behind the rekindling of her authentic stage identity. Every time she collided with Dorothy in the backstage dim between costume changes she was aware of her fated downward route. And maybe one day she would be fine with it. Maybe she really had come to the end of her song and it was getting time to embrace the next phase in her journey. For now, though, she could not bring herself to deliver her lines with enthusiasm. Her arm, while pointing the way through Oz, was limp. The wave of her wand, likewise wilted. If the people of Catford minded that this witch seemed lackadaisical, they didn't show it. In fact it seemed to add to the overall comedy.

Her headline status on the bill took some of the pressure away. On the posters outside the gothic façade of the Broadway Theatre, a block down from the fibreglass cat and the KFC, she held a central position in between Dorothy (played by Robert Tuan who had been in *Eastenders*) and the Wicked Witch of the West (Uma

Burne). Tickets were sold on the basis of her involvement, even if just out of curiosity about what she looked like in middle age or to witness her where-are-they-now story. Stepping in through the stage door, she liked the ghostly dark space that made magic and pictures, it reminded her of what it felt like to be a child, full of wonder, and she had her own dressing room which was more than she had become used to of late. Assessing herself in the mirror with five minutes to go before curtain call, she said aloud, "You are brave you are golden you are you," her pre-show mantra designed to help her focus and banish any distracting thoughts, such as the prevailing stale atmosphere at home and Michael's failure thus far to come and see her as the Good Witch of the South. He kept saying he would come soon and she had maintained a show of nonchalance towards his nonchalance, after all he had seen her on many stages before. But secretly, it was important to her, whether he came or not, for the following reasons: it was her first theatrical part and could lead to others (this might be her new path, maybe it *would* lead to the West End); it was frightening and she would appreciate his support, not to mention his honest opinion on her acting skills; and she would just like it if her handsome husband made his way backstage after watching his wife perform, waited in an armchair while she changed out of her silly bell gown, then took her home and made her feel like a woman. The occurrence, or not, of this wish, had become for Nicole the conclusive straw with the power to decide the fate of the camel's back.

Since the Algarve Soul Weekender things had been teetering on the edge of collapse. Apologies had been made, forgiveness (of him, by her, for spoiling it) had been professed, but an undeniable wedge had entered their cushioning, a line had been crossed. They were in that cheerless place of civil, sometimes pitying communication, arrived at through a growing understanding that in the absence of regular sexual intercourse they got on each other's nerves. They had different preferences for toaster settings—Michael liked to amble and phone-scroll while he was waiting for his, Nicole wanted hers done quickly so that she could proceed to buttering and devouring. There was many a time when Michael would push down the lever and finish up with burnt toast which really irritated him; he'd had to develop a habit of remembering to check the dial first, an unnecessary inconvenience. Also, they had different attitudes toward evening light—Nicole believed in the wafting gold of lamps and liked wandering into a room where a table or bedspread was bathed in a gentle glow, whereas Michael was mindful of the citizen's responsibility to reduce energy reliance, thus a light should be either on or off, on when you needed it, off when you didn't. There was many a time, for instance, when Nicole would head to the kitchen at 10 p.m. to fetch her *Killing Eve–*accompanying ice cream which she had intentionally left melting in a bowl in the soft half-light coming from under the cabinets, to find that Michael had switched them off and she was entering darkness—yet at the same time, if he then needed to use the kitchen himself he would snap on the blaring overhead spotlights, destroying all ambience and mellowness. She had blurted yesterday evening, "You have no understanding of light! You're too binary when it comes to light!" He had defended himself, mentioning the ice caps and ecological catastrophe, and the altercation had from there advanced into harsher weather. It seemed that they were making together a perilous ascent to the summit of their end, and when they reached it they would topple away from each other into the intimidating rubble where they would have to rebuild their lives. Neither of them wanted this to happen. They wanted to go back to Saturday morning loving and sharing ice cream. It would take some amount of crisis-management to return to that utopia.

"I feel like you don't really value who and what I am," Nicole had said this morning, a Saturday morning, in the living room when they had met eyes and longed mutually for how it used to be on this day of the week.

"I feel the same way," he had said.

"Like, what I do is just frivolous to you. It doesn't change anything."

"Well, *I* feel like I bore you," he said.

And that was true, on one level, though she didn't say this, she said that people's work, to other people, *was* boring. If you put a dentist in a room full of Hollywood actors talking shop, that dentist would be as bored as if it were vice versa.

"Anyway, I still want this to work," she said.

"Me too."

"Are you going to come and watch the show tonight?" There was a note of passive aggressive threat here.

"I can't tonight, I've got a meeting in town."

"Michael it's Saturday!"

"I know but it's with one of my patrons from the US and she's on a flying visit."

"What patron? How old is she?"

"Around seventy-eight. Why does it matter how old she is?"

"Are you serious?"

"About what?"

"Her age."

"I don't *know* how old she is, Nic. I don't care, and neither should you." And this too escalated into the harsher weather, she accused him of prioritising everything else but her, he accused her of being childishly jealous and stifling, to which she said how could she be stifling when they hardly ever saw each other and that on the Algarve Soul Weekender she'd seen a nasty side of him that she'd been hoping wasn't really him but as time went on she was realising that it was. The summit loomed again. She went upstairs and slammed into the bathroom to get ready for socaerobics with Leona, he did some press-ups and spent the morning watching basketball. Before he left to go into the West End, he offered, out of guilt, "I'll come to the show next week, ok?" "Sure, whatever," she said, and went back to her *Vogue*, where she had been studying a spread on nature-inspired accessories.

The meeting with the patron finished at eight, she was an heiress who supported social causes, "I *would* say let's have coffee but you know at my age my bladder is the size of a peanut," she said as they were wrapping up. Outside the restaurant Michael thanked her again for extending her donations which would keep the organisation running for the next three years. Walking up towards Bond Street among the milling weekend crowds and the blue Christmas lights, he reflected on what the picture of other aspects of his life might look like in three years' time— Ria would be twenty-one, Blake would be thirteen, a teenager, in pivotal need of him, and he, a vertiginous fifty-two, with a shrinking bladder and less time ahead than behind. He thought about Cordelia's lost son, the reason for his work, and the reality that anything can be taken from you, at any moment, by the cruelty and trouble of the world. He remembered again, suddenly, it still shocked him whenever it came into his mind, Damian's daughter Avril, the incomprehensible idea that she was no longer here. When Ria had told him the news he had tried to get back in contact with Damian—he'd wanted to offer his support, he could feel the acute pain of it in his own bloodstream—but hadn't been able to. He felt a strange kind of guilt that if they'd stayed friends things might have turned out differently somehow, maybe she would still be alive. Then he felt ridiculous for over-imagining his significance in another man's life. He knew it had affected Ria deeply, that she carried a similar sense of guilt.

"I wish I could've helped her," she'd said. "I wish she hadn't just fallen away into the darkness. It's like she slipped off the earth. Anyone can slip off the earth. There's so much death."

Michael had wanted to say something to reassure and comfort her, to allay fear. He'd told her, "It's harder to get lost if you follow yourself. Follow what you like, whatever feels good, go that way. If you ever get lost, I'll be here. I'll help you remember." Perhaps Damian had said a comparable thing to Avril, and yet she was gone.

Oxford Street these days was full of candy shops and toppling brands, the flailing House of Fraser, the fall of Jane Norman where Nicole used to buy her fitted jumpers. Even John Lewis was at threat, which according to Michael's mother was a very, very grave thing for British retail, the prospect of not being able at some point in the future to experience that pinnacle of customer service and appliance guarantee. At one of the souvenir emporiums doubling as a sweet shop he dropped in to buy some Pop-Tarts. He paid in cash. "Can I have the change in 20ps?" he asked. "I'm doing this Smarties thing with my son. He's got to collect twenties and fill a tube for his school—they're the same shape." The cashier was not interested in these details but handed over the change in twenties. Before stepping back out into the street, Michael got a message from Melissa on his phone, a pointed, stirring message, one that seemed to be offering him a choice, that caught him right in the centre of his current marital doubt and suggested a clear onward place from the rubble at the bottom of the mountain, a place he already knew, which shone from this angle in a renewed auspicious light. Can I see you? it read, unusual in its sparseness and singularity. It did not make any reference to the children. It had none of the spontaneous levity of the Algarve balcony kind with an innocent kiss at the end. This was a profound, direct and fundamental question. He could feel all her soul in it, requiring a direct answer. First, he wrote, Hi. When?

Now.

Oh. Now? Where?

Where are you?

Oxford Street.

I can come and meet you.

Where?

By the river. Embankment. 45 mins.

Is everything ok?

Don't worry. Will you be there?

Ok, yeah.

And he knew, on sending those two words, that another line had been crossed. A line of intention, of willing regression. If Nicole were aware of those words and the accompanying swirling in his lower abdomen, it would have added to the wilting in the empty movements of her wand. As she skipped and pranced, without lustre, before her husband-devoid audience, she had no reason to suspect that he was at that moment walking through Soho, in a jagged route towards Charing Cross Road, along Dean Street, left onto Old Compton Street, in the foreboding direction of his unfinished love at the water. He was thinking, if she wanted him then, right there at the river if she asked for him, if she could promise him that she would stay with him and not turn away and he could see that promise in her face, he would go on back to her, he would fold back into her. They would all be together again. They would live in their house, a new house, and go out into the garden when all their labours were done. Crossing Long Acre with ever-quickening strides, the memory flashed before him of holding her hand and leading her through the city to a secret, they would descend the stairs beneath the Covent Garden piazza, they would eat a meal together, she would say to him that the only thing she ever wanted on her birthday was to sit with him in a restaurant and talk. Now they would go back to that place they made, the place that did not exist anywhere else. It would hold fast this time.

Down St. Martin's Place, left onto the Strand, crossing to the sepia pillars of the station forecourt with the people going by and a man walking alone coming towards him, a stranger, yet familiar, something in the face, they looked at one another and looked away, but his eyes were drawn back to the sloping desolate walk, the gaze fixed at a point beyond the world, and the face, he knew that face.

When this happens in the vastness of London, you run into a friend, there is a sense of the universe colluding. The angels are telling you something. They are showing you corridors. They are asking you if you are going the right way. Damian did not want to stop and talk to Michael that evening near the river in December and Michael did not want to believe it was him, his old friend who had once betrayed him and whom he had never told that he was forgiven, so at first they simply did not wholly recognise each other. He looked to Michael like one of the black people who had been destroyed by the country, the fallen shoulders, the close madness. He looked like Damian's father had looked to Damian himself all those years ago on Railton Road, when he was sick and near the end of his life and his clothes were shabby and his body was haggard and spent. "Damian?" Michael called, hoping he was mistaken in thinking it was him, but Damian decided, in the instant their shoulders made a single wavy line across the lane, that he could not answer, there would be too much he wouldn't be able to hear and say and too much of the past he wouldn't be able to bear the reminder of. So they walked on, both of them, in opposite directions, and Michael began to doubt whether it was him after all, it could've been a moment of déjà vu, or a transposing of one face onto another by a quirk of the mind. Yet it weakened him. As he got closer to the water, he felt something leaving him, a worry flowered outwards around his courage like a net. Going through Embankment tube station he came out the other side meeker, less mighty in his resolve, heeding the message of the angels—and there she was, waiting for him at the river wall, wearing her forest green coat.

After leaving the restaurant, Melissa had driven her mother home with Carol, a heavy silence between them. She told the children that they would be spending the night at Nena's and then messaged Michael. She wanted to tell him how lonely the family can make you feel, the ones you are supposed to feel closest to, that it's the people we find in our lives along the way whom we form the deepest relationships with, outside of the family and what it does to you. She and Carol left Alice's flat together, leaving the car and heading for the tube station.

"What did you mean, I have no empathy?" Carol said, her head down, looking at the paving stones and their edges. "This whole thing is about my empathy for her."

"I meant for Adel," Melissa said.

They walked in silence for a while. Carol began to speak again. "Mum asked me, personally, two years ago, to finish the house, and I told her I would. I promised her. That's why I can't leave it alone. She wants to go where she'll be at peace. She wants to leave a legacy when she dies and she asked me to help her achieve it. That's important to me. That's what family is. You don't seem to care about that much."

They had left each other at Baker Street, still a new coldness between them, and Melissa knew that she was wrong. She did care. She understood, that you can have a dream but you might need someone you have chosen to help you meet it, to make it stand up, to give it doors and windows and sunlight flowing through. And that someone must be the right person, otherwise it will never come true.

She turned and saw him, his tall and graceful figure, the lumbering quality to his walk that she now realised she loved. He crossed over. She took a few steps forward. "Hi," she said. "Hey," he said. She hugged him upwards. He hugged her downwards. "What's wrong?" he said, and she told him clearly, in no uncertain terms, the awareness in which she found herself. She wanted to have him back. She wanted to look out on the river at Greenwich in white and electric blue and live together ever after in their house.

"We're meant," she said. "You're my home. It's you, Michael. When I'm with you, everything's in proper focus. I thought you obscured me but it's really the opposite. You make everything beyond seem possible."

He did not know what to say. He smiled because he didn't know what to say. Some twenty minutes before, he would have sunk with her into this dream. He would have changed everything. But now, as if just awoken, he heard the traffic on the street and the lapping of the water in the stone arches of the bridge. He saw the face of his old friend who had left his life and lost his way, lost so much. It was cold by the river. The Sunday sleet was moving in. He thought about Nicole and felt that he should go to her, for it was cold and dark and they were written down in black and white.

"Say something," she said.

Instead he wrapped his arms full around her, squeezed her against him as though he were trying to imprint her outline onto his own. He whispered, "You're my home too." But then he said louder, "I can't."

"You can't?"

"I'm sorry." She had begun to cry. "I can't."

When he walked away from her she was still with him in transposition, carried within. She refused his offer of a cab and told him to go, she wanted to be by herself. She slipped away a little as he waited for the train at Charing Cross, climbed up to his heart again when they were pulling out of New Cross, it continued like this, his tears came and went, and he arrived at the Broadway Theatre just as the Good Witch of the South was granting her final wish. He found her backstage after barging his way in, a cloud of stars, blinking out of her make-up, surprised to see him there while en route to the dressing room. Initially, she glared at him, until her mouth began to tremble.

"I bought you some Pop-Tarts," he said.

21

Sisters Katherine and Beatrice were arranging the Bibles. A small congregation today as usual, the nucleus, it being January which offered little chance of newcomers. On the piano Maurice was playing a suspiciously jazzful rendition of Here I Am to Worship but they let it slide, they had become more accepting of his taste for colourful worship. Along with the Bibles they distributed the hymn books and some photocopied handouts featuring a word search, quiz and comprehension exercise on the Last Supper. They always made sure to cater for the absent youth, in case any one of them might wander in, for it remained among their priorities to grow the flock and call the heathen future to the fold.

In the vestibule Alice and Winifred were taking off their coats, having walked along the bend together past the boundary walls and front yard hedges. Winifred had been telling Alice about her time in St. Vincent, the warm oceanic Christmas by the black volcano sands and the weeks spent relaxing in the new house. She had been going to the local church on Sundays as a way of getting to know the neighbourhood while staying close to the Lord, although of course the Lord is everywhere and His blessing is without locale, He is the only thing that exists everywhere and in every form, wherever you pray, He hears you. They moved through into the hall to take their seats, Alice in her turban headwrap with the gold ring at the front, Winifred in her black knee-high socks and pleated skirt. She was glad to be back, though, she said, back in her familiar place with the primary school across the way and the sounds of the children's voices floating through the air at break times, and this particular house of our Lord which had been her sanctuary and community for so many years. "I'm not even sure I want to leave anymore, for good. I've been here for such a long time now that it feels like home, you know, Alice? Well, it is home."

Alice didn't quite know, there was only one true home and it wasn't here, but Winifred's wavering made her think; she was not too old to be impressionable. No firm plans had been made yet for her to return to Benin, despite Warren's offer to take her—would Adel ever let him go even now that he is a grown man? Some women hold too tight to their sons and it doesn't help them, Alice thought. Anyway, the house was still not ready. There was not enough money in the bank to pay the three thousand-naira daily rate for the plasterers and she had not yet won the lottery. The house, she felt, was becoming a phantom structure in the cosmos. The only way to reach it was in dreaming, she would leave through her window in the night, drift over the satellite dishes of Kilburn, across the seas, towards the Delta, descending to Edo, in through the almost finished roof, and there she would sit alone in her kitchen and wait. Who was she waiting for? Who would come to her door and eat at her table, while here the children would grow taller into themselves and make houses of their own, homes of their own, and have babies, build family? Melissa had said to her the other day over rare eba, "It will be sad if you go. You'll only get to see the kids maybe once a year." The discussion persisted agonisingly down phone lines, through inboxes, in the parlour while Alice absconded in the kitchen heating up akara or making pancakes. "Stay," they said. "It's her life," said Carol, who would not forgive

Adel about the money but they must make it up, Alice was angry too yet had forgiven, it was atonement. "Let her go," they said, "You're being selfish," everyone was being selfish, in different ways. It was the discussion that had no conclusion, and the result was that the house itself had no conclusion. Perhaps the circle of her life would indeed not be completed. Maybe after all she would not end where she had begun but would stand before God in the heavenly light a little bent, a little twisted, and through Him, rather than through British Airways, she would return to her first language. "We could *bury* you in Nigeria," Melissa had said, "after you pass." It was easier to entertain this idea in the presence of Winifred's unexpected fluctuation.

"What about you?" she asked now. "I think when we last spoke about it they were going to finish the roof?"

"No. They are still building," Alice said, and it occurred to her that she had been either saying or thinking a variation of these words for a very long time.

"It's such a complicated thing, especially from so far away. It can take forever. I suppose I'm lucky Herbie works in the construction business."

They stood to sing Abide with Me. During the hymn a young, freckled woman came in with two children, causing a flurry of excitement in the Sisters. Now there would be someone to do the word search. Sister Beatrice could conduct her Sunday school in the other room, a scarce occurrence in this era where for most youngsters Sunday school was *an alien concept*. Winifred as well was glad to see some visitors, and it made her feel even more that here was her place, she wanted to help call the people, to rescue if not the world then at least this little part of London, oh the wandering boys, and the meandering girls, and the burgeoning theys, didn't they all need the care and wisdom of the disciples, to help deliver them into the maze of life? These were hard times. Even when the sky was quite blue and lifted there was a lowness, a tremor, a distrust, a meanness, and you could feel it when you walked along the streets. You could feel some kind of attack wanting to come, and you looked around and you don't know when it's going to attack you, but you can feel it, an old woman of the islands especially can feel it. Yet it still didn't make her want to go, because the other side of it was salvation, the other side of it was hope, and really, now, anyway, it was too late to go.

The plain fact of this hardened during the hymn, making Winifred sing louder in her quivering voice. Alice sang along with her more quietly, her neck bent in that bird-like way, then the vicar gave his sermon and they read from the Psalms while the word search went on next door. The children's mother reminded Alice of Frances, from the house on Bantem Street, the pale, freckled skin and the worried expression. She would like to get in touch with her and find out how she was looking after herself.

"I can go back to St. Vincent on holiday," Winifred said as they continued their conversation after the service was over, "and you know, Alice, I did find it a bit of a bother, all the fussing and flapping they do. It's nice to be around the family but I'm used to my own space. I don't like to be asked all the time what I want to do today or to share my kitchen. I like my kitchen. Did you like the jam, by the way?"

"The what's it call, blueberry? Yes, I eat it with bread. Nice taste."

"I'm going to try and make one with nectarine."

"And maybe some peach you mix them."

"Peach and nectarine, oh yes, that's a good idea."

"Put sugar. Not too much. My daughters they say you shouldn't use sugar on fruit. I put it on apple they get annoyed." Alice laughed. It was good to be here; Winifred was right, it was a sanctuary and a place of friendship. The Sisters provided

331

biscuits and Quality Streets which pleased the two little boys, the air fizzed with unwrapping, Maurice played a game with them involving coins and a piece of string that he kept in his pocket, while the mother, she couldn't be more than thirty, told them that she had just moved into the area and was agnostic, but when it came to raising children she believed in showing them a moral code to steer them even if she didn't believe in Jesus herself, which she didn't, "I mean it's kind of implausible, isn't it." They all looked at her with sympathy, gazing twinkle-eyed from their warm faith, and Sister Katherine offered that faith could be a gradual building of surrender to the way, she might learn it from the children one day, they might give back to her what she had given to them. "Just make sure you read the Bible with them whenever you can. The Lord is patient." As Alice was leaving she encouraged her too to bring the grandchildren again some time, it was right what their visitor had said about a moral code.

They went back along the bend in their overcoats and winter boots, pausing here and there to reflect on a notion, Alice often paused when she was walking because forwardness occasionally distracted. She told Winifred about her friend Frances whom she hadn't heard from in a long while, that the boys' mother had brought her to mind. "You should try and find her on the internet," Winifred suggested. "Everybody does that nowadays, finding their family and old friends, even ancestors from centuries ago. I watched a programme about it."

Carol, lately, had been trying to teach Alice how to use a computer. It was a strange language, the tapping of symbols, the jumping arrow. Her hands felt like a crab trying to fold itself backwards. She was supposed to practise every day, tap it, type some words, log in, not log out. The laptop was always kept open to make it easier for her, next to it a notebook containing passwords and usernames. "Access, Mum," Carol said. "It's about power. This is the way the world works now." She'd helped her set up an email address, directing over her shoulder while Alice sat at the screen, sometimes Carol would have to wait an inordinate amount of time for her to press the @ but she drew on her best patience. Yesterday they had sent her first email: "Dear Family, I'm online! Send me a message! Love from Mum." It had been met with return exclamation marks and welcomes into cyberspace.

After saying goodbye to Winifred at the gate, with promises of forthcoming exchanges of jam and cake and the sharing of details on the next bench-to-bench walk, Alice went inside and made herself a cornflour lunch, then sat at her kitchen table, contemplating. At this very table she and Cornelius had sat on Wednesdays in their after-marriage, he would arrive at the door, take his seat on the right, facing east, and she would take west. There she would serve him his roast chicken and complex rice. On finishing he would always say, "You'll be coming back home soon, won't you," even though he must have known deep down that she never would. It was him, she realised, whom she was waiting for in the dream. He was the one who would one day arrive at the Benin door, take off his coat, lean on his walking stick, and sit down in her kitchen, just the two of them there in the loneliness they had made with their union. What if the house was only a product of that loneliness? What if it only existed because she had failed to make a whole life here? What if she went there, back home, when she was tired at the end of her life, and all she found was him, while her true life was here, waiting to be all of her? To talk jam and praise Jesus with her church friends and sing in the four-lady choir. To make toys for the traumatised and crocheted vase mats to send to Frances when she contacted her through internet. To remind her daughters to mash the backs, not shout at the children, make them eba sometimes—and the children themselves, to see them grow and prosper. Perhaps all of this was the whole, and the house never would be, or should be, because it was a part of the cage he had made around her. In ceasing to yearn for it, she could be free.

She spent the evening practising on the computer and playing her ukulele. She felt lighter inside, that she had finally let go of something that had been hampering her, and slept that night with a profound peace, wanting nothing, yearning nothing. In the dream, she left through the window and drifted over the satellites, this time noticing the familiar streets and the night sheen of the pavements. Across the seas, towards the Delta, descending to Edo, in through the unfinished roof. In the kitchen she proceeded to cook. She washed the rice. She seasoned the chicken. There were akara and plantain, potatoes and cabbage. He appeared at the opening in the wall where a door was supposed to be. He looked tired, like he could sleep forever, his clothes were singed and ragged. Come in, she said, and he took his seat at the table.

How was journey? she said.

I got lost, he said. I couldn't remember where it was.

Still work to do.

I'll get that roof fixed.

No rush.

They ate, one last supper, while children climbed among the ruins, swinging from the scaffolding, wafting in the emptiness, and the sun was setting in the west. Alice watched it falling down the land, a long star, never to be extinguished. When they had finished eating, Cornelius stood up and put on his hat. He could hear his father calling him. He had been hearing it for some time in the flames and the wretched walking, but had not been able to determine its direction. Now he could hear it clearly coming from the north and was eager to go to it in case it faded again. Behind the voice he could hear the booming sound, he could picture Sidney and their mother waiting in the light beyond the precipice and the colourless gate. It's time, his father called, and so he tipped his hat at Alice, thanked her for the tasty meal, and went in that direction. It was a long walk. Maybe he would never make it, Alice thought. She watched him until he was out of sight. The following morning she took off her wedding ring.

⸙

On the ground floor of the Langham Hotel on Portland Place, a waiter moves among the tables of a restaurant, balancing champagne. It is an opulent, well-known place, a hit of the French chef Michel Roux. There are tall arch windows in a circular row, an island in the centre, on the ceiling chandeliers dripping crystalline bright from an impressive distance. The waiter arrives at a table occupied by a couple, a man and a woman, and sets down their flutes. She is dressed in black and gold, long gold earrings and a layer of shine across her eyelids. He is also in black, a shirt and blazer of slightly different shades, both of them are wearing wedding bands. He has chosen this restaurant for her birthday because they watch the signature chef on TV sometimes and have long talked about coming here, plus he wants to make up for things, many things.

They laugh about it now, but the beginning of this year, New Year's Eve, for example, was not among their favoured festive memories. She had wanted to go to Nuvo Lounge across the road from the Broadway Theatre after her Good Witch shift and shock out, but when the queue was long and cold and her status didn't flap the bouncers, he had suggested homely cosying instead with a boxset and take-out. The butter roasted chicken they were going to eat tonight, flavoured with lemon and herbs and served with an arrangement of fregola sarda, pickled pear and Jerusalem artichoke, is another galaxy compared to the culinary plummet of that disappointing night, an awfulness of poultry, a scrambling for something open at that late hour. "Not even KFC, you know," she says, "*Morleys, Morleys,* on NYE!" "I felt so bad, man," he enthuses, but she reassures him, "It wasn't your fault, babe. You weren't to know everything would be shut down, I mean who knew," and she touches his cheek before taking another sip from her flute.

Then the other things, the Weekender, the bringing his work home too much, the sitting on joy. Michael has made a firm commitment to the survival, indeed the flourishing of their mutual joy. The trees are wearing blossom. The spring is pink and light. With time and the thawing of winter, Saturday mornings have almost returned to what they used to be and he wants to keep it that way, which is why he has booked one of the rooms above this restaurant for the night, so that tomorrow, Saturday, they can wake together in a nest of luxury at the start of her fifty-second year and begin again as they mean to go on, they might go shopping in the afternoon, or they might just eat room service and relax. Whatever they do, it must engender happiness, for a decision has been made within him that they will endure.

"You're my flame," he said. "I want us to keep burning. I don't want us to go out." "You're my flame too," she said, and they ate the divine poultry, marvelling at its softness and the ingenuity of Roux. As well as a gesture of reconciliation, tonight is a celebration of good news: Nicole has been offered a leading part in a West End musical.

For dessert they had kalamansi mousse with Tanariva cream, sablé, and citrus garnish, a house speciality. Afterwards they went out into the lobby and up in the lift to the seventh floor. The room was calm green tones and dark wood, floor-length mustard curtains, white linen. It had a cavernous, secluded quality, magnifying every emotion. He took off his jacket and laid it on a chair. "Are you all right?" "Yes I'm ok," she said, but in the intense stillness of the room, they could feel a certain unnatural pressure. Doubt crept upon her, that they would never be fully alone together when they were alone like this. There would always be another presence. There would always be the thing they couldn't pass, and something just wasn't right for the long haul, she could feel it, every time he bent down over the cooker to listen to the rice, she knew where that listening came from, that he would never let her go.

When they lay down she forgot about this and was released again. He liked her like that, on her back with her legs closed, a small space between them, raised by the muscle for his tongue, the owner of the key. She felt herself moving towards the vantage point upwards and onwards, and she could hear a faint music playing in her veins that went streaming through her body, and when she arrived in the open there was a booming sound all around her in which she believed that everything would hold. Then the floating, the balloon descending to the earth. They fell asleep. He dreamt.

He is sitting on the sand in the twilight and he hears her voice. It's ok, she says casually, as if in the middle of a conversation. He looks up and sees her walking away from him towards the ocean in her black and white swimming costume with the diagonal stripe across the centre. She walks into the waves with her body for days, the water reaches for her, she swims out. She goes further and further out, her mermaid flow, her strong brown arms wheeling in front crawl. The sea takes over in its expanse. A titanic wave curled like a spoon and scooped her up and away. "Come back," he said. "Come back."

This time, Nicole did not wake him. She lifted the covers and quietly got out of bed. He did not hear her moving about the room, picking up items of clothing. Somehow she knew he wouldn't wake up, and it is possible that Michael knew, in the depths of this very deep sleep, that she was leaving. She did not linger or stand and watch him lying there in the dark. They had done all the things. They had had all the conversations. She put her belongings in her Louis Vuitton overnight bag and went, closing the door with care behind her, to face the empty corridor.

Similarly, Alice had a final change of heart, in the depth of night, when the earth is turning soundlessly and the truth is standing at your side. It was raining. A small tree was shaking in the wind at the coming of a March storm. Something was looming, something was coming. She could feel it as she lay in bed in her long cotton nightdress and headcloth, her feet close together and her knees drawn up. She could hear a booming sound coming from far away around the planets, telling her that no, it must be, it must, the circle must be completed, she must pass over on her red soil dry from the winds of the Harmattan, or moist with the fall of the rains. Whatever the time the Lord chose for her, she must be in the first place to arrive safely at the last. She understood that she must get out.

She sat up and telephoned Carol. "What's wrong, Mum?"

"I want you to take me home in Africa. I want to go."

Carol breathed in, then slowly out. She nodded.

"Ok. Ok, Mum. We'll take you home."

Carol, though, was considering moving to Sweden with her love to escape Babylon, and this phone call sealed her decision. Warren would have to take her. She called Adel and explained it, and they had a long conversation during which they talked about their boys, Carol told her Clay was going to stay here with his dad and she would spend summers with him, Adel revealed to her Warren's time in detention and how she felt he couldn't soar, she wanted him to soar. They would miss their boys, but there was another place, and for Adel, it had become clear that you can hold too much, for too long, and she should let him go. He had said he wanted to help them finish the house.

"Mummy, don't start crying again," Ria said to Melissa on the day of the departure. Melissa was going to be driving Alice to Gatwick. In the early morning they drove across the river to pick her up, along with her suitcases, her boxes, her carry bags, full of trinkets and crochet and ornaments and cloths and Bibles and crockery, her whole life, moving on the earth. Adel was driving too with Warren, Lauren and Clay. Carol was taking the train to be ecological to the last. Winifred and the Sisters Beatrice and Katherine as well as Alice's downstairs neighbour Terry were going to the send-off with Maurice at the wheel. Hazel was going in her Range Rover and taking more of the luggage; when Melissa saw her, outside Alice's flat when they arrived, she again burst into tears. Blake said, "If this was you going away to live in Africa for good, I'd be crying this much," and rubbed her back. The preceding Sunday there had been a goodbye dinner at Naija Taste for immediate family members at which nobody had argued.

Alice wore wide-leg black trousers with a red M&S cardigan, a fringe wig, comfortable travelling shoes and a little swing in her walk. She had made crochet-mats for all of her daughters, "you put underneath vase," a jar of peach and nectarine jam for Terry, "eat it with fifty-fifty toast," foam teddies for her grandchildren even the ones who were adults, and portions of three akara each in plastic bags for as many people as possible, "you put in freezer." Melissa opened the car door for her with trembling hand and kept her voice as steady as possible, once Alice was seated safely behind the driver's seat, Ria in the passenger seat, Blake next to Alice in the back, staring at her at intervals with gravity, "Ready?" she said. Alice looked around her, at the churchward bend and the primary school, at the front door of her flat which would return to the housing association to give shelter to another, at the small tree which blew in the winds and told her the things she knew. "I'm ready," she said, and they pulled out, a four-car convoy, going south.

There goes by the playground and the high street. There goes by the motorway and the English grasses. There go white clouds, grey blue skies and the cold front. She looked out of the window with her head tipped back and her glasses glinting. Everything changes and remains the same. She is going to the beginning. "We're going to miss you, Nena," Blake said, and now he was trying not to cry. He couldn't imagine her not being there on the other side of the river to come to for a good pancake or the best stew. And he was concerned for his own mother not having her mother to come to when she needed to lie down in a cave away from the world; she still needed her mother, he could see that from the way she was after they visited her, sort of whole and relieved as if a weight had been lifted. "We'll all miss you, Nena," Ria said from the passenger seat. Alice said, "You talk to me in computer. We use that Skype."

At Gatwick they unloaded and went towards check-in, the crowd of them, Alice the smallest among them aside from Blake: the oldest and the youngest, he was holding her hand. The black habits of the nuns billowed as they went past W H Smith and the currency exchange, and the crown of Maurice's head gleamed in the strip lights. "I hope you'll find a good little church like ours there, Alice," Winifred said. She had given her, in collaboration with the Sisters, a tapestry of a golden cross to hang up on her Benin wall, and they had swapped email addresses and rarely used mobile numbers, "We keep in touch." "We will, we will!" said Sister Beatrice, grasping Alice's hand in both of hers, "And we hope to see the children at Sunday school," said Sister Katherine surveying their sweet heathenness, so ripe for godly word search and comprehension exercise. There were several conversations going on at once, Hazel was telling Carol about her Sussex moving plans with Bruce, Ria was talking to Clay about some music she was composing, Melissa was telling Adel that she wished their mother felt that she could die here but accepted that she couldn't, and not that she was going to die any time soon of course, that came out a bit the wrong way, which set her off again, thinking about what was going to happen when it actually happened.

The closer they came to the departure gate, the slower they all walked, until there was no further to go and they would have to part, instead they stayed there for twenty minutes stalling. The chatter continued on in the way of major family goodbyes. Adel, a part of her crumbling, reminded Warren to call her when they arrived in Benin, not just text, a call, she wanted to hear his voice. Alice reminded Melissa to use the healing stone on Blake's chicken pox scars and on that horrible mole under her eye getting bigger. Carol told Alice to keep her passport in a safe place at her sister's, where they would stay for the meantime until the house was ready, and to keep on practising her computer. "Don't forget your ukulele!" Lauren said finally, having forgotten she was carrying it, and Warren took it from her in its case and drew it onto his shoulder next to his rucksack. Brother and sister shed tears embracing. The entire party, in the end, was crying, as the old woman and her grandson went away into the lounge. A vacancy established itself in the ground. The world tipped sideways. There would be no north star across the river. The last glimpse they had of her was a turn of her head to the right and the flash of her optical lens, as Warren pointed at something none of them could see and, bending to take her bag, led her in that direction.

$\sim$

On the fourteenth day of every month, another crowd gathered, outside the town hall in Kensington. They brought with them their green hearts and justice placards. They brought with them silence. When the time came, when the voice called, they moved out into the road and headed slowly for Grenfell Tower, the largest green hearts in front. Traffic stopped. People stared out of car windows and from the top decks of buses. The silence leaked towards the shopfronts and the bars along the route to Notting Hill Gate, where the clientele stilled, holding their drinks, and remembered the flames. Walking next to Melissa was an old black man with a white beard and a green heart on his hat. There were three middle-aged people with walking sticks, young people who lived nearby, some people who had travelled from the north or east or south, some who had lost family members and others who had not. All of them silent. All of them remembering. The closer they got to the tower, along Ladbroke Grove, across Oxford Gardens, the deeper the silence. It finally came into view in the distance beyond the black lace of the night trees. When they reached it, they stood at the base and spoke the names of the seventy-two. There was a closing silence of seventy-two seconds. Afterwards, they were offered soup.

Michael joined the walk at Chesterton Road and they reached the base together, walking next to one another. Their shadows made one shape in the shine of the street lights. Melissa registered the coherence of the earth in his presence.

"Are you hungry?" he said, sitting on a wall next to her.

"Yes," she said.

ACKNOWLEDGEMENTS

Parts of this novel were written during a residency in Brussels organised by the International House of Literature Passa Porta and Literatuur Vlaanderen. Thank you for a beautiful place to work and reflect.

Gratitude to Clare Alexander, Clara Farmer, Poppy Hampson, and all the hardworking team at Chatto & Windus, Vintage, Penguin Random House and Aitken Alexander Associates. To Claudia Cruttwell, Bernardine Evaristo and Jennifer Kabat for championing and editorial prowess.

Deepest love and thanks to Derek A. Bardowell and M and M, who sweetly tell me I can when the mountain is too high. And to Theresa Idode Evans, for inspiration and support.